THE PORCELAIN MONKEY

*A Novel of Scandal and Intrigue
in the 19th Century*

CONNIE BARON RING

Jemkap Books
MELVILLE, NY

Published by:
Jemkap Books

MELVILLE, NY
JemkapBooks@gmail.com

Disclaimer: *The Porcelain Monkey* is a work of historical fiction. Apart from the well-known people, events, and locales that are woven into the narrative, all names, characters, places, conversations, organizations, and incidents are either products of the author's imagination, inspired by real persons, or are used fictitiously. When real-life historical persons appear, the situations, incidents, and dialogues concerning those persons are used fictitiously and are not intended to change the overall fictional nature of the work. Some characters and their histories are fictionalized to disguise their identities.

Library of Congress Control Number: 2025922272

ISBN-13:	979-8-9935883-0-8 (softcover)
	979-8-9935883-1-5 (hardcover)
	979-8-9935883-2-2 (ebook)

Cover and interior: Gary A. Rosenberg • thebookcouple.com
Author photo: Dennis Weiss

"Everything can be taken from a man but one thing: the last of the human freedoms—to choose one's attitude in any given set of circumstances, to choose one's own way."

—Viktor Frankl

PART ONE:
1850–1851

CHAPTER 1

Frida

Hamburg, Germany
Wednesday, October 2, 1850

Eighteen-year-old Frida Kuhn took a final look at the humble rooms she shared with her mother, Roshen, and her younger brother, Jakob. Her heart pounded and hot tears stung her eyes as she faced the enormity of what she was doing. Silently, she padded toward the door in the pre-dawn light, fighting the urge to abandon her plans and remain in Hamburg. Memories danced in front of her eyes, some of them sad but many of them soft and warm.

After Papa's death eight years earlier, Roshen, Frida, and Jakob could no longer stay in the large, comfortable home in which Frida had spent her early childhood. Impressive in its size and style, the timbered house of her birth was surrounded by a garden bursting with geraniums and delphiniums, their bright red and blue hues contrasting excitedly with evergreens stretching to the sky. She remembered the swing hanging from a branch of the old oak tree near the back door. Papa had helped her soar into the air on that swing. Her long raven hair had flown in the wind, and her large dark eyes had crinkled with laughter as she flew higher and higher. Her voice, full and rich even as a child, pierced the air with glee as the swing carried her small frame into the air.

The swing was one of the hardest things to leave behind when they had been forced to move. The new rooms were small, dark, and imbued with the odor of mildew. Situated on a narrow street where little light reached their single window, there was no garden and no place to play. Gone were the mouthwatering meals of beef schnitzel and noodles, thick stews, and tasty gravies. In their place were dried salted fish, stale bread, and cabbage. Even the potatoes that Frida had loved—she remembered Roshen's savory concoctions of fried, boiled, and roasted tubers-—had become scarce and inaccessible during the blight that had swept Europe the year she turned thirteen.

As Frida recalled those difficult times in Hamburg, her eyes rested on her beloved cloth doll, Hildegarde, who peeked out from under her small dresser. With horror and relief, she realized that she had forgotten to pack Hildegarde. She swooped down, dusted her off, and gently made room for her in her brocade carpetbag.

The doll had been a gift from her uncle Erwin, Roshen's brother, on her second birthday. Hildegarde was her best confidante and had been by her side for everything. Tears spilled from Frida's eyes as she recalled how Roshen had lovingly patched Hildegarde's disintegrating left arm with a sock, sewed back a perilously dangling leg onto a threadbare hip, and replaced the doll's missing button eyes. Hildegarde had accompanied Frida and Roshen everywhere: to the market, to the park, and to bed at moonrise when Roshen tucked them both in for the night. Hildegarde had, as young Frida always said, just the right "feel good."

Sometimes, Frida and Roshen talked way into the night, her mother listening for hours to Frida's childhood dreams and soothing her fears. She could still feel Hildegarde's soft doll-body against her chest while her mother's high voice filled the night:

"Der Mond ist aufgegangen,
Die goldnen Sternlein prangen
Am Himmel hell und klar.
Der Wald steht schwarz und schweiget."

The moon has risen,
The little golden stars shine
In the heavens so clear and bright.
The woods stand dark and still,
And out of the meadows rise
A wonderful fog.

But that was all in the past. "You are no longer welcome in this house," Roshen had said, turning her back on Frida. Cold fire had darted from her eyes when she learned of her daughter's intention to marry Josef Rosenstrauss. "You are dead to me. Do you hear me? You are dead."

Mother and daughter had not spoken since.

The bleating of a horn from the nearby docks suddenly tore through the twilight reminding Frida that the time for departure had come. She put some chocolate treats for Jakob and a note she'd written for her mother on the splintered table by the front door and slipped out onto the cobblestone street. She wondered how Roshen would react when she read it. Yes, a note was the only way to let Roshen . . . and Jakob . . . know that she was leaving Hamburg for good.

Today, for the first time in her life, Frida felt raw fear. It was a damp and unpleasant October morning, the mood of the new day reflecting Frida's trepidations. Waiting in the long line to board the *Holstein* were businesspeople seeking their fortunes, laborers looking to find work in America, and families noisily embarking on their escapes from the politically charged Germany of 1850. As Frida moved forward, the crowd separated into two groups. Frida watched as first-class passengers boarded amidst much fanfare. Music played, sandwiches and treats were offered, and aperitifs were generously served on elegant trays. Frida's hunger overtook her as she imagined biting into a fried cod dumpling and sipping a glass of wine. She would eat until she could no longer fit in another bite, and the wine would fill her head with dreams of Josef.

Frida was routed into the second line, the one headed for steerage travel. She became surrounded by crowds of noisy men, haggard women, and screaming children. There was no fanfare for this group. Instead, the odors of stale clothing, tobacco, and beer assaulted her nostrils.

"Get going, steerage swine!" shouted the deckhands, pushing the passengers along. "We haven't got all day. Move it!"

An elderly man tripped on his torn trouser leg.

"Get up, old bastard," prodded a stout, mustached crewman. "No time for clumsy donkeys here. Get going. *SCHNELL*, FAST!" he barked, his mouth curled into a sneer.

Frida shrank into the crowd and took a last look at the shore. Hamburg had been her home since birth, its harbor on the Elbe River rimmed by tall trees and low buildings nestled along the shoreline. Smokestacks at the edge of the horizon signaled Hamburg's rise as an industrial center. She remembered playing along the earthen pathways that ringed the harbor, when Roshen and Manfred, her parents, doted upon her. Now she was leaving Germany, perhaps forever. Once again, she thought of Mama. *Has she found the note yet?*

A sharp rebuke from a man behind her snapped her out of her reverie, and she was pushed along with the crowd until they reached the ship's boarding area. All the months of secrecy and furtive planning were culminating, right now. Cold sweat began to gather under her gray knitted jacket. She was sure that everyone could hear her rapid breathing as she fought the urge to turn back to the certainty of home. Images of her escape flooded Frida's mind. Just a few hours earlier, she had lowered herself onto her narrow bed and glanced around her threadbare room. Terrified to tempt the squeaking of the light wood platform under her, she lay rigid in the darkness, her mother and Jakob unaware of her planned escape.

Yes, leaving Germany was the only answer. Politically, her homeland was in turmoil. The uprising of 1848 had split the population between those who wanted the German states to become unified as one country and those who stood firm with the nobility who wanted to keep the feudal city-state structure that had prevailed for centuries. Violence had raged in the streets, and Frida knew no one who had not been affected. She recalled how just last summer an angry mob had assaulted some neighbors' homes—Jewish homes—blaming the Jews for the failure of the German states to unite and protesting a new political push to grant Jewish civil rights. The pounding of horses' hooves had filled the streets as the protesters screamed epithets at their Jewish neighbors:

> "Jew traitors, Jew traitors!
> You take our jobs,
> You foul our streets!
> Because of you,
> We've little to eat.
> The King's still here,
> You caused defeat!"

Roshen had refused to talk about it. "It will pass," she said. "It always does." But it hadn't passed—nor had Roshen's refusal to acknowledge Frida and Josef's love. "He's your cousin. The Torah may allow cousins to marry cousins, but I certainly can't," Roshen had argued. "Besides, how can you even consider marrying into *that* family?"

Frida's thoughts slipped back to when she and Josef were small and the two families had loved one another devotedly. Her mother and Josef's father, Erwin, were siblings. The families had spent countless hours visiting each other's homes, sharing meals, and celebrating special events—until Papa died, just after Frida's tenth birthday, and everything had changed. Suddenly, she and Josef were not allowed to see one another, and they were forbidden to talk to each other in school. Day after day, she had listened to her mother's rantings.

"He's a traitor, that brother of mine. You stay away from him and from his family. He betrayed us. We will never again have anything to do with any of them," she insisted, leaving her daughter without explanation.

While they were still students, Frida and Josef saw each other regularly during lessons and had spent every recess together, never uttering a word about their school trysts to their parents. As they grew older, they came to treasure each other's friendship above all others.

Frida sighed as she thought now of that early love and how, night after night, she had stolen from the house to meet Josef in the shadows of the evening. Dense trees hid their silhouettes as she yielded to his awkward kisses. Unable to tolerate the tensions behind their secret, they dreamed of escaping to America, a breakaway that just a few weeks earlier had seemed impossible. And then the miracle had happened, and she was now on her way to Josef.

Frida's thoughts turned often to their last night together in Hamburg, just before Josef's departure for America. The two had met in a dense copse of lindens in an isolated area of the park. Josef would leave for America the following day. He would find a job and look for a place to live in New York. She would follow when he completed his search.

"My God, Frida, how I adore you," he had whispered, as his lips sought the tender place behind her ear.

They held each other tightly, unable to end their embrace. Josef's breath was hot as he kissed her eyelids and sought the soft rise of her bosom. Then, the world had fallen away as they fell to the soft lawn beneath the lindens.

"Maybe we should wait," Josef said, as he pulled back and looked deeply into her eyes. "I don't want to hurt you." He winced, confusion clouding his features. "You are my cousin, Frida. The Torah commands us not to indulge in familiarities with relatives. But the Torah does not disapprove of cousins marrying. Which is it? Which is it?"

Frida caressed his face and brought him softly back to her. Her thoughts raced. *Will God be angry because we are not yet husband and wife? But we are one in our hearts. And who knows if our plans will go smoothly? Suppose we never see each other again?*

They held each other tightly, his sweet fragrance filling her until there was only this place, this time, this man. She could feel his breath on her neck and his heart beating ever faster beneath his woolen shirt. She clung closely to him, passion compelling their union.

"Are you sure, Frida, are you sure?" Josef implored.

Frida answered him wordlessly, as she again sought his mouth and clasped him to her with urgency. An involuntary shudder rippled through her body, and tears rolled down her cheeks.

Alarmed, he drew back and cupped her face in his hands. "Are you all right, Frida? What's wrong? Have you changed your mind?"

"Don't ever stop loving me, Josef. Don't ever stop loving me," she cried, as they came together until they reached a crescendo . . . and it was over. Silent and spent, amazed at what had just happened, they lay together in silence under the moon.

"I love you, Frida," whispered Josef, caressing her flushed cheeks. "I will always love you."

A loud blast from the *Holstein*'s bow shook Frida from her memories. She clutched the brocade bag closer to her. It held a few clothing items, her silver hairbrush, and some salted fish she had managed to steal from her mother's pantry. It also held Hildegarde, her knitting needles and lace bobbins, and the delicate, sterling silver Star of David necklace that had been her grandmother's. At the bottom of the bag was a figurine about nine inches in height. It was her most cherished memento and was wrapped carefully in heavy, dark-green paper.

"Next!" shouted the deckhands, herding everyone into narrow lines to face mandatory health inspections. Frida grasped her vaccination certificate, acquired just a few days earlier. Without it, she would be turned away from the wooden clipper ship and returned to shore. "Let's go! Everyone gets screened. Schnell, schnell!" shouted crew members. They ushered the passengers toward medics who would determine their fitness to board. Frida saw many in front of her rejected.

"Too old!" yelled one medic, turning away an elderly man and his wife. The next passenger approached the examination counter trembling with fear. "Denied. Look at that rash. You look like a bag of ground meat."

A strapping young man directly in front of Frida approached next. "No passage for you," heckled a doctor, pointing to the exit ramps.

"Give me a reason," the passenger demanded, showing a German-issued health certificate affirming his fitness to travel.

"I just don't like you, bastard. Don't expect things to go easy just because you want them to. Get rid of him," he commanded the toughs waiting to escort the spurned fellow off the pier.

Bile rose in Frida's throat as she saw how easily she could be deprived of passage. Her stomach heaved as she realized that she would face a second challenge by medics when she arrived in New York—if she survived the cross-Atlantic voyage.

Then, it was Frida's turn. It became difficult to keep herself upright, and she felt detached from her body as the doctor lifted her chin, peering into her eyes, ears, nose, and mouth as if she were a cow in a meat market. He probed her neck, applied his wooden stethoscope to her chest, and examined her exposed skin and scalp. When she was finally approved for boarding, her muscles relaxed, her breathing became less labored, and she rejoined the throng as it crowded onto the ship's deck.

"Come on, move, girlie," a deckhand rasped. "Go, go, go, go," the big man demanded, thrusting himself against her back and catching her off balance. Frida's wool skirt caught between her feet, and the knit shawl she wore around her shoulders almost fell to the ground as she fought to keep her footing.

The man's huge arm caught her. "Where's your mister?" he asked. His small, steel-gray eyes were set in a meaty face topped by a balding head of stringy blond hair. Exposed biceps revealed tattoos of anchors, daggers, and sea creatures. At the base of his neck was a turtle-shaped mole that rippled when he spoke as if it were swimming through a blubbery white sea. Thin lips opened into a grin, revealing yellowed, uneven teeth. The odors of fermented sausage, chewing tobacco, and cheap beer poured from his mouth and filled her nostrils.

Color rushed to Frida's cheeks, and a long moment passed.

"Ah, I get it. There is no mister!" the deckhand shouted triumphantly.

Frida bit her lip, drawing blood, and tried to look past him.

"What? Think you're too good for me? Come on now, sweetheart. Give Otto a kiss."

As Frida cringed, his cronies formed a chorus. "Kiss, kiss, kiss," they chanted, as the crowd looked on, terrified to interfere. He reached down to grab her by the neck, yanked her up in a sweaty grip, and planted his foul-smelling mouth on hers. Pulling his face away, he peered down at her with a lascivious grin." Looks like I've found me some entertainment," he rasped into her ear before he shoved her away, roaring with laughter.

Trembling with fear, but determined not to let him get to her, Frida descended with the other steerage passengers into the bottom hold. Slop pots caked with dried excrement from past crossings made her gag. The odor of damp woolen clothing, mixed with the stench of pickles, salamis, and limburger cheese churned her stomach.

"Get used to it, girl," urged a woman behind her, as a rat scurried between them. "I've traveled steerage before. It only gets worse, but your smeller gets used to it after a while."

How? thought Frida. *Oh, Josef, how did you handle seven weeks of this?* And then Josef's loving face appeared in her mind's eye. *The crossing will end, and we will make a life together in America. We'll have clean sheets and spring breezes visiting us through open windows. There will be space for us to love and to laugh and to prosper. This I promised Josef, and this I promise myself. I will get through this. I WILL!*

As she reached the ship's steerage deck, Frida saw hundreds of multitiered cots placed just inches from each other in narrow rows. They filled almost the entire cavernous hold. Then she saw what she had to do. Clinging to her few belongings, she pushed her way through the throng, her lean, four-foot-ten-inch body easily navigating the small openings between passengers. While most of the emigrants tried to find the more stable center berths, Frida sought the most privacy. A bottom cot along the *Holstein's* starboard side caught her eye. Three young teenagers saw the bunk, too, and they started hurling insults at each other.

While they argued, Frida slipped behind them and took possession of the prized berth. It was the least public of all the cots in the hold. She planted herself firmly at the cot's side, hands on hips, shoulders straight, and carpetbag placed conspicuously in clear view on the thin straw that served as a mattress.

"Get out of my sight," she demanded, her full voice assuming a defiant, authoritative tone. "This is my spot. Nobody takes it from me. Is that clear?" She shook her fist and curled her lip, until the youths noticed adults eying them, and they slinked away.

Passengers continued to stream into the *Holstein's* bowels. Clothing, rations, and keepsakes filled every crevice, and people could barely move. Savoring her victory in keeping her bunk of choice, Frida began arranging her things in the tiny space allotted.

A woman in the next berth leaned over and offered Frida advice. "They'll give out some eats from that iron cauldron over there. But you'll have to be cunning. The men grab as much as they can. And water?" She pointed to an area opposite the bunks that was lined with two four-foot-long water troughs. "They're for washing, drinking, cleaning. And don't even think about bringing water to the berth. The guards will beat you if you're caught." Grateful for the advice, Frida smiled and offered the woman a small piece of cheese from the bottom of her stash; she grabbed the cheese and stuffed it into her toothless mouth, grinning with triumph and retreating to the depths of her bunk, where she turned her back to Frida.

Finally, steerage filled to capacity and a horn bleated hollowly on an upper deck. As the *Holstein* pulled out of its mooring, it tossed its occupants against its damp walls. Children cried, and passengers competed for the slop pots as nausea overcame them. *Remember Josef, think of America,* she willed herself, grateful when a huge wave lurched the ship upright. The *Holstein* fought rapidly swelling seas until, finally, the ship was able to make her way onto calmer waters.

That night, as Frida fought nausea in her narrow cot, she tried to block out the moans and curses all around her. At last, the voices quieted, leaving only the sounds of the sea slopping up against the ship's wooden frame to occupy her drifting thoughts. Suddenly, she was jostled from a hard-won sleep.

"Don't even think about fighting me, missy," a voice she recognized from earlier hissed into her ear. He snatched her brocade bag and rifled through it. A glint of silver caught his eye. "Well, look here," he croaked, as he extracted it from the carpetbag, "if it isn't a *Jüdischer stern*, a Jewish Star. I guess you're not just a bitch; you're a *Jewish* bitch. Get up, *Jude Bitch*. Do what I say. And keep quiet. You make a noise, and my Bowie knife does its job. Like this!"

He grabbed her from the back and grasped her chin in one meaty hand as he held the jagged 12-inch blade to her throat, just below her jawline. Frida fought back a scream as the brute cut a two-inch-long slice into the base of her neck, tearing her skin and drawing blood onto her pale throat. She prayed that someone would come to her rescue but knew that no poor soul in this wretched place would take a chance with becoming another victim.

"And that's just a warning," croaked Otto. "Do anything rash and the knife knows to go a lot deeper." The thug's iron hand slapped over her mouth. "Oh, we're going to have a good time, you and me."

He dragged her by the throat, her blood seeping between his fat fingers, into a hidden storage closet illuminated by one dim lantern. He locked the door and threw her to the floor. His watery eyes widened as he ripped open her blouse and squeezed her breasts. "Sweet," he groaned, as he raised his shirt to reveal rolls of sweaty fat covering his massive chest. His hands went everywhere. "Jew whore," he panted. "I bet a whole week's pay that I'd claim you as mine, and I did. I love winning gambles, don't you?"

Terrified and overpowered, Frida tried to scream, to scramble away, but her limbs froze, and her throat was too dry to emit a sound. She fought to breathe. Her eyes fell on an extinguished brass lamp on the wall of her prison, and she put her focus on that, to think of anything other than what was happening to her. The brute's huge belly covered her fragile frame, and he tore into her. Rigid with terror, Frida felt his grinding thrusts from somewhere outside herself. Finally, they stopped, and he laughed that terrible laugh of his. "Go back to your miserable cot, *Jude Bitch*. You'll need your rest for tomorrow night. And the next, and the next. If you're lucky." He laughed again and left Frida alone and bleeding on the floor.

After he was gone, she curled into the wall of the ship and lay there, motionless, for what seemed an interminable amount of time. Suddenly, Josef's face appeared in front of her. She reached out to touch his fading cheek, her fingers barely visible in the dark. Memories of the lindens came to her and filled her senses. Slowly, she pulled herself up and waited for her heart to stop pounding. When her breathing returned to normal, she made herself a promise. "I will survive, and I will thrive, no matter what it takes."

CHAPTER 2

Josef

It was finally November 20, the day that Frida would arrive in New York. With a pounding heart, Josef hurried through the streets leading to the South Street pier where the *Holstein* was due to arrive. His mind slipped back to the months of dreaming that he and Frida could put the terrible judgments of their families behind them and hoping that they could come up with the means to be together in America. He, the son of a wealthy banker, laughed wryly as he reckoned with the financial dilemma he had faced.

The home he had shared with his parents was in the wealthiest part of Hamburg, a large timbered house with fireplaces in every room, comfortable furnishings, and a vast dining room that echoed often with revelers joining the family to dine. Money had always been plentiful, and a banking career awaited him—until the rift occurred, and Josef was faced with the choice of an extraordinary financial future by succumbing to his father's demands or surrendering the comforts he knew to pursue the love that meant his very soul. When Josef refused to abandon Frida, Erwin had cut off his allowances and managed to freeze his deposits, leaving Josef with no financial resources. The situation had appeared to be hopeless.

And then, the brooch had appeared, lying in a Hamburg gutter muddied by recent rains. Its brightness, shining through street debris, had caught Josef's eye as he knelt to tie his shoe. A deluge suddenly burst forth from purpled skies, chasing pedestrians into their homes and leaving the neighborhood deserted and gray. Overcome by the realization that the storm may have provided a gift of freedom, Josef looked around to be sure the street had emptied and bent to scoop the brooch into his pocket where it would remain until he could find a safe place to examine it.

"If this is real—if it's not counterfeit—the brooch may have been placed in the gutter by God. It could be our miracle," he murmured aloud, fingering the heavy piece.

He hurried home and headed straight to his room, not bothering to remove his wet coat. He lit the gas lamp on his bedside table, trembling with anticipation. Gently, he removed the piece from his pocket and placed it under the amber light. It was an ornate gold pin embedded with rubies, rare pearls, and rose-cut diamonds. Josef examined it, cleaning it as well as he could. His mother's father, his beloved Opa, had been a goldsmith in the old days. As a young boy, the two had spent many hours at his jeweler's bench, and Josef had been a keen learner. Even without jeweler's tools, Josef could see that this was a genuine piece, certainly a valuable one. For a fleeting moment he thought of trying to find its owner, imagining a widow distraught over the loss of a gift from a lover long gone.

The moment passed quickly.

When the brooch was dry, Josef wrapped it in his finest mono-grammed handkerchief and placed it under his pillow. Reluctant to be away from his find, he declined dinner, claiming that he felt ill and would take to his bed for the evening.

The next morning, he rose early to greet another dreary day. Huddled against icy rain and wind, Josef made his way through nar-row streets to the shop of Herr Solomon, a jeweler on the opposite side of town who would not know him. The store was situated in a long lane lined with gabled shops whose windows were framed with white lace curtains and painted window boxes. Josef pulled the bell chain over the entranceway and waited nervously for someone to admit him inside. After a few minutes, an elderly man with a long white beard opened the heavy wooden door.

"*Guten Morgen,*" said the wizened shopkeeper, adjusting his suspenders and peering through thick spectacles. "I am Herr Solomon. Come in and tell me what I can do for you today."

The shop was simple, consisting of one whitewashed room with a long oak counter. A fire grate, a small table with two chairs, and a straw bed along the back wall indicated that it was here that Solomon worked and lived. The jeweler took his place behind the counter and waited until Josef removed the brooch from his pocket. Josef's slim body tensed and his dark brown eyes hooded as he told Solomon that the brooch was 24-carat gold, a valuable family heirloom that he would be willing to part with for the right price.

With great ceremony, the old man reached for the piece. "Let's have a look," he said, his eyes betraying him with their brightening. "It's dirtied up. Can't tell for sure."

It seemed to Josef an endless wait as Solomon turned the brooch over and over, examining it with his jeweler's glass from every angle.

"Well, my boy," he finally declared with a shrug. "I like you, so I'll be good to you. I am willing to give you fifty *thalers*. That's an excellent price. You won't do any better than that."

Josef glared at the jeweler, shaking his head.

"I'm offering you a fair deal. The brooch needs a lot of work. See this chip? And this one?" Solomon questioned, pointing to supposed damages Josef knew weren't there. "That's going to cost. The whole thing needs reworking."

"Fifty thalers? That's it?" Josef exclaimed, his eyes flashing and his deep voice threatening. "The gold alone is worth more than that. But I understand," he added, "you're a rascal. You want a big profit when you sell it." He reached for the brooch. "Thank you for your time. I'll see what someone else will give me."

"Wait, young man," said Herr Solomon, once more putting the brooch under his glass. "I suppose I can fix it more easily than I first thought. I'll offer you ninety thalers, but that's it. A good offer it is," he stated. "You should take it."

Noting the narrowing of Solomon's eyes, Josef reached out again to retrieve the brooch.

Solomon stroked his beard nervously. "No, it's not necessary to go elsewhere," the jeweler sighed. "I'll give you one hundred thalers right now. If you leave, the deal is off."

Josef silently considered the offer. *I never expected more than sixty,* he thought, his heart racing. Blood rushed to his face as he recalled the Torah's command that one shalt not wrong the stranger in buying or selling. *But one hundred thalers will bring enough money to cover two forty-thaler steerage tickets to New York and, hopefully, a place to stay until I can find some work.* "Done," Josef agreed, as Solomon doled out the treasure that would give him and his beloved Frida a new life.

Josef's recollections were interrupted when the crowd behind him thickened, pushing him toward the wharf. A small man, he stood at five feet, four inches with sinewy legs and arms, slender hands, and thick, oiled-back black hair stylishly piled into a wave at the center of his forehead. Never one to be physically aggressive, Josef allowed himself to be carried along until he came across a wooden bench where, as luck would have it, he was able to claim a place to wait. It was in plain sight of the dock, and Josef was relieved to be out of the throng.

As he waited, his heart filled with the memory of his last evening with Frida. He recalled how a gentle kiss under the trees had swelled into an urgency he had never before experienced. He blushed as he thought of his own awkwardness under the moonlight. *If only I had been surer of myself. Or maybe we should have waited until we marry. Was I gentle enough? Was God okay with what we did?* But then, as he had told himself a thousand times since, their love was strong. In their hearts, they were already husband and wife and would always share the bond they had created that night. He thought of Frida's trust in him. *We will never abandon each other,* he swore, *never. But what if I did hurt her?* Uninvited shame rose through him. *Maybe I should not have allowed passion to overwhelm us.* His thoughts started to spin. *How will she be when we see each other? And has she made it through the trip safely and without regrets?*

Together, Josef and Frida had discussed the hardships they would encounter on the Atlantic. Steerage travel was known to be difficult. Josef had tried to convince Frida to wait until he could raise enough funds in New York to provide her with a second-class ticket. "No!" she had declared. "I won't hear of waiting. I will join you in America as soon as you find a place for us to stay. I will *not* live on the streets, and I will not be without a place to sleep."

And so, they had decided, together, that their parents' refusal to support them in any way left them no options. Forging a new life away from the political strife in Europe and away from their families' harsh judgments outweighed everything else.

Excited cries from the dock brought Josef back to the moment. Far on the horizon, the faint outlines of the *Holstein* appeared. A loud cheer went up as the ship came into view, its sails billowing in the wind. After what seemed forever to him, tugboats and barges finally started to cross the harbor to ferry the passengers and their belongings to the pier. Minutes became hours as travelers were subjected once again to health examiners who would determine each passenger's fitness to disembark. Josef watched as more and more voyagers were refused entry to the country and sent back to the *Holstein*'s decks.

Nausea ripped through him when he realized how easily a fever or a cut or some other infraction could destroy their lives. Finally, he caught sight of Frida as she was herded into a large, roped-off registration area. There would be more waiting, Josef knew, as the *Holstein*'s thousands of passengers were processed by officials of various agencies.

As the hours passed, the crowd around Josef became more and more impatient. Frida slipped in and out of view as Josef paced.

Where is she? Maybe she's sick and won't be approved for coming ashore. Will she be sent back to Germany? The unstoppable thoughts raced through his mind.

At long last, Frida emerged from the staging area, and Josef pushed through the crowd until she fell into his arms, trembling. Her knees gave way as she held on to him. Shocked, he realized how thin she was. He pulled her up gently until she could stand on her own. "It's all right, Frida, it's all right," he whispered. "I love you. We're together. That's all that will ever matter."

As he held her, Frida said nothing, but started to relax. Josef trembled as her soft breath caressed his neck. As he reached for her chin, tilting it so he could look into her eyes, the chinstrap on her bonnet opened.

And then, he saw the scar.

The lesion terrified Josef. *What was the steerage crossing like? Why is Frida so terribly thin? So pale, so quiet, and withdrawn?* His stomach turned, and guilt overcame him as he contemplated what may have happened to her. He had been fortunate. He had fallen in with a group of youths on the Hamburg piers as they were meeting their ship, the *Kronsprinz.* "Josef!" a familiar voice had called out just as he was about to head up the ramp to steerage. Hemmed in by the hordes attempting to embark, it took Josef several moments to see through the throng. In the distance he saw a tall, robust young man with a head of thick blond hair, a square jaw, and huge shoulders waving to him.

"Wait, Josef, wait!" the youth shouted as he elbowed his way to where Josef was having trouble standing firm against the crowds.

As the fellow got closer, his burly companions accompanying him, Josef broke into a grin. "Stefan Hartmann!" he shouted, his resonant voice booming. "What are you doing here?"

Sounding out of breath, Stefan replied, "I am on my way back to New York. I've been working and living there for two years and returned to Germany to attend my sister's wedding."

Josef reached out to shake Stefan's hand. "It's good to see you. The last time was when we apprenticed together at my father's bank."

Stefan introduced his companions, friends from Hamburg who would be traveling from New York to Cincinnati where there was a large Jewish enclave. Greetings were exchanged until the crowd threatened to pull them apart. "I'm headed up to second class," said Stefan. "How about you, Josef? Are you also second class? Or is it first class for you today?"

"Neither I'm afraid," answered Josef. "My circumstances have changed. It's steerage for me."

"No such thing!" exclaimed Stefan, his features registering surprise. "You'll stay with me in second. Another fellow who was to travel with us couldn't make it so there's a bunk waiting for you. C'mon, I know the porters on this ship, and we'll have no trouble smuggling you in."

"Thank you," said Josef, consternation crossing his face as he realized that Stefan was thinking of the wealth his former classmate assumed he still possessed. "But I'll be fine in steerage."

"I won't hear of it. You'll be comfortable with me, and we can catch up on old times," Stefan said, smiling broadly and taking Josef's elbow.

As small as Stefan's stateroom was, it was well equipped with upper and lower berths, soft mattresses made up with fine linens, a washbasin, and several drawers built into the walls of the narrow space. The room's ventilated doors opened directly onto the saloon, a common area for eating and socializing.

"What do you think?" Stefan grinned. "It's not as fancy as first class, but we'll be fine. The food is simple, but plentiful, and I have cards with me. Do you still play Skat and Doppelkopf? I remember how much you loved those trick-taking games."

Josef's face lit up. "Doppelkopf is my favorite," he said, smiling broadly. "Best game I know. Remember how we used to make up rules up as we went along?"

Stefan laughed. "Ah, yes. I'll never forget those games. But now that you're with us, we can also have some finger-wrestling tournaments. I used to beat you all the time in school. Bet I still can. Let's try after we get out to sea."

The next forty-two days had seen mild conditions and, after a brief stop in Cork to pick up some Irish passengers, the *Kronsprinz* sailed into New York earlier than anticipated.

One evening, after they had retired to their cabin, Stefan approached Josef. "Where are you staying stateside?" he asked.

Josef blushed deeply. "I don't know," he stammered, "but I'm bound to find someplace."

"Absolutely not," answered Stefan. "You'll stay with me."

"You've done enough, my friend. I couldn't impose further," said Josef.

"I have a room over a grocer's shop. You'll stay with me until you marry your Frida. I remember her well, and you've talked about her so much I feel like I last saw her yesterday instead of a few years ago when we were all in school."

"I have seen her, a lot!" laughed Josef.

Stefan joined Josef's merriment but then grew serious. "I can get you a street-sweeping job. It doesn't pay much, but at least it's a start. And there's a ladies' boardinghouse around the corner from my place. I know someone there who will take Frida in without the usual long wait. Consider it done," he said, extending his hand.

Breathing a sigh of relief, Josef returned a firm handshake. "I must admit I was a bit worried. So, yes, it's a deal."

It was to that boardinghouse on Mott Street that Josef now steered Frida. Horses neighed and dropped their excrement on the earthen roads. The fumes combined with black smoke from burning coal stoves to sting their nostrils. Conversation in strange languages filled their ears, and rushing bodies pressed against them, making navigating difficult.

Frida moved as if she were in a trance. As Josef pointed out sights along the way, Frida did not respond. Her silence hung heavily between them. *Something isn't right. Did something go wrong on the Holstein? Or what if she is upset about our night under the lindens? Or what if the shock of the city bustle is overwhelming her and she wants to return to Hamburg? What will I do if I've lost her?*

"Frida, please talk to me. I know the streets are different from home, but you'll get used to them. I promise." Panic filled Josef's chest. Just a few short weeks before, she had been ebullient in her excitement about coming to America. Now, she rejected his questions and refused to meet his gaze.

As dusk started to settle in, they arrived at a three-story frame building with a covered porch stretching along its ample width. It was an unusually mild autumn day and children played on the sidewalk, savoring the last few moments of daylight. Merchants peddled their wares, clamoring for buyers to purchase fruits and vegetables, pots and pans, and used clothing before they packed up their wagons for the evening. Women were sitting on the front steps and standing in small clusters on the porch, chatting noisily. Dogs barked, cats scurried, and the street seemed that it could not contain another living thing.

Frida grasped Josef's arm tightly as they made their way through the double door to a small first-floor room that served as an office. A buxom, German-speaking woman with gray hair tied back in a severe bun was sitting at a rickety desk. The door was open, and she beckoned Josef and Frida to come in. "What can I do for you? she asked.

"I'm Josef Rosenstrauss, and this is Frida Kuhne, my fiancé.

Stefan Hartmann told us to come to you. I understand you may have a room for Frida. Stefan has secured a job for me as a street cleaner. It doesn't pay much, but I can pay you two dollars a month."

"Ah, yes," the woman replied. "I am Frau Schultz, and I am in charge here. I have something on the third floor. My normal charge is two dollars and fifty cents a week, but since Stefan sent you, I will meet your price. You will give me four weeks rent in advance." She walked over to a wall filled with large iron keys hanging from a shelf and handed one to Frida. "You are welcome, if you obey the house rules. You will share your quarters with two other young ladies. There will be no men in the room, no alcohol, no smoking."

The matron's eyes bored into Frida's as she continued. "Meals are given in the basement. Breakfast is from seven to seven thirty, dinner from six to six thirty. If you are late, you won't eat. You must be in your room by eight p.m. when the doors are locked. Lights out at ten. Warning bells will ring exactly one-half hour before each event. We are all Germans in this house so you will attend the Evangelical Lutheran Church of St. Matthew every Sunday morning at eight. You will share chores with the other boarders, and fighting is strictly forbidden. Any violation will be cause to turn you out. Do you understand?"

"Yes, Frau Schultz, I understand," said Frida. "You will have no trouble from me."

"All right, then. The first two months' rent is due now and on the first of every month after that," said Frau Schultz, extending her hand.

Josef felt his insides heaving at the thought of Frida being required to go to church, but he also realized that the price at Frau Schultz's was all they could afford. He took four dollars in coins from his pocket and placed the money in the matron's meaty palm.

"Say goodbye to Miss Kuhne now," the matron instructed, "unless you would like to sit in the common area for fifteen minutes. Not a moment more."

"Yes, we would like that very much," offered Josef. He took Frida's arm and followed Frau Schultz. She opened the door to a cluttered sitting room with peeling whitewashed walls and a few shabby chairs. It had no windows, and the two gas lamps on either side of an ancient sofa cast very little light. Musty odors rose from an ancient rug, and dust swirled through the air like moths on a summer evening.

"Remember, you have fifteen minutes," instructed Frau Schultz, crossing her arms in front of her ample chest. "I will be back then to escort the fraulein to her room."

When they were alone, Frida slumped and fell into Josef's arms. He held her for a few brief moments, stroking her hair and whispering softly into her ear, "I love you, *mein engel.* We're in America, together. Please, please talk to me."

After a few moments in Josef's arms, Frida pulled away. "We must get married right away," she said urgently. "We cannot wait. It must be now."

"Of course, we'll marry," Josef said, as he reached for her face. His fingers gently brushed the river of tissue at the base of her jaw. "You realize, Frida, that we have not talked about this wound. It's red and raised and raw. What happened to you?" he asked, his eyes brimming with tears. "Are you in pain? My God, I never should have let you travel alone, Frida. I should have . . ."

Frida backed away. "It's nothing. We will talk about it another time," she said, steel creeping into her voice.

"Nothing? Please, tell me."

"Truly, it's not important," Frida insisted. "The *Holstein* hit rough seas, and I fell against the sharp edge of a railing. It's over and done with."

"But . . ." Josef started to say.

Frida stared into his eyes. "I told you; there's *nothing* to talk about. It was an uneventful voyage. And here we are, in America." she said, her tone softening as she reached for his hand. "Now, let's talk about your trip."

Josef's face brightened, and a smile crossed his lips.

Relieved to have Frida with him again, he told her how he had met Stefan.

"I remember him," said Frida. She smiled when Josef explained how Stefan had sneaked him into second class, and how he had helped him with lodging, to get a job sweeping streets, and where to get food and other necessities. Then Josef grew serious, looking deeply into those beloved brown eyes. "And so, we begin our new life. We have all the time in the world. No family, no politics, just us."

Fear clouded Frida's eyes. "No. There's no time to wait. I don't want to wait. We must marry right away. You don't understand, Josef. I've no time to waste."

She is overwrought, exhausted. She must be afraid to be alone. "Of course, we will marry right away," he said, cupping her face. "We have only to wait until we find a rabbi."

"A rabbi?" Frida gasped. "Josef, we discussed this before we came to America. What are you suggesting? There will be *no* rabbi."

Josef sat on the edge of the sofa, running his fingers through his hair. Back in Hamburg, he and Frida had talked often of the anti-Jewish sentiment pervading Europe. Jews had thrived after Napoleon moved into German lands at the turn of the nineteenth century. The invading French emperor needed men for his army and tax income for his coffers, so he had lifted sanctions that had been imposed upon Jews for centuries, and the formerly restricted Jewish population had flourished. After Napoleon's fall from power in 1815, the populace was angry at Jewish successes achieved during the Napoleonic years, and trouble boiled like oil in a cauldron.

Josef thought back now to a street brawl he had witnessed a few months before he and Frida had made their escape. He had been walking home from Sabbath services when he heard glass breaking behind him. When he turned to see what had happened, he saw an elderly storekeeper in the doorway of his shop. He was bleeding from a head wound, his beard stained red. Josef ran over to him, helped him indoors, and stopped the blood with a towel.

The man had pleaded with him not to report the incident. "They will be angry and come back to seek revenge. My boy, on the surface things have been good for Jews during the last few years. But be careful. They don't like our success."

Rattled, Josef had taken the man's caution to heart, disturbed by what he recognized as truth. Unable to erase the scene from his mind, he had mentioned the incident to Frida. She listened carefully, and a discussion had ensued. "The shopkeeper was right," she had said. "If we get to America, we can start fresh. Not a soul will need to know we're Jewish. Think of how much simpler life would be."

Josef had brushed off her response, certain that it was a raw reaction to the incident. He had given it no further thought—until now. *Had she been serious?* The enormity of the situation crashed down on him. "But, Frida, you know how I feel about tradition. We are Jews. How can we turn away from our people?"

Frida looked solemnly into his eyes. "Don't you see, Josef? If we are openly Jewish in New York, we could go right back to living as we did before we came here, afraid and looking over our shoulders for the next anti-Jewish incident. Things here that may seem good for Jews now could change. You heard Frau Schultz insist that all her women attend church. Not synagogue, *church.* No, Josef, I won't face that again."

Heavy silence filled the small room. "We gave up our families to come here," he said. "How can you expect me to give up Judaism, too? Never to light Shabbos candles? Never to daven and pray? Never again to join a minyan or chant the *Schema?*"

Josef was caught in a quandary. *How can I change who I am . . . a Jew with centuries of tradition and love of Torah behind me. I live to honor God . . . but I live to be with Frida. Mine is a lonely choice. Think, Josef, think. . . .*

CHAPTER 3

Frida

Precisely fifteen minutes after she left the young lovers alone in the parlor, Frau Schultz returned to escort Frida to her room. Frida gathered her things, bid Josef good night, and followed the stern matron to a narrow staircase with uneven risers. She accompanied Frau Schultz down a long hall lined with rooms on each side. The floors creaked in protest as they made their way toward Frida's accommodations.

Frau Schultz stopped at Room Fourteen and knocked. A tall, pale young woman, not much older than Frida, wordlessly held the door open and motioned them inside. Another tenant, a short, dark-haired girl of about seventeen, was lighting the room's single gas lamp. Frau Schultz made the introductions, never crossing the threshold. She started with the tall tenant.

"Miss Frida Kuhne, meet Miss Bertha Albrecht. Miss Albrecht is the senior tenant in this building and is the house captain. She is in charge of making sure that all tenants follow procedures. You will obey her instructions to the letter."

Bertha nodded her head slightly.

Frau Schultz pointed to the second resident. "Over there, by the dresser, is her sister, Amalia. Look up from what you are doing immediately, Miss Albrecht, and say hello."

Amalia managed to gurgle a greeting. Frau Schultz turned abruptly and disappeared down a back stairwell. Neither roommate met Frida's gaze. Bertha pointed to the top tier of an iron bunk bed painfully reminiscent of the cots on the *Holstein*. "You sleep there," she commanded.

Frida assessed the windowless room. A cracked washbasin and pitcher sat on a small bureau, wrinkled garments poking out from drawers unable to close against their tightly packed contents. A broom and dust mop took up the corner near the door, and a single hard-backed oak chair filled another.

"We certainly didn't need, and didn't ask for, another roommate, especially one who smells the way you do. You'll have to keep your things on your bed," announced Amalia. "There's no more storage available. And you can do the sweeping."

Frida grimaced but held her tongue. *Yes, I do smell terrible. I hope Josef didn't notice! He didn't seem to, but what if he did?* She quickly put that thought out of her head. *Anyway, I won't be here long. Josef waits,* she thought. *We will rise above all of this. We WILL!*

Within minutes, a bell rang, beckoning the boarders to dinner. The sounds of shuffling feet filled the corridor. Bertha and Amalia went to join them, neither one offering to guide their new roommate to the basement dining area. Frida hoisted her carpetbag onto her mattress, briefly washed her face and hands in the basin, and followed the crowd.

Several long tables and backless benches were aligned along the room in rows. The seating filled to near capacity quickly, the boarders sitting shoulder to shoulder with barely enough space between them to lift a utensil. Frida sighted an opening at the nearest table and headed toward it. Without acknowledging her, the occupants closed the seating gap, declaring that the table was already too crowded.

"No room here," they barked. Several times, the situation repeated itself. Finally, when Frida had had enough of their posturing, she placed herself wordlessly between two residents, standing closely over them until they reluctantly made room for her.

Chatter ceased as trays of bread, followed by platters of gray meat, boiled potatoes, and peas were passed, and everyone began to eat. As bland as the unseasoned food was, it was warm and filled Frida's belly, for which she was grateful. Accustomed to the plain fare, the women hurried to finish their meals within the half hour allotted. Dinner ended when Frau Schultz entered the dining room at precisely half past six o'clock. Wordlessly, the women arranged their plates and utensils into high piles and stood. They formed a single line and exited the basement to return to their rooms. Frida started to follow them when Bertha grabbed her arm and steered her toward three boarders waiting near the kitchen.

"You're new, so you get to work in the kitchen with the three miserables who are assigned to permanent duty because they're hellions who have gotten into lots of trouble. New girls, like you, get cleanup duty with those witches," she said. As Bertha started to leave the room, she stopped, turned, and pointed to the piles left on the tables. "You can start with clearing the dishes."

The kitchen was large, its stone floor covered with droppings embedded from years of meal preparation. A brick fireplace spanned the entire wall at the back of the kitchen. Pots and pans hung from thick dowels bored into its surface, and a large cauldron filled with hot water was suspended over the fire. Much to Frida's dismay, the three kitchen assignees stood to one side, obviously expecting her to singlehandedly perform the overwhelming task.

"New girl, new girl," they taunted.

Recognizing a crisis building, Frida glared, daggers flying from her eyes. Against her will, *Jude Bitch* invaded her mind. *NO. I will NOT put up with insults and degradation ever again.* She paused a moment. Then she climbed up on the nearest table, pulled herself up as much as possible, and glared. Stunned, the kitchen trio had no time to react as she admonished them.

"You *will* do this *with* me. I *will not* do this by myself. If Frau Schultz exacts revenge, we will go down together. Is that understood?"

No one was more amazed than Frida as the three scurried to retrieve pots of sand and baking soda stored near the cauldron. They showed Frida how to use the coarse mixture to perform their task. With all four working together, the dishwashing was completed quickly and, at last, Frida was able to use the outhouse and return to her room.

"Shut the door behind you," commanded Bertha.

Frida did as she was told. She took her carpetbag down and began to determine where she could place her few things. At the bottom of the bag were her two treasures. One was her Star of David pendant, once cherished, but now repulsive to her. . . *Jude Bitch, Jude Bitch.* Despite all that the star represented now, she folded it gently and hid it under her straw mattress. The second object was her figurine. Terrified that it may have broken during the *Holstein*'s crossing, Frida turned her back to Bertha and Amalia, lifting the porcelain figure from its paper nest. Trembling, she held it to her heart. As if it were yesterday, she could see her Grandfather Wilhelm's beloved face and hear his resonant voice.

She recalled the day when, as a seven-year-old, she had first noticed his damaged leg. "Why do you walk so strangely?" she asked one night when he was tucking her into bed.

"My sweet child," he answered, putting his arms around her, "that is a story for another time."

That time came when Frida was ten years old, shortly before Papa died, as Grandfather was pouring tea on a cold January day. The dampness made his limp more pronounced than usual. "Grandfather, your leg is hurting you. It's always given you trouble. It's time you tell me why."

Reaching for her hand, he had looked deep into her eyes. "You are right, *libeling*. It is time." He took a deep breath, a sigh rattling in his chest, and began his story. "When I was a boy, things were going well for Jews. Napoleon had invaded our German lands and caused a lot of bloodshed, but he also revoked terrible laws Jews had lived with. *Mein Gott*, Frida, before Napoleon came, we couldn't own homes or shops. There were laws in Germany that decreed that our people couldn't marry until Jewish marriage quotas had openings. Most of the time, only one Jewish son could marry after the father's death. My own parents—your great-grandparents—had to wait for years to marry, and even then, they had to pay residence fees that allowed them to have a place to live. In those days, a man had to be at least twenty-four years old, prepay three years of taxes, and prove that he possessed at least three hundred *florins*. Those who married illegally were threatened with physical punishment or even exile."

Then, Grandfather had picked up his cane and walked slowly across the room. He picked up a porcelain figurine from the top of a battered bureau near the fireplace. The piece depicted a bearded monkey wearing eighteenth-century clothing and a black three-cornered hat. It stood in a humble stance and held a violin and a bow. Delicately painted in tones of brown, cream, and green with small accents of yellow and magenta, it looked out at an unseen landscape. Frida knew it well. It had always occupied a special place in her grandparents' home, but she had never paid it much attention. He handed the figurine to Frida and asked her to look at it with new eyes. She examined it carefully.

"Why did someone make a monkey statue, Grandfather?"

"The monkeys were popular art objects, libeling, especially those playing musical instruments and participating in bands. People were looking for answers to human behaviors in animals. Monkeys fascinated them."

Frida nodded. She recalled seeing monkeys in a traveling troupe visiting Hamburg Park. Their abilities with their hands and arms, the way they carried their babies, and their expressions had enthralled her. One had been particularly human-like.

"I can understand that, Grandfather. When we saw the Hamburg monkeys, there was a baby who tried to walk away. The mother reached out and grabbed it by the waist, pulling it back into the safety of her arms. My mother used to do that with Jakob when he tried to wander. I guess she must have done it with me, too."

Frida turned the monkey over and over, examining it as never before. Then she pointed to its chipped hat, some bubbling in its glaze, and a crack on its base. "Did the monkey get damaged when you moved to Hamburg?" she asked.

"No, quite the contrary," Grandfather explained, settling in his chair. "Originally, Frederick the Great enacted a rule forcing young Jewish couples applying for marriage to buy defective pieces *because* they were damaged. The factories got paid for imperfect seconds that way. There were other pieces my parents were forced to buy, too, but this one has stayed in the family all these years for a reason."

Grandfather leaned forward in his chair and caressed the figurine his granddaughter was holding. "I want you to have this statuette and to keep it always. Let its fragility and imperfections represent the vulnerabilities and troubles we Jews have always faced; but also allow its delicate craftsmanship, varied hues, and musical theme to remind you that the beauty of life gives us the strength to overcome evil."

Then he had gotten up, poured some more tea, and continued his story. "When Napoleon came to power, porcelain rules and other laws like them were lifted. For many years, we Jews were finally free to become anything we wanted to be. My father opened his own dry goods store, and we were able to move into our very own house. It was a miracle—"

"But, Grandfather," Frida interrupted, "you don't have the store or the house anymore. What happened? Especially to your leg?"

The old man paused to take a sip of tea, his eyes darkening. "In 1815, Napoleon was exiled to Elba, and we worried. The people were upset with Jewish successes. They wanted our rights taken away, to go back to the old days before they had to compete with us. The riots started four years later. I was a youth then. My parents and I were sitting in a popular coffee house enjoying a beautiful summer day. In fact, it was August second, my father's birthday. Suddenly, horsemen came storming into town, their red, black, and gold flags flying. They were yelling, *Hep, Hep!* at the top of their lungs. We were terrified. Commandos were shooting their guns and shouting orders like 'Beat the Jews to death!'

"The sounds of breaking glass were all around us as rioters tore cobblestones from the street and tossed them into Jewish homes and stores. Old men were assaulted, and women screamed as they were pushed and shoved to the ground. Babies were torn from their mothers' arms and thrown to the gutters. At one point, a particularly aggressive group thundered across the plaza, their guns blasting. The horses were terrified and reared up, screaming, almost crushing us.

"The ruffians pulled me out of my chair. 'Teach him a lesson. Show him Jews can't take over our cafés!' they shouted, pulling me to the pavement. 'Get the Jew boy!' they yelled, as they punched me and jammed their knees into my gut. I tried to get up, but they knocked me down again and stomped on my legs. My right knee was broken. All of this happened while my parents looked on helplessly. There was nothing they could do. When we got home that day, we saw our house had been burned to the ground, and the store had been reduced to rubble. Except for a few charred items, everything was gone. The monkey was one of the few things we managed to salvage. It was covered with soot and ash, but it survived."

A harsh bell sounded from the hallway, disrupting Frida's thoughts. "Lights out in fifteen minutes," Bertha instructed. "You'd better get ready."

Frida rewrapped the monkey and hid it in the bottom of her bag. She straightened her shoulders and fell into bed, half asleep before her head reached the pillow.

New days are coming, she thought. *I will marry Josef. There will be no more fear.*

❧ ━━━━✦━━━━ ❧

CHAPTER 4

Josef

After bidding goodbye to Frida at the boardinghouse, Josef started back to Stefan's, feeling overwhelming despair. He had never seen this side of Frida, never known that she could be cold and demanding.

She's been through a lot, he assured himself. *She was injured, but was it more serious than what she told me? And I don't really understand why she wants to shun Judaism; it has been part of our lives since childhood. Will it pass? It must! I know my Frida. She is gentle and loving. We have always loved each other. We always will.*

He thought back to when they were both little. He was four years old, just two years older than she, when he fell in love with her. They had been at a family gathering at Josef's home. The two children were playing a game of tag, chasing each other with abandon when Frida tripped on a stone and fell to the ground, shrieking in pain. Josef had run toward her as fast as his little legs could carry him. Pleased with himself that he had gotten to her before any of the adults, he put his arms around her. "Don't cry," he had pleaded. "I will help you."

Josef's heart soared with the memory. He had touched her silky hair, the color of blackbirds' wings in sunlight, and marveled at how soft it was. Her tears had stopped immediately.

The present rudely interrupted his memories when he reached the room he now shared with Stefan. Darkness had descended, and he had to grope his way to the gas lamp to the right of the door. The soft amber light illuminated the small space. Stefan occupied the only bed, so Josef settled for a thin straw mattress on the floor. There was a potbellied stove that provided heat and the means to prepare a simple meal. A wardrobe stood in the corner near two narrow windows looking out on a light shaft surrounded by the brick walls of an adjacent building. Shoes, clothing items, and containers of food littered the floor.

When Josef had first seen the room, he wondered how he would get used to it. He was accustomed to his family home, a large three-story dwelling in the *Neustadt*, the New Town, near the center of Hamburg. It was one of only thirteen homes that Jews were permitted to own. Most Jews were confined to overcrowded rooms in shoddy, multiple-family dwellings. His grandfather, Werner, the grandfather he shared with Frida, was the descendent of bankers who had first served as moneylenders in the imperial court of Frederick II, often known as Frederick the Great.

When Napoleon lifted Jewish restrictions, Erwin's father, Werner, had been able to join other emancipated Jews to create the Hamburg Municipal Bank and Trust. Housed in a fine stone building on the *Ferdinandstrasse*, it had quickly surpassed M.M. Warburg & Company, the bank that had dominated Hamburg since 1798. Noted for its ability to forge both domestic and foreign commercial relationships, Werner's bank had become a vital player in the Hamburg financial sector.

When Erwin was old enough, his father put him through a strenuous financial apprenticeship, and he did exceedingly well. Hamburg needed finance men, so the family had escaped the riots of 1819 unscathed. Josef was the natural successor to the bank's management. By the age of twelve, he had become an apprentice under his father's tutelage, working at the bank whenever his school schedule allowed. Erwin and Josef's mother, Sara, believed in Josef's abilities and talked to their son often about his promising future.

Josef had always taken wealth and prestige for granted—until a few months ago.

Erwin had argued vehemently against a union between Josef and Frida. "First of all," he reminded his son, "you are much too young. But you have been promised to Edith Heymann, the daughter of Heinrich Heymann, the grain merchant, when you turn twenty-seven. She is attractive enough, and her family has substantial wealth. Heinrich and I agreed that there would be a marriage after you complete your apprenticeship."

"I don't want to marry Edith," protested Josef. "I've never met Edith. I don't know her. More important, I love Frida. Have you no mercy, Father? Have you no understanding at all about how we feel? How much we want this marriage?"

"You dare to defy me?" Erwin roared. "You are my son. You will do as I say."

With all the courage he could muster, Josef locked his eyes on his father's. "I will not marry Edith," he said, his voice reduced to a whisper.

Erwin froze, his blue eyes turning to ice. Then he raised his right hand and slapped Josef's face, sending him flying across the room until he fell in a heap on the floor. "You are as bad as your Aunt Roshen. My sister's stubbornness and lack of respect are what created the chasm between our families."

It took a moment for Josef to gather himself. When he stood, he was shaking. "What do you mean?" he asked, his breath becoming labored.

Erwin broke the heavy silence that had fallen between them. "You don't understand, do you?"

"No. What could Roshen have possibly done to sever all of us from each other? Please, tell me."

"You know there's been bad blood between our families for a long time. You also know I am against this relationship, and I certainly will not tolerate a marriage. If you marry that girl, your mother and I will have nothing to do with you. Your brother will be forbidden to see you or talk to you. I will cut off my financial support, and I will disinherit you."

"But, Father," Josef managed to stammer. "I know you and Aunt Roshen are on bad terms. But why, Father? Why?"

Fury crossed Erwin's face. "Okay. You are old enough to know the truth. Your aunt did not behave like a proper woman. She questioned my inherent right, my legal right as the eldest man in the family, to make decisions that women are not equipped to make. When your grandfather Werner died, I, as his eldest son, inherited all his worldly goods. His wealth became my wealth—mine to do with as I choose, his estate mine to administer, not Roshen's. She dared to question my authority and to demand that I give her half. That is not how a proper Jewish woman behaves. It is contrary to the laws of nature for her to do such a thing."

Erwin paused to collect his thoughts, his lower lip thrusting forward, his color deepening to purple, the veins in his neck bulging.

"Roshen even used her husband's early death as an excuse for her irreverent behavior, claiming that her poverty should affect my decisions. *My* decisions. Is it my fault that her husband died? Is it my fault that he left her with nothing? He should have been a better provider, a provider like me. Your mother doesn't want for anything because I made sure she is well taken care of and that she always will be. I guarded my money carefully. Roshen should have insisted Manfred do the same."

Josef was stunned. He had never seen his father so enraged. All he had ever known was that Erwin had always been there for him, always been the pillar of his family. *Should I ask him about his duty as a Jewish man to protect his sister?* he thought, trying to work up enough courage to confront the furious man. *No, I can't. What good could possibly come from questioning him?*

And so, the moment had passed. One night, when he met Frida under the stars, he had told her about the conversation. It had stunned her, just as it had stunned him.

"Now I understand," she whispered, teardrops running down her pink cheeks. He gently wiped the glistening tears away.

"Yes," Josef had agreed, "both of us now know what they fought about. To me, he was a strong father, a good husband to my mother. Yes, he was demanding in what he expected from all of us. Like most Jewish men, he determined the times to rise in the morning and retire in the evening, when to do the wash, when to go to the market, and what would be on the week's menu. He was always a devout man who prayed regularly and taught us to observe tradition. How could he not have helped your mother—his *sister*—when she found herself impoverished? She was a widow with young children. Jewish doctrine commands that widows and orphans must not be mistreated, or God will rain down his wrath. I don't understand him."

Josef and Frida had held each other silently for a long time. Moonlight wrapped around them like a halo, while the cooing of birds in their nests filled the soft silence between them. When Josef finally spoke, it was with resignation. "We will make our love work, Frida. We will find a way to go to America, my darling girl. I know we will."

At that moment, Stefan returned to the room, interrupting Josef's memories. "How goes it, my friend? Is there a wedding coming?"

Unable to keep his thoughts to himself, Josef poured out his heart to Stefan, telling him in detail about the conversation he and Frida had had before he left the boardinghouse. Sitting on the edge of the bed, Josef held his head in his hands. "My life has but two things in it: Frida and my Judaism. Now I must choose between them. How do I do that?"

Stefan pondered Josef's situation for what seemed to Josef an interminable time. He ran his fingers through his hair and gazed at the floor until he finally spoke. "Josef, my friend, I wish I could advise you. But you must make the choice. If you choose Judaism, you may lose Frida; if you choose Frida, you may, in time, come together and find a mutually comfortable solution."

Stefan paused while Josef absorbed his words. Then he grinned, throwing Josef off guard for a moment. "Something happened today that may help the situation."

"What could possibly have occurred to make things better? I find myself at a hopeless standstill," Josef said despairingly. "I want to marry my Frida. I want to someday have a family. Even that seems impossible right now. I don't speak English. I haven't found a way to make a decent living here. The word at home was that there were thousands of jobs available in America. I cannot find one that will support us both."

Stefan nodded. Then, to Josef's surprise, he clapped heartily. "That's the good news. I found better work for you . . . if you want it."

"Of course I want it! Whatever it is, I need enough money to save for a child someday."

"Well," his friend teased, drawing out the suspense. "Many stores are opening on Chatham Street. A friend of mine is the manager at the Emporium, a dry goods store. He asked me to find a new puller-in, someone who gets people from the street to come into the store."

"But I don't speak English!" exclaimed Josef.

"That's exactly why the boss wants you. The store is in a neighborhood where new German immigrants are settling almost every day. You'll be perfect. You're a friendly fellow and would be a tremendous help. And you'll earn more money!"

Josef jumped off the bed and shook Stefan's hand. "When can I start?"

"How about next week?"

"Good. I am an up-and-coming puller-in! I'll take Frida to the Emporium and surprise her with the job when we take our next walk. I only pray that we can settle our differences."

CHAPTER 5

Frida

That first night in America, when Frida finally crept into bed, thoughts of Josef filled her mind. As she started to drift off, she was suddenly jolted awake by the realization that things in this new country may not be as easy as she once would have thought. The cold reception she had received from the boarders was horrifying. *Is this how it will be in America? Do people suspect I'm Jewish and hate me for it? I was afraid that might happen! Is my fear coming to be? Oh, Josef, don't you see what we must do to stay safe?* She tossed and turned on the uncomfortable mattress until, exhausted from travelling and settling into the boarding house routine, she finally fell into a fitful sleep.

All too soon, the breakfast warning bell woke Frida from her restless dreams. She wasn't surprised to see that Bertha and Amalia had left the room, probably for breakfast. Quickly, she washed her face in the basin on the bureau, dressed, and hurried to the dining hall. When she entered, silence fell as she started to make her way toward the tables.

"Good for you!" one of the boarders suddenly shouted. "Someone overheard you in the kitchen last night. We're proud of you. It's about time someone put those tyrants in their place."

To Frida's amazement, the girl began to clap. Others joined in until the applause reached a crescendo. Across the room, Bertha and

Amalia stood and waved, making room for her to sit between them. As she made her way to their table, others requested she sit with them, all impressed with their new boarder and anxious to make her a friend.

As Frida took her place between her roommates, they smiled warmly. "Never thought you had it in you," declared Bertha, Amalia nodding in agreement.

Others quickly agreed, hurling questions at her faster than she could answer them.

"What did you really say to them?" asked one.

"Are you always so sure of yourself?" probed another.

"It's a good thing someone stopped those menaces," declared someone else.

Astounded by the women's offers of friendship, yet somewhat skeptical of their motives, Frida instinctively held back her answers but allowed their approval to fill her like a riverbed receiving spring rains. *This is how it should be,* she thought. *This is how it must always be.*

After breakfast, Bertha and Amalia walked upstairs with Frida, gossiping about this one and that one and how she had put the kitchen bullies in their place.

When they reached the room, Amalia removed some of her garments from the bureau and offered Frida space to store her belongings. As she cleared items away, she handed Frida a fresh blouse and a light woolen skirt. "Here," she said, as she turned her nose away from Frida's clothing. "You need these more than I."

"Oh, no," Frida smiled. "I couldn't. But thank you."

"I insist," said Amalia. "Please let me do this for you."

Frida accepted her roommate's offering, gagging as she realized how her clothes reeked of Otto and slop pots and sweat. *I need the garment change. Besides, Amalia owes me for the way I was treated when I arrived. It's justice.*

Before she changed, Bertha filled the washbasin so Frida could sponge bathe and wash her hair. Noting the silver hairbrush still lying on Frida's bunk from the morning's rush, she gently groomed the thick dark locks and arranged them into an upsweep. If she noticed the scar, she tactfully ignored it.

"There, that's much better," Bertha announced when she was finished, bringing Frida an ebony-trimmed hand mirror. "Do you like it?"

"It's lovely," Frida agreed, coaxing a tendril into place and enjoying the newfound intimacy.

A knock abruptly sounded at the door. One of the boarders had come to tell Frida that she had a gentleman caller waiting for her in the common area. Frida quickly dressed and said goodbye to Bertha and Amalia, leaving them with their faces arranged in astonishment.

Frida closed the door behind her and pranced down the stairs to the common room. There was Josef, holding a small bouquet of yellow chrysanthemums. He handed them to Frida and beckoned her to sit down next to him on the sofa. "You look beautiful," he said, his face lighting up. "The outfit becomes you. Did you bring it from home?"

Josef listened intently as Frida told him about the kitchen, the change in the boarders since the cleanup incident, and Amalia's clothing gift.

"It seems we are off to a good start in the New World," said Josef. "But right now, please listen to me. I've done nothing but think of our conversation last night. I love you with all my heart. But you are asking too much of me when you suggest giving up Judaism. I don't know—"

Frida stood and interrupted him. "What are you saying? That you are abandoning our agreement?"

Josef stammered, "No, I didn't say that. We will be married. But being a Jew is who I am. It is my blood, our blood."

"You agreed back in Hamburg that in America nobody would need to know we're Jewish. I thought you were serious."

Josef's voice started to break. "I agreed, against my beliefs, that I would give up my yarmulke and my tefillin. I thought that once we were here, in America, you would drop the notion that we should hide our Judaism, that we could live our lives openly without religious reprisal."

"Yes," said Frida, as she paced back and forth, "without religious reprisal. That is why we must avoid standing out. At any cost. Even, if necessary, at the cost of abandoning our heritage."

She watched Josef struggle as his face contorted in pain. *Jude Bitch, Jude Bitch. What if we stay openly Jewish and our children fall victim to tormentors like I did, like my parents and grandparents did? The boarders did not seem to single me out because I'm Jewish, but what will happen when and if they do find out?* "My God, Josef, don't you see we have opportunity here? We can be anyone and anything we choose. How can we take chances? I don't know if you noticed the help-wanted sign in a shop window while we were walking away from the ship. *Jews Need Not Apply*, it said, in German, no less. What if New York becomes like Germany? Think about it."

A heavy silence fell between them. When Josef looked at Frida, the steel had returned to her eyes. He shuddered. "You really are going to make me choose, aren't you? You are willing to split my heart in two? Do I still know you?"

Frida avoided his gaze, staring at something imaginary on the floor. She had missed her monthly and knew it meant a baby might be coming. Terror flooded her. *I cannot raise a child alone. Where is my mother when I need her? I need you, Mama!* Frida's thoughts raced back to the last conversation the two had had when she tried to reason with Roshen.

"Mama," she had pleaded, "I know you disapprove of my marrying Josef. But can you not see how I love him? How he loves me?"

Roshen had pulled herself up to her full height. She was taller than Frida by at least six inches and now towered over her daughter. "You must not marry Josef," she had admonished. "Terrible things can happen when cousins marry. And marrying my brother's son after all these years of estrangement? He abandoned us when we needed him most. No, if you must marry Josef, I cannot stop you. But if you do go ahead, you will be dead to me. Do you understand that? I will consider you dead!"

Frida's mind numbed with the memory of that final encounter with her mother. Right now, she felt alone. Her family was estranged, her future with Josef suddenly seemed tenuous, and her path in a new country was uncertain. As she looked at Josef, it crossed her mind that he might indeed leave her. *I cannot let that happen. He must marry me . . . no matter what.*

"Your thoughts have taken you far away," Josef implored. "Please, let's resolve this now. I cannot bear to argue like this." He reached out and took her hands in his.

Frida forced herself to change her tone. *If I need to, I can bring this issue up later. After we are husband and wife, I won't need to worry about being alone or my child being a bastard.* She stood and caressed his cheek. "If it means so much to you, we can find a rabbi and marry quickly—but quietly." Her heart softened when she saw the fear in Josef's eyes retreat as he sighed deeply, then stood to embrace her.

"All right," she said. "We'll start looking for a rabbi right away. Now, let's go for a walk and enjoy being together."

Frida ran upstairs to get her shawl, returning moments later ready to go out into the street to begin her future. Disappointed that Josef did not yield to her wishes—at least not yet—she allowed herself to step into the sunshine. It was a beautiful day in New York, a stark contrast to the day before, which had been overcast and chilly. The sky was a brilliant blue and boasted just a few clouds floating high above the city. A cool but dry breeze caressed the earth, and a few brilliant red and gold leaves still clung to their lacy branches.

It seemed that all the world had gathered on these streets. Still overwhelmed by the size of the crowds, Frida was happy to be on Josef's arm as he maneuvered his way toward a second-hand clothing shop. On the way, they passed the Ansche Beth Shalom synagogue on a side street. Impossible to miss, it was a three-story building that featured a center doorway topped by gothic windows and arches. It dwarfed neighboring buildings. Unexpectedly, the synagogue's heavy wooden doors were open for a special morning service. Excitedly, Josef took Frida's elbow, and they climbed the front steps into the shul, gasping when they saw the sanctuary. Its ceiling vaulted fifty feet above the floor and was painted an iridescent blue punctuated by yellow stars. At the end of the long central aisle was an elaborate bimah, or reading platform, where the Torah was being read. The ark of shining carved wood stood at the back of the bimah; arched windows on either side allowed sun to stream into the sanctuary in a ribbon of filtered light.

Frida could see how elated Josef was to be in the presence of God, but she was torn. As she heard the words of the service, her heart felt as if it had been torn in two. *Like the porcelain monkey, it is beautiful and comforting, like familiar arms wrapped around me . . . but those arms could be deadly if America hates us.*

As the cantor's voice soared, her heart filled. The rituals rendered a sense of timelessness but also raised her fears. Without warning, *Jude Bitch, Jude Bitch* rang in her ears. She froze, unable to move forward or to retreat to the relative safety of the street. Her heart racing, she could feel Otto rip into her, fouling her senses and rendering her helpless. *Otto should be dead,* she thought. *He should hang from a linden tree while I stab his neck, over and over again. . . .*

Perceiving Frida's change of mood, Josef took her elbow and gently led her to the synagogue's exit. "You're trembling," he whispered as they climbed down the steps onto the street. "Are you well?"

The warmth of Josef's voice brought Frida back to the present. "Yes," she managed to say. "I suppose I'm just exhausted from the trip. It is good to be off the *Holstein*." She forced herself to smile. "Let's continue our day."

As they walked, Josef talked about the service. His voice seemed to come from far away as he spoke about the comfort of the rabbi's words and the fulfillment he felt as the cantor's melodies surged through the synagogue. "Surely you felt the beauty of the service. Didn't you?"

"Yes," Frida admitted, torn between the comfort of Judaism and the appeal of the Christian world. "I still believe our lives would be easier if we take on a new identity, give up our Judaism. But I will agree to find a rabbi to marry us."

Reassured that, if she were with child, her baby would have a father, Frida began to relax and look around. Buildings as high as five stories lined the dirt roads, many of them sporting colorful awnings. Rejoining the pedestrians rushing here and there, the couple became immersed in the sights and sounds of the city. Street vendors beckoned passersby to purchase their wares. Smells of fresh bread stacked high in straw baskets and meats cooking over coals masked some of the unpleasant street odors, tickled their noses, and made their stomachs growl in anticipation.

They stopped when they came across a pretty girl of about fifteen barking her wares. Small and frail with long blond hair and cat-like green eyes, she was dressed in spotted calico with a thin plaid shawl around her slender shoulders. Heavy black boots, worn from long hours spent peddling on the streets, protruded from under her frayed skirt. Carrying a cedar bucket of hot roasted ears of corn, she barked out her wares in a high-pitched song:

"Hot corn, Hot corn,
Here's your lily-white corn.
All you that's got money,
Poor me that's got none.
Buy my lily-white corn,
And let me go home."

Josef had no idea what the English ditty meant, but it was obvious that she was selling a treat. He stepped up to peer into her basket. "In Germany," he said to Frida, "corn was fed only to livestock. This is something we haven't eaten before," he laughed. "It smells delicious. Let's try it."

After they finished chewing the sweet kernels and had sucked out the last moisture from the cobs, Frida excitedly led Josef to a barrel of dill pickles being tended by a young boy. "Let's get one," she pleaded.

Josef pulled a penny from his pocket and handed it to the child who retrieved a fat, bright-green specimen from its murky brine. He handed it to Josef in a paper wrapping, which Josef immediately pulled back to expose the pickle's warty skin. He floated it in front of Frida's nose while she tried to grab a bite. When she managed to capture a big chunk of it in her teeth, juice rolled down her chin and dripped onto her shawl, reducing them to helpless giggles and forcing tears of merriment from their eyes.

As they continued walking the crowded streets, they came upon the Emporium. A middle-aged man approached them and urged them to come inside. Frida was surprised when he seemed to recognize Josef.

Smiling and extending his hand in greeting, the mustached man said, "Hello, lad. So pleased to see you again."

"Josef," Frida asked, "do you know this man?"

"As a matter of fact, I do. He is a surprise—for you," he said, his eyes sparkling,

"What do you mean, a surprise for me?"

"Frida, meet Gottfried Baum, the manager of the Emporium and my new boss. This is where I will be starting work in just a few days!"

A man of medium stature with black hair and a thick chin-strap-beard, Gottfried's lean body carried an air of authority reinforced by his clear green eyes.

Astonished, but pleased at this turn of events, Frida listened as Josef explained the job of a puller-in and how it would provide them with a modest, but adequate, income until they could improve their situation. "But now," Josef said, leading her into the clothing section of the store, "let's get you a wedding dress. You're going to need it."

Excitedly, the two began to comb through racks of gently used dresses. It had been a long time since Frida had been able to pick out a dress for herself. It was right before her eighth birthday. Papa had taken her to buy a new frock for her party. She remembered the dress perfectly: it was a knee-length pink-and-white-plaid silk with a thick sash and ruffled sleeves coming just to the elbow. Starched, white-ruffled pantaloons and slender black boots completed the outfit. She had never before—and never since—felt so beautiful. Recalling the adoring look on Papa's face as she twirled and pranced and curtsied, her eyes misted. *What would he be thinking now?* she wondered. *Would he have felt as Mama does about Josef? Or would he be happy for me? Would he have supported our marriage?*

Suddenly, Frida's eye caught a pale-yellow taffeta gown and a few frocks designed for everyday wear.

"Try them on," urged Josef, smiling at the bright expression in her eyes. "Let's see how they look."

Frida nodded and took the garments to a makeshift changing area near the back of the store. The yellow dress was the first to try. *This will be my wedding dress. I never dreamed that I might be married in something so beautiful.* As she gazed into the mirror, her pulse quickened when she saw the delicate young girl dressed in yellow taffeta looking back at her. She patted the fine fabric lovingly, thrilling to the rustling sound it made as she ran her hand along its length. Despite the scar on her neck, she felt beautiful again, just as she had on the last shopping excursion with her father shortly before he died. *If only Papa could see me now,* she thought, missing him fiercely. *But Josef will see me, and quite amazed at his Frida he will be.*

When she exited the dressing area with the yellow gown and a blue merino day-dress in her arms, Josef greeted her with a puzzled expression on his face. "I thought you would show me how you look," he said. "Especially the yellow. I was looking forward to that."

"No," teased Frida. "You will have to wait like any other bridegroom."

"As you wish, Madam. I suppose I'll need to be patient. But mind you, it will not be easy. I suspect I shall be tortured with anticipation until the time comes when I finally see my bride."

As they walked toward the counter to pay, they passed a table piled with accessories. Despite knowing she should be content with the two dresses she had just selected, Frida could not resist looking at a stylish paisley shawl and a wide-brimmed bonnet in soft cream tones. It tied under the chin with a broad ribbon perfect for hiding her scar in its folds. Josef urged her to take them, as well.

"How will we pay for all of this?" Frida asked.

"I have a little bit left over from the brooch," Josef replied. "The day will come when we accomplish all the things we dreamed about in Hamburg. A thriving business, a beautiful home, and lots of little ones. Right now, though, we have but one wedding to plan for, and the bride will be lovely."

Just then, Gottfried Baum appeared at Josef's side. "I see your lady has good taste," he said. "If you like, I can ask the big boss to take the receipts out of your first pay."

"That sounds good," countered Josef, "but how about stretching out payments over the next few weeks? I'll be here every day, so you know I'll make good on it."

The manager smiled calculatingly and accepted Josef's offer. "That's what I like to see in an employee," he said, "a man who enjoys barter. You and I are going to do just fine." Motioning to an aged woman behind the counter, Gottfried Baum told her to wrap Frida's purchases and to throw in a few hairclips and ribbons. "These will complement the lady's wardrobe," he said. "I'm sure they will be put to good use."

By the time they left the store, the sun was nearing the horizon, heavy clouds had moved in, and it was getting chilly. As they headed back to the boardinghouse, they once again passed Ansche Beth Shalom where the rabbi was just leaving the temple. Dressed in a black coat with fur trim at the collar and sleeves, he seemed an elegant figure as he reached the sidewalk and started to walk in the opposite direction from Josef and Frida.

Summoning all the courage he had, Josef called out to him in German. "Rabbi, I wonder if I may have a word?"

The rabbi turned, motioning to Josef to speak up.

"Thank you, Rabbi. I will take but a moment. I am here with my fiancé who just arrived from Germany yesterday."

"And what can I do for you?" the rabbi asked.

"Rabbi, we have gone through long hardships to come to New York. We have survived because our love is strong and everlasting. Will you marry us?"

Something in Josef's plea stirred the rabbi. After a long, thoughtful moment, his deep voice seemed to Frida to roll over them like a soft embrace. "I am also an immigrant. Come back at three o'clock on Sunday afternoon, and I will talk with you in my study. For now, good evening," he said, and walked away into the dusk.

CHAPTER 6

Frida

At exactly 6:30 a.m. the next morning, the breakfast warning bell rang. Frida awoke trembling from a dream in which Otto was assaulting her. As always after dreams about Otto, it took several moments for her heart to stop pounding and to gain control of her breathing. Her roommates were already up, and Frida somehow managed to get her feet on the floor and walk to the washbasin. The water had been used by the sisters, but there was no time to think about that now. She scrubbed her face and arms, almost drawing blood, but, as always when she washed, it was of no use. Otto lingered in her hair, on her skin, and in her nostrils. *Jude Bitch, Jude Bitch. Will Otto ever get out of my mind? His thick breath is everywhere. He smells of vomit and sweat. His tongue is all over me. His blubber covers me. I cannot move. Somebody help me! There is no one to help. . . .*

"Stop dreaming and get ready," said Bertha. "It's Sunday. We need to eat and get to church."

Church this morning, shul this afternoon. No more monthlies. With child, but no one knows. Jewish, not Jewish. The cascading thoughts dizzied Frida until she exploded with harsh laughter. Tears rolled down her cheeks as she realized the incongruity of being pulled in so many directions.

"What's so funny?" asked Amalia, wearing a puzzled look as she headed for the door with Bertha.

Shrugging off the question with a brief wave, Frida pulled herself together. "I'm coming," she said, as she slipped the paisley shawl over her shoulders and joined her roommates to go to the dining hall.

Frida was amazed when neither Bertha nor Amalia, usually full of chatter, said a word. Wearing grim expressions, the sisters' silence continued through the bland breakfast of oatmeal, white toast, and black coffee. A few lucky boarders managed to grab an apple or an orange from understocked baskets. Frida was not one of them.

When they finished, Frida stepped outside with the Albrechts where unseasonable warmth bathed their faces. As they walked toward the Evangelical Lutheran Church of St. Matthew with the other boarders, Frau Schultz at the lead, Frida wondered if she would get away with her ignorance. She knew nothing of Lutheran proto-col, nothing of what would be expected of her. Her stomach churned with the idea that she may be angering her God. She tried to stay behind so that she could mimic what the sisters did, but they inter-fered with her plan.

Bertha turned, looking directly into Frida's eyes. "What's wrong?" she said, consternation flooding her features.

Frida's mouth was dry, making it difficult to speak. Finally, she shrugged and shook her head. "Nothing," she muttered, forcing her-self to calm down. "Just a bit of fatigue." As they made their way, the two accepted Frida's excuse, and there was little conversation. Frida followed as Bertha and Amalia climbed the front steps to enter the building. It seemed to her that they hesitated ever so slightly before they crossed over the threshold into the nave. While others went to the front of the church and kneeled, neither of her companions fol-lowed suit but promptly sat in the back. Frida followed their cues. She swallowed hard, shrank into her seat, and tried to stop herself from shaking. *What if I'm found out? If people realize I'm an imposter? This is all strange to me!*

The thoughts went round and round in her head until the Divine Service began. The pastor, a lean young man clothed in a long white robe, wore an ankle-length stole around his neck. Made of emerald silk damask, it was adorned with a gold-leaf Latin cross on each end. In an electrifying voice, he motioned to the congregation to join in the recitation of prayers and hymns. Like the other congregants, Bertha, Amalia, and Frida rose and sat when the pastor commanded they do so. Frida couldn't help but notice that neither Albrecht uttered a sound. They were silent during the sermon that called for verbal responses from the congregants, and they declined to participate in the taking of communion.

The service ended with announcements and much handshaking. Glad to be done with the pretense of the morning, Frida walked outside with her roommates. Surprised at her own sense of relief, she held her face to the sun, breathed deeply of the fall air, and closed her eyes to shut out the sounds of worshippers gathering in front of the church to praise the sermon and to catch up on one another's news. She started to dream that she could stay in the sun forever but jolted herself back to reality when the crowd began to disperse.

As they started back to the boardinghouse, all three remained quiet until Amalia broke the silence. "I'm taking a chance, Frida," she said, "in what I am about to say. I'm not certain of your persuasion, but I don't enjoy Sunday mornings. I don't enjoy them at all."

The two young women stopped walking and turned to Frida, nervously checking her reaction.

Frida hesitated in her response. *Do they simply dislike going to church? Are they Jewish? Did they find the Star of David I hid under my mattress? Do I tell them my truth?* Her thoughts spun, and her heart beat fast and hard in her chest. She could feel nausea rising in her abdomen, threatening to spill out right there in the street. After careful consideration, she finally spoke. "Why don't you enjoy the services, Amalia?" she asked. "And why would you think I did not enjoy them today?"

"To be truthful," Amalia said, "I thought that you might be ill at ease."

"Whatever would make you think that?"

Amalia's expression clouded, ever so slightly, as she looked intensely into Frida's eyes. "Well," she said, "you did not offer responses during the service—and you did not take communion. Tell me, have you ever been to a Divine Service before?"

Frida's cheeks turned crimson as she realized how precarious her position was. *They didn't respond either,* she thought. *Why not? But how can I trust them? Protect yourself, Frida, protect yourself!*

"Not in America," she finally answered, hoping that her roundabout answer would put an end to the questions. "Definitely not in America."

Quickly, Frida changed the direction of the conversation. "And where did you go to church in Germany?" she asked Amalia and Bertha. "You speak German. Surely you weren't born here."

"No, we weren't," answered Amalia.

Frida waited patiently for an answer while her roommates exchanged glances. "We came to New York from Berlin in forty-eight, after the March Revolution," offered Bertha. "People were demanding their civil rights, and the situation became violent. We got out as soon as we could." She paused slightly, then continued, her tone suddenly abrupt and leaving no doubt that she wished to end the conversation. "But now, Amalia and I will leave you to return on your own to Frau Schultz's. We have errands to run."

Frida was pleased that she remembered the streets well enough to navigate back to Frau Schultz's to meet Josef. As she walked, she thought about her roommates and realized that they had to be guarding stories of fragile times. Her mind strayed to the porcelain monkey and how it, too, seemed to guard countless secrets of valiant causes rooted in ugly violence. She thought of the terrible March Revolution that had spread through Germany. There had been incidents in Hamburg, but

Berlin had been particularly bloody. Bands of protesters had clashed over civil rights and whether the German Confederation should combine its thirty-nine kingdoms, principalities, and city-states into one nation. A lot of blame for the unrest had been placed upon the Jews for several reasons.

During the recent potato blight, bread riots and hunger revolts circulated through much of Europe. In 1845, rumors had spread that Germany's shortages were the fault of Jewish grain merchants who were accused of hoarding and price gouging. Additionally, many Jews, along with the revolutionaries who were demanding civil rights, wanted representation and rights equal to those of the Christian population. By 1848, when the French king was overthrown by violent insurrection, panic occurred throughout the continent, resulting in widespread unemployment, bankruptcies, and economic crises.

Germany had been hard hit. The king, Frederick William IV, had given in to the rebels who created a popular assembly. Soon, however, Frederick regained control, dissolved the assembly, and established a new, reactionary constitution and parliament. Just recently, he had permitted the establishment of a Christian State that granted civil rights to all citizens but barred Jews from high government positions and educational institutions.

Frida let out a sharp little laugh when she recalled how, to everyone's shock, Frederick had refused the Imperial Crown. He claimed he would not "share his power with a representative body made up of butchers and bakers," and he refused the crown as being unworthy of his consideration because it wasn't ordained by God.

When she got back to the boardinghouse, Frida ran upstairs to get ready for Josef. Breathing a sigh of relief to be away from the tensions of the morning, she rested for a moment on the room's single chair, trying to make sense of all that had just happened. She seemed to have gotten through the charade of church attendance, the secret of her Judaism hopefully still intact. But was it? Bertha and Amalia had asked disturbing questions that, if answered, would reveal the truth.

It was a matter to ponder at a later time. Frida rearranged her hair, adjusted her skirts, and buffed her boots to remove dust that had settled on them during the long walks to and from the church. On impulse, as she was about to leave the room, she lifted her mattress to check on her Star of David. Although tarnish was threatening to set in, it was still there, undisturbed. Memories flooded her mind, unbidden in their intensity. Her grandmother's loving touch when she first arranged the pendant star around Frida's neck had always filled her heart—until Otto. *I won't think about that now, I won't, I won't,* she promised herself. *Today is a day about Josef and me . . . and our unborn child.*

Hurriedly, she set the mattress back down, smoothed the covers, and adjusted her hair. Glancing in the mirror, she was amazed to see a high-cheeked, seemingly calm young woman whose brow failed to reflect the turmoil going on within its owner. She pinched her cheeks, smoothed her dress, closed the door behind her, and pranced downstairs to meet her fiancé.

As promised, Josef arrived at Frau Schultz's at precisely 12:30 p.m. He was freshly shaven and was wearing an immaculate white linen shirt with a stiff, upstanding collar and a broad black tie arranged in a thick bow at his neck.

"How handsome you look," exclaimed Frida, sweeping her approving eyes over his form. "You are quite the stylish one, aren't you?"

"Nothing but the best for my future wife," Josef said proudly, offering his arm to Frida.

As they stepped out into the bright sunshine, Frida took stock of her situation. Surrounded by the sights and sounds of a strange new land and propelled by the secret life growing inside of her, she clung to Josef as they made their way toward Ansche Beth Shalom to meet with the rabbi. The morning's Divine Service still filled her mind as if to remind her of the non-Jewish life she had promised herself back in Germany.

"You know, Josef," she blurted out, breaking the comfortable silence they had been enjoying, "it's not too late to change our minds about a civil wedding." She paused for a moment, removing her arm from his elbow. "Do you remember how Frau Schultz told us that Sunday morning church services are required for all boardinghouse residents? She assumes that all her boarders are Lutheran. If she realizes that some are Jewish, she doesn't care. Her unspoken message in that requirement scares me."

"Yes, of course I remember," answered Josef. He was quiet for a long moment before he spoke again. "Was the service difficult for you today?"

"I don't know if you would call it difficult. It was foreign to me, of course, but really quite beautiful. The music, so different from the minor chords of Jewish hymns, filled the church with a resonance I felt compelling. I could get used to that."

Josef took a few steps backward, almost tripping over his feet. His face clouded and his dark eyes burned. "Are you still thinking about hiding our Judaism? How can you even bring this up again? I thought the issue was resolved, finished."

At that moment, a wave of nausea made its way to the back of Frida's throat. "No, Josef, don't worry," she forced herself to say with a smile. "We are on our way to see the rabbi. We will be married in our faith." Wordlessly, she placed her hand on her belly. *What choice do I have?*

Josef's expression relaxed as they continued toward the synagogue. Frida became intensely aware of the number of shops that boasted German-Jewish names, but also of the fluent German and Yiddish that was spoken, in addition to English, that filled the street. Although her Yiddish was limited, she understood enough to see that people were relaxed and involved in daily tasks and concerns. Absent was the tension that had been present in Hamburg. Peddlers boasted their wares, and Jewish foods and religious items were displayed on the sidewalks and behind plate glass windows.

While they walked, the autumn sun started its descent. A sudden chill in the air caused Josef and Frida to quicken their steps toward Ansche Beth Shalom. Frida tightened her shawl and looked down toward the sidewalk as she hunched against the chilly breezes of the darkening hour. Her mind churning, Frida suddenly stumbled, and Josef closed his grasp on her arm. "Be careful," he reminded her. "I certainly don't want my bride to trip before her wedding."

Frida laughed, accepted Josef's arm, and started to head toward the synagogue stairs.

And then, she froze. Appearing at the building's front doors were two familiar figures. It was Bertha and Amalia, and they were deeply engaged in animated conversation.

"Turn away, turn away," she whispered to Josef. "They mustn't see us."

"But why?" asked Josef, his expression incredulous as Frida's urgency rose. "We will be late for the rabbi."

"Just do it," Frida hissed, as she pulled him away, her pace quickening.

At that moment, the sisters saw Frida and Josef.

"*Guten tag*," they each called out, motioning Frida and Josef to wait. "What are you doing here?"

"We are out for a walk," Frida called back coldly. The shrewd curve on Frida's lips made the sisters step back. As she glared at them, Bertha and Amalia seemed to shrink in size, and they scurried away in the opposite direction. When they were clearly out of sight, Frida again took Josef's arm.

"All right," she said, "I am ready to go inside."

CHAPTER 7

The Rabbi

Rabbi Leo Kohn of Congregation Ansche Beth Shalom straightened his desk before his next appointment. Tall and slender with a head of thick dark hair, large hazel eyes, and chiseled features, the thirty-five-year-old rabbi was possessed of a kind and compassionate nature. Involved with Jewish reform efforts in Germany before he came to America, he was passionate about modernizing Jewish life. "Yes," he murmured aloud, "to survive here we must fit in with the bustle of Manhattan culture."

As a clock chimed the hour, interrupting his thoughts, Leo walked across his simple office to the adjacent waiting room and brought in the young couple he had met on the street. "*Shalom aleichem.* Welcome to Ansche Beth Shalom, and welcome to America," he said in German. "I am Rabbi Kohn. Please, come into my office where we can talk."

As Frida and Josef lowered themselves onto two plain wooden chairs facing the rabbi's desk, they looked around the office. It was a small space with a single window on an adjacent wall. Degrees and letters hung in plain black frames, and books filled a large bookcase.

Leo lowered himself onto the carved mahogany chair behind his desk and said gently, "Let's talk about what can I do for you." *How much like Tilly and I were when we first became betrothed. We were anxious to wed; they seem to be, as well. They are new to America, as were we . . .*

"I am Josef Rosenstrauss, and this is my Frida, Frida Kuhne. I have been in New York a while, but Frida has just arrived. As I told you when we met briefly outside, we want to marry."

It seemed to Leo that Josef became alive with anticipation, while his fiancé seemed reserved. "Tell me a bit about yourselves," said Leo, concerned about Frida's guarded affect.

"We have known each other since childhood, Rabbi. We are sure of our love."

"And you, Frida? Do you want this union as well?"

Frida blushed deeply, a flicker of angst crossing her face.

Leo pressed on. "My dear," he said, searching her eyes for a hint of what might be disturbing her, "marriage is a deep commitment not to be taken lightly." He paused and glanced at a large, black-rimmed clock on the opposite wall. "It so happens that my next appointment has been canceled so I have time to talk this afternoon. Tell me your story."

Frida froze, her body visibly tensing.

"What is it?" Josef asked, imploring Frida to speak. "Something has been troubling you since you arrived in New York. You do want to get married, don't you?"

"Yes, of course, I do," Frida answered. Just then she turned pale and started to sway.

"What's wrong?" Josef and Leo both asked, almost in unison.

"It's nothing," Frida stammered, her complexion blanching by the second. "It may be something I ate." She pressed her hand to her mouth and wiped a bit of spittle from her lip. When she composed herself, her voice was strong and urgent. "I want to be married right away. Can you marry us today, Rabbi?"

"Are you sure you are all right?" Josef asked.

"I said I am fine," Frida replied, her tone clearly closing the topic. "I just want to be with you as husband and wife."

Leo's voice was warm. "I understand. Really, I do. But I cannot marry you today. There are arrangements to be made and things we must talk about first. For instance, do you plan to keep a Jewish home?"

Josef answered immediately. "Of course, we do. Back in Germany, both our families followed Orthodoxy. True to them, and to our faith, we will honor our tradition."

Leo nodded. "You seem devoted to Judaism," he said, encouraging Josef to continue, even as he noticed Frida flinch. An almost imperceptible frown crossed her forehead, and the rabbi wondered what caused her reaction to Josef's words. *Something is wrong here,* he thought. *I will address Frida after I hear Josef's story.*

Seemingly impervious to Frida's discomfort, Josef continued. "Yes, I am devoted to Judaism. My family was repulsed by the number of Jews in Germany converting to Christianity. Many even took Christian names, forsaking their loved ones and their identity so they could escape bigotry and find equality. The irony is that many converts spoke a few empty words that reaped them privilege and status, so the Christians often mocked them. They laughed behind their backs. The converts sold their souls is what I think."

"You know, Josef," Leo said, "keeping the tenets of Torah is righteous and just. But things are changing. Some convert, yes; but others are reforming Judaism, bringing the modern world into its practices. This all had its beginnings at least one hundred years ago when machines and factories began to spread through Europe. The serfs began to leave their servitude so that they could work in the cities where there were growing opportunities to grow financially and socially.

"One of the first was Uri, a Jewish peddler, who had spent years trying to feed his family by traveling through Germany selling goods for meager prices. He was often turned away from lodging and had to sleep in the forests. For sustenance, he foraged for berries, mushrooms, and roots. When he returned to Berlin after peddling trips, he was forced to go through the city gate reserved for cows, goats, pigs—and Jews. His was the fate of Jews who were forbidden to own homes, to establish businesses, or even to worship in a synagogue—if, of course, building a synagogue was permitted by local authorities."

Josef and Frida nodded in recognition of truths with which they had grown up. Leo gave them a moment to reflect and then went on with his tale.

"Uri was a prudent fellow and learned all he could about the trade routes, currencies, languages, and commodities of Europe. His reputation grew, and soon nobles of the land, now without the support and expertise of serfs, called on him to help navigate their commercial affairs. One of those nobles was so impressed that he invited Uri to become part of his court. He needed Uri to advise him on economic and political issues, and to secure sources of labor, food, munitions, and money for his principality. The noble also needed Uri's knowledge of Europe's trade routes, his fluency in multiple European languages, and his mastery of the money systems throughout the continent. Uri agreed and signed on as a *Hofjude*, a Court Jew.

"Uri became known for his usefulness. His ease with the courtiers, who were enamored of his quick wit and worldly manners, became legendary. He became so essential to maintaining the noble's estate that he was rewarded with a hefty income, splendid clothes, the right to live outside the Jewish ghetto in the noble's court, and to share the privileges of Christian courtiers. He dropped his Jewish name and was given the title of Count Conrad Ferdinand of Rhineland."

"There were Court Jews in my family," Frida interrupted. "They served Prince Ludwig of Brandenburg, a favorite of the emperor. For that role, they had to convert. It was a major issue for generations."

"Of course, conversion broke up families," said Josef, his voice rising. "How could it not?"

Leo took a moment to respond. "Yes," he said, "religious differences caused rifts in Jewish families. But there were positive aspects to the roles of Court Jews. Although they risked the wrath of nobles who could dismiss them on a whim, they often acted as Christianized intermediaries between the Jews and the ruling classes in gaining Jewish privileges or even in easing some restrictions."

Josef listened intently, fidgeting in his chair and strumming his fingers. "That's all well and good. But it was just the start of traditional decline!" he exclaimed.

Noticing Frida's increasing discomfort with the direction of the conversation, Leo paused to address her. "And you, my dear? Do you agree with Josef?"

Frida turned her head, averting Leo's eyes. "Maybe some people leave Judaism to protect themselves or even their future families," she said, her voice so low Leo could barely hear her.

Concerned with the tension building between the two young people, Rabbi Kohn steered the conversation in a different direction. "Not everyone agrees with conversion, that is true. In fact, most Jews want to keep their religion, but, over the years, some recognized the successes of the Court Jews. Gradually, many came to believe that the time had come, perhaps not to convert or enter a noble's court but to compromise. They saw that it was time for us to adapt to society—not for society to adapt to us—if we want to be accepted as equals in a Christian world."

Leo noticed that Frida was avoiding Josef's gaze and was taken aback when she quietly said, "Josef, this is exactly what we've been talking about. Please listen to the rabbi with an open mind."

Leo pondered her reaction for several seconds. He steepled his hands, sighed, and finally said, "Let me tell you another story. A personal one. When I first came to serve in New York, I believed strongly in Orthodox ways and traditional ritual. Practicing my faith the same way generations before me had seemed the only path to follow." He smiled wistfully, recalling past times. "Ah, tradition, how sweet it is! I can still smell my mother's Friday night chicken roasting over the fire. The chatter at our family's table after she lit the candles to welcome in the Sabbath still warms my heart."

He chuckled, recalling one eventful Sabbath night. "We were gathered around the hearth when sparks flew out of the fireplace. They ignited a glove puppet my mother had cherished since childhood. We jumped up, grabbed a cauldron of water from across the room, and threw it over the flames that were distorting the puppet's face. Only after the threat of fire spreading to engulf our home was over did we remember that the Torah forbids us to carry or extinguish on Shabbat. Our house was a mess but cleanable, nobody was hurt, and we simply realized that there must be exceptions to Sabbath mores."

When he finished his story, Leo noticed a shift in Frida's expression. A hush fell across the room. When neither Frida nor Josef moved to fill the silence, he pressed on. "So, you see, we must each decide when survival is at stake and do what we need to do. In fact, Ansche Beth Shalom has made some radical changes in the traditional approach to Judaism just so that we can survive in this evolving world."

Frida's interest seemed to spike, but Josef squirmed, wringing his hands. "You support changing tradition?" he asked. "I think I'll never understand what kind of Jew does that."

Leo's heart filled with empathy for all those caught between tradition and changing times. He had often questioned himself as he pondered changes to the rituals he had practiced and advocated most of his life. When he answered Josef, it was with solemnity in his voice. "That kind of Jew is one who believes that God wants his people to be free. Has it occurred to you, Josef," asked Leo, "that by adapting our religion to changing times, we might keep more people within the folds of Judaism?"

A quiet moment passed while Josef and Frida absorbed Leo's words. Enlightenment seemed to appear on their faces, encouraging Leo to share more of his thoughts. "As it happens," he continued, "we Jews are getting along well with most of our Christian neighbors."

Frida's interest continued to pique, her stiffened posture easing as Leo spoke. "You have truly noticed brotherhood in New York?" she asked.

"Yes, I have," said Leo, "because those of us—Jews and non-Jews alike—who have come from Germany are all newcomers to this country. We all want to succeed in America, and we all welcome the support of others who share our German language and German history. We are neighbors and colleagues who get along well. We do business, and we live and work together without fear." He felt his eyes filling with tears. "Whatever happened in Germany is behind us. In America, I am free to follow my heart and to raise my family in a place that accepts us."

Suddenly, the atmosphere in the study relaxed, and the tension between Josef and Frida lessened. Leo rose from his chair, grinning. He walked out from behind the desk and sat casually on its gleaming mahogany surface. "Perhaps you would like to attend our services next Friday evening? You will enjoy our new choir."

"Ansche Beth Shalom has a choir?" Josef asked.

Leo smiled. "Yes, we do. And it's a good one. Quite beautiful, really. We follow other reforms, too. The women in the balcony no longer sit behind a lattice; why should they be estranged? Our services are conducted in German and English, as well as in Hebrew, so our congregants can understand them.

"But we also uphold traditional beliefs. Although there are changes happening in Jewish practice, we study the Torah, we observe all the holidays, and we remain Jewish in our hearts and souls. Does the addition of music, a choir, an organ to our services diminish our ongoing conversation with God? If He created All, He created music. There are changes happening throughout Judaism. They are happening here at Ansche Beth Shalom, but they are also happening at Ansche Chesed over on Norfolk Street and at the new Temple Emanuel on Grand Street."

Josef put his head back and closed his eyes. After several moments, he reached for Frida's hand. "This sounds like a good place for us. As long as the Torah is sacrosanct here, I could give up some ritual if it means that you and I can get past our disagreements."

Frida drew in a deep breath and a smile crossed her lips. "Good," she said, "good."

As the tension left the air, Leo returned to his chair and sat back, crossing his legs at the knees and folding his hands in his lap. "But enough philosophy. Let's talk about your marriage plans. Have you thought about how you will support yourselves?"

Josef's face lit up as he described his new job, predicting a solid future as he assumed more and more responsibility at the Emporium. "I'm a hard worker, Rabbi. I know I will do well and succeed."

"You are right, Josef. Hard work will get you far. But meanwhile, have you found a place to make a home? If not, I have some thoughts on the matter."

Josef and Frida turned to face each other. Leo realized immediately that the question made them uncomfortable. *Obviously,* Leo thought, *they haven't made suitable arrangements.* He decided to give the young people a moment to ponder the practicalities facing them.

Finally, Frida spoke. "We will manage, Rabbi. Perhaps we can find a boardinghouse that will take us as a married couple. Or we can each stay where we are until we find a suitable home."

Leo took a deep breath, adjusted his collar, and placed his hands under his chin. "I think I can help you with that," he said, his eyes dancing. "Fritz Bayer, one of the maintenance men in our Hebrew School, has a vacant room to sublease. He is anxious to have someone move in who could adopt his dog. He cannot provide for her properly because he works a lot of overtime and cannot be home enough to take care of her. In return, he will grant a reduced rent of a dollar fifty per week. Might that be of interest to you?"

Josef nearly jumped out of his chair. Turning to Frida, he exclaimed, "Now what do you think of that, darling? And the dog would be wonderful."

For the first time since they entered Leo's office, Frida grinned. "Oh, yes, Rebbe. A home and a pet. What kind of dog is it?"

Leo smiled. "It's a wiener dog. She's long, like a sausage. Shall I tell Fritz you will take the room?"

Josef reached over the arm of his chair and tenderly took Frida's hand in his. "We finally have a home," he said softly, looking deeply into her eyes. "A place we will call our own."

"All right," said Leo. "And now to the question of a wedding. I have obligations this week, but come to my home next Thursday afternoon, and you shall be married. My wife will prepare a small celebration for after the ceremony."

Leo couldn't help but notice how Josef and Frida moved closer to each other, love filling the small space between them. Yes, they reminded him of his love with Tilly and the delicious anticipation they had shared just before their marriage.

A few minutes later, as Frida and Josef made their way down the steps to the street, he called after them with a last-minute thought. "Bring two witnesses with you. This will be a day to remember."

Frida felt relief bathe over her as she and Josef left Ansche Beth Shalom. At long last, the waiting was almost over—just a little more than a week to go.

As they walked back to the boardinghouse, Josef was elated. "Can't you see us, Frida? Someday we'll have a whole houseful of little ones . . . and yes, a wiener dog. The children will be strong and healthy and happy. Why wouldn't they be with the best mother anyone could have?"

As he dreamed on, Frida loved him even more than she had thought possible. Joining him in his daydreams, she forgot her troubles and got lost in the prospect of a bright future. Rabbi Kohn had seemed optimistic about Jewish life in America. *Wouldn't it be wonderful if he is right?*

Just then, for the second time that day, a wave of nausea jolted her back to reality. *This isn't the first time nausea has washed over me. A baby is coming. Please, please, God, let it be Josef's with his beautiful heart and sweet face.* Involuntarily, calculations invaded her mind. They were taking over the joy she had been feeling and blinding her to the wonderful moments she should be sharing right now, right this minute, with Josef. The familiar bile started to rise in her gut as *Jude Bitch* rang in her ears and played havoc with her heart. *I won't think of it now. I won't. I could never think of my baby as that vile bastard's. NEVER.*

Through the haze of her thoughts, she heard Josef still making plans for their future. As darkness made its descent and the sun cast an orange glow over the city, so did the chill in the air warn them that night was quickly settling in. They picked up their pace against the wind starting to whip through the narrow streets, and they joined other pedestrians all heading for the shelter of their homes. Frida drew her shawl more tightly around her, her thoughts darkening with every step. She imagined various ways to kill her rapist. *I'd strap him down and slice him from head to toe with a Bowie knife . . . or cut him in half with a steel sword. Oh, yes!*

As she knew they would be, Bertha and Amalia were waiting for her in the parlor when she and Josef stepped through the boardinghouse door. "We need to talk," said Bertha, after a few awkward moments. "Perhaps it's best if we go upstairs."

Josef brought Frida's hand to his lips and kissed it gently. Promising to see her soon, he turned to leave, his step lighter than Frida had ever seen it.

When they reached their room, Frida watched with horror as

Amalia went to her cot and took something from under the pillow. Turning slowly toward Frida, her eyes tearing and her lips trembling, Amalia unfolded her fist to reveal Frida's Star of David. Frida's knees gave way. Bertha caught her just before she hit the floor.

"It's okay, Frida. It's okay. We know your secret," she said.

It took Frida a moment to recover. When she did, her cheeks burned with humiliation, and her eyes shot daggers. "How did you get that? You went through my personal things? How dare you!" she shouted, trying to wrest herself from Bertha's grasp.

"It was on the floor when we came in. Neither of us would dream of violating your privacy," whispered Amalia, reaching her hand out to Frida to help her stand. "We know how you feel, Frida. You can talk to us. We're afraid, too."

Something in Amalia's affect rang true for Frida. Perhaps it was the quiver of Amalia's lip or the depth of her gaze. *Maybe she is telling the truth. I was hasty in tucking the star under the mattress. Perhaps it slipped to the floor, and I didn't notice. Still, what is the sisters' reaction to the star? They don't seem upset with my reveal. . .but be careful, Frida. Be careful!*

"Why are you afraid?" Frida finally asked, conjuring up as much annoyance as she could. "What do you have to be fearful of?"

Wordlessly, Bertha and Amalia turned to the bureau. They each lifted something from a drawer, closed a fist around it, and tearfully opened their hands at the same time. A Star of David lay on each palm, the sterling silver shiny, obviously cherished.

Silence filled the small room. No one spoke. Then, wordlessly, the three women came together and embraced. Several moments passed. Bertha was the first to speak. "Like so many others, we fled Germany during the revolution two years ago. We traveled together. You came alone. How did you have the courage?" she asked.

"It wasn't courage," Frida whispered, her voice barely above a whisper. "It was desperation. But tell me about you. Why and how did you make your way here to New York?"

She waited patiently while Bertha and Amalia gathered their thoughts. Their furtive glances told Frida that theirs was a difficult story fraught with fear and doubt.

At last, Bertha, always the more outspoken of the two, broke the silence. "Our brother was associate to Bernard Wolff, one of the founders of the *National Zeitung.* It was a liberal daily newspaper that supported the revolution. In fact, he even fought with Leopold Zunz in Berlin. Have you heard of Zunz?"

Frida nodded solemnly. "Is he not the one who called on a big crowd to storm the royal arsenal at the *Konigstrasse?* I remember hearing about that."

"Yes, that was Zunz," said Amalia. "Bertha and I were teachers in his school for a while. He was a powerful fellow with a strong, persuasive voice. The crowd was ready for a fight. You can't blame them. Food was scarce because of the crop failures the last few years. Famine affected everything. Incomes were down, and people were angry, watching the wealthy carry on as if nothing could, or would, affect them."

Amalia continued, her voice shaking as she recalled the fighting. "Our brother told us how Zunz cried out for more guns and ammunition. 'It's a bloody Day of Judgment for our oppressors. We need weapons and a national guard, twenty thousand strong!' The crowd grew furious, and a terrible energy burst forth. It was like a dam breaking. Bertha and I covered our ears to drown out the anguish in our mother's voice as she begged our brother not to go out into the violence. He wouldn't listen. He said he believed in a united Germany, that it was his duty to help the rebels.

"Cannon fire filled the night, and we huddled in our home watching fires burn holes in the black sky and wondering how Brother was faring. Heavy smoke filled the air and seeped through the house, filling our lungs and burning our nostrils. Just outside our window, the roar was deafening as marchers took up their calls for equality under the law. We heard terrible screams as guns reached their marks, and swords found soft flesh. Horses bellowed in terror, galloping through the streets and throwing many a young rebel into the gutters. Many of the protesters saw their comrades slaughtered in front of them or dragged off to prison."

Shaking, Frida tried to process what the sisters were saying. "We heard about the fighting in Berlin, but we didn't know how bloody it was. How long did it last?" she asked.

Bertha sighed deeply, and her eyes filled with grief. "It went on until at least four in the morning. As things started to quiet down, I went to look out the door and stumbled on something at the threshold. It was heavy, and I almost fell onto the street; I caught myself just in time. When I looked down, there was our brother, a bloodied heap. His hair had been burned off, and his eyes had been gouged. The handle of a sword still showed in his chest, its blade exiting from a deep gash. Blood puddled around his lifeless body. Around his throat was a note: *This is what happens to Jew troublemakers.*"

Seeing the anguish in the sisters' eyes, Frida blanched and choked back her own tears. "How terrible," she said, her voice barely rising above a whisper.

"That was just the beginning," Amalia said, her lips quivering, her eyes widening, and her complexion blotching as she struggled to breathe. Her voice caught as she explained, "The Jews were blamed for the trouble. The population claimed that because they were demanding the same rights as their Christian neighbors, they were responsible for the violence. Rallies were held, and bulletins were posted for huge ransoms leading to the arrests of Jews. Our mother had lost one child; she insisted that Bertha and I go to America as soon as arrangements could be made. We begged her to come with us, but her health was poor, and she refused. When we said we would not consider leaving her, she wept and told us she could not bear to risk our safety. 'You must go to America,' she'd insisted, 'if you want me to live out my days without fear.'

"Unbeknownst to us, Mama had purchased our fares and set a date for our departure from Hamburg to New York. It was a long, difficult trip from Berlin to meet the ship, but here we are, in America, making our way on foreign shores and unsure of what the future will bring."

Just then, the dinner bell rang, bringing the three women back to the reality of the boardinghouse. They freshened up and headed down to the dining hall in silent camaraderie. For the first time since she had left her friends in Hamburg, Frida dared to wonder if she might find peace in her new world.

As they found places at the dinner table, Frida joined the chatter before dinner was served, secure in the knowledge that soon, very soon, she would be sharing her meals—her life—with Josef. She sat quietly through the gray meat and boiled potatoes until, finally, it was time to retire. It was only when she and the Albrecht sisters closed the door of their room that Frida spoke. "I have news," she said, her eyes dancing. "You have met Josef," she said. "And I'm happy to tell you that we will be married in just eleven days."

"But you have just gotten here!" Bertha exclaimed.

"You are leaving us already?" Amalia added.

"Yes, I am," said Frida. "Josef and I have planned to marry since we were children. Rabbi Kohn has agreed to perform the ceremony a week from Thursday at his home." She paused to allow Bertha and Amalia to absorb her words.

When they finally spoke, it was with joy in their voices.

"All right," declared Bertha, asserting her authority. "Our time, Frida, belongs to you. We will do your hair and press your clothes. You do have a dress, don't you?"

Frida nodded, her eyes misting as she thought of the beautiful yellow gown.

"Oh, and you can use my gloves. I just got them at the Emporium last week," Bertha offered.

"You can carry my purse," added Amalia.

"And shoes," suggested Bertha. "Do you have proper shoes for a wedding? You can use my leather boots," she offered excitedly.

Frida laughed, smiling at her roommates' enthusiasm and filling them in with details about Josef's job and their new home. "Will you be our witnesses?" she finally asked, gratified with the new closeness she was feeling and pleased that guests would attend the wedding.

"Of course we will," Bertha answered, a broad grin filling her face. "But now, let's get to work. We will inform Frau Schultz you will be leaving, and we'll shop for something for the dog."

"We will also find a *mikvah* bath for you," Amalia chimed in.

Frida froze. The mikvah. It was a detail she hadn't considered. *Josef would want me to undergo the monthly cleansing ritual. He expects me to do it. But do I want to? Am I worthy?*

She looked into her heart. She didn't like what she saw.

But there really is no choice, is there?

CHAPTER 8

Frida

Bertha and Amalia kept Frida busy all week. First, they went with her to see Frau Schultz, who was none too pleased that Frida was leaving so soon after her arrival.

"You will not, under any circumstances, receive money back from your rent," she had declared, her tone leaving no room for negotiation. She had left the parlor abruptly, her boots tap-tapping furiously as she stomped across the floor to return to her office.

"Frau Schultz certainly didn't waste any words congratulating you, did she?" laughed Amalia, starting off a wave of giggles so merry that Frida could scarcely stand.

It had been the start of a week filled with the kind of pampering that Frida had not experienced since childhood, as several other boarders joined in the excitement of readying the bride for her big day. Early yesterday morning, a warm bath in the tin tub off the hallway had awaited. Her attire had been assembled, her few belongings packed, and a trip to Chatham Street had yielded a fat bone for the dog.

Then came the moment Frida had anticipated with trepidation. Bertha announced that she had arranged for Frida to visit the mikvah. An ancient rite, it was customary for a bride to immerse herself in a designated pool of water to revive original purity and enter marriage in a state of chastity.

"Amalia and I will be glad to go with you, Frida," Bertha had offered, her demeanor more like that of an older sister than a new friend. "The timing is right for you, is it not?"

"Yes," Frida answered. "I am not experiencing my monthly."

Jude Bitch, Jude Bitch! screamed Otto's voice in Frida's mind. *I did not bleed when I should have . . . a baby coming . . . I am NOT chaste. No one must know. Mama, Mama, how could you turn your back on me? Why couldn't you support me? I need you . . .*

The thoughts spun so fast Frida feared she might collapse. Then, seemingly out of nowhere, she heard her own voice calmly reassuring Bertha and Amalia that she wished to perform the mikvah ritual alone. "I want to bask in my love for Josef and savor my anticipation in solitude," she assured her roommates.

Bertha and Amalia had nodded sympathetically while Amalia exclaimed, "How beautiful! But we insist on seeing you safely to the mikvah door."

A short time later, the roommates climbed down the boardinghouse steps to the street. As they walked, Bertha and Amalia each took one of Frida's arms and chatted happily about commitment, marriage, and love. When they reached their destination, the sisters embraced Frida and asked if she were sure that she wanted to go into the mikvah by herself.

"I am fine from here," said Frida. "Go, go. I will see you later."

Reluctantly, the women turned away while Frida slowly climbed the risers to the building's entrance. When she got to the top step, she stopped, saw her roommates turn the corner, and went back down to the cobblestones. It would be several hours until she could return to Frau Schultz's without suspicion. She walked aimlessly, her eyes searching for faces from the boardinghouse or anyone who might recognize her. Wary, she waited until the sun started to go down in the cold November sky, pleased that she had not seen anyone of consequence. Finally, her feet throbbing, she headed back to the boardinghouse and to the approval of the boarders who bestowed her with praise and good wishes. *I did it,* she thought, *no one will know otherwise, but I kept true to myself. Hopefully, God will understand that I did what I had to do.*

The streets in New York always amazed Frida. They twisted around each other like balls of yarn, and she marveled at how the rushing pedestrians seemed to know exactly where they were going. She found herself envying even the horses that seemed so sure of themselves in this strange city.

When she arrived back at the boardinghouse, the women were streaming into the dining hall for dinner. Frida receded into their camaraderie, grateful not to be alone with Bertha and Amalia. By the time they returned to their room, Frida pleaded exhaustion, climbed into bed, and feigned sleep until she finally drifted off into a restless night.

The following morning, after some sleepy moments nestling into her covers, the sisters' excited fussing about roused Frida and thrust her into the moment. There were many last-minute preparations, and Frida was determined to occupy herself with thoughts of her new life with Josef. She missed her mother but Josef would be waiting at the rabbi's home. Her heart soared at the prospect.

All morning, the boardinghouse women continued to stream into Frida's room to help her bathe and to wish her well. Some brought small gifts. There was a sachet of sweet-smelling rose petals, slender candles to someday adorn a table, a small box of chocolates, and, from Bertha and Amalia, a china wedding cup adorned with cupids and delicately painted doves.

When it was time to leave, Frida took a long last look around Frau Schultz's establishment. The porcelain monkey seemed to speak to her from the depths of her brocade bag: *When you came here, this house gave you ugliness; as you leave, it offers the beauty of friendship. Remember my lessons and treasure them always.*

"I think I will miss this place," she commented to Bertha and Amalia, as they closed the heavy front door behind them.

Overhead, gray clouds moved in swiftly. Frida's cheeks flushed a deep pink, and her eyes gleamed as the three picked up their pace against the winter chill. For the first time since her arrival in New York, the crowds seemed to fade into the background as they wended their way through the narrow streets.

When they arrived at the rabbi's home, the rebbetzin was waiting for them at the front door. "Hello," she said warmly. "I am Matilde Kohn. Most people call me Tilly. And this is my daughter, Lotte. She's our eldest child. Her two sisters are too young to be here. With your permission, she would like to attend your wedding. Lotte, say hello to the future Mrs. Rosenstrauss."

The four-year-old shyly extended her hand to Frida. "I'm Lotte," she said. "My mama says today is a special day, so I have on my most special dress. It's yellow, like yours. Do you like it?"

"Oh, yes," said Frida, warmed by the child's sweetness. "I like it very much."

"I like yellow," offered Lotte, "because it's the color of the sun."

"Please, come in," laughed Tilly, "or she will be here all afternoon chattering away."

Tilly ushered Frida, Bertha, and Amalia into a graciously furnished parlor and offered them seats on a curved green velvet sofa. Plants of every size occupied tables and the floor, and books lined shelves that reached to the ten-foot-high ceiling. Rising from a deep leather wing chair toward the back of the room, Leo stood and walked toward them, his deep voice booming greetings and congratulations.

At the corner of the room, standing in front of two tall, six-paned windows adorned with damask curtains, was Josef, dressed in his best black suit. A white carnation was tucked into his jacket pocket, and he sported a tall black hat in the newest men's style. When he saw Frida, his eyes filled and he nodded gently, his lips silently forming "I love you" as he gazed upon her.

"Since we are a small gathering, we have dispensed with most formalities today, as you may have noticed," Leo said. "But before we begin, Tilly would like to have a word with you, Frida."

"Of course," said Frida nervously, as she followed Tilly to an adjacent sitting room.

"My dear," said Tilly, "let us sit and chat for a moment. It must be difficult entering marriage in a strange new place without the benefit of family guiding you. Is there any way I can be of assistance before you wed?"

Without warning, Frida drew in her breath, and hot tears came to her eyes. How she had always yearned to share her wedding day with Roshen. *But Mama is in the past. I won't think of her now. I won't.* "I miss my family but having us to your home today is quite enough. I am greatly honored, as is Josef, and deeply appreciative."

"We are happy to do this for you, my dear," said Tilly. "My husband is quite taken with you both, and I am delighted that Lotte will take part in your happiness. Thank you for including her. But let us chat of some practical matters. I imagine you have attended the mikvah?"

Frida hesitated, her mind spinning. *The baby,* she thought. *I must think of the baby. Say what you have to say, Frida. Do what must be done.* When she finally answered Tilly, her voice was cool and even. "The mikvah is tradition," she said. "It is tradition."

Tilly smiled and took Frida's hand. "Good," she said and began to speak of a Jewish wife's obligations. Frida listened with half an ear, her mind darting about and seeking respite from her tumultuous thoughts. *Josef's baby or that dreadful Otto's. The Holstein, Jude*

Bitch, the lindens . . . no one knows the truth . . . even I don't know the truth. . .Mama, Mama, Mama!

When, at last, Tilly completed her talk, the two walked back to the parlor. As they entered, the few guests present stood to greet them. There were Bertha and Amalia and, much to Frida's delight, Josef's old friend, Stefan Hartmann, who was certainly older than the last time she had seen him but still had his wide grin and kind eyes. After a few brief greetings were exchanged, Josef walked across the room to meet her, and they stood to face Leo.

"Shall we begin?" Leo asked, as he silently pointed to everyone's places for the ceremony. "You have come alone to this country, so this is not a traditional wedding," he said. "But you are committed to each other, and that is tradition enough for me."

As he officiated, Leo spoke of the joys of Jewish marriage, as well as of its expectations. When he offered the last prayer, he bestowed blessings upon them and placed the traditional glass, wrapped in a fine white linen napkin, near Josef's raised foot.

"Mazel tov!" shouted everyone in the small party as Josef stomped on the glass, shattering it in accordance with thousands of years of Jewish practice.

As she heard the glass breaking into shards, Frida involuntarily winced. *The shards are like my life. There they lie, wrapped tightly in a swaddling cloth. They are contained but can never be made whole again. The question is, can I?*

After the ceremony, everyone retired to the Kohns' dining room. Frida was taken aback by all the trouble they had seemed to go through for them. The table was set with a silver tea service, fine Gold Band china, and orange chrysanthemums arranged around a small white wedding cake, which sat in the center. A repast of tea sandwiches, raisin crumpets, and plump red grapes beckoned the wedding guests to celebrate.

"Let us toast the bride and groom," announced Leo, as Tilly poured white wine from a crystal decanter. "I've known Frida and Josef only briefly, but they have shown me their courage, their wisdom, and their hearts. Their strength will carry them through hard times; their devotion to each other will bolster them; and their love will carry them through all their lives. Mazel tov, Mr. and Mrs. Rosenstrauss!" After the toast, congratulatory hugs and kisses followed, and everyone helped themselves to the beautifully arranged treats waiting for them. When it was finally time to depart for home, Stefan, Bertha, and Amalia bid the newlyweds all the best, exacting promises for visits to be paid soon.

As darkness fell, Josef and Frida spoke in soft tones to Leo and Tilly.

"You have done so much for us," Josef said. "How can we ever thank you?"

Leo grinned. "Just be as happy as Tilly and I have been, and that will be enough."

As they left the Kohns' home, Josef gathered Frida close to him to shield her from the cold of the December night. Rain had started to fall, diffusing the light from the gas lamps atop their black wrought-iron poles. The effect made the usually harsh streets assume a soft, protective aura. Frida breathed in Josef's scent, his sweet smell filling her senses and quickening her heartbeat. *Mr. and Mrs. Josef Rosenstrauss! We are one. At long last, we are one,* she thought.

When they arrived at Fritz's building, he beckoned them into a front parlor furnished with odds and ends of mismatched furniture. Clearing a pile of papers from a threadbare blue sofa, he motioned to

Frida and Josef to take off their wet outer clothes and have a seat. He was a short, balding man in his early thirties. With a belly starting to overstay its welcome under his high-waisted pants, Fritz's mellow voice belied his appearance.

"Welcome," he said heartily, "to your new home. I am delighted you are here, and I am sure that we will do well in our new arrangement." Just then, he whistled, and a plump chestnut-colored wiener dog with long ears and the shortest legs Frida had ever seen wiggled its way from behind an overstuffed brown chair.

"Good girl," Fritz Bayer crooned, rubbing the animal behind the ears. The dog turned over and stretched her paws in the air. Laughing, Fritz squatted and rubbed the dog's abdomen until she had enough and rolled back onto all fours. "Get used to this routine. She insists upon it many times a day."

Frida grinned and stooped to pat the dog, her eyes lighting with delight. "What's her name?"

"Her name is Brunhilde. It means 'Glorious Battle Maiden.' Do you think it suits her?"

Josef answered Fritz with mock seriousness. "Obviously, the dog has the fierce temperament that her name implies!"

Fritz grinned. "Oh, very fierce," he said. "About as fierce as a potato dumpling!"

As they chatted about Brunhilde, Frida relaxed in Fritz Bayer's company, settling into the comfort of Josef's casual embrace around her shoulders. By the time Fritz took them to their room, the dog trotting along happily, they were comfortable and at ease. "I'll leave you now," said Fritz, after he lit a gas lamp. "We can talk more tomorrow."

As Fritz closed the door behind him, Josef and Frida came together and wordlessly looked about their new surroundings. The lamp's soft flame cast a glow over the room, illuminating its contents. Two feather beds stood against an adjacent wall. A small oak dresser, a rocker with a fat upholstered cushion, and an iron potbellied stove easily filled the small space. A single window took up the far wall, lights from the street filtering in to create dancing shadows on the tin ceiling as passersby hurried along the cobblestones.

Josef was the first to speak. "We are home, Frida. At last, we are home."

He removed the damp shawl from Frida's shoulders and placed it on a warming stand near the stove. While Frida trembled, Josef untied her bonnet, dismayed when she let out a small cry and her palm flew to the scar tissue under her chin. Gently, he removed her hand and placed his warm lips on the raised flesh. He lingered there a moment, then cupped her chin in his hands. His touch was warm and soft, and Frida felt herself give way as they pressed together, seeking each other with urgency.

As she felt him against her, Frida shuddered. *Jude Bitch, Jude Bitch* crowded her senses. She fought to push Otto out of her mind, refusing to let him destroy these precious moments. Cold sweat ran between her breasts, and her knees threatened to buckle.

"It's all right, Frida, it's all right," Josef whispered, his voice low and soothing.

As he kissed her, Frida tasted salty tears spilling from Josef's eyes and falling to his lips. They mingled with her own and filled Frida with longing. Several moments passed as the beating of their hearts flooded their senses, and the outside world ebbed away. Frida swayed as Josef pulled her ever closer, wrapping his arms tightly around her. With a deep sigh, he removed the clasp holding back her luxuriant tresses and buried his head in their fragrant perfume. He soon found the silk-covered buttons that reached from Frida's slender neck to her waist. When the gown fell to the floor, its yellow silk shimmering in the glow of the flames, he kissed her again and lifted her to the softness of the nearest featherbed.

Removing his waistcoat and shirt, he climbed in beside her, cradling her in his arms. They lay quietly together for a while, basking in the newness of their marriage. As the moments passed, they again became aware of the closeness of their bodies and reached for each other with quickened pulses, devotion, and trust.

Later that night, Frida awoke with a start to someone pounding on the door. Her body began to shake, and she burrowed under the blankets to block out the sound, but it was of no use. To her horror, Josef was oblivious to the insistence of the hammering fists. Unable to wake him, she cowered into a ball and tried to block out the intruding noise. Suddenly, the door splintered, and a huge hand reached for the inside knob, twisting it until the latch clicked open. The battering of her heart filled her ears as she lay in helpless wait.

When she dared to open her eyes, a shadowy figure stood at the foot of her bed. It loomed over her, its form unclear. A shroud covered its head and minuscule, faceless babies swarmed over its hairy chest. She tried to scream, but her throat was soundless with fear. As the figure approached her, Frida tried to reach for Josef, but he was gone, a hollow gash in the bed appearing where his sleeping form had been only moments before. The figure loomed larger as its shadows dominated the room.

Drawing up all the courage she could muster, Frida finally broke out of her paralysis. "Who are you?" she screamed. "Who are you?!"

As she tried to crawl away, her limbs spasmed and froze, and she was held down by an iron arm. Hot breath pushed against her cheeks until, suddenly, she heard an urgent voice that seemed to come from nowhere. It was Josef, holding her tightly against his chest.

"You shouted of babies, darling. There are no babies," he assured her. "There's no one here but you and me."

But there is a baby, Frida thought. *God help me, there is a baby.*

CHAPTER 9

Josef

More than a month had passed since Josef and Frida celebrated their wedding. The workday at the Emporium had just ended, and Josef was battered by blustery weather. When conditions were fair, he enjoyed being outside as a puller-in; he did not enjoy his job at times like this when sleet whipped his face, frigid winds cut through him, and the icy pavement stung his toes through worn-out shoes. Sometimes he thought that the only thing that kept him going through these conditions was knowing Frida was waiting for him.

He had taken just a few steps to head home when Mr. Baum called out to him. "Josef, I know you are in a hurry, but I need to see you before you leave. Please come back into the building and meet me at my office in a few minutes."

Josef nodded his agreement. He rushed back into the store and shook the snow from his threadbare coat, grateful for the warmth that enveloped him.

Mr. Baum was almost done ringing up a purchase with a customer that everyone knew to be difficult. "I'll be there as soon as I finish with Mrs. Goldstern."

"Is . . . is everything all right?" Josef managed to ask.

"I have something important to discuss with you," Mr. Baum replied, turning his attention back to the customer. I will be right with you."

When Josef reached the office, he paced back and forth and wondered if the boss was angry with him about something. Against his will, he conjured up a scene in which he would get fired. He wondered how he would tell Frida that they were now penniless.

Finally, Mr. Baum appeared, unlocked the office door, and sat at his oak rolltop desk. "Come in," he said, motioning to a wooden chair next to him.

"Mr. Baum," Josef said, clearing his throat and trying not to shake. "If I did something wrong . . ."

"Wrong?" Mr. Baum interrupted, his eyes starting to twinkle. "Quite the contrary. I couldn't be more pleased."

Josef took a deep breath and sat further back into his chair, the chill in his bones dissipating. "Thank you," he said, his breath catching with relief.

"No, no. Thank *you*," said Mr. Baum. "I am amazed by how many customers you have brought into the Emporium. After the last fellow we had, I wondered if it was even worth having a puller-in." He paused for a moment and then added, "The thing is. . ."

Josef stiffened. *The thing is. What thing?*

". . . business is growing. An associate just retired, and I need another salesman on the floor. Without a doubt, I'll lose my best puller-in, but, as I said, we're busier than ever and you have demonstrated true talent."

"I'm not sure what you're saying, Mr. Baum," Josef stammered, as he involuntarily clenched his fists and tried to hide his growing confusion.

"Josef," Mr. Baum said in German, "I'd like you to be our new salesman. There's more money in it if you agree. Furthermore, because I have great hopes for our affiliation, I am offering you a commission on every sale you complete. The position also offers the attractive advantage of keeping you indoors on days like this."

Josef beamed as he shook the manager's hand. "Thank you," he grinned. "I will be pleased to accept your offer and will be the finest salesman you have ever had." As he breathed a sigh of relief, his thoughts raced to the future. *It looks like someday, Frida and I will have all the riches that we had once in Hamburg, that others have even now . . . a gracious home, plentiful food, luxuries . . .*

"Very well," Mr. Baum replied, reaching out to accept Josef's handshake. "You will start tomorrow."

When Josef left the Emporium, sleet had started to pelt the city, stabbing its victims with bullets of ice. Josef hastened his step, stopping only for a few minutes to purchase Frida's favorite pastry from Cooper's Bakery. Such delicacies were saved for special occasions, and this was an event worth celebrating. The thought of Frida sharing his news and biting deliciously into the sugary Linzer torte warmed his heart and spurred him on until he finally reached the house.

With freezing fingers, Josef unlocked the front door and bounded up the stairs where Frida was waiting. As usual, he found her in the rocking chair, knitting shawls that she would later trim with exquisite bobbin lace. Brunhilde was curled at her feet on a rose-colored rug. Frida had always excelled in crafts, skills she had learned from her grandmother when she was a small girl. Recently, she was spending many hours with her knitting needles, humming as she deftly transformed balls of woolen yarn and fine silk thread into garments of unique design.

In appreciation for their kindnesses, Frida had made matching, yellow-knit jackets for Lotte Kohn and her younger sisters. They featured flared bodices and long, bell-shaped sleeves falling from dropped shoulders. Each was trimmed with a wide border of rose-patterned lace. A knitted yellow silk shawl for Tilly and intricately patterned yarmulkes for Leo bore the same borders.

"You know, my dear," Tilly had told her when she first saw some of Frida's creations, "people would enjoy these items. Perhaps some of our congregants would consider purchasing similar things. I can inquire for you."

Tilly was right. The winter had, so far, been a bitter one and, in many households, there simply was not enough time to create ample supplies of warm garments. The congregation had responded to Frida's talents, and orders were coming in steadily. There were even requests for tablecloths and challah-coverings for the Sabbath meal, so many that Frida brought in the Albrecht sisters and a few of the boarders from Frau Schultz's house to help. The knitters spilled over from the kitchen to the parlor when necessary, but the more orders they received, the more crowded the small space became.

"Josef, I've been worried about you in this storm," Frida said, as Josef came in from the street. She placed her knitting aside and stood. "Come, sit by the stove."

"It's bitter out there," Josef said, shedding his coat, scarf, and wet shoes. "But I have news that's kept me warm. Do you want to know what it is?" he teased, as he took her in his arms.

"I gathered that something good was afoot," Frida laughed. "You've brought me a pastry."

Josef hugged her tighter, loving the close warmth of her body. "You are no longer talking to an Emporium puller-in," he whispered. "You are now the wife of a salesman. I've been promoted, and there's more money in it, too."

Josef let his words linger while Frida took them in, her dark eyes suddenly filling with an unreadable expression. "Are you not happy, Frida? I thought this news would bring you joy," he said, worry in his voice.

"It's just in time," said Frida, her cheeks flushing. "Come with me."

Gently, she took his hand and led him to her bed. Standing at its side, she reached to the buttons at the side of her dress, releasing them one by one. Slowly, she pulled the garment away from her until it puddled on the floor. Looking directly into Josef's eyes, she removed her undergarments and climbed onto the soft feather mattress.

Afraid to break the gentle silence between them, Josef lay quietly next to her until she took his palm and slipped it against her naked belly. There was a small bulge there that he had not noticed before. "I don't understand, Frida. Are you well? I don't like that lump. The new money is coming just in time. We'll be able to bring you to a doctor to find out what the swelling is."

"No, that will not be necessary," she said, so softly he could barely hear her. She lay her hand on top of his. "It is your child you are feeling, Josef."

An unbidden gasp escaped from Josef's throat. "Are you sure, Frida?" he pleaded, his mind reeling.

"Yes, I am sure," she said. "I've suspected for a while, but I wanted to be certain before I told you. This will be a big change for us."

Suddenly, it seemed to Josef that the room was turning upside down. *A baby. It is a miracle. But so soon? We aren't prepared.* The cream-colored walls that had seemed so assuring to him just moments before seemed to be closing in on him. The furniture appeared to take up the whole room, and the window seemed as if it could never let in enough air.

A knock sounded on the door, startling them both.

"Who is it?" Josef called out.

"It's Fritz. I need to speak to you about an urgent matter."

Hurriedly, Frida dressed, clumsily avoiding Brunhilde, who was barking excitedly and running around in circles at the sound of Fritz's voice. When Josef finally opened the door, Fritz said, "I have some troubling news. The first of February is almost upon us, and I am unsure of what that will mean for this house."

Josef and Frida exchanged puzzled glances. "Does that date have something to do with us?" asked Frida.

"May I sit?" Beads of perspiration appeared on Fritz's brow.

"Of course," said Josef, hurriedly pulling the rocker over to accommodate Fritz's portly frame.

"Yes," said Fritz, "it may have everything—or nothing—to do with all of us. We won't know until the first of February, or Rent Day, as it is called in New York City."

Fritz took a large handkerchief from his pocket and wiped his brow. "On Rent Day," he explained, his voice choking up, "landlords post their annual rent changes. It takes place all over the city, and we tenants won't know until that day if our rents will go up or down over the next year. I rent this house from a fellow who owns many like it. He is an unpredictable sort, and I never know from year to year what will be. I hope you can forgive me if the rent is raised so high that we must move on May first. That's Moving Day for everyone in the city. Those who cannot afford their new rates move to less expensive quarters, and those who can afford more seek finer housing. I should have told you when you first arrived."

As suddenly as he had come, Fritz stood and let himself out, leaving Josef and Frida to stare at each other in astonishment.

"What will we do, Josef, if we must move? We have a child coming."

"Don't worry," he said, putting his arms around his wife. "Think of what your grandfather would have said."

Josef walked over to the porcelain monkey sitting on a shelf near the stove. He handed it to Frida. "This may prove to be a difficult time. But there is beauty in it, Frida. We have a child coming. I have my new job, and your knit goods are selling well. We will find ways to meet expenses."

That night, Josef lay awake listening to Frida's soft snores as he tossed and turned. When he finally fell into a fitful sleep, he dreamed that he was back in Hamburg in his father's house and enjoying every luxury conceivable. He was a child again, oblivious to matters of money and responsibility. He and Frida were playing on the terrace, pretending they were a grownup mother and father with perfect little children lined up in a row.

The children were dressed in satin and organdy, the boys with brocade ties at their necks and the girls with velvet bows in their hair. They were all smiling, bowing, and curtseying to one another, when they started to sing. Their sweet voices filled the air as they sang the song, *"Leise Rieselt der Schnee"* ("Quietly Flutters the Snow"). Then, without warning, dense snow began to fall, sending the children fleeing for cover. A screeching wind blew until it broke through the walls of the room and started to bury them in a blanket of ice.

"We want to eat!" the children screamed, as they became shrouded in yellow-lace jackets. "Feed us, feed us!" they demanded.

Their insistence sent Josef scurrying along the baseboards of a tiny room, searching without success for any scrap of food that may have fallen from an earlier meal.

"Josef, Josef," shouted Frida, "get up from the floor! What are you doing down there, my darling? Why are you crawling like that?"

"I must feed them. They are hungry," Josef cried, his eyes still shut against Frida's frantic efforts to rouse him.

When he finally awakened, huddled in Frida's arms, her kisses covering his face, he was pale and shaken. They sat rocking each other for a long time until they finally slept. When the small black clock on the dresser woke them in the morning, they found themselves still on the floor, their arms wrapped tightly around one another.

"We will think of something, Frida. You and our child will be safe." Abruptly, he got up and dressed for work. As he put on his overcoat, he lingered for a moment at the door. "I may have an idea, Frida," he said, then kissed her cheek and went out into the dawn, not giving Frida a chance to question him.

The day was cold and raw, but Josef was preoccupied. Deep in his pocket, he fingered a crumpled card that had lain dormant since he first arrived in New York. A half-smile crossed his face as he remembered the eager young man who had insisted he take it.

"I'm Peter O'Flanagan," the fellow had said when Josef disembarked the *Kronsprinz,* introducing himself with a strong handshake. "I'm from the Society of St. Tammany, or Tammany Hall, as most people call it."

O'Flanagan was a powerful fellow whose lean, muscular frame was almost six-and-a-half feet tall. He had a shock of red hair, freckles, and blazing blue eyes. His slightly off-center pug nose gave him the aura of someone much younger than his thirty-seven years. He had towered over Josef, taking advantage of his height and brawn to stop Josef in his tracks and force him to listen. "We greet passengers such as yourself when you first step foot on American soil," he had said in a booming voice, speaking German tinged with an Irish brogue. "America's a bit terrifying when you first get off the ship, no?"

"Thank you," Josef, said, averting his eyes, "but I am meeting my companion in a few minutes. He is picking up his luggage."

"Very well," O'Flanagan had said, "but take my card. I'll be glad to help you find lodging, or a job, or anything else you might need."

As Josef had walked away, the Irishman fell in with him, talking about Tammany's political pull and how the simple promise of a vote for a Tammany candidate at election time could earn Josef English lessons, introductions to local businessmen, and access to financial institutions and local commercial establishments. Josef listened but was fearful of becoming involved with political affiliations that might put him in a precarious position in this strange new land. O'Flanagan backed off when Josef finally met up with Stefan.

"This fellow is with me, and we are set in our plans," Stefan had told him. "Now please, thank you. We'll let you know if we need you."

As Josef neared the Emporium, his pace quickened. He would work hard and wait until the time was right to approach Mr. Baum—and to seek out Peter O'Flanagan. It was a good plan, and it would work.

It had to.

After just two weeks, the new position at the Emporium was working out well. Combined with sales of Frida's knit goods, Josef and Frida were experiencing a modest but welcome upward change in their ability to pay bills. In fact, Gottfried Baum had talked to Josef just a few days earlier about promoting him into the bookkeeping functions of the store.

As he reached the top step of his apartment house, Josef hesitated to go in to see Frida. It was Rent Day, and people all over *Kleindeutschland* were reacting to their rent changes. Josef sighed deeply as he thought of a wretched fellow who was standing on the street sobbing. The man had received news of an insurmountable raise on the rooms he shared with his sickly wife and five children, rooms that had already been compromised with downward mobility from previous Rent Days. He held a handmade sign begging for help in finding a place to live. Such had been the scene throughout the city as Josef made his way home to learn of his own situation.

When he reached their room, the door was open. Frida stood silently by the window, Brunhilde in her arms. She did not turn to face him as she whispered, "Fritz Bayer just left, Josef. His news was not good."

Josef walked over to Frida and put his arm around her shoulders, hugging her to him. They stood for several moments until Josef broke the silence. "Did Fritz say what he will do?" he asked, knowing what the answer would be.

"We will have to be out by May first, Moving Day. The landlord's demands are too great."

Leading Frida to the chair, Josef took her on his lap and stroked her hair. When he finally spoke, his voice was strong. "Frida, dearest," he said, wiping her tears. "Please. Don't worry," he managed to say in English.

Frida's face lit up. "You're learning English! How wonderful. I'm trying, too. It's not easy," she laughed.

"We are learning though, aren't we?" Reverting to German, he said, "I've been making inquiries, and I think I have a plan. I had hoped to wait until we become more accustomed to our new life, but we can start to implement the plan now. It will involve other people, and we will need to work very hard, but let's see what you think. . ."

On Monday morning, Josef rose before dawn and headed for Tammany Hall on the corner of Nassau and Frankfort Streets. It was a five-story corner building distinguished by rows of double-hung windows and winged cornices. Two large chimneys on the roof belched smoke into the air. They seemed to warn visitors of the tobacco haze they would find inside.

Confused at first by the large Tammany Hotel sign affixed to the facade, Josef was assured by a passerby that he had, indeed, arrived at the offices Peter O'Flanagan had indicated several months earlier. "Yes," the helpful stranger had assured him, "Tammany conducts its business in a suite of downstairs rooms. The upstairs floors are used as a hotel, especially for guests doing Tammany business. Just ask for O'Flanagan, and the clerks will direct you to him."

As Josef approached the front door, he reviewed his proposal. It was a daring one, but he had discussed it with Stefan, who had enthusiastically agreed to join him if details could be worked out. Josef felt certain that he could enlist Gottfried Baum, as well. The manager was impressed with his work and seemed an eager sort of fellow who would relish the thought of advancing his career.

Once inside, the earthy smell of sock-strained black tea made Josef gag. His nostrils rebelling, he made his way to a vast room with long lines of desks where clerks were answering questions and barking directions. When Josef asked for Peter O'Flanagan, one of them pointed to a makeshift cubicle in a far corner of the room. The clerk never looked up to see his inquisitor. "That way," he ordered and went on to someone else waiting in line.

When Josef reached the cubicle, a crude wooden screen emblazoned with the image of a cartoon-like tiger, the Tammany logo, offset the private space. He knocked tentatively, half expecting to be turned away. He waited for a few moments, heart hammering in his chest—and then Peter O'Flanagan emerged.

"*Kann ich Ihnen helfen?* (Can I help you?)" O'Flanagan asked.

Josef introduced himself, pleased when the big man shook his hand and invited him into the musty five-foot-square area he used as an office. The windowless space was furnished with a wooden desk whose chipped surface was hidden under piles of papers.

Josef reminded Peter O'Flanagan of their brief encounter at the South Street pier. He caught O'Flanagan up on his short but promising career at the Emporium, his recent marriage, and the child who would be arriving in a few short months. "I've come to you today to accept your offer of help in adjusting to the New World," Josef said, pulling himself up as much as his small frame would allow. "I've a plan in mind that would add a new market to the industry of this great city."

A subtle flash in O'Flanagan's brilliant blue eyes encouraged Josef to continue. Josef caught himself just before he started to wring his hands, a habit that had been with him since childhood whenever he encountered a difficult situation. "Josef," his father had warned him all those years ago, "*never* let a colleague detect uncertainty. Whatever you do, regardless of what you are feeling, assume a confident stance."

"I'd like to rent a residence with extra space that could accommodate several craftsmen, Mr. O'Flanagan. My wife is an accomplished knitter and lacemaker, and she is developing new prototypes that combine lace and wool into specialized products. They are selling well. I've brought you some samples," he said, as he placed finished pieces on the desk. He also provided a ledger showing Rosenstrauss business transactions.

O'Flanagan's interest heightened. "I have a wife and a house full of wee ones," the big man crowed. "Me mum, God rest her soul, was a lacemaker back in the old country. I know quality when I see it. Your exquisite lace goods would be welcome in people's homes. Perhaps your establishment would consider creating Christening gowns for our parishioners' little folk?"

"I am certain that could be arranged," agreed Josef, his pulse racing at the explosion of opportunity that could open in the Irish community.

As they continued to talk, O'Flanagan's enthusiasm grew. Finally, the Irishman stood and walked to the door, grabbing his coat from a tall coat-tree.

"Come with me, Josef," he said. "I may call you Josef, yes? And you call me Peter, for sure."

Peter took the lead as the two men walked onto Nassau Street, then turned right onto Frankfort Avenue. They went a few paces until they reached a brick-fronted, three-story building with a store on the first floor. "This should do well for you," beamed O'Flanagan. "There are two rooms available over the store. A basement area is also available that might do for a workspace. I can talk to the owner for you."

"It sounds good," said Josef. "But what is the rent?"

O'Flanagan took a deep breath. "I can get it for you for fourteen dollars a month," he said, wincing at Josef's consternation. "Of course, if you help with maintenance, it could be less."

Josef's mind raced. *If I can get Fritz Bayer to take one of the rooms, together we could manage the rent. Maybe we can get more of Frau Schultz's boarders to help with production and Mr. Baum to work in sales. It could even start with just a few hours for Baum if he doesn't want to leave the Emporium completely for now. It would be a potentially upward move for the manager. The plan could work. It must work.*

He tried to contain his excitement and managed to compose himself long enough to arrange his features in a serious countenance. *But there must be something O'Flanagan wants from me. Perhaps some of my profits. This is too good to be true.* "And what do you want from me in return?" Josef asked.

O'Flanagan laughed and, in a gesture of reassurance, flung his arm around Josef's shoulders. "Well, you see, Josef, I'm running for alderman, and my prospects are excellent. Your business will attract customers. You'll get them to vote for me and for our Democratic Tammany candidates. We like to keep our people close. We'll send one of our boys to fetch you in November to vote."

"But," Josef stammered, "I'm not a cit—"

O'Flanagan flashed a cold smile, his blue eyes boring into Josef's. "You're not a citizen? Is that what you want to say?"

Josef nodded, speech eluding him as his stomach churned. There didn't seem to be a choice if he wanted his plan to succeed.

"Sure, you're a citizen," O'Flanagan said. "If Tammany says you're a citizen, you're a citizen. You'll get your papers at the polls. Now, let's get you over to see about those rooms. You'll keep in touch. You'll help us keep our people in charge."

CHAPTER 10

Otto

The *Holstein* limped into port in the afternoon on a late spring day. Her sails, beaten by months of winter storms, hung loosely from the masts. Buffeting winds had prevented the crew from remaining in the rigging for the long periods required to do repairs. Exhausted, their numbers had been reduced by an outbreak of scurvy; the victims had endured severe joint and leg pain, open sores, hemorrhaging, spongy gums, and death. Hungry and disheartened, the remaining men were forced to work around the clock to keep the *Holstein* sustained. To make matters worse, the weather was deteriorating rapidly. Black clouds swept the skies and hailstones compounded the misery of the hapless creatures on shore trying to make their way to shelter.

Otto Krause had escaped scurvy's wrath, but he had been forced to scrub decks and empty slop when he wasn't aloft in the *Holstein*'s rigging. The scut work reminded him of the almshouse where his prostitute mother had deposited him after he was born. He shook with rage thinking about those years when he was beaten regularly and raped by the older boys, the custodian, and even the cook. With recent storms leaving no leisure time onboard, there had been no time to play the dice and cards he loved. What's more, the captain had restricted liquor because of shortages. Food had been tightly rationed after the ship took on water and destroyed bags of rice and potatoes. Drinking water was in short supply. Otto was not happy.

When the *Holstein* arrived in New York ten days late, land was a welcome sight.

"Time for some sport!" he bellowed, as the promise of whores and drink obliterated his self-pity. He and his mates descended to the pier, shoving their way through new arrivals crowding the docks. They spilled into the surrounding streets that were already over-crowded with tenants pressing on for Moving Day. Carts filled with furniture and household goods, clothing, and iceboxes clogged the cobblestones, and curses filled the air as people tried to get to their new quarters before dark.

The crewmates elbowed and pushed their way through the throng toward Sweeney's House of Refreshment on Ann Street, just a short distance from the *Holstein*'s berth. The brick-and-wood frame building had once been a fine townhouse but now played host to drunken sailors, thieves, gamblers, and members of the rival gangs, Bowery Boys and Dead Rabbits. Worn and shabby, it sported a large bar on the ground floor. Dancing girls in black satin bodices, scarlet skirts, and boots laced with red ribbons wound themselves around sailors just in from the sea.

Otto made his way to the noisy saloon where singing and swearing in many languages reigned. A long wooden bar, pitted and scarred by raucous drunkards pounding heavy tankards of beer and corn whiskey on its surface lined one side of the narrow space. Tall stools swaying on uneven supports were crammed under the bar's wooden lip, and sputtering gas lamps cast long, eerie shadows onto the tin ceiling. Mariners sat shoulder to shoulder while newcomers queued behind them waiting for vacated seats.

Behind the bar, rows of heavy wooden shelves held bottles of spirits ranging from cheap rums to expensive bourbons and whis-keys. It was the beer barrels perched on the wide lower shelves toward which Otto headed, pushing and shoving until he grabbed one of the slender rubber hoses protruding from the largest keg. He plunked down the required three-cent fee, pushed the hose down his throat and, to the chants of his mates, began to guzzle the beer until nature demanded that he take a breath. As soon as he stopped, the bartender cut off the malt until he paid another three cents, and another, and another. Well-practiced at guzzling, Otto soon attracted the crowd's attention.

"Drink, drink, drink!" they roared in many languages, delighted at Otto's seemingly endless capacity.

After several long rounds, the crowd suddenly parted as William Poole, otherwise known as Bill the Butcher and a leader of the Bowery Boys gang, strode in from the street and made his way to the bar. Six feet tall and weighing two hundred pounds, his stovepipe hat made him look even taller than he was. His black frock coat and red silk shirt reflected the fire-brigade origins of his gang. True to the Bowery Boys' dress code, his dark hair was cut short in the back with soaped-down ringlets in front of the ears. A perfectly manicured handlebar mustache topped his upper lip and emphasized the narrowness of his nose. It gave him a scowl that had the ability to threaten even the most stalwart thug.

"I'll take that hose," Poole announced in a chilling tone as he approached Otto.

"Ya think so? Well, think again," rasped Otto, defiantly grabbing a second pipe.

"Yeah," declared Poole. "I think so. In fact, I'll take both of those." As he edged closer to Otto, deadly silence settled over the saloon. Poole was known for drawing on skills from his former life as a butcher, carving his enemies into slabs of meat and gouging their eyes with his thumbs. Not just once in his famed past had he bitten off ears or chomped chins so deeply that his victims were scarred for life. Taller than Otto Krause by several inches, Poole loomed over the deckhand with a drawn knife. "I'll carve you up, I will. Now gimme those pipes."

As the tension in the barroom escalated, the drunken crowd gathered around, ripe for a fight. Reaching into his pocket, Otto jumped to the floor and drew out his Bowie, pointing it directly at Poole's midsection. Poole went in for the kill, grabbed Otto's forearm, and pulled him to the floor.

Whipped to a frenzy, a dozen or so men started to pummel the downed deckhand with fists, bottles, and chairs, stomping on his belly and pounding him with anything they could grab. Gashes and cuts quickly covered Otto's huge head, blood pouring onto the floor in a shimmering puddle. He curled into a ball under Poole's feet, seeming to surrender to his tormentor, when, suddenly, he pulled a second knife from under his shirt and rammed it deep into Poole's calf.

Poole howled with rage and pain, almost collapsing onto Otto's belly. The stunned crowd gasped as attention turned to the wounded Poole, and Otto saw his chance. He leaped to his feet, grabbed a nearby spittoon, and jammed it into Poole's skull. Poole started to sway, blood dripping onto his shirt. Staggering to the bar, the Butcher turned deathly white. Perspiration soaked his waistcoat, and he almost heaved his dinner onto the floor.

Suddenly, from the back of the saloon, Isaiah Rynders, a wiry fellow with dark wavy hair, penetrating black eyes, and a narrow face punctuated by a long straight nose, pushed his way to the front of the conflict. Rynders was boss of the Dead Rabbits gang, which was named for the impaled rabbits they carried on tall spikes and tossed menacingly into a ring to begin a fight. A Hudson River boat captain in his earlier life, he was a strong leader, respected by his followers and feared by all. He watched while Otto pulled the almost unconscious Poole to his feet, drew back his fists, and aimed straight for the bloody gash opening on Poole's head. Otto's knuckles were about to make their mark when Rynders stepped in.

"That's enough," he commanded, as he pulled Otto away from Poole. "I'd like to see the Butcher go down as much as anyone, but we'll save that for another day. I have great interest in keeping you alive for now."

While Poole staggered off, his cronies wiping blood from his face, Rynders threw his arm around Otto's shoulders and maneuvered him to the bar. "And just who are you?" Rynders inquired.

"Who's asking?" Otto managed to demand, his voice gurgling with blood.

Rynders stood back, crossed his arms in front of his chest, nodded to his cronies, and snapped his fingers. "You all know what we do with a recruit," he directed. "Do it."

The Dead Rabbits crowded together and pushed Otto against the bar. Chains, bottles, fists, and feet flew until Otto lay nearly unconscious on the floor. "Carry him upstairs and call a doctor," Rynders barked. "Now that we've taught him who's boss, my affiliates at Tammany Hall will have use for him. Nothing can happen to this fellow, understand?"

When Otto finally revived on an upstairs cot, holding his ribs and spitting blood, Rynders was standing over him, grinning. "I have intentions for you. Before you sail again, I want you to get in touch with me. I'm here most nights. If not, my associates will always know where to find me . . . and you."

CHAPTER 11

Josef

On May 1, Moving Day, Josef glanced around the room he and Frida had shared since their wedding the previous December. Hurriedly, he packed Frida's carpetbag with a remaining few treasured items that couldn't be trusted to a moving wagon. As he closed the door behind him, Josef passed into the crowded hall. There was barely room to move as old tenants hauled furniture and clothing down to the street, and those just moving in pushed to bring their belongings up to vacated rooms.

"Move yer arse!" shouted an elderly matron, as she jabbed Josef in the ribs.

"I'm moving, I'm moving," said Josef, clinging to the carpetbag and trying to adjust his eyes to the dark passageway.

What little light might have reached the stairwell from windows in the apartments was blocked by the mass of humanity trying to move through the building. Holding on to the worn oak banister, Josef inched his way to the first landing where a fight was breaking out. A large man surrounded by his wife and four crying children was hurling curses at a younger fellow trying to manipulate a bedstead past the crowd. A large slat had fallen from the heavy wooden frame and landed on the big man's foot.

"Watch where you're going!" the man yelled, pumping his fists as he sprang toward the offender.

Josef was caught in the middle as the men dropped their

belongings and lunged toward each other. The wife screamed when her husband's clenched fist made its mark on his adversary's jaw. Suddenly, several youths joined in the fray, and fists went flying. Josef fell to the ground, screaming in pain as a booted foot slammed against his face, tearing a bleeding gash in his cheek. He managed to upright himself quickly and wrested through the tangle of moving feet to the narrow staircase.

As he made his way to the building's exit, Josef was grateful that he had no large or bulky items to move. The Frankfort Street room he and Frida would share came furnished with twin beds, a dresser, and a stove. They planned to buy the few other furnishings they would need from Blume's, a used furniture shop on Chatham Street. Josef had visited the store recently and found a suitable table and chairs. He also had his eye on a fashionable secretary desk with intricate leaded-glass doors that provided room to display treasures; Frida would be pleased to feature her porcelain monkey on its shelves. The secretary had been badly damaged in a fire, but it was being offered at a bargain price. He had done some furniture restoration in Hamburg and hoped he would be able to do the repairs necessary to give it new life.

When he finally exited the building, Josef was greeted by more pandemonium. The streets were crowded with carts piled high with beds, chests, tables and chairs, clocks, pots and pans, rugs, and all manner of household items. Right before his eyes, a carter swore loudly as he crashed into the side of a horse with a heavy packsaddle and full side bags. The horse whinnied, reared up on its hind legs and pawed violently at the air, coming down just short of Josef.

"You're a lucky one!" shouted a youth nearby. "My cousin got killed like that last May."

Shaken, but intact, Josef separated himself from the bedlam and wound through the streets, heading for his new home. As he approached Spring Street, his heart started to beat wildly as he heard a posse of sailors noisily catching up with him. Keeping his head down and his eyes averted, Josef quickened his pace and placed him-self as close to the buildings as he could. Instinct kicked in as he hunched his shoulders and shifted the carpetbag to his right side where it would be less accessible to the gang approaching on his left. As he did so, the yarmulke he always kept in his pocket without Frida's knowledge fell to the street.

The ruffians were a noisy lot, singing loudly in German and swearing with abandon. As they increased their pace to catch up to Josef, one of the sailors shouted, "What do you know? Look at that flat hat. Looks like we have us a little Jew. I thought all Jews were big so they could hold up their huge noses!"

"Yah," laughed another, "so they can smell their own stench!"

Feeding on each other, the sailors looked to their leader, a large man with a massive belly and stringy blond hair hanging to his shoul-ders from a balding center. "Let's say hello to the little guy. I'm sure he's lonely," the big thug said. "Yeah, he wants company so bad he's shaking. Let's give him what he wants."

Jeering and cursing, the gang crowded around Josef so that he was forced up against a wall with no place to escape. The leader flashed a Bowie knife and crouched down to Josef's height, breathing foul breath into his face. "You're a Jewish bastard, aren't you?" he sneered. "Maybe we should check and see for ourselves, mates."

Josef sucked in his breath and the air left his lungs as a tough grabbed Josef's feet and another yanked at his pants, pulling them down around his ankles.

"Hey, what do you know? The balls are there, but his ding has been cut up. I guess he really is a Jew." The leader flashed his knife and drew it across Josef's upper thigh, drawing blood. Josef could feel it slice his flesh.

"And look at that," another hoodlum said with a grin. "His blood's red."

Fighting terror, Josef tried to wriggle away from his tormentors, but they tackled him to the ground. One of them thrust a knee into

Josef's privates. Josef retched as an avalanche of vomit spilled out onto the street and the gang danced around him, chanting anti-Jewish obscenities.

"Should we take another slice of him to be sure his blood is still red? It could be purple. You never know," suggested a tall ruffian with a pimpled face.

"Nah, let's just see what's in his sack," said one of the mates as he grabbed the carpetbag.

"Yah, let's see," they chorused, spilling the contents of the bag onto the sidewalk.

The leader sneered, odors of limburger cheese and cigar smoke spilling from his narrow lips. "Give Otto the bag," he commanded. "Give it now."

Josef tried desperately to crawl away, but Otto clamped his foot down on Josef's leg.

"You don't like me? Everybody likes Otto," he cackled, spittle pouring from his mouth. He grabbed the carpetbag and tore it open. "What? Just a bunch of Jew rags," he exclaimed.

Frida's carefully folded yellow dress was the first item to fall to the sidewalk.

"Ah, what do we want that dirty Jew's things for?" said Otto. "Let's give it all back. But maybe we better wash everything first, in that puddle over there."

Laughing, they scooped up Frida's precious gown and dragged it to the street where they threw it into a spill coming from a nearby night-soil depository.

"That's better," Otto laughed. "Those filthy rags needed washing."

As the sailors walked off, arms around each other and resuming their raucous singing, Josef huddled on the pavement, trembling uncontrollably. Grateful that there was no one on the street to see his crumpled form, he managed to wriggle his pants up to his waist but was unable to upright himself.

After some moments, a drayman hauling a flat-bedded wagon of furniture passed and stopped at the curb. A big man with flashing blue eyes and a coarse black beard sprinkled with white whiskers, he jumped down from his cart with a nimbleness belied by his thick legs and large feet. "Are you all right?" he asked, noting the spillage on the street and Josef's bloodied face.

Josef was unable to respond, silently shaking his head from side to side.

In the distance, the carter's eyes followed the marauding sailors as they were about to turn a corner. "They did this to you, didn't they?" he said in halting German, squatting to Josef's level. He extended a work-worn hand to Josef. "Come," he offered, pulling Josef to his feet. "I'm Colin Byrne. Let me take you home."

Too stunned to refuse, Josef managed to stand shakily for a few moments while he collected himself. When his bleeding legs could hold him up, he and Colin gathered as much of the carpetbag's spilled contents as they could and climbed up onto the wagon's wooden seat.

"You are too kind," Josef offered. "Why are you doing this?"

"They're a bad lot, some of these sailors," he said. "When they get to shore after months of seafaring, they can get real nasty. I don't like that. And so, here I am. Where can I take you?"

While they made their way through the teeming streets, Colin told Josef about his family. Newly arrived in America from famine-torn Ireland, he was the father of three with another on the way. "We came here a few years ago with nothing," he said, his voice choking with emotion. "The harvest in Ireland failed, and our potato farm became worthless. There were times when there was so little food that people were reduced to eating grass and putrid potatoes, which brought on fevers and death. I lost my parents, a sister, and a few cousins to starvation. With a wife and babies to feed, we sold our land, little as it brought, and here we are. I've been learning German and hauling for a while. The pay is too little for too many hours, but we are managing. At least, we have a room, and we manage at least one meal a day."

When they arrived at Frankfort Street, Josef pulled a few hidden pennies from his shoe. The gang had taken the rest from his pocket. "It's not a lot," he said, offering the money to Colin, "but I am much obliged. Perhaps we will meet again.

After Colin drove off, Josef stood in front of the new house for a few moments, still shaking from his encounter with the sailors. He knew he was a sorry sight. Blood had soaked through his trouser leg, his clothes were dirty and crumpled, and his usually coiffed hair was in tangles.

As he was mustering up the courage to go inside, he heard a familiar voice calling from the upstairs window. It was Fritz Bayer. "My God, Josef, what's happened to you? Stay right there. Stefan is here, too. We'll be down in an instant."

Josef could hear Fritz's and Stefan's pounding footsteps on the stairs. He allowed them to help him up to the apartment where Frida was waiting for him. She let out a shriek when she saw him, hurrying to his side as quickly as her now bulky body would allow. "I'm sorry, Frida. I'm so sorry. Your beautiful yellow dress—your carpetbag and your shawl—are ruined."

"Pooh," she said, brushing hair away from Josef's eyes. "I only care that you are hurt. What happened, Josef?"

"It's nothing," Josef said. "A small accident in the street is all."

Frida took a deep breath and straightened her shoulders. "That's not all, Josef. You tell me what happened."

Ignoring her orders, Josef sighed and limped across the small room. Sparsely furnished, it had, in its favor, two large windows that let in the pale light of the descending dusk. At the back of the room was a windowless sleeping alcove. It was just big enough to accommodate ancient mattresses settled upon frames, each rising three feet from the floor. Frida had found some construction blocks in the area and asked Fritz Bayer to place them between the beds for Brunhilde so the dog could climb up for naps.

"Here, let me help you," said Stefan, following Josef to his bed and guiding him up the block steps. Gently, he and Fritz laid Josef down while Frida scooped water from a basin on the stove into an old ivory-colored enamel pitcher decorated with a floral design. "I'll take care of him from here," Frida commanded.

As she removed his damaged clothing and tended to his bleeding leg, Josef's trembling lessened, and his breathing slowed. In his mind's eye, he saw his attacker's blade and felt it pressing his flesh. He heard the sailors' taunts and recoiled at the image of Frida's beautiful dress drenched in sewage. Unbidden tears of humiliation filled his eyes, and words eluded him.

Frida took his hands in hers and brought her face close to his. "Who did this to you, Josef? Who beat you?"

"No, no, there was no beating," he answered, pausing as if to gather his thoughts. *She's my Frida, my heart. We've shared everything always. I must tell her. But I can't. She could lose faith in America. She could pull back from the temple and live in fear again. I mustn't . . .*

When Josef finally spoke, his voice was soft, but his eyes were anguished. Frida listened while he told her about the bedlam of Moving Day and the near miss with the horse.

"Shush, shush," she whispered, as she climbed into bed beside him. Holding him close, she stroked his brow and sang softly until he fell into a fitful sleep, Brunhilde snoring gently at their feet.

The next morning, Josef woke to find Frida already up and about the apartment, scrubbing every corner and placing their few things, including the porcelain monkey, on shelves lining the living area. Fritz and Stefan were cleaning the basement when Josef joined them. The two had brought with them a handmade awning sign that they had completed just days earlier. At six feet by four feet, it was designed to fit perfectly over the basement store window. Painted a deep golden yellow, it read ROSENSTRAUSS & CO: KNIT GOODS MADE TO ORDER, in bold red and green lettering.

"We're not going to use the sign," declared Josef.

Stefan and Fritz were stunned. "We've talked about this for weeks, Josef," said Stefan. "Surely you are not going to give up your dream, are you?" A heavy silence fell over the room. "No," said Josef, after several moments. "The business will go on as we have discussed over these last few months. It's strong, and it's growing. But Frida is right. Rosenstrauss is a Jewish name.

Josef paused to gauge his friends' reaction. "*Jewish bastard*" played repeatedly in his mind, and he felt the knife against his flesh. *Never again,* he swore silently, *never again. Not if I can help it. But it is a terrible thing to change one's name. Honor thy father and thy mother. On the other hand, God will understand. He must understand.* When he spoke again, his expression was defiant. His eyes burned, and his jaw was determined.

"We will redo the sign. From this time forward, we will be known as Rose Industries. And someday, the sign will not just be a wooden awning. Rose Industries will be housed in a large stone building that dominates the landscape, a force to be reckoned with on Wall Street."

CHAPTER 12

Frida

By the end of July, the cellar of the new house had been converted into a workroom. Colin Byrne, the man who helped Josef on Moving Day, had come to work for the business in the last few weeks hauling materials to refurbish the building. A skilled carpenter, he had installed white wall panels, intricate molding, and a windowed door to the street that he painted a welcoming yellow. Latticework outlined its edges and reflected the motif in Rose Industries' new sign.

As she looked over the transformed space, Frida was pleased. Amalia and Bertha were sorting lace-making supplies in a far corner. In recent weeks, Frida had started offering lace-making classes and had several students eager to learn the craft. There were eight such students so far, all of whom had heard about Rose Industries from the Albrecht sisters. Several of them were still boarders at Frau Schultz's house.

"Come," Frida called, slowly walking to the kettle whistling on the potbellied stove near the door. "Time for tea."

Over the last two weeks, she had grown clumsy, her bulk making walking or sleeping almost impossible. *My big belly means the baby will be especially strong and healthy,* she reasoned, counting backward to the night beneath the lindens. *Everybody's late for the first baby. Yes, that's it. That's the answer.* Tweaks and twitches rippled unevenly through her body at all hours of day and night, and a foul taste stubbornly clung to her palette. Tea was an excellent antidote. It calmed her insides and soothed her spirits.

As the women gathered around the large worktable in the center of the room, they admired the still-warm German plum cake that Bertha had prepared using her grandmother's recipe. A buttery pastry made with grated almonds and lemon zest, the top was embellished with a circle of caramelized red-skinned plums. "Looks wonderful," said Frida, as she made her way to the stove.

"I'll get that," one of the women said, urging Frida to sit. The woman picked up the cast-iron kettle, now whistling urgently, and poured the contents over a teapot of blended Assam, Ceylon, and Darjeeling leaves. As was the custom in Hamburg, she added rock sugar and poured the steaming water over the mixture. She added cream and did not stir the savory liquid until a pale amber cloud formed.

The delectable aromas of pastry and tea wafted through the work area, and Josef, Stefan, and Colin were soon drawn to join the women in the late afternoon repast. Fritz Bayer and Gottfried Baum, Josef's former boss who—much to the Emporium owner's dismay—had left the Emporium to join Rose Industries, came in from sweeping the front pavement to join the group.

Despite the gloom of an unusual summer chill and intermittent rain that had descended upon the city, the conversation turned to how much had been accomplished in just a few short months. Shortly after Moving Day, Amalia and Bertha had joined Frida in turning out completed shawls and jackets. They were talking about drawing on their knowledge of Berlin fashion and extending Rose's inventory to include embroidered gloves and hats. Frida had mentioned the idea to some of her customers, and they were enthusiastic at the prospect. Sales had been brisk, especially as the summer season started and Rose Industries began to create light cotton-lace garments. Tilly Kohn had occasionally joined in production, as well, and the ladies of Ansche Beth Shalom had become loyal customers.

As they ate and talked, Frida became aware of a dull ache building in her back, right below where the baby was kicking. As quickly as it came, it left, only to return minutes later. *It's nothing,* she thought hopefully. *The cake is probably sitting too heavily. Either that, or the baby was made on our wedding night and is just growing a lot before it comes next month.*

When the clock struck five, Bertha and Amalia gathered up their things and went to the door. The other women took their cues, talking excitedly about the future of Rose Industries, and left Frida and Josef for the night.

"I'm tired, Josef," Frida said. "I'm going up."

"I'll be with you soon," Josef replied, wrapping his arms around Frida's shoulders and kissing her cheek. "There are some accounts I need to go over before I go to the bank in the morning."

Frida returned his kisses and turned to leave the workroom. As she climbed the stairs, she held tightly onto the railing as a cramp wound like a snake to the bottom of her belly. This one did not dissipate the way the earlier pains had; it held on for several seconds, leaving her breathless.

No, no, no. The timing is wrong, she thought, the *Holstein's* odors invading her nostrils. *It can't be that bastard's. I won't allow it to be that repulsive man's child.* Quickly, as she had so many times before, she recalculated the months. *Josef's child would arrive in June, already passed. . . or September, not yet here. That thug's would be due now, at the beginning of August. But it IS Josef's. I know it. Just a little late or a little early. It MUST be.* Suddenly, Frida broke into a cold sweat. Nausea was making its way to the back of her throat. She groaned, fighting against a fast-shooting pain, and made her way to the bed.

By the time Josef came into the apartment, the cramps were worse. "Frida!" he gasped when he saw her. Her hair had come undone and hung in damp tendrils around her neck. She was lying on her side, legs drawn up and panting as another spasm traveled through her body.

Josef turned white as Frida's cries pierced the room.

"Get me out of here!" she howled. "Get me out of these clothes!" She reached for Josef's arms, lowering herself to the floor and pulling at her dress. As she loosened the garment and it started to fall, unfamiliar moisture startled her as it crept down her inner thighs. Starting as a trickle, a clear water-like substance suddenly exploded onto the floor in an odorless puddle. She clutched her abdomen as unbidden tears covered her cheeks.

"The baby!" Josef cried, excitement and fear mingling in his tone and in his eyes. "Our little one has decided to make its appearance early."

Frida groaned and allowed Josef to help her into a birthing ensemble she had found at the Emporium. Made of white muslin and embroidered with daisies, it consisted of a short undershirt, a blouse, and a skirt with a full-length flap running down the front. She had wondered what baby had been born under its folds.

Alarmed at the sudden change in Frida's condition, Josef ran to the hall and called for help. "Fritz, Fritz!" he shouted. "Get the midwife!"

A short while later, a tall middle-aged woman with white hair and wide brown eyes arrived. She was carrying a folded birthing chair and a large bag bulging with ointments and tools she needed to ensure the safe delivery of a child. "I'm Mrs. Stein. Hilda Stein. Do you remember me, Frida?" she asked gently. "We met a few weeks ago when you first engaged me to deliver your baby. You are just as I remembered—a slip of a girl carrying a large burden to her front."

The midwife placed her bag at the foot of the bed and bustled about the room to get it ready for delivery. She straightened the wrinkled sheets, lit a lemon-scented candle, and set a pot of water to heat on the stove. "Mr. Rosenstrauss," she said, turning to Josef. "Fetch your wife's Circle of Women. She will need their distraction, and I will need their assistance. While you are out, get some wine to bring your wife comfort and ease her confinement. A fragrant white is best.

Light on the pallet and soft on the stomach. A bit would be good for you, as well," she said.

Tilly was the first of Frida's Circle of Women to arrive at Frida's bedside. Bertha and Amalia followed shortly. They brought a basket filled to overflowing with sweet summer fruits and small cakes. "What can we do?" asked Amalia, anticipation filling her face.

"You can set up the birthing chair in the corner," answered Hilda Stein. "Bertha, you can tie this towel to the bedpost. Frida will need it to pull on when the pains become hard. And crush some of the peaches and apricots you brought. Their fragrance will soothe her as she labors."

The midwife poured olive oil from a jar and rubbed some over her hands to generate heat before she went to Frida's side to examine her. As she bent to ascertain the progress of Frida's labor, Frida let out a piercing scream as a new, stronger contraction wracked her body.

"I can't do this!" she cried. "I can't! I won't!"

As dusk turned to night, and night to dawn, the women soothed Frida's brow, fed her morsels of berries and pastry, and held her white-knuckled hands as she fought the pains of her labor. By noon, summer heat had returned, and the air in the small room became heavy with humidity. Lines and dark pools had formed around Frida's usually intense eyes, which were now dulled with effort.

"What's happening?!" shouted Josef, pounding on the door. "Can't you let me in? I can't bear her suffering!"

Mrs. Stein finished applying a poultice to Frida's female parts and opened the door slightly. "She is in hard labor, Mr. Rosenstrauss. You must be patient. You will be informed as soon as your child is born," she said, closing the door against Josef's anguished pleas.

After several more hours, Frida's pains escalated and were soon coming every two minutes. With some effort, Mrs. Stein, Bertha, and Amalia managed to walk her to within inches of the birthing chair. Suddenly, Frida's legs buckled, and she fell to the floor. She curled onto her right side, pulled her knees up as close to her chest as she could, and screamed.

"This is too much!" she cried, her voice so shill it seemed to cut the air. "What have I done? I don't want this baby. Make it stop!"

Mrs. Stein dropped to the floor. She placed her hands under Frida's arms and turned her on her back. "Almost time to push, Frida!" she shouted. "Amalia, bring me more warm oil. Bertha and Tilly, help me get her onto the chair. She must be situated right over the opening in the seat."

Frida's howls filled the room as the women got her into position. The midwife crouched and palpitated her abdomen to hasten the contractions.

"Get away from me!" Frida shouted, as Amalia tried to soothe her brow with a damp cloth. Like a cornered cat, she clawed at Amalia's cheeks, drawing blood in long straight lines.

Suddenly, Mrs. Stein grinned. "The baby is crowning!" she shouted. "Push!" Setting aside the flap in the skirt, Mrs. Stein felt for the baby's head in the birth canal. She reached for Frida's hand and brought it to the emerging child. "This is what you are working for," she said.

Frida's eyes filled with hot tears as she felt the warm, waxy substance covering the infant's head, its pulse strong and steady under her touch. *Jude Bitch* sounded, unbidden, into her thoughts as she tried to rid her mind of Otto. *Who are you, child of mine? WHO ARE YOU?*

Frida's howls filled the room as the baby's head showed. Her body relaxed, then tensed again as a contraction ripped through her. Then another. And another. Suddenly, the contractions changed. Alarmed, Mrs. Stein felt for the baby's progress.

"What's wrong?!" Frida cried. "Nothing's happening."

"Now, listen closely. The baby's shoulder is wedged in the birth canal. We need to release it. You must be brave and endure what's next." The midwife went to her bag and pulled out an ornate box that housed the separate parts of a wood-handled forceps. Quickly, with a speed born of experience, she assembled the instrument and brought it to Frida's bed.

"No!" screamed Frida when she saw the device. The large scooped-metal blades of the forceps loomed before her like torture instruments. As the women reached for her, she kicked out at them, knocking Bertha down. While Amalia rushed to pick her sister up from the floor, Mrs. Stein drew herself up to her full height and stood over Frida.

"Enough!" she commanded, her tone stern but caring. "I am also a mother, Frida, with six children of my own. I've prevailed over many births, some of them with worse complications than yours." She accepted a fresh, damp towel from Tilly and placed it over Frida's brow. "It's almost over. Just a bit longer, and your child will be here."

Tears filled Frida's eyes as she acquiesced to Mrs. Stein. She stifled her screams as the forceps entered her. Her body contracted repeatedly as the instrument worked to free the baby. And then, release came as the infant entered the world, and its cries filled the room.

"It's a boy, Frida. You have a son. And a big boy he is, too," announced the midwife. She cut the umbilical cord, sponged and wrapped the child, and placed him on his mother's chest. Gently, Frida peeled back her infant's swaddling clothes to examine his brand-new body. "What's this?" she cried out. "Mrs. Stein, what's this mark on his neck? It looks like a flattened turtle."

Mrs. Stein walked calmly over to the bed and solemnly peered at the baby's neck. "That is a flat mole," the midwife concluded. "It's harmless. It may fade or it may get bigger over time, although most likely it will remain as it is. He can always let his hair cover it, but I'm betting it will never bother him in the slightest."

Exhausted, Frida sighed deeply and instinctively tightened her arms around the new, warm body. Unbidden, *Jude Bitch, Jude Bitch* screamed through her mind. Her eyes clouded over, revulsion rising from deep within. The turtle mark. *Where have I seen it before? Or have I? Whose child is this? Will I ever know? Should I ever know?* She looked into the baby's still unseeing eyes. *But you are an innocent. I can't let that bastard do any more harm. I won't think about it. I'll do what I must do to take care of you. We will survive. No one must know . . .*

The infant fussed, soft gurgling sounds rising from his chest as he squirmed against his mother's warmth. As he snuggled into her, the child placed his wrinkled hand on Frida's cheek. *Yes, he had to have been conceived under the Lindens. He's a big boy; that's why he's late. Yes, that's exactly why.* Frida covered his hand with her own, amazed at how small and warm it was. *He knows already that he's my son. And Josef's. I won't have it any other way.* Tenderness overcame her, and she cradled her baby tightly. Tears of joy mixed with fear tumbled down her cheeks as she struggled to bring order to her thoughts.

"Bring Josef in," she pleaded, in a hoarse whisper.

A few minutes later, Mrs. Stein had delivered the afterbirth and brought Josef to Frida's side. He reached down to stroke his newborn's downy head. "He's ours, Frida. Did you ever in your life see anything so beautiful? He may have come early, but look how robust he is. Mrs. Stein says he's seven pounds, four ounces. Imagine that." Josef spent several minutes gazing at the baby, visibly moved when the infant curled his fingers around his thumb. "He trusts me already," he crowed. He bent down so that his face was even with the child's. "I promise you, son of mine, I will live up to your trust. Yours and your mother's." He stood and gazed at Frida. "We must name him," he said.

Frida nodded. "How about August?" she offered. "In honor of his August birthday."

Josef furrowed his brow while he gave the name some thought.

"The name means *esteemed, venerable*," urged Frida. "Like you."

"I like it," Josef finally said, a wide grin. "August Rosenstrauss. Our son."

Frida froze. She turned to Bertha, Amalia, Tilly, and the midwife who stood to the side. "Please. Give us a moment."

When they were gone, she stared at Josef, her expression momentarily unreadable. "No, Josef. Rosenstrauss is no longer our name." *Jude Bitch, Jude Bitch!* "Our business is Rose Industries, and we are the Rose family."

Josef took a step back from the bed, his face ashen. He glanced between his wife and son, then closed his eyes. For a few moments, Frida watched his eyes moving under their lids as if he were living through an event only he could see. Finally, his countenance relaxed, and he bent to stroke Frida's hair. "I understand," he said. "We are the Roses; Frida and Josef Rose, and our son, August."

With great effort, Frida placed August on the bed. She lifted her hands to Josef's face and pulled him to her. Wordlessly, they sought each other's lips.

August's cries interrupted their kiss, demanding to be fed.

"We're not on our own anymore, are we?" Josef laughed. He stepped away from Frida and turned to get Mrs. Stein. August was making it clear that he needed to eat. "I'll see you later," he said, blowing a kiss to Frida from across the room.

Frida listened to the commotion in the parlor. Squeals of delight filtered in as the women cooed about the child and marveled at the birth process. They came back into the room with Mrs. Stein and listened attentively as she gave Frida feeding instructions and brought August to her breast.

When the baby was sated and put down to sleep, Josef came

back into the room and gazed adoringly at his slumbering son. Tilly brought a chair over to the bed and sat down, her hand resting on Frida's. Anticipation filled her eyes. "We have a bris to prepare for," she said, her eyes twinkling.

"We'll see, Tilly. We'll see," said Frida. Her skin grew cold as Josef's face twisted and his expression became distant. She suspected he would want the bris, but she intended to talk him out of it. Surprisingly, Josef took a long time to respond. When he did, his voice cracked as he echoed her exact words: "We'll see."

After the others had left and August was sleeping, Tilly's assumption that August would be circumcised loomed large between Josef and Frida.

After some awkward moments, Josef leaned in close to his wife. He gently brushed her tangled hair away from her face and looked deeply into her eyes. "This is a difficult decision," he said, his eyes filling with pain that Frida had never seen before. He seemed lost in his own thoughts. Finally, he spoke, his voice tremulous. "I am torn between having our son be dangerously recognizable as Jewish and following the Old Testament's command to circumcise male children as a covenant with God."

"Why do you say that, Josef? It seems a change has occurred in you."

"It's just that I have heard of people being brutalized when circumcision reveals their Judaism. But how can we defy our God? To avoid circumcising August would deprive him of participating in any Jewish rights. I cannot fathom that," said Josef.

A frown crossed Frida's forehead as she contemplated Josef's shift from his former insistences on following tradition. Despite herself, his discomfort made her think back to her Judaic roots, the comfort of her early years at the synagogue, and her brother's joyous bris. She heard Papa's voice whispering to her soul about the ancient tradition and how circumcision was essential to belonging to the Jewish community.

"This is a new dilemma, Josef," she said. *Jude Bitch, Jude Bitch* raced through her mind, but Papa's persuasions were compelling. Driven by Papa's ghost, Frida reached for Josef's hand. "Let's do the bris," she said, pushing her own fears aside. "I just hope we won't be sorry."

CHAPTER 13

Josef

It had been a busy three months since August's birth. Orders for Rose products had come in not only from Ansche Beth Shalom and from Peter O'Flanagan's parish, but also from individual neighborhood women. Rose Industries had recently hired more workers to keep up with demand, and the shop hummed from morning till night.

The boarders from Frau Schultz's house were happy to secure steady employment in exchange for the piecework they had been producing on their own. A natural with handcrafts, Frida had pursued making bobbin lace, a skill she learned from her maternal grandmother in Hamburg. She was teaching the women to be proficient in fashioning intricately patterned creations, many of which were based on a rose motif for which Rose Lace, as it was now branded, was becoming known. Created by braiding and weaving lengths of cotton thread or silk on spool-like bobbins, the work was kept in place with pins set into pillows. When several artisans were working at the same time, the gentle hum of clicking spools filled the room. Usually, one of the women read aloud to pass the time. Frida kept a pot of tea readily available on the stove, and Rose Industries was becoming a workplace to be envied.

When Josef arrived home from his office, he hung his jacket on the coat-tree near the door, kissed Frida, and crouched down to embrace August. At three months, he had become a plump, rosy-cheeked baby with blond fuzz starting to cover his pink scalp. His almond eyes were small but flashed behind long lashes, and his full cheeks were dimpled. His nose, stubby at birth, was becoming long and narrow. Rolls of dimpled baby fat covered his stout body.

While a juicy chicken roasted in the oven, Josef and Frida set the table in preparation for the Sabbath meal. Wistfulness filled Josef's soul as he realized how far his little family had strayed from the traditional Friday nights of his youth. Yielding to Frida's wishes, they no longer attended Friday night services, but Josef had insisted they light candles and recite the prayers that were so much a part of him. He had talked with Leo Kohn about pulling away from the synagogue and had been amazed at the rabbi's response.

"Josef," he had said, "you have a new family and a new business that have brought priorities that demand to be met. God understands, and Ansche Beth Shalom will be here for you when you wish to return."

"August laughed today," Frida said, interrupting Josef's thoughts, as she laid out silver flatware she had found at the Emporium. "He was fussing when one of the women began to make silly faces for him. He has been irritable for the last few weeks, so it was a wonderful sound."

Suddenly, a howl went up from the dresser drawer where Frida and Josef had created a makeshift cradle.

"Do you see what I mean about his fussing?" she said, fatigue reflecting in her eyes. She picked August up and held him to her bosom. As she smiled and sang, August's face calmed and he reached for her nose, holding on to it with his now-dimpled hands.

After a bit of playing, Josef and Frida finally sat down to enjoy their Shabbat meal. The chicken, roasted with onions until its skin was crisp and its flesh moist and aromatic, was accompanied by challah, sweet potato pudding, and string beans garnished with thick slices of sautéed mushrooms. A stew of cinnamon-spiked apricots and freshly baked sponge cake rounded out the meal.

"We've come a long way in a short time," Josef mused, as he speared his second helping of chicken. "When we first arrived in New York, we were lucky to share a Sabbath meal of potatoes and garlic pickles. Now, we even look forward to dessert."

As Frida cleared away the main course and brought a pot of steaming tea to the table, she became solemn. "Josef," she said, slicing the still warm cake, "we need to discuss an important change in our lives."

Noting her serious expression, Josef nodded. "What is it?"

"What I have to say is not so much a concern as it is a practical matter. You see, it has become clear that we can no longer attend Ansche Beth Shalom on Saturday mornings."

Josef sat back in his chair and pushed away from the table, leaving a half-eaten piece of cake on his plate. He felt the blood drain from his face as he pondered Frida's declaration. "Not attend Saturday morning services? We've already given up Friday nights. Now you're asking me not to attend Sabbath rituals, to disobey God's commandment to keep the Sabbath holy."

"I can understand your concern, Josef. I've thought about this for a while, but the shop demands our attention. Orders are coming in so fast we can scarcely keep up. We are both needed to oversee daily operations. Please don't argue with me. My mind is made up."

While August fidgeted in the background, heavy silence filled the room. "You are sure of this?" Josef finally asked. His clenched hands had turned his knuckles white.

"Yes, I am," Frida declared, placing her hands on her hips and jutting her jaw. Fire flashed in her eyes, and her lips drew into a tight line. "This has been a long time in coming. It is imperative that both of us tend to matters that simply cannot be interrupted for the Sabbath. Just yesterday, the warming pot under the new apprentice's skirts was kicked over. The red-hot coal rolled out onto the floor, and the poor girl's skirts caught on fire. In the haste to put out the embers, the table candles on her station were almost knocked over. The incident convinced me that we must always be on the premises to avoid disasters and make sure the workers are not distracted. Besides," she added after a brief pause to allow him to take in what she said, "Rose Industries is not widely considered to be a Jewish enterprise. While the long summer days enabled us to keep up with Christian companies' hours, winter's short days demand competitive change."

Josef remained silent while he considered Frida's concerns. His part of the business had become increasingly demanding as he maintained Rose Industries' financial books, secured supplies, and hired workers. Unwelcome *Jude Bastard* chants entered his mind, his brow furrowed, and his usually soft mouth hardened into a grimace as he recalled the gang attack on the street. His mind raced. *But God commands us to honor the Sabbath and keep it holy. . . .*

After several moments of uncomfortable silence, he finally managed to reply, "The Sabbath is dear to me, but so are you, Frida. I suppose ritual could be maintained in the privacy of our home. I do agree Rose Industries must thrive; we must maintain our acceptance into commercial circles as a business on the rise. We have a child to support and protect. I remember how Rabbi Kohn explained that changes in tradition can be essential to Jewish survival here in New York. I suppose that if we remember our roots and continue to observe the Sabbath on Friday nights at home, I can relinquish Saturday services at the synagogue. I will do so with a heavy heart, but I will accompany you tomorrow to our shop."

As Frida bustled about preparing for bed, Josef sat for a long time recalling the easy Jewish life of his youth. Tradition had been a comfort, albeit one he had taken for granted. He remembered getting dressed in his best frock coat and tallit to accompany his father to synagogue. His mother, adorned in her Sabbath finery, had walked with them, too, leaving them to join the women in the upstairs gallery while the men prayed downstairs in the sanctuary. Their voices had filled the synagogue with a power gleaned from centuries of tradition, bringing him shivers of joy. He had loved reciting the Torah scripts that countless generations had performed before him, and he had welcomed the peace of the Sabbath with all his heart.

But thoughts of unrest in Germany inserted themselves and mingled with memories of the trouble Judaism had brought him both in Hamburg and in the street encounter with the sailors. *Tradition didn't help me then,* he thought, *and it didn't help when Father deserted Tante Roshen, or when our families rebuked the love Frida and I share.*

After some time had passed, Josef retreated to his office. A while later, he returned upstairs. Frida was just putting a cranky August down for the night.

"I've been going over our books, Frida. We need to take on more people. The future—our future—is in textile production. Tomorrow, after I check in at the shop, I will go to see Peter O'Flanagan. He told me he could help with introducing me to financial establishments. It is time to purchase lacemaking and knitting machines and to move Rose Industries to bigger quarters."

Frida reached for Josef's hand, her cheeks growing pink with excitement. "It's a wonderful idea. Let's do it."

The next morning, Josef arrived at Tammany Hall just as it was opening. It was as he remembered it from a few months earlier, but today it was crowded with hundreds of men preparing for the upcoming 1851 elections. All 233 seats in the House of Representatives were up for grabs, and Tammany was in a frenzy. There were signs supporting the Tammany-supported Democrat candidates running against the Whig Party for offices ranging from New York Secretary of State to commissioners, inspectors, and members of the New York State Assembly.

Peter O'Flanagan was in the thick of it, barking orders and directing poll workers, sign-handlers, and volunteers determined to beat out the Whig candidates. Clouds of cigarette and cigar smoke hovered in the air and assaulted Josef's nostrils as he made his way to see the Irishman.

When he finally managed to corner O'Flanagan, Josef was brief and to the point. "Good morning, Peter," he said, extending his hand. "It's good to see you again. I didn't realize when I came here this morning that you would be so busy. I can come back another time if that would be more convenient." Josef shifted his posture, embarrassed that he had interrupted the tall man. He had never seen such a frenzy of political activity, and he wasn't sure of what to make of it. *Is this how it is in America? Are people this free to express themselves? Will Mr. O'Flanagan think unkindly of me for coming to him at this time? Will he turn me away with a warning not to bother him?*

"No, it's good you are here!" O'Flanagan bellowed, his voice rising above the din. "We'll put you to work straightaway. There is scaffolding to be built and tables to be set up with patriotic bunting. Later, after today's preparations are completed, we can meet about whatever it is that is concerning you. Volunteers for our great cause are to be celebrated."

Overwhelmed by the politician's enthusiasm and determination, Josef allowed himself to be led to a group erecting scaffolds that would be used to access ballot drops on Election Day. The foreman, a slender fellow with dark eyes, a headful of unruly black hair, and biceps that bulged from his upper arms like bratwurst hiding under the skin, handed Josef the end of a wooden plank and directed him to help carry it to a partially erected scaffold.

The crew was just one of several working on preparations for Election Day, but they wordlessly accepted Josef as one of them. While they worked, they chanted Democratic slogans and laughed raucously at the expense of Whig candidates whom they berated with abandon. Josef could not understand everything they said. He had been working on his English, but it was still halting. He was unable to grasp the meanings of their slang, but he fell in with their labor and gave it his all. By later that afternoon, the scaffolds were complete, and work stopped for the day.

As he was leaving, Peter O'Flanagan fell in beside him. "Thank you for your help today," he boomed, placing an arm around Josef's shoulder. "We need all the workers we can get. You're obviously good with wood; that problem you solved with adjusting the scaffold rigging did not go unnoticed. But you have business to discuss with me? Let's walk a bit, and you can tell me what's on your mind."

"I couldn't intrude on your free time. I can return next week if that would be better."

"'Tis okay. I was taken with your business ideas when we last met."

The sun was fast dropping into the horizon, and an orange glow bathed the streets. *I must get home to Frida. I've already been gone too long. And on the Sabbath, no less. But God has not struck me dead,* he marveled. *Am I still a Jew? Will my family be there when I get home? Or will they have been stricken by an act of God so terrible that I will mourn this day forever?*

O'Flanagan's hearty voice snapped Josef back to the moment. "Tell me what's on your mind, Rosenstrauss. I trust you have been doing well with your lace. The ladies in our parish have been quite smitten with your christening frocks. Perhaps you can produce some trims for our church vestments? And a cloth for our altar table? I assure you they will be well received."

"Ah, yes," Josef replied, his tone revealing enthusiasm. "We can do that. Have your representative come to see me about your needs. And by the way, Peter," he added, "it is Josef Rose now, and our firm is known as Rose Industries." He paused, wondering what O'Flanagan's response would be. Amazed, he listened as O'Flanagan took the name change in stride.

"And so, Rose Industries it is," O'Flanagan proclaimed. "An easy, quick name to remember. It will serve you and your business well. And is it the business you wish to talk to me about?"

"Yes, it is," Josef said, as they sat down on a nearby bench.

The streets were overflowing with workers hurrying home for the evening meal. Others were singing and laughing their way to bars, celebrating the end of the six-day workweek.

"Is New York always this busy on Saturdays?" asked Josef, regretting the question as soon as it left his mouth. *Does he realize I'm Jewish and have never been out and about on a Saturday? Will he help a non-Irishman, a Jew?* A flush of color covered Josef's face as time seemed to stand still while he waited for O'Flanagan's response. He fought the old urge to wring his hands, a habit he despaired of ever shedding.

"Yes," laughed Peter, "it always is. But Saturday nights are special, particularly for those looking forward to their rest on Sunday. But tell me what I can do for you."

Reassured by O'Flanagan's warm tone, Josef caught him up on the progress the business had been making. "It's time for us to expand. Orders are coming in fast for our lace and for our knit products. In fact, we need to hire more people in production, stock, and bookkeeping. We are also considering bringing in workers to help with building maintenance, custodial care, and even advertising."

Josef paused to gauge O'Flanagan's response.

"Go on," O'Flanagan urged, "I'm listening."

Josef clenched his hands behind his back and fought to keep his voice even. It was a few moments before he could finally speak. "I also want to purchase a lacemaking machine. The new Leavers machine would allow us to do five-by-seven-yard runs of patterned lace. Just think," he said, his demeanor brightening. "We could expand into mass curtain production and table products of all kinds."

O'Flanagan looked at Josef inquisitively. Before he could say anything, Josef anticipated his question. "Yes," he said, his confidence growing, "with a Leavers machine, anything would become possible, from producing draperies to lining luxury stagecoaches to creating lace wall coverings. We would continue our handmade lace line. Don't you worry about that."

"It sounds well thought out, well planned," said O'Flanagan. "But you seem to have other ideas, as well."

"Yes," said Josef. "Sometimes my eagerness gives me away. I also want to procure a knitting machine. Rose Industries has two paths to follow. I plan to pursue both lace and knit goods manufacture—and a combination of the two, as well."

O'Flanagan's face lit up. "You're on to something, Mr. Josef Rose, something very big." The Irishman stood, stretched, and reached into his pocket for a card. "Here you are, Mr. Rose of Rose Industries. This is Mr. Edward Reilly's card. He is the chief loan officer of the new Immigrant Savings and Loan Bank on Chambers Street. It is a short brick building that just opened last spring. You can't miss it. It will be refreshing for Reilly to work with a foresighted businessman like you. Immigrant was founded to help Irish famine victims, but it has lent money to German clients before. With my recommendation, Mr. Reilly will be open to your needs."

As the two stood to part ways, O'Flanagan grinned. "A lucky thing it was that I greeted the *Kronsprinz* last year. Tammany doesn't always meet ships from Hamburg, but we had an envoy from Cork coming into New York on that vessel, and I was sent to meet him. It was a blessed day. With your business expanding, I suspect we will have many dealings with each other in the future. Meanwhile, we will send someone to fetch you on Election Day. The Democrats must win, and we will do everything in our power to make that happen."

When Josef arrived home, darkness had fallen, and the Sabbath candles were extinguished. Frida had saved a meal of beef flanken, roasted potatoes, and stewed beets for him, but it was cold and turning gray by the time Josef entered the flat. Frida was nowhere to be seen.

"Frida!" Josef called. "Where are you?" When there was no response, he scampered downstairs to the shop where he found Frida sitting in the dark with August, trying to get him to sleep. Sometimes a change of scene helped to calm him when he became restless.

"Where have you been, Josef? Your morning business meeting seems to have turned into a whole day affair."

"Frida, I'm so sorry to have kept you waiting. But you will be astonished when you hear what's happened."

As Josef recounted the day's developments, Frida relaxed. "So, you will see this Mr. Reilly next week after the election?"

Josef paused thoughtfully. "No, why wait?" he said, grinning. "I'll see him first thing this week. Things are looking up, my dear, and someday we will have it all. We're on our way."

Josef was waiting at the bank when it opened on Monday morning. Located on the edge of the Irish district, which was sometimes called Little Ireland, the small office was, as Peter O'Flanagan had promised, easy to find. When he arrived, the bank was already crowded with domestics, laborers, and tradesmen eager to establish savings accounts to send money back to relatives in their home countries— or, like Josef, to build reserves for new businesses.

After a lengthy wait, Josef was finally called into Edward Reilly's office. A man of average height and stature, Reilly wore an aura of confidence blended with compassion. Self-possessed, resolute, and keen-witted, he put Josef at ease immediately.

"Peter O'Flanagan has already contacted me about you," Reilly said, as he sat across the desk from Josef. "I understand you are doing important things, things that are going well for you. Peter and I go back a long way. We were classmates in County Kerry, a bonny place of crystal blue waters and verdant forests. We came to America a few years ago and we are neighbors to this day. Peter was of considerable help when I was president of the Irish Society and the bank was just a hope on the horizon. A good man he is, indeed. We attend mass together quite often. Just recently, we attended a christening at Trinity Church. My wife was with me and commented on the baby's gown. Peter told me it was made by your company and said you might be coming in to see me. Well, here you are. What can Immigrant Savings and Loan do for you?"

Josef explained his plans for Rose Industries. Reilly listened attentively, nodding in approval and asking practical questions. A half-hour later, Josef stood and gathered his coat. "I've taken enough of your time, Mr. Reilly."

"No, not at all. Please sit. I am interested in your ideas. In fact, I'll ask my assistant to fetch us a pot of tea and crumpets. I take it you enjoy tea."

"Yes, yes, of course," said Josef, lowering himself back into his chair.

Within a few minutes, a steaming teapot bundled in a green-wool cozy was on the table. The scent of warm sugar filled the air from fat scones bursting with golden raisins piled in a straw basket next to it. Small jars of creamy Irish butter, bright yellow lemon curd, and a pitcher of fresh cream completed the offering. The scents filled Josef's nostrils and made his mouth water.

"We don't do this for all our customers," offered Reilly, "but it is time for the morning repast, and we still have more to discuss."

A while later, the banker rose and offered his hand to Josef. "Your word and Peter's recommendation are good enough for me. You will get your funds immediately. Immigrant will be proud to be part of your burgeoning business. And so will the Irish workers you'll be sure to employ. Yes, we will get along quite well together."

Josef all but flew home to share the news with Frida. "We will have enough money now to invest in equipment and hire more workers. And—what do you think of this idea? Let's expand the business into our present apartment and find a more suitable place for us to live, a place where August can have his own room and maybe even a small yard to play in."

"We won't have increased income for a while," Frida protested, her brow furrowing.

"It won't be long until we do," said Josef. "I've been going over the books. I think we should start looking right after Rent Day in February.

"Are you sure?"

Josef took Frida in his arms and held her tight against his chest. His pulse quickened as he shared this moment of promise with her. Visions of a busy home and a towering brick factory played in front of him like the flick books he had enjoyed as a child. Not much bigger than the size of a fist, a flick book contained a series of drawings that subtly changed from one page to the next. When one flicked through the pictures, they appeared to move. He could almost reach out and touch the images that now played in front of him; his family would have the finest of everything. They would enjoy a spacious home with lots of room to entertain; children would laugh and play in a garden . . .

A shriek from August brought Josef back from his reverie. Laughing, Frida pushed away from his arms to tend the baby who was turning red in the face demanding his next meal. "Yes, it's a good idea. But now we have work to do," she said, as she put August on her hip and went to the rocker to breastfeed. "Immigrant Bank has money; we should expand the business NOW."

CHAPTER 14

Josef

Josef was up most of the night studying Rose Industries' books and projecting revenues versus costs over the next five years. From every standpoint, prospects were excellent. Pleased that he could draw upon his apprenticeship with Erwin back in Hamburg, he realized how much of that training was now giving him the expertise to move forward. When he finally went to bed, he thought how wonderful it would have been to confront his father with his success.

He fell into a restless doze just as the predawn November light peeked through the curtains. Suddenly, a pounding at the door reverberated throughout the house. Trembling, Frida bolted upright and cowered into Josef's arms.

"Go back to sleep, darling," he whispered, covering her and tucking her back into the safety of the bed. "It's probably the milkman with a delivery," he murmured, as he threw on a wool dressing gown to protect himself from the autumn chill pervading the apartment and raced down the steps.

The pounding got heavier with the passing moments, and Josef recoiled at the memory of an incident that had occurred in Hamburg years earlier. Then, as now, he had been asleep when loud knocking woke him. He had heard Erwin race down the stairs to open the heavy wooden front door. Harsh voices had floated up to Josef's room. He hadn't been able to make out all the words, but *Jude aufgepasst* (Jew beware) was at the essence of the encounter. His father refused to discuss the incident the next morning, but it had sent terror through Josef's soul.

As Josef fumbled to open the door, his heart beating heavily, someone called out loudly: "My name's Gus Cairny, and I've come to fetch you to the polls. Today is Election Day, and your vote has been promised to Tammany."

Cairny was a thick-set fellow with beaver teeth, a huge chest, and arms massive enough to crush a wall. A head of wiry black hair reached almost to his wide-set dark eyes, and the mustache above his narrow lip grew seamlessly into a thick beard. Dressed in a gray-checkered coat and black pants, his brawny body exuded strength. "Get dressed right now," said Cairny, his husky voice insistent. "We've not a moment to waste."

Trembling, Josef managed to meet Cairny's demands and followed along a few paces behind him under the rising sun until they reached the polling plaza. Even this early in the morning, there were thousands of people in haphazard queues lining the streets. Cairny took Josef's arm and steered him toward a makeshift wooden station where they were sucked into a crowd of new immigrants.

"Stay on this line until you are called," Cairny instructed. "Your citizenship papers are waiting for you. We'll send someone to escort you to the ballot boxes."

Josef waited for what seemed like hours. Across the plaza, in the full light of the new day, candidates and workers were delivering heated speeches and spouting campaign slogans. While he fought to hold his place against the pushing and shoving around him, a fight broke out between the Whigs and the Democrats. Fists flew, barriers were knocked down, and the mob became increasingly rowdy as speakers from both sides spurred them on.

Finally, Josef reached the front of the queue. A skinny young worker with a sparse beard sat behind a long table where new immigrants were being processed. "Name?" the clerk inquired, without looking up from the roster spread out in front of him.

"Josef Rose," he said, keeping his hands in check.

"I take it you have renounced allegiance to your former country?" the worker asked.

"Yes," stammered Josef, unprepared for the question.

"Do you have a witness who will swear you have obeyed the laws of the United States? Someone who has referred you to us will do."

Heart beating wildly, Josef felt trapped. Just then, Peter O'Flanagan appeared, seemingly out of nowhere. In his booming voice, he vouched for Josef authoritatively. "I am glad to certify Mr. Rose," O'Flanagan said, staring down at the clerk. "He is a valuable member of New York society who is worthy of citizenship."

"He needs proof of residency," the worker said, starting to dismiss Josef.

"Not necessary," said O'Flanagan, drawing a thin packet from his breast pocket and handing it to the clerk with great exaggeration. "These are his eligibility papers. You will find them in perfect order."

Josef winced as he saw O'Flanagan slip a sealed envelope under the table. The clerk snatched the envelope and stuffed it into his hip pocket. His bland expression never changed, and his eyes revealed nothing of the clandestine exchange. He threw the residency guarantee onto a haphazard pile and then searched through a large box of papers on the table. The pages were in no particular order, but he finally retrieved a frayed document about five-by-seven inches in size. Long words Josef could not read were scrawled in black ink. The clerk filled in Josef's name, stamped the document, and, with a flourish, signed it as a witness.

"You are now a United States citizen, Mr. Rose. You may proceed to the ballot box," the clerk instructed, waving Josef toward a mass of waiting voters who would decide, among other things, the next mayor of New York City and a slate of candidates ranging from alderman to New York State governor.

"Come with me. I'll match you up with one of our Tammany people who will walk you through the voting process," O'Flanagan declared, taking Josef's arm and chattering about Rose Industries' bright future.

Suddenly, a hush fell over the crowd as a sinewy man with a prominent nose, blazing black eyes, and a distinctive swagger climbed onto a packing crate that had housed the lumber used to build the plaza podiums. Without words, his very presence drew hundreds of men dressed in long, rough overcoats and stovepipe hats. Emboldened by drink, they pushed and shoved through the already-dense crowd to surround the podium. A tense hush came over the horde of humanity as the man shouted in a voice that seemed to split the air with its intensity.

"I am Isaiah Rynders!" he cried, sending a wave of fear through the crowd. "My Dead Rabbits Club is here, scattered among you. We know you. Five hundred of you are from Philadelphia, brought here to vote the Whig ticket. Damn you! If you don't leave these polls in five minutes, we will *dirk* every mother's son of you."

Within moments, the crowd scattered in fear as opposing party members turned to each other with fists flying. Bill Poole's Bowery Boys gang arrived and joined in the fray. As the fights intensified, bullies—lumps of lead wrapped in handkerchiefs—flew. Jaws were broken, eyes were gouged, and blood lined the streets in rivulets as men crumpled to the ground.

"Josef," said O'Flanagan, seemingly unfazed by the scene unraveling around him, "I'm needed in the office, so I am going to hand you over to that young man over there." He steered Josef to a mustached fellow with a huge head, solid chin, and brick-like legs. "This is Tommy Mulden," he said, as he pointed to voter lines more than a block long. "He'll make sure you vote right."

Tommy threw a huge arm over Josef's shoulder and steered him toward the scaffolds that Josef had helped to build. The thug said not a word, but pulled Josef through the battling throng, setting anyone in his way into speedy retreat. Josef had no choice but to trot along, his short legs struggling to keep pace.

"Where are the police?" Josef managed to stammer.

"The coppers? Yellow-bellied blokes, they are, afraid of offending anyone and losing their jobs. Besides, we don't need them, do we?" Mulden laughed. "We take care of ourselves just fine."

As they made their way, Tommy kept a heavy hand on Josef's shoulder. The queue was dense, and voters squirmed under the arms of fierce men making sure their votes were cast properly. When it was Josef's turn, Mulden shoved him roughly to a table loaded with ballots where Josef was supplied with a party ticket imprinted with the Tammany Tiger logo. Josef saw that the Democrat boxes had already been checked, canceling any possibility that he could support a Whig candidate.

"See that platform against the wall?" Mulden said, pointing to a particular scaffold. "You'll climb up and pass your ballot through the window to the election judge." He tightened his grip and steered Josef to the ballot depository.

"Good. One more vote for Tammany," he said with a grin, as Josef's ballot thudded into place. "Now just hand over the required three-dollar polling fee, and you'll be free to go. A voter who's made an excellent choice."

Terrified not to comply, Josef reached into his pocket, his knees shaking when he thought of what might have happened if he hadn't had three dollars with him.

Tommy laughed loudly. "Now that's a good lad. A very generous donation you've made, indeed. Now go find Peter O'Flanagan. He tells me you're needed to help count the ballots."

As Josef turned to make his way back through the crowd, he heard a commotion behind him. A familiar voice assaulted his ears, churning his stomach. He turned to see a hooligan with stringy blond hair and a raspy voice pulling along a voter carrying a Whig flag. The ruffian's bulky sailor's coat and thick high-necked sweater barely concealed the huge belly that rippled as he exerted himself. As quickly as he could, Josef crouched under the red-white-and-blue bunting affixed to a table piled high with ballots. Nausea nearly overtaking him, he watched through a tear in the skirting and listened in horror.

"You don't want to vote that way, mate," the thug said to his victim, grabbing the Whig sign out of the man's hand. "Do ya?" The brute knocked the would-be voter to the ground, raised his huge foot, and stamped on the man's knee where a red stain immediately appeared and spread to his thigh. Howling with laughter when the man screamed in agony, he grabbed his victim's hair, dragged him upright, and forced a party ticket into his hand. "There, now, that's a good man," he rasped, taking the man's three dollar fee and dragging him over to stacks of ballots on the table just over Josef's head.

From under the bunting hem, Josef could see the Whig's feet and hear him grunting. The man's howls of pain filled the air as his tormentor twisted his wrist and forced him to drop the ballot into the box.

"That was a good vote you made, fella. Tammany thanks you. You see? Otto did well for you. Saved you the trouble of having to mark the party ticket paper. Now, get your cronies over here to vote—or you'll have Otto to deal with."

Josef froze, breaking into a cold sweat as Otto started to saunter away. Suddenly, an orange alley cat scurrying toward the ballot table caught Otto's eye. He bellowed in glee and turned to stalk the hapless creature. Taking a shriveled piece of pork jerky from his pocket, he squatted and held out the meat. Josef could see Otto's feet and smell the dried seawater caking the soles of his worn leather shoes. Slowly, one paw at a time, the starving creature approached the jerky.

Just then, a tribe of sailors turned onto the street. Their raucous voices terrified the cat and sent it scurrying into the shadows right past Josef. Sweat soaked through Josef's shirtwaist and his eyes widened in fear as Otto screamed curses.

"You wretched creature! If I ever come across you again, I'll have your head!"

As Otto turned away, his pleasure thwarted, Josef waited under the table until the hooligan was out of sight, grateful that he had remained unnoticed. When he stood, his knees creaking in painful protest, his shirt and pants were soaked through with perspiration despite the chilly breeze that had started to fill the voting plaza.

Slowly, Josef made his way to Tammany Hall to see O'Flanagan. As he walked through the smoke-filled building, he spotted the tall redhead standing with a group of men dressed in stiff white collars, tight black trousers, and black topcoats. Some wore stovepipe hats, but all sported pocket watches on thick gold chains peeking out from the perfectly aligned buttonholes on their form-fitting vests. O'Flanagan spotted Josef immediately and waved him toward his office.

Josef waited there patiently while the Irishman was finishing his meeting, glancing around the room and noting the frenzy of activity taking place. Ballots were piled on every surface, and overflow crates cluttered the floors. As counts were determined and loudly announced, Josef was reminded of the carnivals he used to visit in Hamburg where barkers shouted above the din of busy crowds.

"Let's keep it going, keep it going!" counters shouted, as ballots were dumped in piles without regard to any perceivable order. "Whig votes?" they commanded. "The discard pile is over there. Tammany will bring in the vote for our people. Do you all understand?"

Finally, Peter O'Flanagan made his way to his desk and sat down across from Josef, his blue eyes filled with merriment. "It's quite a day for Tammany!" he exclaimed, seemingly oblivious to the disorder around him. He extended his hand to Josef and shook it vigorously. "We are grateful for your help," he said. "Let's get you counting over there with Cairny and Mulden. We'll raise a glass when our Fernando Wood is voted in as mayor, and I become a full alderman."

The next few hours passed in a flurry of activity as Democrat votes were loudly proclaimed, and Whig votes were booed and hissed. By the time the sun set, Tammany burst into applause when the projections came out in favor of their candidates. Peter O'Flanagan was jubilant and stood before the hall, a large beer stein in hand, and declared the results. "Tonight is a great victory for Tammany Hall and the Democrats," he asserted. "We've won almost every race— except for mayor. But rest assured, fellows, in the next election, even the mayor's office will be ours. Fernando Wood will triumph in fifty-four!"

Again, a great roar erupted in the hall as the workers met Peter's toast with approval. As soon as he had completed his rounds of congratulatory handshakes and pats on the back, he found Josef standing at the back of the great hall. "Yes, my lad," O'Flanagan beamed as he greeted Josef. "Precincts outside our jurisdiction defeated Fernando Wood. But he will prevail in the next election, isn't that correct?"

"That sounds right," Josef stammered.

"Oh, yes, that's exactly right. It is with the help of generous donors like yourself that we will succeed." O'Flanagan paused for a long moment, then hovered over Josef so closely that he was forced to step backward. When Peter finally spoke, his words came in a hoarse whisper. "We can count on you for three percent of Rose Industries' profits every year to support our great cause, yes?" He stared unflinchingly at Josef—then, suddenly, he relaxed, his familiar grin replacing his icy stare. Even his voice resumed its booming quality. "Now, let's join the lads at the pub and celebrate our great victories."

When the evening finally ended, Josef walked through the darkened streets toward home. Discarded ballots gathered against the curbs and occasionally floated through the air on stray breezes. Candlelight from parlor windows and the lonely clip-clop of an occasional horse provided the only relief from the desolation of the descending night.

Is this what I'm coming to? thought Josef. *Is paying Tammany off, and saying nothing about their election methods, what they mean by selling one's soul? Frida would say we're doing what we must do to survive. But are we, or are we doomed in God's eyes? I don't know. Heaven help me, I don't know . . .*

When Josef arrived home, Frida was waiting for him. August was sleeping soundly, and the flat was quiet as she sat in her chair knitting by the stove. She placed her needlework in a basket on the floor and rose to greet him. "I know you were voting, Josef, but you've been out all day. It will be dark soon."

"Yes, I know," answered Josef. "But there have been some developments."

As Josef told her most of the day's events, Frida listened without interruption. Her eyes grew glacial as Josef told her of O'Flanagan's payment demands.

"How can we do this?" Josef implored.

"How can we *not* do this?" Frida responded. She reached for his hand. "All we have hoped for is coming true. O'Flanagan has made our situation clear; we are obligated to meet his demands."

The Torah would say otherwise, Josef thought. *Remember the Sabbath and keep it holy . . . Thou shalt not bear false witness . . . Thou shalt not covet.* Lessons of his youth hammered in his head as he fought the shame rising in his belly.

As Frida prattled on, her voice rising with anticipation as she detailed their growing proficiency in English, their acceptance into local society, and, especially, Rose Industries' glowing future, Josef retreated deeper into his thoughts. *If I had followed the Torah, obeyed God's commandments, would I be facing these terrible choices? Would I have allowed myself to take part in deceiving my neighbor? To scheme and to let my ambitions overcome me?*

"Are you listening, Josef?" Frida asked, jolting him into reality. She let a few moments pass before she spoke again. When she did, her voice was iron. "You must go along with Tammany, Josef. If you don't, I will."

PART TWO:
1856

CHAPTER 15

Josef

Just as he had so many times since his introduction to Tammany politics five years earlier, Josef left Tammany Hall to head home for the evening. A sultry pall hung over the city as the thermometer climbed to ninety-seven degrees by noon and held on all day. Even at this late hour, heat clung to the cobblestones and radiated from buildings at every turn. An uneasy quiet hovered over the usually noisy streets, the populace too drained to hawk their wares or hurry to evening destinations.

Fernando Wood had won the mayorship in 1854, and Peter O'Flanagan had ridden his coattails to become a member of the New York City Common Council, which was the upper house of the Board of Aldermen, a legislative body. The public had revolted against the old board, colloquially known as the Forty Thieves, accusing it of improprieties in granting ordinances and dispersing monies to favored politicians.

Josef made his way through the oppressive air, his thoughts centered on his late-afternoon meeting with Peter O'Flanagan. The Tammany kingpin had called him in to discuss the launching of the 1856 mayoral campaign, slated for the fall, just a little more than two months away.

"Your support has been appreciated over the last several years," O'Flanagan said.

They sat across from each other at a long oak conference table surrounded by sixteen red-damask chairs. Vases of late-summer roses, wilting from the heat, stood in the middle of the table next to a tub of beer. A large map of New York City occupied the wall behind Josef. It outlined the wards of the city and was pinned with scraps of paper indicating the politics of various neighborhoods.

"Can I offer you a cucumber sandwich?" O'Flanagan asked, adjusting his tall frame into his seat and passing a plate to Josef. "And there's beer in the crystal decanter over there, if that suits your fancy."

"No, thank you," said Josef, taking the plate and setting it aside. "I have little time tonight. What's on your mind?"

Peter took a bite of sandwich and then shuffled a pile of papers, looking for a particular document. "It has come to my attention," he said, reading from a parchment letter emblazoned with the Immigrant Savings and Loan logo, "that Rose Industries has turned unprecedented profits. Quite an accomplishment in only five years." He paused to take a swig of beer, then continued. "I understand you have requested additional funds to finance more equipment."

"Yes," replied Josef, whose English had vastly improved over the past few years. "We have one lace machine right now and two knitting machines. We'd like to expand our sheet-lace production to accelerate lace apparel and home decoration production. Demand for knit goods is also up, and we have started to sell wool yardage for coats and suits. We'll need machines." Josef wondered if it would be wise to tell O'Flanagan of his plans for supplying the military with cloth for uniforms. He decided to wait until demands came in.

O'Flanagan grinned, sitting back in his chair. "I'll talk to Reilly. I'm sure additional loans can be arranged." He crossed his long legs and steepled his hands under his chin. "But onto another matter. As I am sure you are aware, Josef, Mayor Wood has made extraordinary strides in the city. The streets are cleaner, saloons are closed on Sundays allowing our residents to enjoy quiet church days, and crime is down. The rowdies certainly aren't missed on the Sunday Sabbath." O'Flanagan winced, catching himself too late. "My apologies to you, lad," he stammered. "I think 'tis not your Sabbath, but surely you enjoy a quiet weekend day as much as the rest of us."

Josef pushed his thoughts away as *Jüdischer Bastard* and the fat seaman's blade sprang, unwanted, into his thoughts. He cringed as the assault invaded his mind, and he willed himself to smile. "It's fine," he said. "Sundays are busy for us. Our machines are going seven days a week to meet customer quotas."

"So I am told," the big man said, downing the last of his cucumber lunch. "You are in need of more Irish workers then, I'm sure."

"To be truthful, right now we are all right."

O'Flanagan stood and walked silently around the table to take a chair next to Josef. A moment passed before he spoke. "My dear lad," he finally said, his eyes narrowing. "Don't be modest. I will be sending you additional workers in a few days. 'Tis certain you will find positions for them. Isn't that correct?"

Peter suddenly stood to greet a visitor, his face breaking into a wide grin.

"Gus Cairny," he beamed, extending his hand to the guest. "You remember Gus, don't you, Mr. Rose? He helped to guide you in your first election. You spoke so little English then, but look at you now. 'Tis quite an accomplishment."

Suddenly, Peter's eyes lost their warmth. He stared at Josef, then looked toward Cairny again. "Gus, please, sit down. Josef and I were just talking about you and the support Tammany has thrown behind Rose Industries. He has expressed his deep gratitude and wishes to know what else he can do in reciprocation."

"It is good to see you, Mr. Rose," said Cairny, settling himself into a vacant chair. Cairny had recently become a leader in the Dead Rabbits organization and was a Tammany cohort. "As Peter has told you, Edward Reilly speaks highly of you. And, yes, he has said there are some things you can do for our great cause."

"What do you have in mind?" Josef asked, his apprehension rising. He fought the impulse to wring his hands.

Cairny crossed his sturdy legs, his black linen frock coat opening at the knees. He grinned as he reached for a cucumber sandwich from the plate beside Josef, took a few bites, and downed some beer. "The sandwich isn't the bacon and beef I like," he laughed, "but it's a hot day, so it will do." He paused and leaned in toward Josef. "I'm what you call a sporting man, I am. I love food, cards, and the ponies, with a bit of culture thrown in. Can't get enough of any of it. I'll count on you to join me and my friends one of these days at the tables."

Josef blanched. He had come to understand after years of dealing with this lot that this wasn't an invitation but a directive. As long as he did what they said and as long as he looked the other way when necessary, he was in their good graces. Cross them, and he could lose everything. They could destroy him. When he composed himself, he managed to nod in agreement. "That will be fine, Mr. Cairny, that will be fine."

"And so," Cairny continued, "we need your contributions in reelecting Fernando Wood. We'd like you to work closely with our William Tweed in overseeing the books and getting out the vote when the time comes. Tweed was a United States congressman. He's running for a position on the Board of Aldermen and needs your vote. He supports Tammany Hall and everything we stand for."

Cairny and Peter shared knowing glances as they exchanged anecdotes about the two politicians. Josef swallowed hard and finally agreed. "I'm here for whatever you need me to do."

"Good," said Cairny. He started to get up from his chair but stopped abruptly. "Oh, yes. One other thing. The missus would like to fill our new house with lace draperies. You'll come for dinner next week. Surely, you'll want to give us a house gift, isn't that so?"

"That can certainly be arranged," Josef said, trying to hide his consternation. "I'll be happy to come by and take measurements whenever you wish."

O'Flanagan's loud voice, jovial once again, changed the course of the conversation. "So, it is settled. Tweed will contact you soon, and I'll be sending you new employees. Let me know how they are working out." As he stood to dismiss Josef, his eyes once more turned icy gray, and his lips thinned. "I welcome the token of appreciation I know you are offering—your finder's fee for the workers, so to speak. Cairny will come by tomorrow to collect it."

Forcing a smile, Josef nodded.

"Very well," O'Flanagan said, offering his hand. I look forward to advancing our interests together."

That night, Josef tossed and turned in his bed.

"What is it?" Frida asked, as Josef turned his back.

"Go to sleep, darling," he said, avoiding her inquiries. "I will see you tomorrow afternoon. I have business to attend to early tomorrow."

At 8:00 the next morning, Josef walked over to Norfolk Street to Ansche Beth Shalom. As he climbed the steps of the synagogue, he was overwhelmed with shame. Between the growing demands of the business and the births of six more children, including identical twin girls, the relationship between the Roses and the Kohns had drifted. The Roses had not attended services or synagogue functions in years. Tilly's time had also become limited to bringing up her family and attending to synagogue duties, and Josef was unsure of what the rabbi's reception would be when he arrived at the temple.

As Josef opened the heavy wooden doors, the coolness of the synagogue greeted him. Its stone walls offered protection from the climbing heat of the day and seemed to envelop him with the promise of peace a synagogue had always provided. He entered the sanctuary, his heart filling with a combination of longing and regret as he remembered the joy that being close to God had once given him. Silently, he slipped into one of the long oak pews. As he slid his hand against its smooth wood, he gazed up at the bimah. In his mind, he heard a cantor's resonant voice rise above the uttered prayers of men clad in white damask prayer shawls, davening in devotion.

Leo will help, he thought. *He will help me find my way again.*

Lost in his thoughts, Josef was jolted out of his reverie when he heard the click-clack of footsteps on the stone floor. He stood to see who had entered the sanctuary.

"I am Assistant Rabbi Mayer Jacobs. May I help you?" a young man asked. Dressed in a black suit, the only sign of his religious affiliation was a yarmulke of woven black and blue braid covering his thick brown hair. He was beardless, and bright blue eyes sparkled behind steel-rimmed spectacles displayed on his aquiline nose.

"Yes, thank you," said Josef, taken aback by the man's lack of religious attire. "I am looking for Rabbi Leo Kohn."

"Oh," said Mayer Jacobs, nodding his head solemnly. "I hope it is nothing serious you wish to discuss. You've missed him. He left just last month for Chicago to serve as rabbi of the new B'nai Israel. Would you care for his forwarding address?"

Josef felt his knees go weak. The color drained from his face, and he started to fall backward. He caught onto a pew just as he was about to collapse. "No, no, thank you," he said. *It's too late. I think I belong to the devil.*

PART THREE: 1859–1865

CHAPTER 16

Frida

Where are you, Frida? You're dead. You're supposed to be here with me! Roshen screeched, as she stretched out a skeletal hand. Her mother's eyes had sunk deep in their sockets, and a few wiry white hairs sprouted from her withered scalp. Ashen lips caked with blood smirked as they wordlessly mouthed old childhood lullabies meant to lure Frida away from life.

"I'm not dead, Mama!" Frida screamed as she bolted upright in her bed. Shaking, she called for Josef to no avail. He had risen early to tend to urgent business at the shop. It was February 1859, and Rose Industries had become a major business force in New York City in the past five years.

Waiting for her heart to stop pounding, she pulled back the covers and wrapped herself against the cold in the wool-lined, lace night coat she had recently crafted. When she stopped trembling and the nightmare receded, she lit a candle. She shuffled silently to the dresser, picked up an elaborately carved ivory box, and padded downstairs.

The velvet-lined case had been a recent gift from Josef on the eighth anniversary of Rose Industries' first year. It held her Star of David, locks of hair gently gathered from her seven children on the day each was born, and a stack of correspondence wrapped in fine blue satin ribbon. They were unopened letters that she had sent to Roshen but had been sent back to her from Germany marked *Veigert*

(Refused) in her mother's tight handwriting. All Frida's letters had contained questions about Roshen and Jakob, news of her marriage to Josef, news of newborn children who now ranged in age from three to seven years, and details of the life she and Josef were building in America. Money had been included with every letter and remained in the returned envelopes. None of the letters had been opened; none of them had been read.

Tears rolling down her cheeks, Frida untied the ribbon and placed the letters on her lap. She started to count. *One, two, three . . . eight . . .thirteen . . . twenty . . . thirty-one.* Thirty-one times she had reached out to her beloved mama, and thirty-one times those letters had been returned. Mama didn't know that she had seven grandchildren. Frida sat silently for several moments, recounting the details of her dream. *One more letter, Mama,* she vowed. *I am not dead. Maybe this time . . .*

As the clock chimed six o'clock a.m., Frida went downstairs to the secretary Josef had bought when they first arrived in America. He had refinished it beautifully, his meticulous work revealing maple and ebony inlaid patterns in the piece's rich mahogany. After she checked the porcelain monkey to remind herself of the fragility and of the hope of life, she opened the drop-front of the desk. As its patina picked up glints of moonlight streaming in through the window, she reached into one of the cubbies to retrieve sheets of linen writing paper. Adjusting her gown, she sat on the burgundy leather desk chair they had recently purchased for Josef, picked up her pen, and began to write:

Dearest Mama,

It is, again, with a mixture of joy and sorrow that I am writing this letter—joy because of good news, and sorrow because my many letters to you have gone unanswered. Our estrangement hurts my very soul, and it deeply troubles me that the years pass by without each other.

You have seven grandchildren who are all doing well. The eldest, August Manfred, his middle name chosen to honor dear Papa, will be eight years old in August. He is a big boy for his age, strong and muscular, with a shock of blond—yes, blond— hair (we have no idea where his tallness or his fair coloring came from!). August is quite a prankster, Mama. We caught him just a few days ago trying to cut off half of Josef's handlebar mustache as he napped after dinner. Thankfully, Josef woke as soon as the scissor came near his whiskers, and he hastily sent the boy off to his room without his nighttime snack. It was a doleful sight but an amusing one, as August pleaded for his rice pudding (his favorite), especially when it is topped with cinnamon and chocolate shavings.

Wilhelm, my beloved grandfather's namesake, turns seven in June and is a rebellious child. He adores his older brother. They get along splendidly, even though he is half August's size. They play together for hours. I worry when it gets too quiet; they get into mischief very easily, especially if they get into the kitchen. Left to their own devices, they would tear through the house, jumping on furniture and sending dust flying from the cushions. Wilhelm has just announced that he is a big boy now and wishes to be called Willie. He loves everything and is becoming quite an athlete. Even at his tender age, he can go many rounds with the hoop, his sturdy little hips whirling around for an hour at a time. He loves to play ball with his brother and his friends, and he can run as fast as the wind.

And Bessie. Bessie has turned six. She is a small, slender little girl with a graceful figure and silken black hair, but she is ashamed of several birthmarks that cover her face. The doctors say there is nothing to be done, and the poor child is subject to teasing by other children. She is self-conscious and doesn't smile often, but she has already discovered the joys of music and finds great refuge in poetry.

Louise and Gertrude, who is named after your mother, are five-year-old identical twins, and they keep us busy. They look exactly alike. Their hair is long and dark, and their eyes have turned such a deep brown that we can scarcely see the pupils. They want only to be together and cry pitifully whenever they are separated even for the few moments when we must tend to their individual needs. We've been a bit troubled by swelling and coldness in their fingers, but they smile a lot and love to be tickled despite their sensitive stomachs.

The children are much taken with Burkhardt. At four, Burke, as we call him, is a content little boy and laughs easily. He loves to be outside and breaks into delightful giggles at the sight of his pram. When he is happy, he flicks his wrists, and his dimples all but cover his whole face. He looks a little like you, Mama, with dark eyes and a tall, slim build. He was recently playing on the parlor floor, and he spotted, of all things, Hildegarde. Remember my old doll, Hildegarde? I have had her with me all these years, and she occupies a place in the big basket I keep near my knitting chair. I think I may need to surrender her to Burke. He has become quite attached to the dear old thing.

When Elsie was born, we were concerned with her very small size, but she is a beautiful child with a full head of curly dark hair and bright pink cheeks. At almost three, she is still small, but Josef and I are small, so we are not too worried about that. She is not speaking yet and is a bit withdrawn, Mama. I wish you were here to tell me what to do with her.

The older children are learning to read and write. There is a German American school nearby where their studies are presented in both languages. They revel in sharing their skills with Josef and me as we become increasingly proficient in English. We have come a long way in learning English (we attend classes regularly), but how they giggle when we mispronounce or misuse a word.

And Mama, our business, Rose Industries, is thriving. I wish you could see how busy the workshop is. Lace and woolen cloth manufacture are our specialties. Orders pour in, and production increases almost daily to keep up with demand. We recently moved the business into new quarters. Two floors are devoted to production, and 350 workers operate lacemaking and knitting machines in ten-hour shifts.

Our profits have allowed us to move into our own home, too. It is on Twenty-third Street and has enough bedrooms to house our growing brood. We recently acquired our own horse and carriage, and it is of great help in getting around the city to tend to business and to the family's needs. We've hired Ida Burmann, a young woman from Berlin, to help us in the house. She went to school with Bertha and Amalia Albrecht, dear friends and board members in our business. Ida helps with the household chores and with keeping track of all the children. Next week, Liesel Didelsheim, who has been working in our shop, will join us in our household as our children's nurse. It is a big relief to have so much help. I could never have imagined having such a life.

Mama, dear, I have enclosed a sum of money for you to use as you see fit. It saddens me that you have sent back all the funds and letters I have sent to you in the past. Despite the economic downturn that started worldwide last year, we are well able to help you. Josef has great business skills, and he has started to manufacture woolen cloth for which the military, in its quest for uniforms, has acquired great interest. America is experiencing great tension between the northern and southern states, especially as issues of slavery become increasingly widespread. There are rumblings that civil war could erupt if things don't change soon, and Rose Industries is prepared to do our share for the North if war should occur.

Mama, I am not dead. The children aren't dead. Please, please think of coming to America to see your family who will offer you all the love in the world and revel in your visit. I have enclosed a first-class ticket for you on the recently launched steamship, SS Bittern, for June 24th when the weather on the Atlantic will be favorable. The voyage to New York will take about ten days. You will have a private stateroom, and I will be waiting at the new Castle Garden terminal to meet you and to take care of you. Every comfort will await you in our home. You will have your own room where you can seek peace at the ends of lovely days seeing America and getting to know your grandchildren.

Please, Mama, take this journey so we may see each other at long last. If the date is not good for you, I will change it to suit your needs.

Loving you always,
Frida

When she finished, she held the letter to her heart before she placed it in an envelope. Her thoughts were uplifting as she thought about her mama. *This letter contains new promise that things might, at last, change.*

Early Tuesday morning, Frida left the children with the new house-keeper and made her way to the Middle Dutch Church on Nassau Street where mail was collected and sorted for both transport and delivery. As she huddled into her velvet cape, her brocade boots scarcely protecting her frozen toes, she couldn't help but wonder how long it would take for her letter to reach Hamburg. From the church, it would be placed on a packet ship to go to London where it would be stamped and placed in a bin until transport space became available. It would then be transferred by steamship to Hamburg, a process that could take weeks. Frida prayed that her beloved mother would answer the mail summons and open her letter. *This letter . . .*

As she approached the wood frame building, now almost two hundred years old, she found herself unwittingly imploring God to help. Furious with herself for allowing God to come into her thoughts, she walked through the weathered front doors to an open space where postal workers were collecting and sorting mail.

When she reached the outgoing table, haphazardly stacked high with letters and packages, she hesitated, suddenly unsure of herself and how she would feel if *this* letter came back to her. She considered the possibility for a few moments. Then she threw back her shoulders and held her head high. *For nineteen cents in postage, the chance is worthwhile. Perhaps this time will be different. Maybe, just maybe, Mama will come.* She drew a deep breath, placed the letter on the table where it would be sent to Hamburg, and walked away.

CHAPTER 17

Roshen

Relentless March winds tore over the Elbe River, reminding Hamburg citizens that the long winter season had not yet passed. The last few days had been sunny but cold, holding forth only an occasional promise of spring for the winter-weary city. The day had started out with sunshine, but by late morning, dark clouds started to roll in. Gulls squawked overhead, their raucous cries warning of impending bad weather. Roshen had warned Jakob not to go ice-skating on the river.

"The ice is thin!" she shrilled, as Jakob, now a tall young man who resembled his mother in height and build, headed out the door, skates casually thrown over his shoulder. Once a compliant and affectionate child, he had grown into a headstrong fellow of twenty-two. He reminded Roshen of his sister. *Frida was a sweet child once,* she thought, memories of her estranged daughter rising to the forefront against her will. *She is dead, she is dead,* Roshen scolded herself. *Don't think of her. She is DEAD.*

Roshen stamped her feet, exasperated at her inability to influence her son.

The rest of the morning had been an uneventful one, filled with cleaning and preparing bread for the evening meal. Suddenly, pounding at the door interrupted her chores.

"Frau Kuhne, this is the constable. Open immediately! There's been an accident. Come to the shore at once; something has happened to Jakob."

Roshen threw down her dough, grabbed her cloak, and rushed out the door to the constable's wagon. As soon as she was seated next to him on the hard wooden driver's seat, he whipped his horse, pushing it to go faster and faster. An icy mixture of snow and sleet started to fall, and Roshen clutched the wagon rail, praying that the horse wouldn't slip and fall before she could get to Jakob.

While they drove, the constable filled her in on the scant details he had about an accident on the river. As they approached the Elbe, she was struck by the crowd that had gathered by the gazebo near the lindens. "Let me through," she begged as she jumped off the wagon. "Let me help my son!" She reached the shoreline just as Jakob was pulled from the water and placed on the ground. Ice had started to form on his hair and lashes, and his usually high-colored cheeks were gray and sunken.

"I'm a doctor!" Roshen heard a man shout as a heavyset, bearded man in a beaver coat rushed to the scene. He fell to the ground, trying to resuscitate Jakob, his breath clouding his silver spectacles. Jakob lay still, his limbs stiff and unresponsive. "C'mon, boy, wake up," implored the doctor, alternately raising Jakob's arms to expand his chest and take in air, then crossing them to force him to exhale. "Who saw what happened here?" the doctor demanded, frantic at Jakob's lack of response.

"We were skating and having a great time," said Edgar, one of Jakob's companions, a lanky fellow with a shock of blond hair and a full mustache. His brow was furrowed, and he avoided Roshen's gaze as she stood over Jakob's still body, her eyes wide with shock.

"There were three of us—Jakob, another fellow, and me. Suddenly, we heard a loud crack. When my friend and I looked back, a hole had formed on the river and blue ice was floating in the exposed water. Jakob was gone. We heard thrashing for a few seconds, then nothing. We tried to get to him, but the ice was too thin. That's when we waved to shore for help. The patrollers hauled a boat over to the hole and got to work." Edgar paused for a moment. Tears ran down his face, and his shoulders heaved. "They hammered through the ice and somehow found Jakob. Is it too late, Doctor?"

"Come on, come on!" shouted the physician, ignoring the young man as he desperately worked on Jakob. He was still crouched over the unconscious boy and trying to get him to breathe. After endless moments, he stopped his maneuvers. He fell back on his haunches, sighed deeply, then stood to face Roshen and Edgar. "Yes," he said gently, looking at them with tears clouding his eyes. "It is too late. He is gone."

Roshen fell to the ground, her body covering her son's. Her sobs came in convulsive gasps, and her cries pierced the air. The crowd stood back, reluctant to stay and unwilling to go.

Edgar was the first to break the silence. Slowly, he walked over to Roshen and pulled her up from the ground. She leaned against his chest, her thin body heaving in grief. Edgar wrapped his arms around her and held her. Roshen finally pulled back and kneeled. "You can't be gone, Jakob! You can't be!" she screamed, as she slapped her son's face in a fruitless attempt to revive him.

When her sobs finally subsided, Edgar offered his hand. "I'm Jakob's oldest friend," he said. "You can't be out in this weather much longer. I'll take you home."

As they walked, Edgar held Roshen's elbow tight against his ribs. They moved in silence, their feet crunching the ice forming on the cobblestones. When Roshen finally spoke, her voice was cutting. "Tell me, Edgar, why did you let Jakob drown? If you had been paying attention, he wouldn't be dead."

Edgar did not respond, and they walked the rest of the way without talking. As they went, the young man gradually released Roshen's arm. Once they reached her gate, Roshen walked abruptly into the house, ignoring Edgar, and slammed the door behind her. She removed her cape, shook snow from its folds, and smoothed her threadbare skirts. Then she threw out the crusted-over dough, wiped down the kitchen, and prepared to go to bed.

"Jakob didn't listen to me. I told him not to skate today. He got what he deserved," she muttered aloud. "That's right. He should have listened to his mother."

After the mandated seven days of shiva passed, Roshen was alone to confront her solitude. The seven-day Jewish ritual of mourning had been a time of desolation for her. As she sat on her shallow wooden box, mandated low by tradition to symbolize the depths of mourners' grief, anger overwhelmed her. Her husband was dead, her brother was estranged, and both her children were gone. Jakob had been the last of her family. Friends from her former life—that life of ease and comfort—hadn't contacted her in years. There had been only a trickle of neighbors, and some of Jakob's friends, coming in to offer condolences. In the traditional effort to ensure that the bereaved are cared for emotionally, spiritually, and nutritionally, just a few had brought food to show their concern. None had stayed to share Roshen's grief; none had offered distraction or comfort.

"Good, that's over with," she said aloud to the empty room. "Good riddance to nosy people stopping in. I don't need anyone but myself."

The first thing to go was the cloth covering the room's only mirror. Roshen laughed a short, bitter laugh. Jewish tradition required the covering of mirrors to remove distraction from mourning and allow the bereaved to concentrate on spiritual rather than secular concerns. *As if a mirror could take away all that's happened to me,* she thought, as she started to fold the covering. *Everyone's gone. Worse, God has abandoned me. Why should I stay with Him?*

An unexpected knock on the door reminded Roshen that Jakob was already gone more than a week. During shiva, the door had been unlocked to allow visitors to come in without distracting the mourners. There had been no callers since then. Anticipating the possibility of more bad news, Roshen threw a shawl around her shoulders and pulled the door open.

A courier dressed in a snappy blue uniform handed Roshen a note saying that mail awaited her in Town Hall. "If you come with me now, I will be happy to take you to retrieve your mail. That is, if you're not too busy."

Roshen was expecting nothing, but agreed to accompany the messenger, mostly to break up the day. Within moments, she was dressed and climbing onto his wagon. Suspecting it was yet another routine letter from Frida but unwillingly frightened it might be bad news about Frida, she broke into a cold sweat that rolled down her neck into the collar of her cape. When they arrived at the post office, she disembarked from the wagon and went into the building where a long line of patrons waited to receive letters and packages. After endless minutes, it was finally her turn. She gave the clerk her name and, after what seemed an interminable time, was handed a small envelope addressed to her in Frida's distinctive handwriting.

Roshen's heart pounded, just as it did every time she heard from her daughter. She examined the envelope, its thin paper fragile and tenuous. The front was covered with the expected postage-due marks, but on the back was an unusual message. It was scrawled along the envelope's bottom, outlined by a black-ink box: **THIS LETTER COULD BE LIFE-CHANGING. PLEASE READ.**

All right, Frida, you win. I'll read your letter when I get home. We'll see what a dead daughter has to say.

That night, after a paltry supper of dark bread and old cheese, Roshen sat down on the only chair left in the parlor. She had been forced to sell the old oak table, her small but serviceable sofa, Frida's bed, and now even Jakob's clothes. Jakob's bed would have to go, too. After Germany's financial downturn the year before, there had been almost no income. She had started to take in laundry and, although her hands had turned red and cracked from lye soap, there had been few customers. Any money she had had was spent, and Roshen worried daily about how she would procure her next meal. Jakob's meager earnings were gone. Flour and yeast were often too dear to purchase, and the dried fish that had sustained her for so many years had become too expensive.

Her body weary from bending over tubs of hot water, Roshen closed her eyes and reviewed her options. She could return the letter as she had done with countless others—or she could open it. *It might provide a good laugh,* she thought, bitterness curling her lower lip. *My daughter is dead; dead people don't send letters. But maybe, just maybe, she has gotten rid of Josef. Maybe she realizes how she has wronged her mother. I gave her only love; abandonment is all I received in return.*

Roshen sat quietly for a long time, her thoughts rambling like a wanton river through the forest. Finally, she got up, her knees squeaking in protest and her back shooting spasms of pain along her spine. The letter was sitting on a ledge near the lone window. It let in thin shafts of late-afternoon sun, too scant to provide light to the dreary room. Clouded with age, the glass panes provided little view of the outside. Only the vague shadow of a single bare tree swaying in the evening breeze gave any indication there was life outside her four walls.

Blood racing through her veins, Roshen picked up the letter and returned to her chair. She held it on her lap for a long time, thoughts of self-sacrifice and resentment flooding her mind. Finally, she turned the envelope to its back and slowly withdrew the letter. She held it on her lap for a while, glancing only occasionally at the elegant script that filled its pages. Curiosity finally overwhelmed her and, despite herself, she read on to the end.

When she reached the last page, a wry smile crossed her lips. *A ticket to America. It could be the answer to my prayers.*

CHAPTER 18

Frida

Finally, it was July 5, 1859, the day Mama would arrive in New York. Frida tried to get out of bed, but the sound of the sea crashing against the wall behind her grew louder and louder. She shivered compulsively, burrowing under the blankets to block out the sound, but it was of no use. In their fury, waves broke through the side of the ship. They came faster and faster, washing over her and pushing her under their murky shadows. She tried to breathe, but her mouth filled with suffocating brine that traveled to her nose and eyes, rendering her helpless against their relentless assault. *"Jude Bitch!"* screamed a voice from above her as a knife cut into her neck. "Not even a virgin, you Jew whore!"

Startled awake, Frida clutched at the scar on her neck. No longer red after eight years, it was still a raised cord that stood out from her flesh like an elongated burl on a willow branch.

"Are you all right, Frida?" asked Josef, still half asleep. "You were thrashing about. . ."

"Hush," Frida said, her heart still pounding. She laid her fingers gently across Josef's lips. "I'm okay. I'm up early to meet the *Bittern*. If Mama is on the ship, she will be docking in just a few hours. I never heard back from her, Josef. I just hope with all my heart she will be there."

For weeks, Frida had pored over first-class advertisements for the SS *Bittern*, a brand-new steamship, one of the first of its kind to travel across the Atlantic as clipper ships receded from the seas. Pleased that she did not need to concern herself with steerage or even second-class travel descriptions, she read about the *Bittern*'s premium amenities. Roshen would be able to enjoy finely presented hot meals, a comfortable mattress dressed in Irish linen, and facilities for bathing every day. The ship's Grand Saloon was a forty-foot-long, high-ceilinged room walled in imported mahogany and furnished with plush love seats, gas lighting, fine paintings, and large mirrors that amplified the space and made it feel endless. First-class passengers could enjoy many hours in the salon reading, listening to music, and enjoying fine wines served in crystal goblets. There would be no slop pots, no shortage of rations, and no straw berths for Roshen. She would have the finest that a new, modern ship had to offer.

As the coachman pulled up with the horse and carriage, Frida slipped on her white lace gloves and adjusted her indigo Rose Lace gown. A horsehair crinoline held the skirt out from her body in a fashionable circle, the wire hoops supporting it caressing the floor like a soft whisper. Her ecru day cap complemented raven hair stylishly parted in the middle; it was tied with a wide, matching taffeta bow that allowed her curls to hide her scar.

Frida's skirts rustled as she climbed into the carriage to make the trip to the new Castle Garden Emigrant Landing Depot where the *Bittern* would arrive shortly. As the horse—*her* horse—clopped through the streets, Frida marveled at how much the city had changed since her arrival in New York. She remembered how she and Josef had discovered hot corn and pickles and how astonished they had been when they came across Ansche Beth Shalom. They had been amazed that such an imposing synagogue could be allowed to peacefully dominate a neighborhood. Since that time, most of the small two- and three-story row houses Frida had known had been replaced by five-story brick buildings that housed up to forty families each in 350-square-foot apartments.

Yes, Mama will see a different New York than I saw when I first arrived. She will not need to use an outhouse, she thought, thinking of the newfangled indoor plumbing she and Josef had recently installed inside their home. *She will have food kept cold in the iceboxes Colin Byrne made for us. She will enjoy windows that open wide to let in sunshine and the perfumed air of summer.*

Excited cries from the dock brought Frida back to the moment. Far on the horizon appeared the faint outlines of the *SS Bittern* as it headed toward the pier. A loud cheer went up as the ship came into view, its chimneys bellowing white steam into the sultry summer sky. Its sails, used only when necessary to propel the engines through heavy currents, were in full view as if to say, "I bring your Mama. She has journeyed to you, at last."

As the driver pulled up to a dockside area designated for those waiting for first-class arrivals, Frida's thoughts raced. *Will she be here? Has she come?* Against her will, she found herself making a promise she wouldn't have thought possible. It came from the depths of her being, seemingly from another lifetime when living had been uncomplicated. *God, I swear that if you have brought her to me, I will return to your fold. I will.*

Time seemed endless to Frida as she waited for the ship to pull into port. She paced endlessly, her feet screaming in protest as her blue satin slippers blistered her toes and their thin soles scarcely guarded against the pebble-strewn ground. The treeless plaza gave no respite to the climbing heat and puckered her taffeta in protesting ripples.

At long last, first-class travelers began to emerge from the ship. Amidst much excitement, they made their way out of ten-foot-high doors emblazoned with the *Bittern*'s insignia to the gangway. The ship's crew, dressed in their finest whites, formed a double line to bid farewell to the departing passengers. Ladies were dressed in colorful summer finery, their crinolined skirts swinging gently across hand-knotted carpet runners lining the descent to the pier. The diamonds and rubies they wore caught the rays of the August sun and flashed their radiance into the cloudless sky. Their escorts wore the latest wide-legged trousers and checked, double-breasted vests under long jackets with lapels that reached almost to their shoulders. They hovered protectively over their women and guided them down the steep walkway to the broad plaza where Brazilian leather steamer trunks were being unloaded in one area, and loved ones awaited the new arrivals in another.

Amidst promises of reunions to come, the departing passengers embraced and shed tears as they sought waiting family and friends. In the background, containers of yellow freesia, pots of purple allium, and stately raspberry-colored Stargazer lilies provided a fitting foreground to a small stage where a nine-piece orchestra played popular tunes from both the German Confederation and America.

As reunited families departed the arrivals plaza into waiting coaches, tears burned Frida's eyes. Roshen was nowhere to be seen. *She hasn't come; she hasn't come . . .*

Suddenly, she spotted a tall woman dressed in a tattered shawl and a worn black dress that hung from her gaunt figure like an old mop. The woman toted a single bag, its broken handle making her struggle to hold it against her body in one arm while the other held a cane that seemed to be the only thing keeping her from falling to the ground.

At first, Frida assumed the stranger had somehow wandered into the plaza from the surrounding streets. Then, suddenly, she recognized the high cheekbones and gray-green eyes. Once bright, those eyes were now faded and darting frantically.

It must be Mama. But she's so old . . . Mama's not old. "Is that you, Mama?!" she shouted, gathering her skirts and rushing toward what seemed like a caricature of the mother she had left behind. Frail and gray, Roshen possessed none of the fire in her posture and none of the passion in her eyes that had marked her early years. Instead, she was a withered shadow of the imposing heroine Frida had treasured.

Frida ran toward Roshen, her feet seeming unable to move quickly enough. Suddenly, her pace slowed, her arms open wide in readiness for the embrace she once thought would never come. Her mother stood before her, motionless except for the darting of her eyes. They narrowed as Frida approached her.

"Don't touch me," she said. "The dead don't embrace."

Roshen followed her daughter out of the plaza in silence, her breathing heavy and labored. When they climbed into Frida's waiting carriage, Frida tried again to engage her mother in conversation. "Mama, please. I have waited so long to see you, talk to you. You came. You must have forgiven me! I want to know everything," she pleaded. "Have you been well? How is Jakob?"

Frida tried unsuccessfully to suppress the tears that spilled over when Roshen's silence remained unbroken. *Mama just needs time,* she thought. *It's all too new.* As they traveled silently through the streets, she became acutely aware of how the city must be affecting Roshen. The iron-clad wheels of carriages and surreys screeched against cobblestones and thudded when they hit ruts in the street. The plopping of horse manure and the cacophony of voices shouting in English, German, and Yiddish added to the din. Dogs barked as they ran unfettered through the streets, and children shouted as they chased balls that landed in the heaps of garbage piled up around doorways and lampposts. The summer heat brought flies that buzzed around compost piles and amplified the odors of cooking sausages, fried potatoes, and hot onions wafting through the air.

No, thought Frida, *Mama can't see past all of this. She's not noticing the camaraderie of children playing, the crowds of neighbors gathering to talk peacefully, or the new Jewish businesses that had opened throughout the city. She's not seeing the absence of fear.*

When the driver finally left Frida and her mother at the front door of the family's new home, Roshen had still not uttered a word. The thirty-foot-wide townhouse was in a row of recently constructed brownstones on West 23rd Street. Set back ten feet from the road, it boasted a front garden filled with lavender and roses. A broad, five-step stone stoop led to a double door of ornately carved imported ebony topped by a chiseled marble cornice featuring baskets of fruits. Beneath the stairs was a simple door for access by servants and deliverymen.

On the first floor, the parlor featured a marble fireplace, three tall windows, and French doors leading to a back garden. A kitchen with a wide cooking-fireplace and two rooms for servants made up the basement. Five bedrooms occupied the two floors above the living area. The house was sparsely furnished, but Frida and Josef looked forward to decorating more as their profits grew.

"Liesel will take your bag, Mama," Frida said as she introduced the nursemaid to Roshen. "She lives with us and helps with the children. And this is Ida," offered Frida, as she introduced the kitchen helper. "She also helps sometimes with our brood." By prearrangement, the children were dressed in their finest and lined up in age order in the foyer. As they had just been taught, they bowed and curtsied as their grandmother made her way down the line.

"Guten Tag, Grossmama," they said, almost in unison, as Roshen approached them.

Roshen ignored their greetings, looking them each up and down with a scrutinizing eye. When she finally got to the end of the line, August was starting to shift restlessly from side to side. Taller by far than the other children, at nearly eight he stood four feet, three inches tall. His body was starting to shed its baby fat, and the beginnings of finely tuned muscles were emerging from his athletic body. Almond-shaped gray eyes under heavy eyebrows accentuated a narrow nose, and his mouth, while thin, now set itself into a wide smile.

"Why do you look different from your family?" asked Roshen, her stern mouth forming a straight line.

"I don't know," the boy answered, looking toward Frida and Josef who averted his eyes.

"Just say hello to your grandmother," said Frida, in an icy tone that revealed her disapproval of Roshen's question.

"Welcome, Grossmama," August finally said, his husky voice tinged with amusement. "My birthday is coming soon. But why are you wearing black when all the other ladies wear bright colors?"

"August!" shouted Frida. "Don't be rude to your grandmother."

Josef, standing behind the children, reached out and placed a firm hand on August's shoulder. "That is impertinent," he admonished, his face turning various shades of crimson.

"I wear black," Roshen said, looking August straight in the eye, "because my children are dead."

"But," August stammered, reaching for the fringe on Roshen's shawl, "my mama is right here."

As the shawl yielded to August's curiosity, Frida noticed a small, deliberate tear in the bodice of Roshen's dress. It was on her left side. According to Jewish ritual, a mourner's garments are torn to symbolize grief. For parents, the tear must occur on the left side, over the heart. "What happened, Mama? Tell me!" Frida cried, fear clouding her thoughts.

Roshen stared ahead, her lips still straight and narrowed. "Jakob is dead," she said flatly. "Just like you."

Frida's hands flew to her cheeks. She stifled the hulking sobs threatening to spill from her chest, and her hands shook like scarlet leaves in an autumn storm. Josef and Liesel gathered the children quickly and led them from the hall.

When they were gone, Frida gave in to her grief. "How, Mama, how? When? Please, Mama, tell me what happened."

When Roshen spoke, her voice was distant. "Take me to my room at once," was all she said. "And leave me to myself."

Frida fought to keep her knees from buckling as she led the way to the small bedroom where Roshen would be staying. Sun streamed in through the tall window overlooking the street, its brightness amplified by a large mirror hanging on the opposite wall. Usually Bessie's room, Frida had moved the six-year-old in with the twins and removed the child's books and toys. Originally designed to be a guestroom, a single bed, a simple nightstand, and a small rocking chair stood on the wall next to the door, and a wardrobe occupied the far corner. A porcelain chamber pot peeked out from under the bed, placed there for emergencies, and a rose-patterned washbasin on the nightstand completed the furnishings.

Frida watched from the hall as Roshen dropped her bag heavily on the floor and made her way slowly to the narrow bed. Time seemed to stand still as Roshen posed motionless by the side of the bed. Finally, she reached for something perched on the pillows. It was Hildegarde, and she had a note around her neck:

Welcome to our home. I have missed you all these years. May your visit be warm and long. Your loving old friend, Hildegarde.

"Close the door and let me be," ordered Roshen, keeping her back to Frida.

The firmness in her voice brought Frida back to a time when her mother's commands had required instant responses. "Yes, Mama, I will. And I'll have dinner sent up to you shortly. But, Mama, tell me about Jakob."

Frida's pleas were met with stony silence, its depth seeming to shut out familiar household sounds and the chirping of birds through the open window. Roshen stood transfixed, never turning to face Frida.

The noises of the children clamoring for dinner finally broke Frida's mood. As she turned to leave, she started to close the bedroom door behind her. When it was about to click into place, she froze. Roshen's sobs echoed through the empty upstairs hall. Alarmed, Frida pressed herself against the door's slightly open space and peered, soundlessly, into the room. Roshen had thrown herself onto the bed and curled her knees up to her chin. Her face lay buried deep in the pillow, and her shoulders heaved.

After a few moments, Roshen reached for Hildegarde and clutched the doll tightly against her chest. "What have I done?" her thin voice wailed. "What have I done?"

CHAPTER 19

Frida

The night was long. Several times, Frida left her bed to check on Roshen. Dismayed when Roshen's sobs turned to labored breathing, she tried to gain entry to the room, but Roshen had engaged the deadlock near the top of the door, and silence met Frida's pleas. In the morning, the empty water pitcher and the chamber pot were in the hall, but the dinner of roast chicken and potato kugel that Ida had brought up was still there, untouched and congealed.

Over the next two days, meals were brought to Roshen, but they never made their way into her room. There was quiet from within, broken only by the sounds of heavy breathing and stifled cries.

"Mama," pleaded Frida, "Please. You must eat, Mama. Please, open the door."

Usually well dressed, coiffed, and groomed, Frida suddenly lost interest in her appearance. The curls that customarily clustered in ringlets around her neck fell into sheaths of uncombed strands. Her large dark eyes were clouded and red-lined.

With tears streaming down her cheeks, she sought solace in Josef. "I can't bear what's happening with Mama," she wept, grief overcoming her. "I wish I had never put that deadlock in. It was meant for Mama's privacy, but how I regret it now!"

"Give it time," he whispered, cradling Frida in his arms. "She will come around. Come back to work, my darling wife. The women at the shop need you. The children have Ida and Liesel to take care of their daily needs, but they still need you. *I* need you."

Frida didn't hear a word. She sat in her room, knitting and reading a bit, but mostly rocking in her chair by the fireplace. Brunhilde was her constant companion. The old dog never left her side and placed herself at Frida's feet for hours.

It was Bessie who changed things. A fragile child, her pale skin, though marred by birthmarks, stood in stark contrast to her glistening black hair and round dark eyes. Long eyelashes brushed against her high cheekbones, and her small nose formed a perfect profile. She bore a serious expression offset only by the dancing in her eyes when she was pleased. She spoke with a soft voice that rose in high, sweet tones when she sang. A child with few friends, she was devoted to her music and was already showing astonishing ease with the piano.

On the third morning, Frida was about to again appeal to her mother. As she started to approach Roshen's room, she saw Bessie knocking gently on the door. She flattened herself against a wall, intrigued by what might happen.

"Grossmama," Bessie said softly. "You must be lonely. I get lonely lots of times. I would like to come in to visit you and Hildegarde. And guess what? I have a song for you. Maybe you will like it and will sing it with me. I have a strudel for you, too. It's made with apples."

Undaunted by her grandmother's silence, Bessie began to sing:

"I dream of Bessie with the dark brown hair,
Borne, like a vapor, on the summer air.
I see her playing where the bright sunshine plays,
Happy as the clouds that dance on her way.
Oh, I dream of Bessie with the dark brown hair,
Floating, like a white cloud, on the summer air."

Frida froze, afraid to move as the child's sweet voice filled the hall. She stifled a chuckle when she heard how Bessie had personalized the popular Stephen Foster tune with her own words. *Leave it to Bessie to make the song her own. And thank God for the music that fills my daughter's life.*

When the song was finished, Frida let out an unbidden gasp as the doorknob began to move, slowly at first but completing its turn in due time. Bessie stood at attention, straightening her shoulders and smoothing her hair. Her eyes brightened as the door creaked open. Then, the child reached out and took Roshen's skeletal hand in her own. Unbathed and still in the clothes she had been wearing when she departed the *Bittern*, Roshen's face was ashen.

As Frida stared, she noticed, for the first time, the thickened red skin on Roshen's hands and the arthritic bends in her fingers. Most of all, she saw pain and surrender in Roshen's eyes. *Has grief done this to my mother?* she wondered. *Where is the tall, assured woman of my childhood?*

Frida stood in the hall, unable to move, while Bessie slipped into her grandmother's room. Almost immediately, the door shut, and Frida heard the scraping of the deadlock. She strained to hear Bessie's and Roshen's conversation, but all that came through were indecipherable murmurs. She finally gave up and retreated to the kitchen to discuss preparations for the upcoming Sabbath when Bessie burst in, babbling excitedly. "Grossmama let me stay with her for a long time. She liked a song I made up for her, and then she said that she will eat some dinner tonight if I bring it to her. She says that she will meet with August and Willie, and all the others, too. Isn't that wonderful, Mama? Isn't that just grand?"

"You are a very grown-up girl, Bessie," said Frida, taking the child in her arms. She kissed Bessie's fragrant hair and stroked her cheek. "Thank you, my sweet girl. I will gather up the children, and we will go to Grossmama's room this afternoon. Please tell her to expect us after lunch."

The meetings took place at Roshen's open door. Each child lingered for only a moment while the old woman looked them up and down. She demanded that each one report his or her name but offered only a dismissive wave of her hand as the children passed in an otherwise silent line. August and Willie were particularly upset that she was cold and distant with them.

"Why won't she talk to us, Mama?" Willie asked later. "Did we do something bad? Is she angry with us?"

"She's our only grandmother," August lamented. "My friends at school have grandmothers who play with them and bake cookies. Why doesn't my grandmother do that?"

Willie echoed August's sadness. "She's just a mean old lady. The twins say the same thing. Burke and Elsie are babies, so they don't count. I don't like Grossmama at all," he said, tears rolling down his cheeks. "August and I wanted her to see us play ball. Why won't she do that?"

Frida tried to comfort them, but she was at a loss for words.

I wish the same things. Why won't she welcome her grandchildren into her life? Why won't she let me talk to her? Why did she even come to America?

Bessie was the only child Roshen would engage, and she took to visiting with her granddaughter for long intervals behind her closed door. Toward the end of the week, Roshen joined Bessie in song. Frida chuckled as Roshen struggled to carry a tune; she had always loved to sing but indulged herself only when she thought no one was around to hear. With Bessie, she seemed to lose herself, and the two spent lazy hours whispering and blending their voices in popular German songs.

Frida tried desperately to learn more about Jakob's fate, but Roshen refused to give Frida the details of her brother's death. "Mama," she pleaded from outside Roshen's door on Friday afternoon. "It's okay if you don't want to talk about Jakob for now. But please, come downstairs tonight for dinner. It is the Sabbath, and a brisket is roasting in the oven. The children will all be there. They want desperately to know their grossmama."

Tears burned in Frida's eyes when there was no response from Roshen. Unaware that Bessie was in her mother's room, she was startled when she heard her small daughter plead with Roshen. "Yes, Grossmama. Please come to the dining room at dusk. It's the Sabbath. I need you there."

Later that evening, the household entered the twenty-five-foot-long dining room. As was their custom, the children were arranged in age order, the youngest seated near Frida and Josef at the head of the table. Hoping Roshen would decide to join the Sabbath celebration, Frida had invited Stefan, Bertha and Amalia, Fritz, Colin Byrne, and Gottfried Baum of Rose Industries' inner circle to meet her; the group had become as close as family would have been had there been no estrangements and no vast geographical differences. There were bright exchanges as the guests greeted the children with smiles and gifts.

It was a glorious New York evening, and the setting sun sent slivers of golden light through the tall windows, bathing the room in apricot tones. Unusual for the city at this time of year, a breeze fluttered the curtains and cooled the remnants of hot air that had filtered in all day. Amidst much excitement, the children started to take their places at the table. Liesel Didelsheim supervised the younger ones to make sure that mishaps were avoided. She was a large woman with long blond braids, big bones, and a generous lap that Elsie, especially, loved to sit on.

As darkness descended, Frida closed her eyes and was about to recite *Shalom Aleichem,* the Jewish welcoming of the Sabbath, when the tapping of a cane on the polished parquet floor interrupted her routine. Roshen appeared at the doorway. Still attired in her black dress, she looked withered and worn, but a slight smile curved her lips.

Bessie jumped up from the table and ran to her. "Grossmama!" she shouted. "You kept your promise. You came to dinner."

Tears rushed to Frida's eyes as she watched Bessie lead Roshen to a place of honor at the far end of the table. Suddenly, as if on cue, August shouted, "Grossmama is here!" and began to clap. The other children followed his lead until the dining room was filled with applause.

"Children," Josef interrupted. "The Sabbath is about to begin. There will be time later to be with your grandmother."

"Yes, Papa," they chimed in unison as they settled in to watch Frida welcome the Sabbath as Jews all over the world had done for millennia before her.

When prayers were completed, Josef said the *Hamotzi,* the traditional blessing of the bread, and passed big hunks of the sweet yellow challah around the table. Ida Burman, her dimpled face sporting a wide smile, brought in heaping platters of brisket surrounded by roasted onions, sweet potato kugel, pickled red cabbage, and bright green string beans garnished with toasted almonds. Big pitchers of savory gravy were passed, and a vat of freshly made applesauce completed the entrée.

For Frida, dinner seemed to stretch out forever as she watched Roshen pick at her food, scarcely eating a thing. Her face was pale, and her chapped hands trembled as she brought her fork to her lips. She drooled slightly, spittle gathering at the top of her chin. Frida wanted to bring the meal to a close quickly but did not want to change the Sabbath routine and alarm her family and guests.

"On Friday nights, Mama, before we go on to dessert, we take turns catching everyone up on the events of the past week. August, the eldest, always goes first."

August climbed off his chair and stood behind it. "This week I learned to play cards with Papa," he said, smiling broadly at Josef. "It's a lot of fun, and I even won a game." He paused, took a deep breath, and continued. "Usually, we just tell one thing. But something else happened that I want to tell. I have a job."

"Oh?" said Frida. "Tell us about it."

"Yes," August declared, pride spreading across his face. "The job is with Papa. He's paying me three cents each to bring advertisements about Rose Industries to a lot of businesses around here. It was my idea."

"Why, that's wonderful, August," said Frida.

"Very impressive," said Stefan. "I'm sure I speak for all of us from the Board who are here tonight."

Josef beamed from ear to ear. "And August is doing an excellent job. He does more distributions each day than he did the day before. I can barely keep up with him," he said, reaching across the table to shake August's hand.

August took a deep bow, drawing laughter and congratulations from the diners.

Willie was next. "August won a card game, but I beat him at baseball. We were playing with our friends in the garden, and I got more hits than he did."

When it was Bessie's turn, her eyes wore a solemn expression as she spoke about the songs she had shared with Grossmama. "She likes music as much as I do. We like to sing together."

Louise and Gertrude were next. Louise spoke for them both. "We were sad this week. Grossmama wouldn't let us into her room. It's not fair. Bessie was there a lot—"

"Now, now, Louise," Frida interrupted. "Grossmama has not been here long. I'm sure you and Gertrude will spend time with her soon."

Frida glanced at Roshen who just stared at her plate, unmoved by Louise's lament. Her complexion had turned waxy, and she turned her head from Frida's glance.

Concerned but not willing to give up the Sabbath ritual, Frida turned to Burke. "And what news do you have, Burke?" she asked, certain she knew what was coming.

The little boy's eyes filled with tears. "I miss Hildegarde. Gross-mama, will you ever give her back to me?"

Frida turned her eyes, again, toward Roshen and hoped for a response that never came. After several moments, Frida looked lovingly at her son. "It's okay, Burke. Hildegarde is just visiting Gross-mama. She still lives with us, and she will always be here for you."

Elsie had turned three in March and babbled incessantly, but had used only single words, a cause of worry for Josef and Frida over the past year. Frida filled in for her. "I have an important announcement about Elsie. She spoke some whole sentences today."

The child blushed a charming pink, but there was pride in her eyes, and she nodded vigorously. "Yes, I did words today," she said. "I like words."

Everyone applauded.

"Good girl. We knew you could do it. Hooray for you!" they chimed, almost in unison.

Elsie picked up her own chubby hands and clapped, too.

After a dessert of flourless chocolate cake and succulent summer fruits, Roshen announced that she was exhausted and wished to retire for the night. With effort, she pulled herself up from her chair, wincing with fatigue and pain. As she made her way out of the dining room, her steps were halting and unsteady.

Alarmed, Frida called for both Liesel and Ida and whispered instructions to them. Following close behind Roshen, whose arm Ida held firmly, Liesel escorted the children from the dining room and brought them upstairs amidst loud protests about having to go to bed.

As soon as Roshen and the children got to the top of the stairs, Josef and Frida answered a myriad of questions about Roshen's health. Then they rose from the table and brought their guests into the parlor. They sipped sparkling champagne and gossiped lightly about events at the shop. Josef was the first to bring up business.

"Let's congratulate ourselves," he said to the visiting Board members, raising his glass. "We have become an acclaimed business. And now we're this close," he said, curling his right thumb and forefinger into a circle, "to getting the military contract for wool uniform cloth from Washington. It will require tremendous expansion for the business."

Applause filled the room as Josef continued. "Look at us," he said and grinned. "We are the Board of Directors for Rose Industries. We built all of this, from scratch, together! As the chief officers, Frida and I both thank you, from the bottoms of our hearts, for believing in us. So tonight, everyone, let's talk about your new titles.

"Stefan, you are officially our comptroller. With your background—how well I remember our times training together at my father's bank in Germany—you are the perfect person to oversee Rose Industries' finances, implement the budget, and manage our payroll.

"Bertha and Amalia, we are so glad you've agreed to be our official design managers for wool and lace, respectively. Your creativity and your impeccable taste will take us far on our business journey."

Josef poured more wine and led the group in raising their glasses, the tinkling sound filling the room with merriment.

"Hear, hear," they said, as they heartily toasted each other.

After a few moments, Josef continued. "Fritz Bayer. How lucky we are that after Leo Kohn moved to Chicago, you left your maintenance job at Ansche Beth Shalom to become our buildings and grounds manager. You are tireless in keeping everything up and running smoothly.

"Colin Byrne. As special projects director, your heroic carpentry talents will not be wasted. It was a lucky day when I met you."

"Hear, hear," said the group, raising their glasses again.

"And Gottfried. Gottfried Baum. You were my former boss at the Emporium, but you've become a good and loyal friend. You are a gifted salesman. Could anyone serve better as our general sales manager?"

A chuckle rippled through the room as Gottfried stood and bowed solemnly.

"On a serious note," said Stefan, after the laughter subsided, "we will need to explore our options to meet shop expansion and labor costs if we take on military contracts."

"The demands will be considerable," Josef agreed. "Let's start with labor. We'll need to do further analysis, but Tammany has been a good source for new workers. We'll need a lot of them. Fortunately, most of the people they've sent to us have been satisfactory. Their wages are minimal, and very few complaints or problems have reached our ears. But we'll need more space, too."

Frida smiled, radiance flooding her face. "Josef and I have been exploring our options. There is a building available next to the shop that we can acquire with a loan. Our numbers are solid. Surely, Immigrant Savings will back us."

"I propose another toast," said Josef, raising his glass. "As soon as we receive government contract confirmation, I will secure funding and let Colin Byrne know that he has his work cut out for him."

Suddenly, a loud thump echoed through the house. From upstairs, Liesel and Ida both screamed. "Come quickly! As fast as you can!" insisted Ida, her voice shrill and commanding.

Josef and Frida jumped up and bolted out of the dining room, the others just behind.

"Your mother is in her room!" cried Liesel, panic in her voice. "I think she's fallen, but there's no response, and the door's locked."

Josef knocked loudly and desperately tried to open the door. It was of no use. Roshen had, as was her habit, locked it shut.

"Move over," commanded Stefan. "I'll knock it down." He hurled himself against the door several times, perspiration running down his neck and spreading across his wide shoulders. When the door refused to budge, he stood back several paces and kicked it until it yielded with a screech, and the wood collapsed in jagged shards across the floor.

Frida and Josef rushed in to find that Roshen had collapsed. "Fritz, bring Dr. Reinhard here at once," Josef pleaded. "He lives just down the street on the corner. Hurry!"

"Mama!" shouted Frida. "What's happened to you? I've just found you again, Mama! We have so much to talk about, so many lost years to catch up on. Please, Mama, you must live!"

CHAPTER 20

Frida

Roshen lay on the floor, her legs splayed. A puddle of regurgitated food had spilled from her mouth, some of it already caking around her lips. Frida fell to her mother's side and placed her ear against Roshen's chest. "She's breathing. That's good. Mama, please talk to me. Dr. Reinhard will be here any minute. I know he will." She lifted Roshen's head to place it in her lap and stroked her cheeks, horrified at how thin the skin had become. "I'm here, Mama. I'll take care of you. Whatever you need or want will be yours. Just please, don't leave us."

"Only one thing to say to you, daughter. Where did August come from? Doesn't look like anyone we know. Shame on you," she rasped, as a shudder wracked her body, and she stopped moving.

Bile rose to Frida's throat, and she involuntarily drew back, her heart pounding. *Mama's right, August isn't like the others. She doesn't know what happened. No one ever will! But he is still my child, and I owe her no explanation. . . .*

Hot tears burst from her reddened eyes, and she felt her mama go limp. All thought evaporated as she realized Roshen was failing. "It's okay, Mama," she pleaded. "Just come back to me. Please, someone, do something!" Josef rushed to Frida and helped her to gather Roshen in her arms. They rocked back and forth, back and forth, but there was no response from the sick woman except a crackling sound that came from deep within her.

Within minutes, Fritz arrived with Dr. Reinhard. As he held his stethoscope to Roshen's chest, his eyes revealed deep concern. "She's unconscious, her extremities are cold and mottled with purple patches, and she's having trouble breathing," he said. "How long ago did the first symptoms start? Has she been eating? How long has the swelling in her feet and ankles been going on? Has she been experiencing weakness or loss of appetite? Has she traveled recently?"

The questions came so fast that Frida had scarcely answered one when another came. Roshen became ashen, her breathing wet and halting, as the doctor continued his examination. "Let's get her into bed," he directed. "I think there is a problem with her heart. Let's make her as comfortable as possible."

The next few hours seemed endless to Frida. She and Josef sat by Roshen's bedside. Dr. Reinhard remained in the room and brought smelling salts to his patient's nose every few moments, but her breathing became increasingly shallow. "I'm so sorry. There's nothing left to do but wait," he said, as he readied himself to leave for the night. "I will be back tomorrow to check her. Meanwhile, if there are any changes, please send for me immediately."

As night passed into dawn, and dawn into sunrise, Roshen's pulse became persistently weaker. Dr. Reinhard was called back and noted that her feet had swelled, and her skin had become mottled. He tried to administer tablespoons of warm brandy, but Roshen rejected it, the liquor dripping from her mouth and spilling onto her neck. Heat built up in the room as the day progressed, but Roshen shivered convulsively, and her skin grew clammy. Then, shortly after sunrise, when the household was still silent with sleep, Roshen's breathing came to a stop.

"Mama!" shouted Frida, tears stinging her cheeks.

She watched in horror as Roshen's lips developed a blue pallor, and her eyelids failed to flutter or to twitch as they had throughout the night. Dr. Reinhard covered Roshen's face with a sheet. As thin as she had become, she seemed to have shrunk in size even since her arrival. She was now almost invisible under the blankets. Except for a small mound lifting the bedcovers, she occupied a fraction of the mattress.

"She's so still," Frida sobbed, as she buried herself in Josef's arms. "She just came back to us. What do we do now?"

"What you do now," Dr. Reinhard said softly, "is say goodbye. Do you have a religious leader to call?"

Frida and Josef stood back and looked at each other. Shame rose in their cheeks as they shook their heads. "No, we don't," Josef said apologetically. "We will need to find someone."

"If you are Jewish, may I suggest contacting Rabbi Samuel Adler at Temple Emanuel?"

"That's the spired, converted church on East Twelfth Street, is it not?" asked Josef. "I've passed it many times. Is it Orthodox?"

"No," said Reinhard. "In fact, it was a church but is now a reform congregation and has many modern changes to traditional Judaism. I, myself, belong there. You would be welcomed as members. If you wish, I will accompany you there and introduce you to Rabbi Adler. He is a recent immigrant from Germany and will be sympathetic to your plight."

Josef and Frida looked into each other's eyes.

"My mother would like that," Frida finally said. *I promised God I'd return to Him if he brought Mama to me. And maybe it's time to go back to my roots. Things are better here than they ever were in Hamburg. I saw one sign—the one that said No Jews Need Apply—when I first arrived in New York. There's been nothing since, and I must honor what Mama would want. But what if I'm wrong and people shun us because we're Jewish? But what if they don't and we don't have to be ashamed or afraid anymore?*

"Yes, Dr. Reinhard," Frida finally said, her voice low. "That's what Mama would want." *Honor thy parents. Honor thy parents. Honor thy parents. . . .*

Reinhard nodded solemnly, kindness filling his eyes. "I will leave you now to let your family and friends know of your mother's passing. We can meet with the rabbi this afternoon to make funeral arrangements for tomorrow. I will send my carriage for you as soon as we set a time."

After he was gone, Josef held his arms open. "Emanuel will be a good thing, Frida," he said. "We will find community again."

Frida pulled back, her jaw jutting out in a defiant stance. *Jude Bitch* screamed in her ears, louder and louder, closer and closer. She could smell the tobacco on Otto's brown teeth, feel his filthy bulk on her breasts as strongly as if all that had occurred on her cross-Atlantic voyage were happening again, right now. Her hand flew to her scar, and she felt Otto cutting her neck.

How can I do this? she thought. *We've come so far. Yet the Ten Commandments tell us, "Honor thy father and thy mother." And I promised God.*

When she finally composed herself, her voice was brittle. "I hope it will be a good thing, Josef. I certainly hope so."

As Sunday's sunshine poured through the children's rooms, they woke noisily and ran out to the garden. It was a humid but cloudless day, and they began to play happily under Liesel's supervision until breakfast was ready. The contrast of their laughter to the darkness in her soul jolted Frida as she mustered up the courage to tell her brood of Roshen's death.

"Let's go into the parlor," she said, after they had finished their meal, "where we can be close together to talk about something important."

The formal room was long and narrow with a double-sided marble fireplace shared with the dining room. Two ladies' chairs upholstered in cream-and-green-striped damask were arranged on either side of the hearth. On the adjacent wall was a square piano designed by the recently established Steinway Company. Frida's secretary desk, the one lovingly restored by Josef years before, stood near the entrance to the room. It held the porcelain monkey behind its glass-paned doors. Frida's gaze fell now on the figurine's complex features. *Remember me in times of sorrow,* it called to her as she remembered her grandfather's words so many years before. *You will survive this. You will.*

Revived by the poignant message the monkey always sent to her in times of trouble, Frida took her place next to Josef by the fireplace while the children sat in a circle on the room's slightly worn Persian carpet. They seemed to sense solemnity, and even August and Willie settled quietly.

"Early this morning, children," said Frida, a gentle expression crossing her lips, "something sad happened. Grossmama passed away. That means she died."

"What does *died* mean?" asked Burke.

Frida mustered courage from somewhere deep inside of her. She sighed deeply. "When somebody dies," she said, "it means that his or her body stops working."

"How can you tell?" asked Louise, her eyes gazing deep into Frida's.

"Well, sweetheart," said Josef, "we can tell because Grossmama grew very still. God looked down at her and knew it was time for her to rest."

"But will she decide to wake up?" asked Burke. "She has to. We didn't get to spend any time with her. You said we would later. She has to wake up and be alive."

"That's silly," August chided. "No one decides to be dead. Right, Mama?"

"August is right, Willie. She can't decide not to be dead. Do you remember when the bird that came to our garden every day died last year? We were sad, but it was time for it not to be sick anymore. Like Grossmama, the bird wasn't moving or breathing, and we buried it in the garden."

"Is that where we are going to bury Grossmama?" asked Burke. His usually happy face was pale, and he held Hildegarde close to his small chest. Frida had returned Hildegarde to him when he woke up, and he tearfully clung to the old doll.

"No, Burke," said Josef. "We will take her to a special place with gardens, and she can be part of their beauty forever."

Bessie wailed. "But who's going to sing with me?" she asked through her tears. "It won't be the same."

"No, Bessie, it won't be the same. Things will be . . . different. But we will always remember Grossmama. We must be happy that she came here and knew she had a big family who cared about her."

"I have just one question," said Burke.

"Yes, Burke," answered Frida. "Papa and I will always be here to answer your questions. You will always be able to talk to us."

"Well," the child asked, "can we take Hildegarde to the park today?"

"That is a splendid idea," answered Frida. "Papa and I must find the right garden for Grossmama, but Liesel and Ida will be glad to accompany you. Now, everyone run along and get ready. It is a beautiful day, and the outing will be good for you."

When the children scampered up the stairs, with Liesel and Ida right behind, Frida fell into Josef's arms, hot tears searing her cheeks. Josef held her tightly, kissed her eyelids, and stroked her hair. "She never forgave me, Josef. She didn't see me as alive."

"No, Frida, darling. You sent your mama passage to America, and she came. Had she had more time, she would have forgiven you. She wouldn't have come otherwise. You can be at peace."

Thoughts spun around and around in Frida's mind. Angst rose from her belly, and her skin bristled as if she were being stabbed by a deluge of needles.

Did she come to forgive me? Did she come because she still loved me? Or did she come out of expedience after Jakob died? Oh, God, I'll never really know.

CHAPTER 21

Frida

Dr. Ernst Reinhard was a man in his early forties. Short, but slim and narrow of shoulder, he wore his light-brown hair long and brushed to the side. The only thing marring his fair complexion was a growth on his left cheek, a growth so small it was noticeable only if one were to stand right next to him. His mustache and full sideburns were meticulously trimmed and, from most angles, hid the growth. Stylishly dressed, his overall appearance was a perfect reflection of the latest in men's fashion.

A compulsively organized and punctual man, he arrived at the Roses' home at precisely noon on Sunday morning. As he was about to ring the bell, the door opened to dispel all seven children, along with Liesel and Ida. Except for Bessie, whose cheeks were stained with tears, the children were excited about going to the park. Brunhilde ran as fast as her little legs would carry her, and Burke clutched Hildegarde. Even Elsie, sitting in her pram, wriggled and squealed in excitement. In their rush to get out, August and Willie nearly sent Dr. Reinhard flying down the stairs.

"We're going to play ball," Willie shouted, proudly displaying his baseball glove and bat.

"And marbles," added August. "Don't forget marbles. They're great. Right, mister?" he exclaimed to Reinhard, who nodded in agreement. The father of three boys, Ernst Reinhard loved children, and his eyes twinkled in merriment as he watched them prance down the street.

After a few moments, when Amalia and Bertha arrived to keep watch over Roshen's body as dictated by Jewish tradition, the Roses came down the front steps, Frida clutching Josef's arm. Usually dressed in colorful attire, her jet-black clothes emphasized her sunken cheeks and ashen complexion. A black Rose Lace shawl lay loosely around her shoulders. It emphasized her dark hair, parted in the middle and brushed down to cover the ears—and her scar.

After greetings were exchanged, Dr. Reinhard quietly led Frida and Josef to his waiting carriage. "The temple is on Twelfth Street, and the temperature is rising fast. I thought it best that we drive," he said, as the three climbed into the coach. It was an elegant carriage with gold-toned satin walls, a carved-ebony vanity drawer, and a calling card case featuring burnished mahogany-toned leather.

Nobody spoke as the horses started down the street. The sky was a robin's-egg blue with cotton clouds billowing overhead. Noisy starlings were flying in formation, creating darting silhouettes as they flew high above the city. Children played, dogs chased each other, and women dressed in their Sunday best strolled on the arms of handsome men.

As Frida settled in, Josef's voice interrupted the dark thoughts that occupied her mind. "Dr. Reinhard," he asked, "your coach window coverings are made of Rose Lace, are they not?"

"Yes, they are," Reinhard responded, seeming surprised at Josef's knowledge of needlework. "Are you interested in obtaining some for your carriage?"

Josef smiled. "As a matter of fact, our carriage is lined with our very own Rose Lace. Our firm is Rose Industries. One of our special products is coach lace."

"I'm embarrassed; I should have recognized you," said Dr. Reinhard, his cheeks reddening. "The fact is that my wife and I have Rose Lace not only for the coach but hanging as draperies throughout our home. The lace is beautiful. You have capable tailors—and salesmen."

As they proceeded to the synagogue, Dr. Reinhard steered the conversation to Roshen. "I am so sorry for your loss," he said, his voice filled with compassion. "It was a terrible night for you. Although I regret using a cliché, I wish there had been something that could have been done."

An awkward silence filled the carriage in sharp contrast to the vibrant noises in the street that filled the perfect July morning.

"Look," Reinhard suddenly exclaimed, "there is the synagogue."

Frida looked through her window. "Are you sure that's it, Doctor?" she asked, thinking the temple looked like a church.

"Yes, of course. I'm an active member. Have been since Emanuel was founded in '45."

As they pulled up to the building, Reinhard explained that the synagogue's exterior remained unchanged from its earlier days as a Baptist church. The main entrance featured an arched double doorway centered under a stained-glass window that reached to the tower. The building still featured a square steeple, topped by an elaborate spire that rose above it by several stories, dwarfing the four-story building next door.

"You'll be amazed how the church has been transformed into a Jewish place of worship," Reinhard said. "It's quite a step up from Emanuel's first place of worship in a second-floor room in a loft building."

While the coach driver went to park the carriage, Dr. Reinhard guided Frida and Josef through the short wrought-iron fence separating the synagogue from the sidewalk and into the building. An aura of peace greeted them as sun filtered in and bathed the sanctuary in light and diffused color. Frida's eyes were drawn to the wide central aisle that parted two sets of long, wide pews leading to a raised pulpit. The ceiling soared above them and featured high-wooden cross-vaults and a Gothic ark within the apse. She was overcome to see that the church had, indeed, been altered to include a bimah and an *Aron Kodesh*, a Torah ark. Its paneled doors were open to a silk-curtained interior cabinet, revealing not one, but two Torahs, each housed in an ornamental wooden case and adorned by engraved gold and sterling silver finials and breastplates.

Dr. Reinhard let his charges immerse themselves in the beauty of the sanctuary until he saw that they were ready to move on. "Come," Reinhard said gently. "Let us go into Rabbi Adler's study. He is expecting us, and there is much to do."

The study was of modest size. It featured rich, wood-paneled walls and a large mahogany desk that stood in one corner. Wallpapered in dark-green damask, several gas lamps illuminated the room and gave it a peaceful aura. Bookcases filled with leather-bound volumes and ancient Jewish ritual items offered refuge.

"It's good to be here," Josef whispered to Frida. "Do you think so, too?"

Frida's mind raced. . . . *Jude Bitch, Jude Bitch . . . We were okay at Ansche Beth Shalom; we also left its folds before anything might have happened. But start anew with another synagogue that may be accepted by the public but also may not be? I don't know . . . On the other hand, I should do what Mama would want . . . and I promised God.*

At that moment, Rabbi Adler walked across the polished wooden floor to greet them. A man of average height, he was possessed of slim shoulders and a narrow face. What hair he had left was visible under his dome-shaped black felt hat. His hazel eyes were wide-set and topped by thick, dark eyebrows. A prominent brow fittingly reflected his scholarly air.

"Sit down, please," he said, indicating barrel-backed russet chairs across from his desk. "Dr. Reinhard has told me of your situation. Perhaps we can meet again after shiva is complete so I can learn more about you, but time is of the essence now. As you know, according to Jewish mores, your mother must be buried within twenty-four hours of death."

"How are we to do that?" stammered Josef. "We are not affiliated with a synagogue, we have no burial plots, and probably not enough

Jewish men in our lives whom we can ask to form a minyan. We are at a loss on how to proceed, Rabbi."

"Emanuel is here to help," Rabbi Adler said sympathetically. "But first, let me tell you about our congregation so you can make an informed decision. As Ernst may have explained, we are Reform Jews. Our modern sermons and our hymnal are in English and German, not Hebrew. An organ fills the sanctuary with music to fill the soul, especially when it supplements our choir."

The rabbi paused for a moment, watching Frida and Josef. When they nodded to indicate that they were receptive to the ritual changes he had described, he continued. "Ansche Beth Shalom removed the lattice shielding women from the men's view; here we allow mixed seating so congregants can sit together as families in shared experiences with God."

I like Emanuel's reforms, thought Frida, thinking back to men and women sitting together at the Lutheran Church back when she boarded with Frau Schultz. *Emanuel allows Jews to be more like Christians, to fit in better. But what is Josef thinking?* She glanced at her beloved husband, afraid of what she would see. Instead, she saw his face light up with unabashed comfort. "I think Emanuel may be the answer to our prayers," he said. "What do you think, Frida?"

I must say yes. It is the answer for Mama. Do I have a choice? And Josef seems so happy . . .

Then, unbidden, the memory of her father's funeral in Hamburg played before her closed eyes. Papa had died of pneumonia, and she had had little time to adjust to his early death. Walking to the funeral with Roshen, Jakob, and some neighbors, a gang of hooligans passing bottles of beer among themselves caught up with them. The unkempt youths were singing loudly, cursing and hurling ugly epithets at passersby. As the little funeral party walked along the cobblestones, the gang pierced Frida's heart with their taunts.

"Why are you all wearing black?" they yelled, as they spit at Jakob. "And those little Jewish hats? Must be going to a funeral. Good for us. One more Jew dead," they laughed, clapping each other's backs.

Frida was shaken from her memory when Josef gently placed his hand over hers. "Frida," he pleaded, "please tell me what you think about joining Emanuel."

"Your reforms please me," she said, addressing Rabbi Adler, her emotions rising. "We were married by Leo Kohn of Ansche Beth Shalom and attended that synagogue for a while. But to be honest with you, Rabbi, I have been tortured about my Judaism since I left Hamburg nine years ago. Jews had a hard time there."

"I understand," said the rabbi. "At Emanuel you will find many who have been through horrors in Europe. We have found each other here and have been quick to adjust to New York. There is a strong bond among us."

Frida and Josef exchanged glances, and Frida thought for sure Josef would see old memories clouding her eyes.

"You have nothing to fear from Emanuel," the rabbi said, his voice firm but reassuring.

Suddenly, Frida found herself unable to hold back tears of grief. As she described Roshen's unforeseen death, Adler listened attentively, his hands folded on his lap. Great sobs poured out from deep within Frida's soul, and angry tears cascaded down her cheeks. She told the rabbi about her estrangement from Roshen and how she still knew nothing about the circumstances of Jakob's death. Thoughts, unspoken until now to anyone but Josef, came forth in unfettered abandon.

"It's okay, Frida," Josef whispered, putting his arm around her shaking shoulders. "It's all going to be okay."

"Your husband is right," Rabbi Adler said. "We will support you in your grief for your brother and your mother."

While Frida composed herself, quiet filled the study. As the silence gathered, Frida's sobs subsided. She dabbed at her reddened eyes with her lace handkerchief until her choking tears stopped. "Will you be kind enough to perform my mother's service, Rabbi?"

"I will be honored," the rabbi said. "I can do a graveside service this afternoon at three o'clock. If you join Emanuel now, our members' burial grounds will be available to you immediately." Rabbi Adler's face softened in folds of empathy. "I understand your fears," he said, "but I assure you they will be laid to rest when you enter the bosom of our congregation. We will be here for you any time you need us."

After several long moments, Frida drew a deep breath. As she exhaled, she nodded quietly. "All right," she finally said, tears sprouting anew. "What do we do now?"

When the necessary paperwork was complete and the required membership fee was paid, doubt still lingered in Frida's heart, but she listened intently to the rabbi as he described the temple's Salem Fields Cemetery. It was situated in a bucolic setting in neighboring Queens County. Grass vistas and winding paths had been constructed several years earlier that would eventually offer mature gardens and trees. As Rabbi Adler offered choices of traditional ground-burial sites and mausoleums, Frida and Josef came to a mutual decision.

"We will be grateful to purchase a mausoleum," Josef said. "Our family is already large, and a mausoleum will insure us that we will always remain together."

Rabbi Adler rose from his desk, smiled softly, and called Ernst Reinhard in from where he had been waiting. "Ernst," he said, "I am glad you brought the Roses to us. This is what they have decided."

He caught Reinhard up on Frida and Josef's new synagogue membership and on their chosen funeral and burial plans. Much to Josef's relief, Reinhard offered to help gather the required ten men to pray nightly at the Roses' home during shiva.

"Thank you," said Josef. "Thank you for everything."

The family arrived at Salem Fields about fifteen minutes early. Frida and Josef were pleased to see not just the Albrechts, Fritz Bayer, Stefan, Gottfried Baum, and Colin Byrne in attendance, but many Rose Industries workers, as well. They had gathered in front of the mausoleum's portico and ranged from custodial and clerical staff to production foremen, upper-level supervisors, and chairmen. The men were dressed in mourning black, many of them in silk top hats trimmed with mourning bands and long mourning veils hanging from the rims. The ladies wore black dresses similar to Frida's, their dark crinolines rustling with the slightest movement. All murmured their condolences in whispered tones.

Rabbi Adler had already taken his place before the crowd, and Ernst Reinhard was there with men from the synagogue who would complete the minyan later that evening. He had brought other temple members who were part of the synagogue's hierarchy, as well. Among them were distinguished financiers, business proprietors, and other esteemed professionals. They gathered around Frida and Josef, somberly welcomed them into the Emanuel family, and offered condolences on behalf of the congregation.

God help me, Frida thought, straining to justify the irreverence rising in her soul. *Like Ansche Beth Shalom, Emanuel, with its obviously prominent membership, will be good for business, too.*

Ashamed that such a thought could enter her mind during such a solemn occasion, she greeted the funeral attendees with a sad smile and took in the details of the mausoleum. It was an imposing white granite building, solid and seemingly impenetrable. Ornate cherubs marched along a frieze that stretched across its portico as if to acknowledge that its future occupants were children once and had been loved. The double wooden doors were open to reveal pink marble-faced drawers waiting for their eternal residents. Shafts of light, tinted by the pink, green, and blue hues of a large stained-glass window, gave the mausoleum interior a soft glow and offered peace to mourners.

A hush fell as the rabbi delivered his prayers. To Frida, time seemed endless as Rabbi Adler stood by Roshen's traditional, plain pine casket and delivered a simple eulogy. At the end of the service, he chanted the Mourner's Kaddish, the prayer traditionally recited for the deceased, and announced that shiva would take place at the Roses' home for the next five days until it ended for Sabbath observances.

Except for Frida and Josef, the mourners had all left by the time cemetery personnel placed Roshen into her final resting place. Frida railed against the harsh creaking of the coffin sliding into its drawer and the heavy, final clunk when it hit the back of the chamber. Outside, the sounds of birds and squirrels chasing each other in the trees seemed to mock what was happening inside. Frida fought for equilibrium as her head spun, and her stomach heaved.

Holding each other, the Roses lingered for a while after the drawer was closed. Frida tried not to think of all the business connections that Emanuel might provide. Against her will, those thoughts overcame all others, and her tears finally stopped. Josef put his arm protectively around her shoulders as they left the mausoleum and started down the granite path to their waiting carriage. Young mimosa trees, with their feather-like pink flowers and lacy leaves, cast fragile shadows over the landscape, completing a picture of peace and serenity. They had gone but a few steps when Frida stopped abruptly and turned to look back at the building that would house her mother forever. She would be there, too, one day, with Josef and the children. The family would rest together forever in their love.

Love? I now know the strength of a mother's love. How could Mama cast me aside, consider me dead? Even animals take care of their young. I've watched robins bring worms to their babies, dogs suckle their pups, geese lead their goslings to safety and pull them under their wings to sleep. I would kill to protect my babies, fight any enemy to keep them close and safe. Mama cast me aside so easily; she saw me as dead because of whom I love. I committed no crime. And now even Jakob is gone, but she wouldn't talk about that beautiful boy. Was she cruel to him, too? WHO WAS SHE?

Did Mama ever love me? And yet, she came all the way to America. Why? As Frida wracked her brain, a sickening realization settled in her stomach: *Mama must have traveled all this way to avoid homelessness. She was sick and penniless without Jakob, so she saw me as a way out. . .*

Frida's stomach lurched, her heart turned icy, and her jaw jutted out as she thought of Roshen's cruel manipulations and how much her mother had taken from all of them. Silently, she drew in her breath and straightened her shoulders. When she finally spoke, it was under her breath; her voice was cold and firm. "*Gute Nacht*, Mother. I won't think of you anymore."

The drive home from the cemetery was bathed in stony silence. Frida refused to speak when Josef tried to engage her. She remained wordless when they arrived at the house, as well. The aromas of potato kugel and savory pot roast floated through the air, and the sweet sounds of Bessie singing while she accompanied herself on the piano welcomed them, but Frida hardly noticed. Unwanted thoughts were flooding her mind as *Jude Bitch, Jude Bitch* rang in her ears and Otto's rancid smells assaulted her nostrils. *Have I betrayed myself? Our Judaism was resolved until Emanuel. I'm so sorry, God . . . but I kept my promise. I always do what I have to do. . .*

As they entered the parlor, Josef's voice brought Frida back to the present. The children were all in the parlor—except for two. "Liesel, where are August and Willie?" he asked.

Liesel's hands were full with the twins and Burke, who were all howling for dinner. Elsie needed a diaper change, and the caretaker was close to tears. Distractedly, she pointed toward the back of the house. "The boys have some schoolmates over to play, something with marbles," she said, her attention riveted on Elsie, who smelled quite ripe. "They've been out in the garden for a while. I must say, they entertain themselves very well."

The hair on Frida's forearms rose. She grabbed Josef's hand, and they hurried to the backyard where the boys were squatting on the ground playing marbles with a few others.

Willie screwed up his nose and pouted. "August always wins," he whined. "And I'm always losing my allowance. Someday, I'm going to win, and we'll see how he likes it."

Frida looked at Josef in consternation and then back at the boys. "What do you mean? What you are doing is gambling. We talked about this when you played marbles before," she said. "You promised you wouldn't gamble again."

The children cast their eyes downward, obviously nervous about Josef's and Frida's scrutiny—except for August. Frida cringed as her son's expression changed. His small but usually innocent eyes transformed into narrow slits, and his mouth curled into a sneer. Her mind raced back to the *Holstein* and the brutal card games Otto ran with his cronies. The deckhands played for money, but they also played for rights to the steerage women.

Despite herself, Frida again retreated into her memories, recalling in vivid detail how she and the other young women would seek hiding spots wherever they could, but at least one poor soul would always be caught. On the off times that the crew couldn't find prey, Otto would be particularly cruel on his nightly attacks.

"You're better than any money," he had snarled, drooling. "Ah, yes. At least I have a regular whore. Another good time tonight, *Jude Bitch*, another good time." She had recoiled, her revulsion spilling over into her thoughts. *I will get you for this eventually. I will. No one owns me, and no one ever will. EVER!*

Suddenly, August laughed, his voice loud and brittle, a voice Frida had never heard before. She snapped back into the present. "August, I asked you why you are gambling. That's a lot of marbles you have in front of you," she said, noticing that August's piles were much larger than those of the other boys. She squinted at him with consternation.

"I won them fair and square," the child said, rising to his feet.

"It's gambling, August. You are *forbidden* to gamble."

"Frida, darling, it's okay," Josef whispered, as he leaned in and cupped his hand under her chin. "It is a child's game. You are overreacting."

Frida's vision blurred, and she ignored Josef. "August, you will give back whatever you've collected from the other boys immediately!" she demanded.

"But I like playing this game," August said, squatting back down and picking up a marble. "I will just play where you will not see me." He looked up at her with Otto's eyes, testing her, and her body went rigid.

Josef was stunned to silence by his son's disobedience.

Frida's limbs started to shake. Her hand went to the scar on her neck, and for the millionth time, she told herself that it didn't matter what the biology was. *HE IS JOSEF'S SON,* she repeated until she convinced herself and, once again, it was her truth.

"What did you say, August?" she finally demanded, hands on her hips. "How dare you defy your mother?"

As if a curtain had lifted, August's eyes softened and brimmed with tears. "I'm sorry, Mama, I'm sorry," he said, dropping the marble and climbing to his feet. "I don't understand why it's bad to gamble, but I won't do it again. I promise, Mama, never again."

CHAPTER 22

Josef

A year had passed since Roshen's death, and the family had put her collapse and funeral behind them. Payments to Tammany had become more frequent, but they were offset by a twenty percent rise in profits. Frida and Josef had become active members of Emanuel where they were engaged in the synagogue's philanthropical committees, and their social calendar had little space now that they were seasoned members of the temple. Josef felt closer to God than he had in a long time, and he was grateful that Frida had put most of her religious trepidations behind her when she saw that the anti-Jewish sentiments in Germany had not carried over to their new life. Her resilience amazed him, and he loved her more than ever.

Today, sunshine poured into the bedroom in advance of the special occasion about to unfold.

"Wake up," Josef urged, kissing Frida's neck through the pool of radiant black tresses that fanned around her face.

"Why?" she whispered sleepily, drawing Josef's arm around her waist. "It is your thirtieth birthday. Weren't we going to treat ourselves to sleeping a little late? It's only 8:00. Your party doesn't start until 5:00 this evening."

"That was the plan," Josef said, smiling, "but plans have a way of changing." He pointed to the open window.

Frida sat up. "What's going on?"

❖　203　❖

"We need to check on August and Willie. They have company outside. There's a lot of chatter coming from the garden."

Hastily, Josef and Frida threw wraps over their nightclothes and headed downstairs. Sure enough, August and Willie sat with six other boys in a circle.

August, about to turn eight years old, stood and started to distribute fliers to the group. He barked out instructions, "Okay, fellas, here's today's supply! Remember, all you must do is give a flyer to each address on your list. I'll pay you a penny for every flyer you distribute, and we'll meet again when my father gives me more handouts. That should be in a day or two. Now get going. Meet me back here when you are finished and you'll get your pay."

The boys scrambled noisily to their feet, counting their leaflets and comparing how much each would get.

"August," said Josef, coming on the scene just as the boys ran out of the garden with their bundles. "What's going on here?"

"Oh," said August casually, "it's just business. You give me three cents for every flyer I deliver. I pay each boy one cent and keep two. That's okay, isn't it, Papa?"

Josef glanced at Frida. Both unsuccessfully tried to stifle grins. "He may not have my physical traits, but he certainly inherited his business skills from me," Josef whispered. "I couldn't keep up with his demand for flyers, but I had no idea he had set this up. He didn't ask me for advice; he just knew what to do. He thinks just like his Papa."

Josef turned to August. "You're asking if setting up your own business is okay? My dear son, it's exactly the way business works! And you came up with the idea yourself. Congratulations! You understand the profit principle. You might even be a Rose executive someday."

"Can I go now?" August asked. "I've got to catch up on my records."

"Of course," said Frida. "We'll invite the Board to be our guests for Friday night Sabbath dinner, and we'll make a formal announcement about your new enterprise then. This deserves special accolades."

Wrapping arms around each other, Frida and Josef went back inside and started down to the kitchen where Ida had set out a light breakfast of griddle cakes with warm blackberry syrup. Located in the basement, the kitchen ran the full length and width of the eighteen-by-forty footprint of the house. Shelves holding pantry items and cooking utensils lined the brick walls, and copper pots hanging from long black poles were arranged along the ceiling. Two newly purchased Oberlin stoves occupied most of the back wall. Made of cast iron and metal, and imprinted with pseudo-moldings and panels, they each stood on fluted iron legs that supported both coal and wood bins; either fuel could be used for cooking or baking. Large reservoirs on the stovetops provided a constant source of hot water.

A new cook, Henry Juenger, had been hired as a general helper and to work with Ida in the kitchen. A man of medium build and a high-pitched voice that belied his muscular frame, he was a recent immigrant from Munich where he had been a tavern owner. He and Ida had taken to each other immediately in managing the needs of the large family and the ever-increasing appetites of the children.

As Josef and Frida entered the kitchen, a large cadre of extra workers who had been hired to help with preparing and serving food for fifty guests was already at work. Ida and Henry barked orders in rapid succession as helpers scurried to complete menu items on time. An assortment of imported cheeses, herring, and cold smoked salmon would serve as appetizers. Roast duck with braised shallots, tender beef sauerbraten, and crispy chicken schnitzel would make up the main course, to be complemented by noodles with fresh herbed vegetables and warm slaw made with cabbages, butter, and minced egg yolks.

Dessert would be placed on a separate table and would consist of nut cakes, apple strudels, and pies woven with intricate braids covering beds of succulent berries. A large assortment of sweet peaches and apricots was being prepared and garnished with edible white orchids and bright red nasturtiums. Bottles of champagne and sparkling wines would fill a huge icebox brought in for the occasion.

After they had eaten breakfast, Frida and Josef went upstairs to view the dining and living rooms on the main floor. A few workers were bringing in a small cookstove with a movable top; it would be placed in a far corner to keep extra platters warm. Colin Byrne had brought in workers to hang cascading lavender wisteria on the walls and over the fireplace. Pots of red roses and purple bellflowers that symbolized love and affection were being placed strategically throughout the room, and a long congratulations banner hung conspicuously from the ceiling near the front entrance.

Josef was pleased, but Frida was overjoyed. This was their first big party, and everything was falling into place. Later in the afternoon, when preparations were complete, they stood back to survey the work. The children were being fed and prepared for an early bedtime, the extra chairs they had ordered were set up, and the gas lamps were ready to be lit.

"The guests will be here soon, so we must get ready," said Frida, starting up the steps to their bedroom. Josef followed her, his hand circling her waist as they ascended. "Time to dress," he said. "I cannot wait to see you in your newest fashion!"

Her short-sleeved, sage-green taffeta gown boasted a low neckline and was hung carefully on a hook behind the door. Trimmed with creamy Rose Lace, the fashionable gored skirt allowed for a smooth front and a slightly extended back. Frida loved the floral self-patterning and the way the color complemented her dark eyes.

"You look stunning," declared Josef, gently reaching out to touch her hair. Parted in the middle, it twisted into an intricate pattern at the nape of her neck and deftly hid the scar under her jaw. She wore simple pearls arranged in two strands clasped at the throat; a topaz-encrusted drop fell at her neckline.

"You look rather elegant, too," she said, straightening his snowy-white cravat and brushing a piece of imagined lint from the lapels of his black tailcoat. "Listen to the chatter from the parlor. Shall we go downstairs and meet our guests? I believe most of them have arrived."

As they started down the steps, the sweet tones of the piano, accompanied by a violin and a cello, filled the house.

"What's that?" Josef asked, his brow furrowing.

"Why, it's a piece by Johannes Brahms, the composer from Hamburg whose music you love. A surprise gift from me to you, my dear husband. Bessie's piano teacher brought in her performance group to play all night for us. They've even brought a banjo player to liven things up later in the evening."

Josef's eyes welled with tears. He took Frida's hand and kissed it. As they reached the parlor, waiters passed trays of canapés and offered flutes of champagne to the guests. They cheered when they saw Josef, the guest of honor, and raised their glasses. Someone started to sing, "For He's a Jolly Good Fellow." The others soon joined in until the house was filled with music and camaraderie.

As they made their way through the crowd, Josef was delighted to see not only all the members of the Rose board in attendance but also congregants from Emanuel. It had only been a year since they joined the synagogue, but it had been a good one. Josef had been delighted when he was asked to join several committees, and Frida had befriended several of the women. She was already looking forward to next year when she would join them in preparing for Emanuel's Purim festival. She and Josef had participated in the elaborate celebrations the previous spring, and both had enjoyed the two days of the holiday dressing up in costume, indulging in festive meals, and watching the children's parades.

Josef was musing about his joy of Judaism, and the renewal of purpose Emanuel had brought to him, and to Frida, when Ernst Reinhard and his wife, Martha, made their way through the crowd to their hosts. Frida and Martha embraced, Josef and Ernst shook hands heartily, and the four chatted until other friends, business associates, and synagogue members joined the conversation. He was particularly happy to see Fritz, Stefan, Gottfried, Colin Byrne, and the Albrecht sisters, and he greeted them with enthusiastic handshakes for the men and cheek kisses for the women.

As Josef stood back and surveyed the lively guests, his heart filled as he recalled their small circle before they joined the temple. They had taken to Emanuel, which widely broadened their social life, and Frida showed no signs of regret or fear in following her heritage. *It was worth it,* he thought. *It was worth giving up ritual then—worth it all now—to see her happy.* He was particularly gratified that Frida had not invited Tammany members to the affair; he shuddered to think of what their presence would have done to his state of mind—and hers—had the gang intruded upon their joy. The fact was that he tolerated them only when it was necessary.

As the musical ensemble drifted into popular songs, black-coated waiters served the buffet dinner out of elaborate silver tureens to the appreciative crowd who raved about the festive menu and toasted often to Josef's birthday and to Frida's prowess as a hostess. Between the main course and dessert, Josef addressed the guests.

"Thank you so much for coming," he said, lifting his glass. "I am honored to have you all here tonight. Yes, it is my thirtieth birthday, but we are drinking to other milestones, as well. Frida and I will soon be celebrating the tenth year of our arrival in the United States. As destitute immigrants, we were frightened and unsure of how America would treat us. In fact, it has treated us very well. We arrived here knowing no one except my dear friend, Stefan, who has been by our sides throughout the years. Now, we look around and see all of you who have become so important in our lives."

"Let's drink to that," toasted one of the guests. "Hail to friendship and success!"

When glasses were once again lowered, Josef said, "As you all know, the rumblings of possible civil war between the Northern and Southern states are turning into a roar. The Union will need an abundance of supplies. So, here's the news. Rose Industries has been named the premier contractor for the wool cloth, blankets, and uniforms needed by the U.S. military. If all goes well, we will create standard measurements and use our own cloth to manufacture ready-to-wear uniforms. Our lace-production facilities will also be expanded to include the metal-wire lace and braid used to trim coats, cuffs, lapels, and epaulets. Accordingly, we are opening a new mill next month to accommodate new machines and additional workers. It will be a three-story stone building with Rose Industries etched into its sides and a large red awning covering its entryway. You will all be welcome to join us for a gala opening."

"Hear, hear!" the guests shouted, applauding loudly until Josef announced that dessert was ready and everyone hurried to the buffet tables to feast on the luscious offerings. Hot coffee and tea were served from engraved silver urns. Sherry, cordials, and cognacs were offered by roving waiters. As dessert was winding down and being cleared away, Frida and the women gathered in the garden, now lit with lanterns and bursting with roses in a variety of pink, red, and peach tones, to discuss the fashionable fabrics that Rose Industries was creating. The men pulled their chairs near the parlor windows. Josef handed out cigars, enjoying the companionship and the sounds of twenty-five men all talking at once.

Soon enough, the topic that Josef had been hoping to avoid came up.

"What do you think of Lincoln, the Republican?" asked one of the men. "Do you think he'll win the election in November? He and that Stephen Douglas, who the Democrats are running, certainly have different opinions. Lincoln wants to stop the spread of slavery; Douglas wants the states and territories to decide the issue for themselves. I was at some of the debates those two had back in '58. Even though Lincoln lost that senatorial election, he made a point when he said, 'A house divided against itself cannot stand.'"

A long discussion ensued during which Josef tried to remain neutral. He and Frida had had many conversations about the divisions between the North and the South, and he was afraid that publicly sharing opinions could have hidden dangers in both social and business circles.

"Like the Republicans, I think slavery is wrong," he had told Frida in the privacy of their bedroom. "We Jews, of all people, should understand the downtrodden."

"I agree with you about the moral aspects," she had said, her jaw set and her eyes cold, "but there are practicalities. The country needs slavery to provide cotton. Rose Industries needs cotton, so it needs slavery—to survive, Josef, to survive."

Josef was jolted back to the conversation at hand when several men defended the Democrats' insistence that slavery was an issue to be determined by each individual state.

"Many of us were there last February when Lincoln spoke at Cooper Union. He made some good points," said a Republican.

A Democrat in the group laughed. "Oh, yes," he said, "Lincoln made quite an impression. He looks like he's walking on stilts—even without his stovepipe hat. And his voice is ridiculous. It's high and shrill, and his Kentucky accent made it almost impossible to understand him. He'll never get anywhere. You'll see."

"But," offered a Republican, "looks and voice aside, he won me over in ten minutes. Lincoln is against anything that would destroy the Union. He's tolerating slavery, but only where it already exists—at least, for now. Congress should regulate it, not allow it to spread to the new territories. Lincoln says the founding fathers intended slavery to end over time. It's not supposed to expand."

A buzz spread through the room as tensions between Democrats and Republicans escalated. A neighbor, a large, round man with a shiny bald head and a slightly unkempt beard, broke through the escalating tension. His deep bass voice commanded the attention of the guests. "Let's look at this objectively," he said. "The slavery issue affects the whole country. Like Lincoln says, we must remain one nation. God knows the South needs our manufactured goods—and we need their rice, sugar cane, tobacco, cotton. But all of it depends on slavery that the abolitionists want to take away. If the South secedes, as they are threatening, the entire nation loses."

Discussion on the pros and cons of slavery took over the room. Josef's heart pounded. He tried to stay out of the conversation by passing pastries and liqueurs, emptying ashtrays, and adjusting the oil lamps as darkness descended. His heart raced as opposing realities of the political situation set in. *That new political faction, the Republican party, argues against the suppression of human beings for profit. But Democrats—like Douglas—see the economic chaos that will come if the South leaves the union.*

Nausea rose in Josef's belly as memory interceded. *I know what it's like to be thought of as less than human. Our people have been the oppressed from Egypt to modern-day Europe. But,* he argued with himself, *unlike the slaves in America, I was able to leave Germany, the land that oppressed me. In America, I can go home at night as a free man, to be with my family without fear of being sold. We came here for freedoms that have given us a good life. The enslaved can't do that.*

Just then, a cool breeze carrying the promise of summer rain drove the women inside where they joined the men's conversation. They eagerly accepted Josef's offers of tea and lemonade, and they enthusiastically joined the men in talking about the Roses' burgeoning opportunities.

When the grandfather clock in the corner struck nine, the group started to say their goodbyes. Most gushed thanks for the Roses' hospitality. They raved about the evening and told Frida and Josef how much they looked forward to the next gathering at their home. When all the guests had left, Frida retreated to the bedroom but, as Josef was about to close the front door, he froze. Coming up the walk were three familiar men.

Leading them was Peter O'Flanagan. He smirked, sending a chill down Josef's spine. "You remember Gus Cairny, don't you, Josef?

And Edward Reilly of Immigrant Savings? They came along because they're impressed with Rose Industries' accomplishments."

"Peter, Gus Cairny, Mr. Reilly," Josef managed. "Come in. This is certainly a surprise. Haven't seen any of you in a while. What brings you here tonight?"

As the visitors climbed the stoop and entered the house, Josef was helpless against the urge to wring his hands. His heart was pounding, and it was all he could do to keep himself upright.

The three men strode into the dining room and sat down. They helped themselves to the remains of pastry and fruit, and they exchanged comments about the house and the decor. Josef stood to the side, unsure of why they had made this unprecedented visit.

When O'Flanagan finally spoke, his voice was cold. "We heard you were having a birthday party," he said, looking around at the congratulatory signs on the walls and hanging from the ceiling. "We wondered why we weren't invited but decided to stop by on our own and join the celebration. Isn't that right, Mr. Cairny?"

"Yeah, that's right," answered Gus, picking up a cigar from an embossed ebony humidor and making a show of lighting it. His lip curled and his eyes grew hard.

The veins on Josef's neck stood out as he contemplated his choices. He could ask them what they really wanted—or he could humor them, tell them he was glad they stopped by, and offer them drinks and desserts. "You didn't get my invitation?" Josef managed to lie. "I sent it to you at Tammany Hall. But, happily, you're here now. Can I offer you some coffee? Chocolates? Brandy?"

The three uninvited guests declined more refreshment but looked sideways at each other, their faces opaque and unrevealing.

"Well, Rose, sit down with us," said O'Flanagan. "We'll get straight to the point. It has come to our attention that you've been awarded an impressive contract."

"Very impressive," added Cairny, who had been promoted to Assistant Chairman of the Tammany Hall General Committee. He squinted and nodded ever so slightly at O'Flanagan. When he continued, his tone was firm. "Your business," he said, "has, in fact, become so impressive that we know you will want to increase your Tammany donations from five percent to ten percent of profits. Of course, an inspector might want to come to your factory. He could also inspect the new mill I hear you're constructing. It would be unfortunate if he found irregularities that would make Uncle Sam contract another manufacturer, wouldn't it?"

O'Flanagan sat back and stroked his chin while Cairny paused again, looking directly into Josef's eyes. When he continued, his voice was still frosty. "Mr. Rose, you know all the good work Tammany devotes to helping immigrants—like yourself, just a few short years ago. It costs money to help with their food and shelter and to help our Democrats win this November against that devilish Lincoln."

"Besides," Reilly added, speaking for the first time, "you are going to need us more than ever."

The three men laughed, but their eyes displayed no humor. Gus Cairny got up and placed his hands on the back of Josef's chair. He stood there for some time, allowing an uneasy silence to build up in the room. "My dear Mr. Rose," he finally said, "if the South secedes from the Union and forms the Confederate States of America, Lincoln's very predictable move would be to place strict blockades on the South. Starve them out, so to speak. Just think what that would mean for you. No cotton or wool would mean no business for Rose Industries."

Josef plastered a smile on his face, trying desperately to hide his consternation at the persistent threat in Cairny's voice. "Gus," he said, his voice strong despite his fear, "we've known each other for a while now. Did you really think Rose Industries hasn't thought of that? We've been stockpiling cotton and wool for months. If the time comes to replenish our supply, we've been assured of a federal grant to override the blockades and procure the raw materials we will need for Union military products."

Cairny cleared his throat and drew deeply on his cigar, blowing curls of blue smoke into Josef's face. "Even though Lincoln provides blockade exceptions for companies like yours, it is probable that you'll need to strike deals with blockade runners. Tammany has many connections to companies that would provide those services. It could be bad for you if you don't cooperate."

O'Flanagan spoke up next. "If the time comes, I can put you in touch with Alex Johnson. He's the captain of a blockade-running enterprise called Sea Winds. His fleet of lightweight, low-slung steamships can cruise unnoticed through the Union blockades, especially at night. The ships are fast, quiet, and easily escape detection. In exchange for Confederate cotton, all you would need to do is supply the South with cheap, ready-made clothing for the slaves."

Josef's heart pounded, and he rubbed his hands so hard that later that night he developed ugly red blisters on his palms. *Run product illegally?* he asked himself. *That's tacit endorsement of something I abhor. Go against my country? Never. But if things go awry . . . we are providing a vital service to the Union . . .*

Josef watched O'Flanagan and Reilly adopt sober faces at Cairny's suggestion, nodding in agreement. "Of course," he managed to stammer. "If I need Alex Johnson, I will certainly be in touch."

As Reilly, Cairny, and O'Flanagan extended their hands, Josef reciprocated, their flesh feeling vile against his skin.

At that moment, August appeared at the top of the stairs. "Papa, I can't sleep. Can I come downstairs now? Who are those men?"

Alarmed, Josef answered the boy immediately. "August, these are my friends, Gus, Peter, and Mr. Reilly. They've come for an after-dinner coffee. Now go ahead, like a good boy, back to bed."

"Pleased to meet you," Cairny called up to him. "You're a big chap, aren't you?"

The three laughed as August returned their greetings and retreated to his room.

When August was out of sight, Gus Cairny spoke up. "I'm glad to meet your kid. Especially since there's something that's come to my attention that I was going to speak to you about anyway. A neighbor of ours, about ten years old, plays cards with your son. Says he's a real whiz. Neighbor kid doesn't want to give up any more allowance, though. Apparently, he's lost his whole piggy bank to August."

Josef felt as if his stomach had dropped to his feet. As soon as the three Tammany men had left, he fell to his knees and his head sunk between them. *He promised he wouldn't gamble again. August is our SON. Frida and I believe him. If what they say is true, he could bring on Tammany's ire. Yet how can I criticize him? Aren't I gambling Tammany's rage in every deal I make? Or every deal I don't make? No, this will pass. He's just a boy playing a child's game. It will pass.*

CHAPTER 23

Josef

Although three years had now passed, Josef awoke from a nightmare about Tammany Hall in which he was back at his thirtieth birthday party in '60. In the dream, O'Flanagan, Reilly, and Cairny came to his home, threw a shroud over him, and placed him in a blockade steamship that was doomed to sink. Suddenly, the three took on ghostly forms and chased him into the bank where they took all his money, seized the deed to his business, and shrieked with mocking laughter when he tried to claw their loot away from them.

"Frida!" he shouted reflexively, only to realize that she had already risen and left the bedroom. *Just as well*, he thought when he regained his composure. *It was a long time ago, and we never did run the blockades. We've thrived since then, too, and our profits are increasing every year.*

The dream still vivid, Josef managed to get himself up and dressed. He made his way to a loveseat under the window and sat there for a while until he could face Frida without alarming her. When his trembling finally stopped, he went downstairs to join her for coffee in the garden. He kissed her lightly and took his usual place across from her at the antique wrought iron table near a newly installed fountain.

He put on his best face when he said, casually, "We've become experienced hosts since my thirtieth back in sixty, haven't we? And this year's July fourth celebration topped them all."

"Yes, it did," Frida said, smiling at the memory of the guests in attendance, including a group of prominent professionals who were members of the New York Affiliates, a business consortium of executives, lawyers, and commercial giants that Josef had recently founded.

Josef laughed and reached for Frida's hand. "How far we've come," he said, recounting production expansions that included patriotic flags and supplies such as socks, gloves, caps, and underwear for the military and for the general population. Based on Rose Industries' need for materials to produce military necessities, the company had been granted boycott exemption rights to procure cotton from the South early on. Blockades had decreased competition, and Rose Industries was riding high.

"It's hard, sometimes, to realize that we employ over seven hundred people," Josef mused, his eyes dancing. "At the rate we're going, we'll soon need new hires. In fact, let's talk with the board about erecting additional worker dormitories and employing more company doctors. Maybe we could even add a clinic."

Frida's brow furrowed. "Are more doctors, let alone a clinic, really necessary?" she asked. "Very few businesses—at least that I know of—have even one doctor like we do. As much as the workers could benefit from such additions, I veto those proposals. We can only do so much, Josef."

Josef was silent for several moments. "Perhaps you are right, Frida. But we will continue providing tea for all shifts."

"And simple pastries," laughed Frida. "We can never give those up. Now that the factory is running twenty-hour days, refreshments keep the workers going. Besides, I love nibbling, too." She rose and popped the last few crumbs of a buttered croissant into her mouth. "And now you must excuse me. I have business that needs my attention and the progress of the party we are hosting tonight to check on."

After Frida left, Josef thought back to the changes the last few years had brought. Money was flowing, the family was growing up, and guests came to visit in an endless stream. Back in '61, when their house could no longer accommodate their changing lifestyle, he and Frida had looked for a new home. They spared no expense when they purchased a double townhouse on Fifth Avenue. The bowed facade offered a grand double-doored entrance nestled into glistening white granite blocks. On an upper roof, a turret with incised wooden trim looked out over the avenue and quickly became a favorite place for the younger children to play "lookout." Bessie especially loved the turret and spent hours there, playing her piano, singing, and imagining adoring fans below applauding wildly.

Except for the twins, who refused to be separated, each child had his or her own bedroom while the house staff, now including more cooks, maids, maintenance men, and several tutors, occupied rooms behind the basement kitchen, which was busy from five o'clock in the morning until well after sunset. Whenever she could, Elsie spent time baking with Ida, who spoiled her with Linzer tortes. The child loved to help make the raspberry preserves that filled the cookie-like pastries and emerged after each session covered with confectioners' sugar.

Outside, behind the garden, a stable housed several horses and carriages, wagons, and carts. The children loved the animals and spent many hours stroking and grooming them. August, especially, became fascinated with the creatures' size and power. He spent as many hours as he could learning about their habits, their history, and their prowess at the racetrack. Impressed by August's knowledge, Willie decided that he wanted to be a jockey when he grew up. He acquired storybooks about horses and brought them to the stable where he read aloud to the animals, convinced that the horses understood every word.

There had been much excitement when the family moved. Frida adored shopping for furniture and accessories. There were mirrors framed in ornate gold leaf, richly embroidered tapestries, and statuary in every room. Shimmering silk draperies outlined the windows and intricate Rose Lace covered the walls. "We must have indoor plantings," Frida had told Josef shortly after they moved in. "Everyone in the synagogue's Garden Club has them. Look how just those few ferns in the corner brighten things up. Think of what more greenery will do."

"Don't we have enough plants?" Josef asked, truly bewildered by Frida's newest demand.

"No, there's no such thing as too many," Frida responded, as she ordered urns and Byzantine pots of philodendron, burgundy rubber plants, and colorful African violets. Soon, frothy maidenhair ferns, orchids in many varieties, and elegant palm trees were arranged throughout the house. Her favorite plant was a prized oleander. Placed in a locked greenhouse room where it enjoyed bright sunlight, it was a twelve-foot specimen with lance-like, leathery, dark-green leaves and a profusion of delicate rose-colored flowers that belied its fatally toxic properties.

"Just one touch without gloves, only one tiny taste of the oleander's leaves or flowers, will make you very, very sick or even bring death," Frida admonished the children and the household staff. Her warnings were well heeded when she made up stories about the oleander being like the wolf in *Little Red Riding Hood,* beautiful to behold but treacherous to engage.

Best of all the house features, in Frida's opinion, was the reception room, which occupied half of the first floor. Ornate friezes placed about a foot down from the thirty-foot high ceiling featured carved roses of every variety. The walls were inlaid with wainscoted panels to accommodate floral-themed oil paintings. Mahogany floor planks were bordered with teakwood and arranged in a herringbone pattern.

Since their move, the Roses had hosted two Purim balls for Temple Emanuel, as well as charity events to raise money for wounded veterans and war orphans. Frida immersed herself in the planning and execution of the affairs. In the process, she became the backbone for the congregation's social functions, as well as for New York Affiliates and for the charity organizations to which she belonged. Josef was pleased that although she devoted many hours consulting with him about the business, she was basking in the social frenzy. There were Afternoons-at-Home and calling cards to be given out on Sundays, and Frida loved it all.

Josef had also become immersed in the social scene. He met often with some of the men at Delmonico's Restaurant, otherwise known as The Citadel, at #2 South William Street. Ernst Reinhard had introduced Josef to Delmonico's shortly after their first New Year's Eve gala. "I'll pick you up at five," he had told Josef one afternoon. "Delmonico's offers outstanding choices of entree, a far cry from the fixed menus offered in other eating places. Havana cigars and imported coffees top it all off. We sit in one of their private dining rooms, and the waiters discreetly attend to our every desire. I think you'll be very pleased."

Josef was quickly taken in by the restaurant's rich mahogany and cherry walls, coffered ceilings, subtle gas lighting, and fine Persian carpets. At a Delmonico's gathering one night in '63, war took up most of the dinner conversation.

"This fellow, Lincoln, has gone too far with his Emancipation Proclamation," said a Democrat. "Outlawing slavery in the ten states still in rebellion has caused nothing but trouble. My workers are in an uproar because freed slaves are satisfied with lower wages. 'They'll take our jobs away,' they claim."

"They're not wrong, though, are they?" said the owner of a furniture factory. "I don't care for slavery—it's morally reprehensible—but I'd rather replace my sixteen-dollar-a-week laborer with a freed slave who'll take five dollars. I've already hired former slaves. They're just grateful to be working as free men."

"I don't know about any of you," Josef said, "but I will always pay my workers equally, as I do now. What one worker gets for a particular job, the others get, too."

"It's bigger than that," countered the Democrat, blood rising to his face. "If that kind of thing happens, labor will become too expensive. Businesses like mine could go under."

"But," said a dedicated abolitionist, "there's another issue here. Freed slaves could prove important to the economy, to our whole way of life. Lincoln is allowing slaves to serve in the Union army. The Southerners are furious about that. I say hooray for Lincoln. We'll get more soldiers and maybe get this darn war over faster."

"Faster?" asked Josef, overcoming his reticence to speak. "The North has lost at least seven bloody battles. Something will have to be done faster than fast if the Union is to survive."

"Josef is right," said Ernst Reinhard. "I've treated soldiers coming out of Bull Run, Antietam, Shenandoah Valley, and even the infamous naval battle between the *Monitor* and the *Merrimack* where men were blown up, heaved into the water, and left to drown, blood clogging their throats as they struggled to keep afloat. Soldiers and sailors who survived their wounds have blank expressions that tear at my heart.

"But there is more," he said, his voice nearly a whisper. "My older brother's son, my very own nephew, was eighteen when he enlisted in the army. His unit fought at Antietam last September, and he told me about his experience. The camp was littered with fetid food, vermin, and so much slop that the pits overflowed and soldiers defecated wherever the need struck. The poor lad, like so many of his comrades, contracted dysentery. He became afflicted with abdominal pain so acute that he couldn't stand but was forced to lie on a filthy blanket near a refuse pile crawling with rats. His fever raged to the point where he was delirious.

"We were lucky that he was one of the few soldiers to respond to quinine treatments. It didn't cure the disease, but he was sent home to recover. A skeleton when he was released, he's home now. I tend to him daily and pray constantly that he regains his former strength. It will be a long process."

Silence gathered at the table until an elderly banker, a round, white-haired man in his early seventies, finally spoke. His voice was low, and his eyes filled with tears that flowed, unrestrained, down his wrinkled cheeks. "My grandson was in the frontal assault at Fredericksburg, just last December. He managed to survive, but barely. When he was sent home, he came to my wife and me. His mother succumbed to cholera in '61, and his father is serving as a colonel and cannot leave his post. Thank God he talks to me and doesn't keep it all bottled up inside like so many of his comrades who suffer from soldier's heart. His right arm was blown off when a wounded confederate hidden under some brush thrust at him with his bayonet, inflicting an eight-inch slash across his left thigh. As he looked down, a canister went off overhead releasing iron bullets in a cascade of death. Bullets ripped open my grandson's right leg at the knee, exposing shredded bone and muscle. He lost consciousness and was taken by his buddies to a field hospital. When he regained consciousness, a military surgeon was standing over him with a bloody knife.

"'There's no chloroform left, soldier, but I'll do my best to remove this leg as quickly as I can,' the doctor told him. Six military aides and a field nurse held my dear boy down. They forced brandy down his throat to dull his senses, and bullets to bite to stifle his screams, while the doctor cut open the festering flesh on his leg. Despite my grandson's wails, the doctor sawed off his tibia and threw it into a pile of limbs stretching out four or five feet wide and high.

The old man choked up and started to tremble. "Lincoln must do more to bring this horror to a close. We need more equipment, more medicines, more soldiers, and we need them now."

For months, especially after the nights he met with the men at Delmonico's, Josef wrestled with his thoughts. He tossed and turned in bed, grateful that Frida slept soundly and was unaware of his angst. Relentless thoughts plagued him like hammers pounding his brain. *How do I get to live my luxurious life while so many suffer? I can continue contributing funds to the war effort, yes. I can continue to provide the Union with military goods. But what can I do personally? What can I do, God? What should I do?*

In March, the answer came. Lincoln signed the Civil War Military Draft Act requiring all male citizens between the ages of twenty-two and forty-five, and married men to age thirty-five, to enlist with the Union. A lottery would take place on July 11th. There was much pro-and-con discussion about it at Delmonico's meetings, and Josef listened carefully to all of it. He finally made up his mind.

"I'm only thirty-three years old. I am going to join the Army," Josef told Frida one night after a particularly disturbing meeting. "I owe everything to America. The war must come to an end quickly, before more die."

Frida stamped her foot. "The president is allowing single men to pay substitutes to fight in their place. You contribute huge sums to the military hospital, and you provide vast resources and materials to the Union army. We certainly have the money to hire a substitute, and that is exactly what you will do."

Torn, but unwilling to cross Frida, and fresh with stories of the wounded and dead, Josef succumbed and hired a poor lad from the mill. The father of four was thrilled to receive the $300 substitute fee, a sum far higher than the annual $112 he currently earned as a custodian's assistant. "When you return from the war," Josef promised the young man, "you will be promoted to a higher position. That is, if you give me your word that you will not tell others of our arrangement."

Public reaction to conscription was swift. Throughout the city, resentment ran high. Neighbors snubbed neighbors, workers threatened violence, and families accused each other of treason. Fury had built up among workers who could not afford to pay substitutes. The time was ripe for violence.

"Things are not going well, Frida," said Josef one hot night in July, a few days after the Union won a resounding victory at

Gettysburg. "The drawing for the draft is next week. Just yesterday, I passed a crew setting up a platform where the selection drum will be placed. There is talk that blindfolded election officials will pull chits containing the names of potential conscripts from a spinning barrel. Their names will be published in the papers the next day. I've heard talk about how unfair the Conscription Act is. Already, thousands have met in saloons and bars, living rooms, and kitchens to organize a protest. Agitators carrying "Stop the Draft" and "Don't Give Away Our Jobs" signs are increasingly marching through the streets. I fear for the worst. We should brace ourselves and keep the children here at home. It could get ugly."

CHAPTER 24

Otto

Otto Krause considered himself a lucky man. Most clipper ships, including the *Holstein*, had been replaced by steamships. Faster and more predictable than their predecessors, they had become the dominant form of transatlantic voyage. Otto's livelihood was threatened, and he was terrified of experiencing the pennilessness he had endured as a child. He was despairing of finding work when a representative of Sea Winds, the notorious blockade-running fleet, had come to the pier to recruit workers. An Irishman from Tammany Hall had met the *Holstein* at the dock where he and his comrades were going ashore after a difficult run on the Atlantic.

"I'm Peter O'Flanagan," he said to the group, extending his hand, "and I've come to recruit some of you for a dangerous, but very lucrative, undertaking."

After O'Flanagan had talked about Sea Winds, Otto signed up immediately and had proved to be an asset to the enterprise. He had come to the attention of Captain Alex Johnson, who oversaw the most perilous runs. Otto soon became sought after as a runner who could safely exchange Northern cloth and slave clothing for Southern cotton.

Early on the morning of Monday, July 13, 1863, when draft selections for the war effort were commencing, Otto arrived at a New York City pier after a successful run. As he stepped onto the dock, he encountered a furious mob attacking two hundred Black workers exempted from the draft because they were not recognized as citizens. Additionally, the mob was furious that freed slaves were given jobs that were once exclusively held by Whites. Some of the workers were stabbed and thrown into the river; others were kicked and pelted with stones.

"Vengeance on every Black! They can't take our jobs!" the mob shouted as they grabbed victims, stripped them naked, and dragged them through the streets until they were bloodied or dead.

Unaware of the reasons that the crowds were enraged, Otto went immediately to his old hangout, Sweeney's House of Refreshment, where his favorite wench, a prostitute named Mary, knew his every desire and could satisfy both his thirst and his raging desire. By 10:30, when the sun was beating down mercilessly through the humidity-soaked air, Otto was sated. He found the growing mob and joined its march to the provost marshal's office where all decorum had collapsed. Firemen ignored their duty and set the marshal's office on fire. Even before the first name was pulled from the draft-selection wheel, a Republican-appointed police superintendent was beaten almost to death.

Otto had no idea what the issues were, but he smelled blood and immediately became an instigator in the melee. Armed men, women, and even children soon were rushing up Lexington Avenue. Recalling random beatings from his childhood days, but excited by the mayhem, Otto became a leader. "Rip those streetcar rails up! They'll come in handy!" he shouted, using a heavy railroad tie to beat a young copper senseless. "Get me a telegraph wire!" he yelled to a teenaged thug nearby. "Let's show this guy who's boss."

Within minutes, the two had the unconscious policeman tied into a fetal position and stuffed into a window well.

Emboldened by the crowd's wild applause as they approved his efforts, Otto ran down the street. His English was limited, but after years of going back and forth between Germany and America, he knew enough to get involved easily. "String that Black man up!" yelled someone in the crowd. "Teach him a lesson for taking jobs from hard-working White folk."

Enraged men pumped their fists in the air and set upon the fellow. Otto pushed forward, tackled the hapless man, and pulled him to the ground. While young abolitionists tried to stop the crowd's advances, the mob overwhelmed them, beating them senseless and leaving them lying helpless on the road. The mob roared its approval, and someone grabbed a rope from a nearby hardware store. "This will do the job!" he yelled, as he threw the rope to Otto.

"Kill!" screamed the crowd, as someone tied a noose and threw it over a nearby lamppost. Encouraged by the throng, Otto helped to strip the man of his clothes. "Hang, hang, hang!" the mob chanted until Otto joined other thugs in pulling the man up by the hair and getting his head into the noose. The horde roared its approval as the rope was pulled, stopping just short of strangling the victim to death, when someone threw a burning log underneath the makeshift scaffold. The crowd went into a frenzy.

"Add more wood!" they yelled. "Roast him! He can't take our jobs! Teach the slaves a lesson!"

The flames grew and licked at the fellow's feet. Agony filled the man's face as his neck snapped, and he hung over the flames until his body was burned beyond recognition.

From there, the mob advanced until it arrived at the Colored Orphan Asylum on Fifth Avenue at 44th Street, just a few blocks from the Roses' home. The Asylum provided shelter for children who otherwise would have been sent to live in jails or been left to their own devices as beggars. The enraged crowd surrounded the building, sending its more than two-hundred occupants racing into the streets. "Kill!" thundered the horde. Otto blended into the crowd, brandishing his knife through the air. Excited by the violence, his member pushed against his pants as he tried to separate a skinny adolescent girl from the terrified orphans.

"You're mine!" he yelled, lunging at the child's waist. As she started to fall, she kicked out wildly at his leg, her heavy black boot hitting his shin. Otto doubled over in pain and was pulled back by a matron, a hefty woman with strong arms and unusually broad shoulders who was bringing up the rear of the line.

"You stay away from that little one right now—or you'll deal with me!" she snarled, pointing a heavy rifle at Otto's head. Her terrified brood watched as Otto retreated, and the children continued their flight to a nearby police station.

Enraged by the failure to capture his prey, Otto grabbed a torch from one of the rioters and threw it into the orphanage, whooping in delight as it caught fire. The crowd cheered as ten-foot flames engulfed the building.

"They all escaped, the bastards!" someone shouted, as the last of the children and staff disappeared around the corner.

"But rich folks who buy their way out of this godforsaken war haven't escaped!" yelled a huge man holding a dagger in one hand and a musket in another.

"Let's find 'em!" bellowed Otto, as he followed mob leaders who knew where the wealthy lived. Stately homes of prosperous Republicans quickly went up in flames, their terrified occupants spilling out into the street where they were beaten and left to be trampled.

"More! More!" yelled the crowd, as they spread through the neighborhood, grabbing jewelry and cash from homes just before they were torched. At several abolitionists' homes, wives and children were held as ransom until legal tender and valuables were handed over.

When Union soldiers fresh from the Battle of Gettysburg finally arrived to quell the mayhem, the mob, besieged now by cannon fire, began to scatter. Otto slinked into an abandoned grocer's shop to steal some dinner and started to run toward the nearest saloon. As luck would have it, he came across a boy huddled in the doorway of a known gambling joint. The blond child with the gray, almond eyes was clutching several packs of cards and a large bag of coins.

"Well, well, what have we here?" Otto grinned. "What's a little kid like you doing with a big bag of money like that, eh? We wouldn't want it to fall into the wrong hands, would we, now? Give it over here—for safekeeping, so to speak."

He kicked the youngster's ribs, grabbed the money, and darted away just as several patrolmen turned onto the street. He never noticed the turtle-shaped mole on the boy's neck. If he had, he would have seen that it was precisely the same as the mole on his own neck . . . and in the exact same place.

CHAPTER 25

August

August clutched his bruised side and moaned, not so much from the pain of the goon's assault but from fear of what would happen to him when he got home. He had promised Frida that he would never gamble again but, even more, that he would stay indoors and away from trouble on this day when violence was permeating the streets. Yet here he was, bloodied in the gutter with fire and smoke all around him and the stench of soot clinging to his clothes, boots, and hair.

As soon as he recovered enough, he ran his hand across the ground only to discover that his gambling winnings had been taken by the oily man who had assaulted him. August had come here, as usual on a Monday, to gamble with the orphans. Those Mondays were glorious days filled with the triumphs of wins.

I'm the best, he mused now, remembering how much he had won that day. *Had them all fooled with my straight face. They thought I had nothing in my hand, but I had aces and pairs waiting to surprise them. When I raked in the winnings, their expressions were priceless. I'll get today's bounty back. ALL OF IT and then some. No tough scares August Rose out of a game. NOT EVER.*

August was brought back to the moment that shouting rioters had thundered past him. When he first left the orphanage and the mob barreled down the street, he had hurried into the safety of the nearest doorway where he rolled himself into as small a ball as his big frame allowed. He was now a solid youngster, broad-shouldered with a head of fine blond hair and full cheeks. His tear-filled gray eyes darted wildly as he searched for a way out of his dire situation.

Temporarily immobilized by the thug's blows, August was grateful when he heard voices approaching. Three exhausted men were walking through the ravished streets when one of them noticed August huddled against the doorjamb. "Look," said Peter O'Flanagan, "I think it's August Rose. I'd recognize that blond hair anywhere." He rushed over to August, Gus Cairny and William Tweed coming in right behind him. "August, is that you?" asked Peter, his voice strong and authoritative.

"Yes," whimpered August. "Who are you?"

"I'm Peter O'Flanagan, and this is Gus Cairny. We met briefly at your house the night of your father's birthday party a few years ago, but I've seen you—albeit from a distance—a few times when we've visited your home. And this," he said, pointing to the third fellow, "is our friend, William Magear Tweed."

Tweed, a portly fellow of three hundred pounds, with small, light eyes, a full beard, and a thick mustache, tried, without success, to bring himself down to August's level. Finally, he placed his thick hand under August's face so he could look the child in the eye. "You're the gambling genius, am I not right?"

"What makes you think I gamble?" August asked. He groaned and tried to avert Tweed's grasp, but the big man wouldn't allow him to get away. He tweaked August's ear until the boy finally relented.

"It's the cards you're still clutching, boy, that give you away—and your growing reputation for the games."

"What do you want from me?" asked August, his adolescent voice starting to break.

"We want to get you home, lad, that's all. It looks like you've had enough activity for one day. Come on now, on your feet before more trouble comes."

As terrified as August was, he also welcomed adult support and acquiesced to the men. As they made their way along Fifth Avenue, the spoils of the day were all about. August's stomach retched when they came across bodies of dead and wounded victims who lay in the streets surrounded by pools of blood. Fires burned everywhere, and bullet casings were more plentiful than stones in the roads. Children cried, women sobbed, and men headed to the nearest open saloons to seek relief from their battles.

As they approached the house, August became panicky. "Please," he begged, "don't tell my parents about the gambling. I promise I'll never do it again. Just say you won't tell them what you saw."

Tweed grinned, his eyes gleaming. "Well, son," he said, after a perfectly timed delay, "I'll keep your secret. But we'll have a secret of our own. Come play cards with us, and we'll see for ourselves just how good you are. If you fail to impress, your secret will be out. If we like what we see, your secret will be safe. In return, we'll expect you to contribute part of your winnings for all the good work we do for Tammany Hall."

When they arrived at the Rose residence, the three men left the boy at the front gate where he waited until the posse was out of sight. August's mind raced as he tried to come up with a believable reason he might have been compelled to go out on such a hot—and now-proven dangerous—day with spoils from the riots everywhere. He waited out of view until his scheme was hatched. Then, he threw his shoulders back and opened the front door.

The family was gathered in the front parlor. Mama was crying, Papa wore fury on his face, and Willie was pacing back and forth in front of the windows.

"Where have you been, August?" demanded his mother, her veins throbbing in her temples. His gaze went immediately to where her loosened hair revealed the scar still rising from her neck. It had always fascinated him although he had never conjured up the courage to ask about it.

"I can explain everything, Mama. Just let me wash up a bit first."

"You'll do no such thing," Josef insisted. "You'll tell us right now why you defied our instructions to stay home and, even worse, why you didn't tell us you were going out and where you were going."

Blood rushed into August's ears, and his heart thumped wildly. His eyes clouded, and his lips curled. "Well," he said finally, trying in vain to avoid their eyes. "You will be glad to know that I was off on a business venture. I'm expanding my flier route into a messenger service. In addition to delivering Rose fliers around town, I will pick up packages and letters from businesses and deliver them more quickly than the postal service."

"And when did you come up with this idea?" asked Frida, skepticism creeping into her voice.

"Oh," August said casually, but firmly, "a while ago. I wanted it to be a surprise."

"But why today? It's mayhem out there," asked Josef.

"I went to the Colored Orphan Asylum to pick up some mail—and to hire some of their boys for my new business. There were mobs of people yelling and screaming and fighting, so I hid. I couldn't get my business done. But I will."

Josef and Frida paused, exchanging long glances. After a few moments, Frida spoke, her words firm. "We'll talk more later about what happened in the streets today. But alright," she said, as Josef nodded in agreement. "You'll establish a new Rose Industries service."

"It is a good idea," said Josef. "What will you need?"

August's mind raced. He hadn't thought of any of this until now. "Actually," he finally said, "I could use a bicycle. It'd be a lot faster than walking, and I'd be able to get around the city quickly. I'd attach a basket affixed with *Rose Industries Messenger Services* signs. I know bicycles are hard to get; they're a new thing. But if my idea works, I could buy a fleet of them, hire extra boys, and deliver more and more packages and letters."

"It's a good plan," said Frida, "and I think we should do it. Your father and I will discuss your idea with the board. But right now, we need to continue our conversation about today. You cannot disappear into danger like this again. We have enough to worry about with Louise and Gertrude."

"What's wrong with my sisters?" August pleaded, alarm crossing his face.

Josef and Frida each sighed heavily. "As you know, from the time they were small they have suffered with rashes. At first, the purple blotches seemed harmless—but things are progressing, and we are worried. The doctor was here today to check on them. They are getting a lot of stomachaches, they're having trouble swallowing, and we can all see how they have developed hard, tight patches all over their skin. The condition is spreading and may eventually affect their muscles. He told us that the girls should stay away from sunlight as much as possible to keep the patches from getting worse. That's why we have been using their parasols whenever we go out."

"Does the skin have anything to do with why they have been walking strangely? Or why they are having trouble making dolls for the orphans? Will they be okay?" August asked, fighting tears.

"We don't really know yet. Only time will tell," said Frida.

"And so, August," said Josef, "we have enough to worry about. Just you keep out of trouble. Right now, let's get you some dinner and to bed."

When August finally got into his nightclothes, his eyes narrowed, and his jaw formed a perfect line. *That was close,* he said to himself, as he turned out the gas lamp next to his bed. *And now, I have my work cut out for me.*

CHAPTER 26

Frida

"I've invited all of you here today for two reasons," Frida said to the board members seated in Rose Industries' new conference room. It had been built just after the Civil War Draft Riots had calmed down the year before. "We will begin the meeting after a few announcements."

The chamber was large, almost as long as it was wide. Its floor-to-ceiling windows offered a view of a new patio garden just starting to bloom with the pastel colors of spring. A French conference table occupied the central space and was surrounded by two dozen green damask armchairs. Recessed shelves flanked a marble fireplace and displayed mementoes from business trips Josef had made in pursuit of lace patterns and fabrics. As the meeting started, a hush settled in as a butler brought in sparkling wines, delicate canapés, and a huge cake covered with snowy whipped cream, fresh strawberries, and edible fuchsia orchids. A moment later, Bessie, now eleven years old, entered the room and wordlessly sat at a Steinway piano occupying the wall between the windows. She paused for several moments. Then, to everyone's surprise, she began to play Felix Mendelssohn's "Wedding March." A low murmur spread throughout the room as the board tried to determine what was happening.

Frida and Josef began to clap slowly and then picked up speed. Frida smiled and invited Amalia and Stefan to join her at the head of the table. "There is news," she said. "Stefan, will you do the honors?"

"Thank you, Frida," Stefan said, blushing deeply and putting his arm around Amalia's shoulders. "Yes, we have an announcement to make. Amalia and I have become engaged. And yes, we kept our love secret until we could make this deep commitment. Frida and Josef have kindly offered their home for an autumn wedding. We hope you will all join us in celebration."

At once, everyone applauded, slid back their chairs, and walked over to the beaming couple offering hugs, kisses, and assurances that they certainly would attend the festivities. Bessie continued to accompany herself on the piano as she sang the popular love songs of the day. A few people started to dance, including Bertha, who partnered up with the only stranger in the room, Rose Industries' newest board member. Frida couldn't help but notice that they seemed quite smitten with each other.

"Let's keep an eye on those two," Frida whispered to Josef, her voice crackling with mischief. "You never know! Amalia and Bertha are both late to marry. They've been caught up in the business, so this is all good."

After a while, everyone settled in the seats around the table. Frida lifted her glass. "My dear friends," she said. "First, I would like to introduce the newest member of our board, Arnold Schubert. He has been appointed head of our newly formed legal department. He comes to us out of Harvard Law School and has clerked for several prominent judges. Can you stand, please, Arnold?"

Schubert was six feet, seven inches tall and towered above everyone in the room. Rail-thin, his tapered face sported thick mutton-chop sideburns that emphasized his sharply defined nose. His dark hair was cut to ear level in the back, parted on the side, and combed smoothly to the base of his neck. Large hazel eyes sparkled under thick brows, and he sported a deep cleft chin that somehow emphasized his wide smile. His lips were surprisingly full and offered glimpses of perfect white teeth. "When I agreed to take this position," he said solemnly, "I did so because Rose Industries enjoys a solid reputation as a fair and just employer with a keen eye for the future. Thank you all for this opportunity."

Arnold spoke for a few moments about his extensive legal background. He retreated to his seat after Josef officially welcomed him to Rose Industries. After congratulations were offered by everyone, Frida resumed. "And now to the business of the day," she said. "Battles are still raging, but the conflict will, at some point, come to an end. We can't predict the economy after the war; it could easily collapse, especially if the North loses. Rose Industries *must* be prepared. We must survive—and we will, no matter what the future holds. You've all been asked to come up with ideas that would allow us to flourish when hostilities end."

Discussion became lively and animated. The first suggestion was from Stefan. "We should go public, get into the stock market as soon as possible," he said, starting to present charts and tables and newspaper reports.

"Absolutely NOT!" cried Frida, her face crimsoning with rage. "Stop that thought, right now! I don't care if the market is up, or down, or sideways. I'll never be a part of that nonsense. The stock market is gambling, pure and simple." Her stomach lurched into her chest as she thought of the sailors on the Holstein gambling for rape rights. The memory of Otto bragging about his triumph in securing her for himself during that horrible voyage flooded her mind and threatened to take over her thoughts. *Maybe that's how August came to love gambling . . . but I will not think of that now. I WON'T!*

Aware that Josef and all the board members were stunned by her reaction, Frida mustered her strength and brought herself back to the present. "Let me be perfectly clear," she said, her tone firm and unyielding. "To put the company at the whims of the stock market would be undiluted speculation. This company will never rely on any form of gambling to survive. We will depend on ourselves to continue Rose's growth. We will never rely on outsiders—and we certainly will never gamble with our fortunes. Is that clear?"

A hush fell over the group until Josef broke the silence. "Okay, friends," he said. "Let's move forward." Obviously flustered after Frida's outburst, Josef went through suggested options until several key endeavors were decided upon. "And so," he finally said, "Rose Industries will create upholstery and commercial-grade fabrics that will expand us into new, essential markets. We will also purchase whatever supplies we need to manufacture sheet leather for bags, luggage, shoes, and boots. They're all necessities; everyone needs them, in good times and in bad."

After lively approval, Josef continued, a broad smile on his face. "Inspired by today's engagement announcement, there's another new line we should pursue—that is, Amalia and Stefan's idea to mass-produce bridal fabrics. Amalia, will you explain?"

Amalia took Stefan's hand and smiled broadly as she outlined their ideas. "Queen Victoria made her mark when she married Prince Albert in '40. Since then, brides want to wear white like she did. The days of colorful bridal attire are fading fast. I, for one, will wear white Rose Lace. But everyone is different. Pure white silk, like Victoria wore, is always gorgeous, but some brides may want organza, crepe, brocade, or chiffon. Let's create a fabric for every bride."

"Amalia," Josef said, "if we go ahead with this idea, you will be the perfect person to oversee the new Rose Bridals subsidiary."

Bertha laughed, joy for her sister shining in her eyes. "Don't forget tulle for veils, Amalia. Every bride needs a veil."

Ideas flew for new product lines until Frida glanced at the grandfather clock as it inched toward 10:00 p.m. "We will set up another meeting soon to refine today's decisions," she said. "In the meantime, enjoy what's left of this beautiful evening."

As stars filled the sky and the moon sent rays of brightness to the darkened city, the board members left for home. When only Frida and Josef remained, they sat at the table across from each other and helped themselves to more canapés and wine.

"You know," Frida said, her gaze steady and determined, "we'll need additional manufacturing space—again. North of the forties, Manhattan is wilderness. Land is still readily available, but that's going to change. And soon. The possibilities are wide open. Let's go after them immediately."

Josef's brow folded in consternation. "I don't know, Frida. All this could be too much too soon."

He winced as Frida's jaw set, and she stood. Her eyes narrowed, and she seemed taller than her four feet, ten inches. Her eyes flashed. "This is not the time to be cowardly, Josef. We *will* expand, we *will* buy property, and we *will* be prepared for whatever is to come of this godforsaken war."

Josef shuddered, but he acquiesced. "All right, Frida," he said. "I suppose you are right. I'll work with Stefan and Arnold immediately."

Frida's expression relaxed. "You won't be sorry, Josef. And neither will I."

As they walked home through the balmy night, Josef put his arm around Frida's waist and drew her close to him. Flush with possibility, Frida felt love welling up in her chest. Silently, they approached the house, Frida thinking of how she and Josef would enter their bedroom and gently remove each other's clothing. They would light the candles and sink into the feather bed they had just received from Switzerland, its ten-inch down mattress receiving them like a cloud. Josef would smooth back her hair and kiss her deeply. They would caress each other and breathe in each other's fragrance until they could no longer keep their passion in check. It would be perfect . . .

As they turned their corner, they froze. They saw a carriage speeding down the street. The driver was standing, whipping his horse and screaming at it to go faster. People had gathered on the curb, turning to each other in disbelief at the recklessness playing out in front of them.

"Someone stop that fellow!" yelled a youth, who tried, without success, to keep up with the carriage and take control of the reins.

The horse was glistening with sweat, and foam was pouring from its mouth when the driver finally yelled "HALT!"

To the Rose's horror, the carriage skidded to a stop in front of their home. Before it came to a full standstill, a gentleman climbed out of the passenger compartment clutching a black bag and barking urgent orders to the driver to wait unless otherwise instructed.

It was Dr. Ernst Reinhard—and he was frantic to get into the house.

Frida broke away from Josef and ran to the front steps where a constable was working to keep onlookers at bay. When the officials saw Frida and Josef, they ushered them inside where Gertrude lay on the floor unconscious. The doctor was on his knees applying smelling salts, and his expression was grim.

Louise was sobbing, and August was huddled in a corner with his knees drawn up to his chin. He was shaking uncontrollably. "It's my fault!" he wailed, his face turning red and his small eyes so filled with tears they were all but shut tight.

"It's not!" Bessie cried softly, putting her arms around him. "It was an accident, August. None of us should have been playing the way we were."

"No, no, no," sobbed August. "The game was my idea. It's all my fault."

"What game, August? What game?" asked Josef.

"We always play war, Papa. I'm always Lincoln and give the commands. Willie plays Robert E. Lee. Burke, Elsie, and the twins are the soldiers. Bessie doesn't want to kill anyone, so she plays the nurse."

"That sounds reasonable," offered Frida. "But what happened today? Why is Gertrude lying in a heap at the bottom of the stairs?"

"It's because I commanded the cavalry to follow a confederate platoon across a river. Burke pretended to get hurt, and I told the nurse to go downstairs to get water. Gertrude knew the soldiers were in trouble. She was just standing there, and when she started to walk she tripped and fell down the whole flight. Now she's going to die, and it will be my fault."

Frida gathered the weeping child in her arms and rocked him, assuring the boy that the game may have gotten out of hand, but he wasn't responsible for her fall. Her head throbbed mercilessly as she realized the grim possibilities that could be lurking in the moments just ahead.

As the salts did their job, and Gertrude regained consciousness, Dr. Reinhard continued his examination. For some time now, Frida reported, both Gertrude and Louise had been getting worse. The mild purpling and pitting that had started in their fingers when they were small had appeared on their toes, as well. Hard, wood-like patches on their extremities and torsos had advanced to their faces. Sores had developed everywhere and erupted into raw, open ulcers. Worst of all, for them, their beautiful hair had been falling out in clumps.

"Gertrude's left foot seems to have a fracture," said Reinhard. "I'll apply a splint and suggest bedrest until it heals. But her hardened skin concerns me."

The doctor looked at Louise, who was watching her sister and crying. Her purple fingers dabbed at her eyes.

"Have either of the twins developed any new symptoms other than their sores? Hardened skin? Joint weakness? Fatigue?" he asked.

Frida felt her knees go weak. Many had been the nights when the twins cried themselves to sleep with stomachaches; many had been the days when they gasped for breath, were unable to pick up simple objects, or tripped. She had attributed their problems to growing pains, poor appetites, and clumsiness. Not until this moment did she recognize there might be more sinister causes behind their complaints.

When Reinhard finished his examination, he knew what was wrong. "Frida and Josef, please come with me into the parlor where we can talk."

The pair held hands as they followed the doctor and didn't let go even as they sat down.

"I think," Reinhard said, as the Roses sat on the edges of the love-seat, "Gertrude is suffering from scleroderma. It hardens the skin, and Louise has similar symptoms. We don't know much about the disease, but bathing in hemlock water might give some relief. Leeches and mercurial ointment can also be applied to relieve stiffness."

"Will my girls be okay?" asked Frida, visibly shaken. "And what about the other children?"

"That remains to be seen," Reinhard said. "But eventually you'll need to hire someone to watch the twins full time. The symptoms can become debilitating."

CHAPTER 27

Frida

Two years had passed since the last business expansion, and Rose Industries was booming. When Frida awoke on Friday morning the 14th of April, 1865, she was full of good cheer. Orders for new Rose products were pouring in, and just a few days earlier, on Sunday, April 9, the Confederacy had lost the Battle of the Court House at Appomattox, Virginia. There were still skirmishes in progress, but the conflict had turned in the Union's favor. The North celebrated the end of the war on April 9, just five days earlier.

Josef had already left for the day. He was in early morning negotiations for furniture upholstery, fabric wall coverings, and curtains for new mansions being built uptown. Afterward, he had meetings with Boss Tweed for the new County Courthouse and a new City Hall. The night before, Josef had surprised Frida with coveted tickets for the Grand Sacred Concert at Irving Hall for tomorrow's Saturday matinee. She had yearned to attend the gala affair and was thrilled when Josef presented the tickets over a steak dinner at Delmonico's the previous weekend. That evening, they would attend a Passover celebration at Emanuel, an event she looked forward to eagerly. It would culminate days of joyous victory celebrations.

Slowly and luxuriously, Frida pulled back her creamy satin sheets and donned a caramel-colored silk robe trimmed with Rose Lace and bead pearls. She slid her manicured feet into matching slippers and walked to the open window to check the weather. Some fog and drizzle had gathered over the city, but traces of sunlight and sweet spring fragrances wafted through the room with the promise of a bright day to come.

By the time breakfast was served, the children were ready for school, and the twins were ready for their tutors who had become a necessity as their disease progressed. Frida made a split-second decision. Standing at the head of the table, she made an announcement in her most authoritative tone. "Children, I need you to listen, RIGHT NOW," she announced, and they immediately came to attention, apprehension in their eyes.

"If you look out the window," Frida said, "you will see that it is turning into a perfect spring day—a perfect day to celebrate what looks to be the end of the war. Therefore, I am forbidding you to attend school or meet with your tutors. Instead, I am demanding that you go with Ida and Liesel to visit Barnum's American Museum— unless, of course, you don't wish to see Zingaro and His Monkey, Punch and Judy, or Wooderoff's Glass Blower. If there's time, you may even get to go to Central Park."

Disbelief spread around the table as the children wolfed down their pancakes, scrambled eggs, and orange juice. As quickly as they could, they discarded their books, got out the wheelchairs required now for Gertrude and Louise, and assembled under Ida's and Liesel's directives for the day's outing.

After the children left, Frida dressed, summoned her carriage, and went to pick up Martha Reinhard and several other Emanuel women. Charity work was a matter of duty for a person in Frida's position, something one must do to maintain both social and business relationships. On Mondays, Frida's circle volunteered at the Jewish Hospital, which had opened its doors to Civil War injured and still-suffering survivors of the Draft Riots in 1863. They dressed wounds, read to the blind, and made patients as comfortable as possible. Alternating Fridays were reserved for the Colored Orphan Asylum where Frida and her committee volunteered to help restore the institution's former functions. August had told her about his firsthand view of the mayhem on that terrible July day in '63, and the committee had started their work almost immediately.

Their building destroyed, the asylum had moved into temporary quarters in a dilapidated but usable old house in the Carmansville section of Manhattan at 150th and Broadway. It was a long and bumpy, but beautiful, ride to get to the new location that nestled along winding Hudson River shores. Old-growth trees, expanses of flowering shrubs, and grazing cattle dotted the peaceful landscape and provided a sense of safety to its traumatized residents.

Asylum work had become a Rose family activity. Some of the orphans had become workers in August's messenger service. Willie regaled them with lively stories about horses at the stable where he had found a job, and Bessie sang at special asylum celebrations. Burke, who had developed significant artistic ability, came along sometimes to help the children work with clay, paint, pastels, and charcoals. Even little Elsie contributed by making simple fabric dolls for the youngest orphans. Gertrude and Louise tried to help with the dolls, but their stiffened hands prevented them from doing much.

The day went by swiftly, and Frida returned home pleasantly tired. She napped for a bit, then combed her hair, now peppered with several silver strands, by parting it in the middle and plaiting it into an intricate pattern. She gathered it loosely in a comb at the back of her neck, deftly fluffing it out to cover her scar. By dinnertime, the family assembled, as usual, at the dinner table for the Sabbath meal and for the usual announcements of the week's events. The children were talkative about their surprising day. Frida and Josef listened attentively as details emerged, but Frida was distracted by a strange expression in Ida's eyes.

Sensing trouble, Frida asked Liesel to take the children upstairs to get ready for bed. When they were gone, she addressed the faithful servant with a direct question. "What's troubling you, Ida?"

Ida hesitated, but under Frida's withering glance, she finally gave in. "Well," she said, "we saw three strongmen in the park just before we left. One of them was a beefy fellow with the hugest arms I've ever seen; another one was tall with penetrating blue eyes. They looked familiar; I recognized them vaguely from visits to the house. They said they were from Tammany Hall. They seemed to recognize August—said he was a good boy doing good work with his messenger service. I don't know how they could know that, but they did."

"And the other?" asked Frida, her skin prickling.

"I'd never seen him before. He was a nasty fellow with a huge belly, long stringy hair, and a raspy voice. He didn't say more than 'Good day,' but he sent shivers down my spine. Even August shrank away from him. Then they left, and we made our way home."

Frida flushed, and her stomach heaved. Josef blanched, turned away from Frida, and tried to hide the fear rising in his face. Neither glanced at the other as they dismissed Ida and retreated to the bedroom to get dressed for Friday night services. Absorbed in their own thoughts, they didn't speak until their carriage pulled up to the front door.

When they arrived at the synagogue, the mood was jubilant. For the remainder of the territories still held by the Confederates, it was only a matter of time until their surrenders came about. It was the fifth night of Passover, and the Torah portion Exodus 33:12–34:26, containing the Thirteen Attributes of Mercy, would be read. Calling for grace and compassion, its pertinence to healing the nation was not lost on the congregation.

After Rabbi Adler's Friday night sermon, the congregants gathered at the traditional Oneg Shabbat, the sharing of refreshments following a service. Conversation enthusiastically turned to the next morning when Temple Emanuel would honor a planned National

Day of Prayer to mark the end of the war. Many congregants, including Frida and Josef, came to worship only on occasional Saturdays, but the following morning would be special, and a large, joyous turnout was expected.

The night passed peacefully. When morning sunshine streamed through the window, Frida was surprised that Josef had already risen. She was disappointed that on this special morning he had not held her in anticipation of celebrations just ahead.

He was, as she knew he would be, downstairs sharing breakfast with the children. When she joined her family in the dining room, the conversation was animated as Josef answered a barrage of questions about the end of hostilities.

"Can we still play war?" asked nine-year-old Burke, who loved the authority he enjoyed when the games allowed him to be commander. "It's great to fight for the Union, right, August?"

"Nah," answered August. "I'm too old for that now. I'll be fourteen soon." He stood up from the table. "I'm going out."

"Where are you headed?" asked Frida, exchanging troubled glances with Josef. "You've been doing a lot of that kind of thing lately."

"Just out. I have messenger business to attend to," he said in a tone that left no room for negotiation.

The boy's sudden departure cast a pall over the dining room merriment. Josef was the first to recover. "Of course, Burke, you can still play war. Girls, you can still be the nurses and soldiers while Willie leads the horses to victory." Josef laughed when Burke sighed with relief.

"That's a good thing," Burke responded. "And now can we have our Saturday morning treats?"

As he did every weekend morning, Josef took down a bright red ceramic jar placed tauntingly on the top shelf of an open cupboard. "Okay," he began, "who wants to guess what today's treat is?"

The guesses were shouted noisily and all at once. "Well," said Josef, drawing out the suspense, "close your eyes and you will see . . . a fresh batch of . . . molasses drops. Handmade by the great Ida."

While the children gobbled up the drops and washed them down with glasses of milk, Frida and Josef retired once more to their bedroom to get ready for Passover services at the synagogue. They would join the congregation and then continue to the theater.

They arrived at the temple just as Rabbi Adler began the celebratory service. Moments later, a young man approached him. The rabbi looked at him askance. The man whispered something in the rabbi's ear, handed him copy of *The New York Herald*, and hurried away, visibly shaken.

A silence washed over the sanctuary as Adler's expression changed to shock, then to disbelief. Choking audibly, tears poured down his cheeks. When he managed to speak, his voice was brimming with despair. "President Lincoln is dead by an assassin's bullet."

A hush fell over the congregation. Suddenly, a man began to chant the Kaddish. Others in the sanctuary joined in until a sea of grieving voices filled the synagogue. It was the first time, for Emanuel, that the sacred prayer for the dead had ever been sung for anyone not of the Jewish religion.

That afternoon, members of the temple met in each other's homes to share their grief. Josef and Frida invited the Reinhards, the Rose Board, and prominent members of the temple to share a small repast and to determine what they could do in the face of this tragic turn of events. The congregants discussed how Lincoln had never turned away from Jewish concerns. He had granted multiple civil and military positions to qualified Hebrews; he initiated a law authorizing the first Jewish chaplains into the military; and he pardoned falsely accused Jewish soldiers from unjustified punishments.

Arnold Schubert, who had arrived shortly after the gathering began with Bertha on his arm, listened attentively while Lincoln's friendship to the Jews was extolled. When he spoke up, his voice trembled. "I'm sure you all remember General Grant's General Orders Number Eleven in '62, just a few short years ago."

A hush settled in as Arnold continued. "My parents were living in Paducah, Kentucky at the time. The order was based on claims that Jews were responsible for the illegal cotton trade going on between the Union and the South. It was professed that Jews were profiteers exploiting the boycotts and must be expelled from his military district which included Kentucky, Tennessee, and Mississippi. The fact was never considered that there were only four known Jews among something like two hundred profiteers who were dealing in the black market.

"My father was a retired doctor and was donating his time to healing however many troops as he could. He was treating a young soldier—I don't even know if the lad was Union or Confederate because Papa only saw need, not politics—when the order came that all Jews must leave Paducah."

A gasp rippled through the congregation. Arnold paused, tears filling his eyes. He drew in a deep breath, paused, and continued with a breaking voice. "It was the night before Hanukah. I had come in from New York to visit my family. A blizzard was raging but had not dampened the excitement of the holiday. We were preparing latkes, and scents of the delicious pancakes filled our house. My father had just come home, covered with the blood of his patients, and was about to change his clothes when we heard loud banging outside. At first, we thought that the century-old tree in our front garden had fallen in the storm. Then, we heard loud voices yelling, 'Jews out!' We suddenly realized that soldiers were hammering something on our front door and were screaming vile directives.

"'Jews, get out!' they insisted. 'Under orders of General Ulysses Grant, all Jews are to leave Paducah and take up residence elsewhere . . . immediately.'"

"'American soldiers!' shouted my mother in disbelief. Terrified, we huddled together until the troopers finally left. When we worked up the courage, we ventured outside and saw the notice nailed to our door. It stated that we Jews had twenty-four hours to leave Grant's military zone. There would be no exceptions. The penalty for disobeying the edict was immediate imprisonment."

Frida shuddered as Arnold continued his story. Her hand flew to her scar, and her mind stirred up the sometimes-uneasy security she lived with in America. *Jude bitch* punctured her thoughts as she tried, to no avail, to close her ears to Arnold's story—until Arnold described Lincoln's reaction to the directives. "When Lincoln learned of Grant's preposterous orders, he put a stop to the whole dreadful affair immediately."

Frida's head pounded, and her vision blurred as she fought to appear in control. In her mind, screams of soldiers back in Hamburg driving Jews out of their homes overwhelmed her. She began to shake. *I made a promise to God that I would return to him if he sent Mama to me, but maybe I should have followed my instincts and hidden my Judaism . . . I gave in to Josef and to circumstance. I may have endangered everything: my family, my business, our very lives. What will we do without a Lincoln to right such wrongs if they come again?*

"Are you all right?" asked Amalia, rushing to her side.

"I'm perfectly fine," Frida declared emphatically, willing herself out of fear. "Now let's start making plans to get us all through this terrible event."

Over the days that followed, the newspapers meticulously covered Lincoln's assassination. In articles bordered by heavy black mourning lines, they detailed how John Wilkes Booth was able to shoot the president at close range while he and Mrs. Lincoln were enjoying the comedy, *Our American Cousin.* They detailed how the accomplished actor, who was intimately familiar with the play, timed the fatal shot to coincide with its funniest moment. The audience, Booth knew, would erupt in raucous laughter and mitigate the gun's report.

Frida and Josef became glued to the papers to see if the assassin would be captured and punished, and they met daily with Emanuel members to organize mourning efforts. The word was that a funeral train would bring Lincoln's body to twelve major cities in seven states so people could properly grieve their fallen leader.

The Lincoln Special, as the train was called, would arrive in New York City on Monday, April 24th. It was nine cars long and would carry three hundred mourners. Lincoln's son, Willie, who had succumbed to typhoid three years earlier, had been disinterred and was also to be aboard the train. He would be reburied next to his father at the end of the tour.

Activity at Temple Emanuel was frenzied as the congregation donated money, services, and materials in preparation for the city's funeral efforts. Josef and Frida provided black bunting that would be hung from buildings all over Manhattan, as well as in homes, businesses, and houses of worship as people sought to express their grief. Ramping up production to a furious rate, Josef and Frida directed the mill to provide black plumes, pendant festoons, mourning badges, and huge banners with black crepe borders.

Rose Industries worked around the clock, but Frida managed to spare some moments with the children at home. The boys made small American flags with remnants from the mill, while the girls spent hours in the kitchen with Ida and Henry preparing cookies and small cakes for volunteers working on the funeral effort.

Bessie composed a song for Mrs. Lincoln. "She's so unhappy. Maybe a song will make her feel better," she said. At twelve, she had become a prolific composer and spent hours at her piano.

"We will send your song to the First Lady," Frida assured her daughter. "It will help her in her saddest hour."

On Monday morning, April 24th, Frida and Josef joined the Rein-hards for a small breakfast before making their way to City Hall where thousands were already lined up to pay their respects. The four waited in silence until they were finally admitted to the rotunda.

Frida clung to Josef as they approached the open coffin, which was guarded by an admiral on one end and a general at the other. The face they remembered from Lincoln's speech at Cooper Union faded into memory when they gazed upon the president's now-leaden features. His forehead receded sharply, and his eyes were sunk deep into their sockets. His cheekbones, so high in life, seemed morbidly prominent, and his face was pitted with death. Dressed in stark black, Lincoln's white turned-over collar and bright white gloves provided scarce relief to the engulfing finality of the coffin and seemed, to Frida, to be a mockery of the tragedy at hand.

"I thought he would destroy the country. I thought the war would destroy all we've worked for. I was wrong, I was wrong," she whispered to Josef as she patted her streaming eyes with a black-gloved hand. Shaken, she took Josef's arm and started to return to the carriage for the short trip home. What she saw astounded her. Thousands had arrived and were waiting outside City Hall in a quiet queue; most would never make it inside.

When they reached home, Josef and Frida discussed plans for Lincoln's funeral procession, which was to take place the next day. The temple had invited them to march with the Emanuel contin-gency along with dignitaries from synagogues and churches from all over the city. Still shaken by Arnold's story, and lingering doubts about her decision to be openly Jewish, Frida urged Josef to decline the invitation and to view the event with the children from home. Lincoln's cortege would pass by their house in midafternoon.

The next morning, the Roses awoke to a cloudless sky. Ordinarily, this would have been a school day. It would have begun with enticing the children to leave their snuggly beds. There would have been jostling over wash-up times, protests over which shirts or blouses to wear, and who could get to the breakfast table first.

Today, there would be no school. There was no bickering. There were no protests or discussions over who would get to pat Daisy, the puppy who had replaced Brunhilde after the beloved dog died of old age the previous December. Instead, somber faces gathered around the dining room table. The usual chatter was gone, replaced only by the sounds of clinking silverware and the occasional loud slurp from a glass of milk. The family ate quickly, and the children were dismissed to stay quietly in their rooms until it was time to review the procession.

As the afternoon progressed, bright sunshine bathed the streets. The first trees to bloom after the long winter season, saucer magnolias with their large cup-shaped pink flowers, sent dappled light through the streets and provided stark contrast to the black-draped buildings that lined Fifth Avenue. The air still bore the last crispness of winter but seemed to dance with the promise of spring warmth.

By 2:00 in the afternoon, the Rose household assembled on the sidewalk to await Lincoln's cortege. Dressed in funereal black, they presented a somber sight but blended seamlessly into the black-attired crowds lining the streets. Flags flew at half-mast, bells tolled, and drums rapped their mournful rolls as the procession wound its way north through the city.

August was determined to be the first to see the cortege. He scampered up a tree where he could see the procession approaching. After a long wait, he had news. "They're coming!" he shouted, as he spotted mounted police, state militia, infantry, and cavalry troops. They were followed by carriages, three abreast, that stretched out along the avenue and carried government officials, military personnel, and employees from key city and federal agencies. Religious

organizations, union and trade groups, clubs, and ethnic organizations turned out to march in great numbers.

"Look!" shouted August, as members of Tammany Hall came
into view. "There's Mr. Tweed and Mr. O'Flanagan. They're good
fellas, aren't they, Mama?"

He waved furiously, as Frida looked on with consternation folding her brow into straight lines, thankful that they seemed not to
notice the fourteen-year-old in the tree. *They are certainly invaluable
for our business, but they're not good for my son, not good at all,* she
thought. *I'll have to watch August more carefully.*

As the hearse passed, men removed their hats and children came
to unaccustomed attention. Women wept, and strangers comforted
one another. Many threw flowers. The clip-clop of horses' hooves and
the rhythmic echoes of marching feet were punctuated by drumrolls,
and marching bands delivered mournful dirges. Occasionally, an
early robin flew overhead, its bright spring call offering lonely hope
to the somber procession.

Frida was shocked when she saw that just a small contingency of
only three hundred Blacks brought up the rear.

That night, after the children were in bed, Frida and Josef retreated
to their room. Overwhelmed by the events of the day, they fell into
each other's arms.

"He was fifty-six years old," Frida whispered. She sighed deeply,
clinging to Josef. "Promise me you will live a longer life, Josef. Promise me that."

Josef put his arms around her and rocked her gently. "We'll both
live a long time, my darling girl. Both of us. I know it!"

During the night, Frida woke frequently as images of the last
two days invaded her dreams. Night sounds of the house turned into
death throes; the sputtering of embers in the bedroom's fireplace

became snare drums; a breeze floating through the curtains became the *whoosh* of horses' tails as they proceeded up Fifth Avenue.

When morning finally dawned, Frida gently woke Josef. As she stroked his hair, now sprouting a plethora of silver strands, she spoke softly. "Josef," she said, "I ran into Gus Cairny a few days ago when I was shopping with the girls. He's a manager for John Morrissey, the owner of the new racetrack at Saratoga, and he invited us to be guests at one of the resorts on the lake. I had reservations about accepting—I worry about exposing the children to racing, and to Tammany, but we can keep a close eye on our brood and warn Ida and Liesel to do the same. Saratoga has so much to offer. As Cairny pointed out, the hot springs will be healing for Gertrude and Louise. There's sailing, swimming, horseback riding, and sports for the children, and concerts, balls, and entertainment for us."

Josef rolled over and looked into Frida's eyes. "I don't know, Frida. We already have overwhelming business and social obligations that we must honor. It would mean more obligation to Cairny, to Tammany."

Frida's eyes grew cold. "We have no choice, Josef. We cannot afford to cross Tammany. Gus made it clear that he expects us to join him for a few days in July when General Grant and his wife will be his guests. Mr. Morrissey wants to have them meet us."

The color drained from Josef's face. "But you abhor what Grant did in Kentucky just a short time ago," he protested.

Josef is right, she thought. *I do abhor what he did, but the connection could put Rose Industries in a commanding position.*

"Grant could be very important to us in the future, Josef. It's business. We do in life what we must to survive," she said, her voice firm. Her eyes burned with determination like diamond pinheads in a cloudless night. She lowered her face to within inches of Josef's, her hot breath coming from behind clenched teeth. "I told Gus we will be there. And we will."

CHAPTER 28

Frida

"It's called the Queen of Spas for good reason," said Ernst Reinhard when Frida and Josef told him of their plans to take the family to Saratoga. "Taking the waters will do Gertrude and Louise immeasurable good," he declared. "It's an amazing place. I was there last summer. The geology is fascinating. Hot, bubbling water from miles down forces its way through ancient cracks and makes its way to the surface, as if for our pleasure. The bathhouses are built so that the spring waters merge into tubs—perfect for the girls to soak in. And not bad for you and Josef, either. It's doctor's orders. I insist you go."

By July, the shock of Lincoln's death almost three months behind them, Gus Cairny had made reservations for the Rose family at Saratoga's finest hotel, Union Hall, and the household was ready for the trip. In the past year, business had grown still again. Using newly developed standard men's measurements, Rose Industries now produced complete ready-made uniforms for the armed forces. Profits catapulted, as did increased Tammany payments, when the military seized upon the innovative availability of well-constructed, pre-made jackets, pants, and capes suitable for almost all military personnel.

At home, Frida had hired an in-house seamstress to outfit the girls and herself in the latest fashions. Extra seamstresses were now brought in to complete enough apparel for the Saratoga scene. Bolts of fine, specially designed damasks, silks, laces, velvets, and organzas were stashed all over the house for dresses, and baskets of trims, imported buttons, feathers, and gemstone adornments were stashed out of the reach of curious children.

As the departure date for Saratoga came closer, Frida purchased several huge trunks that would accompany the family to the resort. For Frida and the girls, there were hogsheads for walking and traveling dresses, others for breakfast and teatime, and still more for yachting, horse races, and lawn games. The ball gowns Frida would use for the nightly dances held at Union Hall took up several more hogsheads. Separate luggage pieces were packed with undergarments such as ribbed corsets, pantaloons, and nightclothes. Trunks packed with clothes and accessories for Josef and the boys completed the luggage. Everything would be shipped early by train and delivered to Union Hall in time for the family's arrival.

The day before the July 4th celebrations, the household burst into a frenzy of activity just before dawn.

"Everybody up!" shouted Liesel, as she made the rounds of the children's rooms. "Get dressed and come for breakfast. The carriages will be here in an hour to take us to the pier."

"It's too early," moaned Bessie.

"Up, up, up anyway," said Frida as she walked into her daughter's bedroom. "The boat to Saratoga won't wait for sleepyheads."

By the time the Roses arrived at the foot of Debrosses Street for a 7:00 a.m. departure, the sun was already warming the city streets. It promised a clear day, perfect for the trip up the Hudson River. The *Chauncey Vibbard,* a new sidewall steamboat built the previous year, was known for its incredible speed. At 265 feet long and 35 feet wide, it traveled 25 miles an hour and carried up to 2,000 passengers.

The *Vibbard* made an impressive sight. Thirty-foot paddle wheels on her sides were all but dwarfed by her chimneys, which were already belching steam by the time the Roses boarded. Passengers included those who, like the Roses, would travel to Catskill Mountain resorts, but also those seeking to enjoy day trips to places like

Bear Mountain, Poughkeepsie, and Rhinebeck. In stark contrast, a company of wounded and battle-weary soldiers was lined up to sail north on the *Vibbard*. It would carry them to base camps and hospitals or, hopefully, home.

Once onboard, Liesel and Ida, pushing the twins' wheelchairs, followed the children as they explored the ship. There were card rooms, writing rooms, games for youngsters, and musical groups performing everywhere. Liesel and Ida assured Frida and Josef they would keep a close eye on their charges during the seven-hour trip to its end stop at Albany.

Delighted to have time to themselves, Josef and Frida strolled along the *Vibbard*'s deck to breathe in the fresh air and feel the sun warm their skin. A gentle breeze rolled off the Hudson as the ship churned north up the river. Frida lay her head on Josef's shoulder as they cruised along the river's gentle blue waters.

"I've sometimes thought of home through the years. This feels like Germany, doesn't it, Josef? The gentle slopes, the birds singing overhead, the lapping of the water against the ship's hull bring me back to the Elbe and to the German countryside. Do you ever miss it? Miss Germany?" she asked, sudden tears of homesickness stinging her eyes in an unwelcome invasion.

"Yes, I do," Josef said quietly. "I wonder what's become of my father and mother, my brother. Are they alive? Are they well? I've tried so often to reach out to them, but my letters have gone unanswered. It is a sadness I must bear, I suppose, for the rest of my life."

"We've both had similar sadness to bear, Josef. I wonder if your parents ever read the letters. They didn't return them, so that means that they may have." She paused, tears threatening to spill down her cheeks. "But tell me, Josef. If you had to it all over, would you do things the same way?" Frida asked, half afraid of Josef's answer.

A long hush fell between them. Josef held her closer and kissed her hair. "I wouldn't change a thing, Frida, not a single thing."

As if on cue, August and Willie emerged from around a corner.

"Come quickly!" they shouted. "Bessie is singing, and the crowd loves her."

Frida and Josef followed the boys along the broad promenade into the lounge, which spanned the width of the *Vibbard*. Its ceilings seemed to reach beyond the room's very dimensions. Chairs and sofas covered in fine velvets and brocades were clustered in conversational groupings, and several gas chandeliers featuring crystal pendeloques reigned over the opulent space.

At the far end of the room, a small figure sat at a grand piano so highly polished that it mirrored the walls surrounding it. The young girl smiled and paused, with a nod of her head, to acknowledge Josef and Frida before she started to play Beethoven's "Für Elise." Frida's heart swelled as Bessie's long fingers ran lightly over the ivory keys. A hush fell over the guests as Bessie's sweet, bright voice suddenly broke out above the piano's complex tones in verses she had written to complement the mellow Beethoven notes.

After Bessie completed several pieces, a rotund man with a shiny bald head came over to Frida and Josef. He smiled warmly, extended his hand, and introduced himself. "I'm George Seaman," he said. "The young lady at the piano is extraordinarily skilled, don't you think?"

Josef beamed. "I agree," he said, his posture straightening. He drew close to Frida. "In fact, she is our daughter."

"What a coincidence," George Seamen said. "I've been wondering who she is. I am most gratified to meet you. I have great interest in the young lady. Are you by chance heading to Saratoga today, or will you be disembarking at another spot along the way?"

When Frida and Josef said that they were heading to the Union Hall hotel for a holiday, George Seaman was delighted. "Splendid," he said, smiling widely. "I am the hotelier, the grand manager of the Union and a friend of Gus Cairny's. Are you familiar with Gus?"

"Oh, yes," said Josef, throwing Frida a sidelong glance. "We know him well."

"Good, good, good," said George Seaman.

Frida suspected that the man enjoyed repeating words three times and stifled a giggle.

"Gus is certainly a key part of our endeavors. But on a different note—there's no pun intended here—surely, you've heard of the new Leland Opera House on Union Hall's grounds? With your permission, I will tell Gus and the Leland Brothers, the hotel's owners, about your young lady. They are always interested in angels' voices. In the meantime, will you join me for a peach schnapps on the deck? The views are lovely and the refreshments plentiful."

A few hours later, the Roses arrived in Albany, where they transferred to the Saratoga and Schenectady Railroad for the last leg of their journey. The children had never been on a train before. They spent the ride excitedly looking out the windows and pointing out the sights as they whizzed by meadows, woods, farms, and towns. When the family finally reached Union Hall, dusk had enveloped Saratoga and stars twinkled in a violet sky. As their carriage made its way up the long tree-lined driveway to the hotel's entrance, they passed formal gardens in full bloom and fountains whose waters leaped twenty feet into the air.

As the carriage rounded a gentle bend, the main building appeared. Four stories high in some places and five in others, the H-shaped hotel featured a tall tower on each corner from which large American flags flew.

Gus Cairny stepped down from the columned veranda at the front of the hotel when the Roses arrived.

"I'm delighted you're here," he said, extending his hand to Josef.

Josef returned the gesture in a professional manner. "We are too, Gus. We are looking forward to our visit."

"I've booked a guest cottage for you," Cairny added. "You will enjoy eight spacious and airy rooms especially designed for families like yours. When you are settled in, I can arrange to have dinner sent to you—you must be exhausted—or you can be my guests in the dining room."

Grateful after a long day traveling, Frida and Josef accepted Cairny's offer to dine in.

"Very well," he said. "A butler will accompany the chef when he presents your meal. Tomorrow, however, I would like you to join me in greeting General Ulysses Grant when he arrives on the 7:00 p.m. train from Lake George."

As Cairny left, Frida's thoughts raced back to Arnold's story. *Will Grant realize we are Jewish and greet us with disdain? We have no choice but to meet with him. The military connection will be invaluable and will help immeasurably to promote our products. Besides, I wonder if he has an excuse for what he did. Hmm, that's an interesting thought.*

The next morning, July 26th, dawned brightly. As the sun rose over the lake, blush-pink clouds filled the sky promising another beautiful day. The children awoke early, eager to start their Saratoga adventures. August and Willie were particularly excited.

"Papa and Mama, guess what? Mr. Cairny invited me to the stables," Willie pronounced. "He says I have a jockey's body, and he's going to teach me to work with the thoroughbreds."

"I'm going to the stables, too," August chimed in, not to be outdone by his younger brother. "We're going to watch the horses train and see which one will run the fastest at the races."

"Stay right here, boys, while I talk to your father." She took Josef's arm and the two walked away from the children.

"Josef," she said, "I am concerned about the boys spending time with Cairny and his cohorts. But how can we deprive them of the opportunity to see the horses? Willie, especially, is so excited, and he does have a jockey's slim build."

Josef steepled his chin. "Yes," he said, looking deeply into Frida's eyes. "We're here despite any misgivings we may have had earlier. I agree. We can't reasonably deprive them."

A few minutes later, they returned to the boys who were pacing back and forth.

"We have decided you may go with Mr. Cairny. Just be sure you obey Ida," warned Frida. "Liesel will take care of the other children, especially the twins. They tire easily and may need to rest, especially after they've taken their scheduled baths."

After they all left, Frida dressed in a day gown of white and blue organza. Off the shoulder with short, ruffled sleeves, it presented with a cool effect perfect for the heat promised later in the day. Cairny had sent over a suggested schedule of events that included breakfast in the hotel garden followed by coffee on the piazza, a stroll through the grounds, and an afternoon carriage ride led by horses adorned in elaborate finery. A visit to the lake, where an orchestra would send the sweet sounds of Beethoven, Schumann, Verdi, and Mozart across the water to complete the festivities.

Frida and Josef returned to their cottage in time for a nap before dinner in the main dining room, where they met the children who excitedly reported the details of their day. Under Liesel's watchful eyes, the children had settled themselves under an oak tree on the shore. The beauty of the grounds had captured Elsie's imagination, and she created a tale that caught all their imaginations. Under its spell, they had created a short play combining their talents. Elsie wrote, Burke sketched, and Bessie created songs that brought the "Legend of the Saratoga Fairies," as they called their masterpiece, to life.

Willie and August were jubilant about their afternoon at the stables. "I have decided," Willie crowed. "I am going to be a jockey. Mr. Cairny says there's jockey training in Coney Island back in the city where jockeys will teach me to ride. Can I do it, Mama and Papa? And can August come, too? Please? If you let us, we'll even go to bed early!"

When Frida and Josef broke into wide smiles of approval, the boys whooped for joy and made all sorts of promises to be good forever.

Only the twins were sullen and distant.

"Why do I have to drink mineral water?" complained Louise, scrunching her face. "I don't like it."

"Me either," echoed Gertrude. "It has bubbles in it."

"Yes, I'm afraid you must drink it," she said, kissing the tops of their heads. "Dr. Reinhard says you each need to drink a glass in the morning before breakfast and several times more during the day. He says it will help you to get better." Frida paused. She allowed her eyes to twinkle merrily. "You like to play tickling games, right?" she said.

"Oh, yes," the girls answered, almost in unison.

"Well," Frida said, her mouth arranged in a smile. "Think of the bubbles as tickling you—like this," she laughed, as she reached out and sent the children into paroxysms of giggles.

By dinnertime, everyone had napped, and the family set off to the immense dining room. With its one-thousand-seat capacity, long tables were separated by a ten-foot passageway down the center of the space. Lush carpets, imposing chandeliers, floor-to-ceiling frescoes, and mirrors set off by hundreds of gas lamps created a rich ambience. Salads and appetizers preceded multiple entrée choices that included delicacies such as baked bass with port wine sauce, chicken pie French style, braised duck, and stewed mutton with potatoes.

Much to the children's delight, pineapple pie and Charlotte-Russe-a-la-Vanilla, a chilled confection of whipped cream, lady-fingers, and raspberries, were offered to finish the meal. Happily, they retired to the cottage with Liesel and Ida while Frida and Josef remained to chat with other guests in one of the Union's private parlors until the nightly ball began.

The next morning, July 27, Frida and Josef left the twins and Elsie with Liesel and Ida and headed into Saratoga. The city had been elaborately prepared for General Grant's evening arrival. Oil paintings of the general flanked by red, white, and blue bunting adorned buildings, and a cannon fired welcoming rounds across the lake. A band drummed out patriotic songs, its beat seeming almost to lift the streets in undulating waves as visiting men, women, and children from multiple countries joined Americans in anticipation of the general's visit. Frida, Josef, and the children arrived at the train depot to join the welcoming crowd just as Grant's train pulled in.

"Is that him?" asked Burke, his sketch pad in tow to capture the scene. He pointed to a man about five feet, eight inches tall with a slightly stooped build. The general's 135-pound frame supported a fine head with russet-colored hair, blue-gray eyes, fair skin, and a straight, bearded and mustached chin. His wide, furrowed brow gave him a contemplative affect but softened as he gazed at his wife, Julia, with noticeably deep affection. Grant kept Julia's elbow close to his side as they made their way through the throbbing crowd to a carriage that would take them to Congress Hall, the large hotel on Broadway where they would be staying.

"I thought he would be a bigger man, a man with a cruel face," whispered Frida to Josef, her voice so low Josef could barely hear her. "And his wife? She isn't at all pretty, is she? Her eyes are crossed, and her figure is much fuller than I would have expected."

"Reserve judgment," admonished Josef. "Cairny has arranged a private meeting with the Grants tomorrow evening. We'll see what they have to say then."

The next morning brought a hot day filled with swimming and sailing. After much cajoling from August and Willie, Josef and Frida finally consented and allowed the boys to accompany them to the track. When they arrived in early afternoon, four thousand spectators had crowded into the tiered timber grandstand. Cairny, who was seated with them, had arranged prime seats at center track. The boys clamored to take in every detail of the odds board and the paddocks where the jockeys were saddling and parading their steeds.

"Look, Mama! Look, Papa!" shouted Willie. "There's the jockey who helped me ride on his horse yesterday."

Willie waved to the jockey who was exercising his stallion. Dressed in gold silks and breeches with a blue helmet, vest, and gloves, he cut a dashing figure as he mounted Whisper Nights, a magnificent chestnut thoroughbred. The jockey squatted high in his stirrups, waved to Willie, and pranced in front of the paddock in anticipation of the coming race. The two-year-old animal's coat glistened in the sunlight, and its muscles rippled under its hide, tensing and relaxing with every pace.

Soon, the crowd went wild as the horses and their riders queued up in their assigned places. Willie kept his eye on Whisper Nights as he pranced restlessly in anticipation of the races. Suddenly, a cheer went up as a starter sauntered to the gate. Fifteen thoroughbreds and their jockeys lined up behind the rope barriers and waited until the starter raised—and then lowered—his flag to signal the opening of the race. Then, they were off in the two-and-a-quarter-mile heat, the thunder of their hoofs reverberating throughout the stadium.

Willie and August stood on their seats, fists pumping, and cheered Whisper Nights to go faster and faster and faster—until he was only a half-head behind and burst through the finish line to come in at a close second. The boys shouted and hugged each other in jubilation.

"What would we have won if we had bet?" August asked Gus Cairny after the races were over.

"The purse was twelve hundred dollars," Cairny said. "That's a great deal of money. Winning is everything in racing. That's why we call it the 'Sport of Kings.' "

Frida cringed, trying not to let her alarm show. *He's not a good influence on our sons. We didn't bet, but did we make a terrible mistake exposing them to this environment? I can only hope this will go over the boys' heads.*

The next evening, a string orchestra was playing a waltz when Frida and Josef joined Gus Cairny at a reserved table in the hotel's main dining room. "I expect Ulysses and Julia at any moment," Cairny said, scanning the huge room.

Suddenly, loud applause resounded through the cavernous space as the general appeared with his wife on his arm. The matre'd accompanied the guests of honor to an elaborately set table designated by an American flag, where Cairny introduced them to the Roses and other guests carefully chosen to sit with the Grants. Frida was seated next to Julia. While the men listened intently to Grant's accounts of the war—particularly of the decisive victory at Appomattox—Frida and Julia became engrossed in conversation. Both women wore native flowers in their hair and roses in their sashes which started an intense conversation about their shared love of horticulture. "Have you toured the grounds here yet? The gardens seem lovely," Julia said, her delicate hands whisking stray dessert crumbs from her lips.

"Yes, I have," Frida answered. "They are beautiful. Perhaps we could enjoy a stroll after dinner?"

Julia's face lit up. "We can walk to the lake," she said. "Mr. Cairny has arranged a sail before we attend a performance of *Colleen Bawd* at the new Opera House. Please join us."

"We would be delighted," answered Frida, her mind working. *Spending time with a man who despises Jews will not be easy, but it is important for the business. I knew it would be difficult when I accepted Cairny's invitation, but it is a matter of practicality. I always do what I have to do!*

As dusk settled in, there was time for a private conversation with the Grants immediately after the sail. They met in a private parlor just off the hotel lobby. The fresh air had both invigorated and relaxed the general, and he was in a receptive frame of mind. Frida waited for the perfect moment.

"General," she said, as he settled into a plump sofa, loosening his tie and running his hands through his rumpled hair. "I have a matter of grave concern. It is about what happened in Paducah, about General Orders #11."

An uncomfortable silence came over the small room. Grant shifted his weight and flinched ever so slightly as he spoke. "It is a matter of great consternation to me, as it is to the Jewish population of our great country. I can only explain what happened as an oversight for which I hold full responsibility. I signed the order, which was prepared by a subordinate, in great haste, without reading it. It is an action I deeply regret."

Josef glared at Frida. He wrung his hands and his brown eyes conveyed outrage, as if to say, *How could you bring that up, Frida?*

Frida ignored him, her heart pounding as she contemplated her next move. It took several moments to compose herself. When she finally spoke, her voice was deceivingly calm and firm. "You know, General, I hope you are aware of the great service our company, Rose Industries, has contributed to the war effort. We have provided the military—your armies—with the highest quality uniforms available anywhere on earth. No compromises have been made in making sure your soldiers have every comfort and protection we can provide in facing the enemy on the field. Profit has not been our priority; patriotism has."

"Yes, Mrs. Rose, I am aware of your enterprise, and you have my word that I will do everything in my power to extend your contract indefinitely. I have been urged to run for president after Andrew Johnson's term is over; should I win, you will win, as well."

Julia glanced at an ornate clock on a wall near the room's French doors and was the first to rise from her chair. "Shall we retire for a bit now to change before we go to the Opera House? Frida, I am delighted you will join us for the rest of the evening's events. I am enjoying our newfound acquaintance."

"It will be our pleasure," answered Frida. *This is working out just as I hoped. Rose Industries is rising to national prominence. One must always do what one must do.*

That evening at the Opera House, sixteen hundred bejeweled and coiffed patrons fluttered their fans and soon hushed their conversations. Frida shifted in her shallow seat, the metal of her cage crinoline uncomfortable against her legs. She brushed back a stray tendril from the braided bun at the nape of her neck and breathed in deeply, trying without success to prevail over the stifling humidity.

When the outer curtain rose, her mouth fell open in disbelief. Instead of the gathering onstage of the ensemble, a piano stood singularly under a gas lamp that cast a warm circle of light around the instrument.

From backstage, George Seaman emerged to speak to the crowd. "Ladies and Gentlemen," he said, "before we begin our featured opera, I would like you to welcome Miss Bessie Rose, a young lady who promises to become a goddess extraordinaire in the music world. I am sure you will enjoy her as much as I did when I recently came across her special talent."

Frida's face registered total surprise. She turned and whispered to Josef, who also appeared to be in shock. "This was certainly a well-kept secret; our little girl has astounded us. She's growing up faster than we ever could have realized!"

Josef took Frida's hand and squeezed it. "It's too fast, isn't it?" he agreed, a wide smile crossing his face. "She never ceases to amaze us!"

When Bessie, clad in a white frock with scarlet trim, stepped onto the stage, shallow obligatory applause and murmurs of annoyance rippled through the audience. Undaunted, she bowed gracefully, took a seat at the piano, and allowed the patrons to become quiet before she began to play. As soon as her sweet voice mingled with the tones of the exceptional instrument, restlessness ceased, and the mesmerized audience became enthralled with her performance, tears running down many cheeks. When she finished, a standing ovation thundered through the chamber until Gus Cairny closed the curtain in readiness for the main performance.

Julia Grant turned to Frida, her expression radiant. "She is exquisite, Frida. A welcome addition to the music world."

Frida blushed deeply. "No one could be more pleased at this performance than we are," she said. "Our daughter has surprised and delighted us."

As Bessie left the stage, the curtain closed, then opened again a few minutes later as the opera began. Grant's party stayed through the second act, at which point a military aide accompanied them, as well as the Roses, to the ball given in their honor at the Congress Hotel.

It was a gala affair tastefully decorated with flags and bunting, tables set with the finest accessories, and spirits specially selected to complement sumptuous menu items. Elegantly ornamented women dressed in satins, laces, silks, and velvets whirled in their men's arms as an orchestra played waltzes, quadrilles, and polkas until the guests were exhausted and ready to retire.

As they started to leave, Julia offered Frida her delicate, white-gloved hand. "It has been my privilege to spend time with you, Frida. Hopefully, we will meet again, perhaps even with our children. From what we have discussed, they seem to have much in common."

Grant shook Josef's hand. "A pleasure, sir. We look forward to doing more business with you."

Frida turned to leave, a wry smile on her face. *We have won his good graces. Excellent! It will be worth any discomfort with this meeting. And then some.*

As Frida and Josef headed back to the cottage, they were filled with anticipation and pride in Bessie's achievement. Suddenly, Frida was overcome with a sense of foreboding. The moon had receded behind a cloud and cast long fingers of pale, muted light along the landscape. Somewhere in the distance, a loon sent its forlorn cry through the night, and an owl hooted from the canopy of the trees. Frida held onto Josef's arm, urging him to walk more quickly.

As they approached the cottage, they heard Gertrude crying. Josef burst open the door and ran upstairs, Frida following close behind. Gertrude's swollen fingers, which had recently developed open sores on their tips, had locked in a claw-like grip, and she was howling in pain.

"I was trying to dress my doll," she sobbed. "And then my fingers wouldn't move, and they hurt. Now it's hurting up my elbow and down my legs. My stomach hurts, too. Make the pain stop, Mama, make it stop!"

Frida rushed to Gertrude's side. She put her arms around the stricken child and cradled her head. When Gertrude pulled away, screaming in agony, Frida glanced down at her bosom. A large clump of Gertrude's hair had fallen out and was covering the bodice of her gown.

"Get a doctor, Josef! NOW!" she screamed. "Gus will know one. Just get someone, anyone!"

Twenty minutes later, Gus Cairny arrived with Dr. Edmund Wurman, a young physician who was working in town for the summer. His wiry frame seemed almost to totter as he entered the cottage.

Frida was shocked by his youth but was immediately won over when the physician spoke. His voice rumbled from so deep inside him it sounded as if his very soul was spilling forth. Immaculately dressed, even at this late hour, his deft fingers went to work immediately to determine what could be done for Gertrude—and for Louise, who was complaining that her hands and feet hurt, too. He examined both children, the expression on his chiseled face serious.

"I notice that the skin on their hands and feet has hardened and is quite swollen. These small red spots and the hard lumps on their faces are of concern, as are their weakened muscles."

Frida spoke in low tones as she told Dr. Wurman of Ernst Reinhard's diagnosis. The practitioner nodded in solemn agreement as he reached into his black bag and pulled out a slender bottle of the popular Mrs. Winslow's Soothing Syrup. On the front was a logo depicting a mother cuddling an infant in embroidered, white swaddling clothes; several younger children were at her side creating an idyllic domestic scene.

"If you read the label," Dr. Wurman said, "you will see that the syrup reduces inflammation, gives tone and energy to the system, and provides relief from pain within minutes. It will also relax the girls and reduce their anguish."

With great ceremony, he opened the bottle and poured some of the straw-colored liquid into a silver spoon. He administered the first dose to Gertrude, who wrinkled her nose at the anise-flavored potion but swallowed obediently. Louise did the same.

"I suggest that you prolong your stay here so that Gertrude and her sister can continue to partake of the healing mineral waters. I will be glad to check in on them every day if, of course, if that would be desirable to you," the physician pronounced.

"It would be a welcome development, Doctor," said Josef, relief flooding his features.

Edmund Wurman placed his slender fingers on his chin. "You must realize that both girls will need constant care," he said. "I can be available to you on a daily basis, both here and back in the city if you like."

He glanced at Frida who nodded her head affirmatively. Her color had faded, and her eyes had glossed over. Her hands trembled. *We knew this would happen. But it's too soon*, she thought. *I suppose it would always be too soon.*

"Mrs. Rose," continued the doctor, "I highly recommend that you take Mrs. Winslow's Syrup, as well. It does wonders to calm the nerves and the bowels when they become rigid with nervousness. It consists of morphine, sodium carbonate, and spirits derived from sweet fennel and ammonia water. It will soothe your worries. You can get it at any pharmacy or grocers, or I can easily arrange a steady supply for you when we all return to Manhattan."

As Dr. Wurman promised, Gertrude and Louise relaxed within minutes of taking Mrs. Winslow's syrup. Frida was able to put them to bed without the fretfulness they usually experienced at night. She kissed them both, pulled the covers over them gently, and left their room on tiptoe.

Outside their door, she hesitated. Then, she quietly turned the bedroom doorknob and stole into their room. Soundlessly, she made her way to the high dresser on the adjacent wall. She took the syrup bottle, opened the cap, and poured some of the potion into a spoon. She lifted it to her mouth—and then hesitated.

I don't want a potion to calm me, she thought. *Besides, I can always take it later. I will sleep. And, despite everything, I will sleep well.*

Moments later, she crept into the room where Josef was snoring lightly. Slowly, she undressed and crawled into the bed next to her husband. Spooning against him, she wrapped her arms around his body, her tears tumbling across his back. He stirred and turned to hold her in his arms.

This is the only potion I need, she thought, as her eyes dried and grew heavy. *It always has been. It always will be.*

PART FOUR:
1870–1872

August

It was March of 1870. At eighteen years of age, August had become a full-grown man. He preened in front of the mirror and liked what he saw. In the last five years, he had developed an impressive body with muscles that rippled through his frock coat as he moved. His side-parted blond hair was thin, but stylishly oiled, and framed an intelligent face with close-cropped whiskers and a trim mustache. A large Adam's apple bounced up and down in his thick neck when he spoke, his voice deep and pleasing but with a hint of gravel.

"Yes, August," he said, as he gazed at his image. "For some reason, you don't look like anyone else in the family, but you *are* a dapper fellow, so don't worry about that!"

As he entered his mother's room, August smiled. As usual, she was sitting by a window enjoying the morning sun. She was holding the September issue of *Godey's Ladies Book*. He knew she enjoyed reading the magazine's fiction, poetry, and opinion features, but mostly she loved its tinted fashion plates depicting the latest in women's styles. It was from these plates that, like most women in her circle, his mother derived her fashion inspirations.

With its wide distribution, *Godey's* had inspired August to garner advertising contracts from his clients and to compile ads for prominent newspapers like *The New York Times* and *The New York Herald*. Burke added complementary drawings and elegant script to the copy. The two created Rose Advertising Agency, which now employed eleven workers and was widely sought to create publicity for local merchants. A Rose mail-order subsidiary was in the works and scheduled to open within weeks.

"My son," Frida said happily as August entered the room. "How handsome you look! Shall we go together to this morning's board meeting? By the way, we made the papers again today." She held up newspaper articles that described Rose Industries' newest endeavor.

After Grant was elected president in '68, he kept his promise to the Roses. He continued the military's contracts with Rose Industries that had grown to include the manufacture of uniforms for new markets; coachmen, doormen, and even the police placed recurring orders. "WE MAKE UNIFORMS for EVERY PROFESSION and EVERY OCCASION" now appeared on Rose Industries' signs. Men's sizes and cuts did not require the same degree of customization as women's fashions. The manufacture of ready-made men's clothing, August had convinced Josef, was a natural expansion. A style enthusiast himself, he had found that men liked the idea of forfeiting their tailors in favor of well-made apparel available on demand. New department stores like Lord & Taylor, Bloomingdale's, Brooks Brothers, and A. T. Stewart's were popping up in the city; all expressed interest in buying ready-mades from Rosewear, as the newest division of Rose Industries would be known.

"No, Mama, I will go to the meeting on my own," August replied. "I have an appointment with Willy immediately afterward. As you know, he has accepted an offer as a trainer and jockey at Jerome Park Raceway in the Bronx. He wants to talk to me about manufacturing jockey apparel and horse blankets."

"So, I'll see you at this afternoon's board meeting. Will you join us later for dinner?" Frida asked hopefully.

"No, I have plans," August said briskly, making it clear that he did not wish to be questioned.

Frida winced. She straightened her shoulders and looked unflinchingly into August's eyes. "I hope you intend to see Selma

Richter, who I've been telling you about. As I've told you before, she is a catch, that one. Her father is a top industrialist and very powerful in Washington. You will marry her someday. It will be important for you, August, important for all of us."

August stood tall, straightened his shoulders, and left the room. *I will not let Mama bully me, but she's right. Selma is a catch, and her family ties would be good for business. Mama has said that I would learn to love her. Perhaps she is onto something.*

As August entered Delmonico's, the lunch crowd was just arriving. Joining the diners were bankers, industrialists, and chief executives from all over the city who were gathering to move Manhattan's thriving economy forward. "I'm meeting the board," August told the maître'd who recognized him immediately.

"Ah, yes," he said, bowing slightly to August. "They are all waiting for you."

As August moved through the busy dining room, he stopped to shake hands and exchange greetings with prominent businessmen. When he got to the table Josef always reserved for meetings, Josef, Frida, and the board were already there. August made his way to a seat next to Josef, who was leading the meeting. He stopped to briefly kiss his mother's cheek, shook his father's hand, and sat down.

After a long lunch of roast duck and endive salad, the group began their business agenda. Josef took the floor first. "I am proud to announce that as of this week, August will oversee acquisitions for Rose Industries."

Applause and speeches ensued and continued through dessert. August outlined several new policies. "We want to be known for our customer service," he said. "Therefore, we will institute a generous return policy. 'One hundred-percent satisfaction, or your money back' will be our mantra."

An uproar over such unprecedented policy erupted. Bertha and Amalia were particularly upset.

"Look," Bertha implored, "Amalia and I know what goes into creating bridal fabrics, especially fabrics that are custom designed."

Amalia laughed. "I must have changed my mind a hundred times for my gown. Bertha experienced the same thing before she married Arnold."

Frida chuckled. "Ah, yes," she said. "We went through at least a dozen fabric designs for each of you. But, I must add, you both made gorgeous brides."

Amalia interrupted the conversation, which had turned quickly into a merry discussion of wedding memories for the two sisters. "But seriously," she argued, "suppose each time a bride had an idea for a fabric, she ordered cloth knowing it could be returned. We'd have a backlog of unsaleable merchandise."

"Point well taken," offered August. "So, let's not make returns available for everything. We can implement the policy, though, for specific, ready-made products that can easily be resold."

Arnold took the floor next. "I'll investigate any legal ramifications that may occur. Such a practice is unheard of, as far as I know. But it should be an incredibly lucrative move."

At this point, Josef turned the meeting over to August, who presided over the table with wit and charm. After a few hours, the group left to go their separate ways. When August turned down his offer to share a carriage for the trip home, Josef was visibly disappointed.

I'm a grown man, August thought. *I'll do as I please.*

As Josef's carriage turned the corner, August hailed his own cab. He directed the driver to an uptown address and stopped in front of an imposing, free-standing house. The butler greeted him in front of the mansion's double-doors. "It is pleasant to see you, Mr. Rose," he said. "But you are early. Please wait in the foyer until Miss Richter is ready."

August fumed impatiently while he paced the marble-floored

entrance hall. A large, circular mahogany table with a wide, inlaid rim took up most of the space. Large urns of sunflowers and tall vases of asters, dahlias, and chrysanthemums were placed strategically throughout the room, their funereal fragrance filling the grand entryway.

After fifteen or so minutes had passed, Selma appeared at the top of the elegant staircase. Heels clicking and echoing, she descended, carrying an ermine stole over one arm in preparation for the cool evening expected ahead. Dressed in sapphire blue, her black hair shone brightly against her pale skin and emphasized her icy-blue eyes. She offered August her hand, and the two made their way to a waiting carriage that would whisk them to a dinner taking place in the home of Abraham Oakey Hall, the distinguished mayor of the city of New York and a close affiliate of Boss Tweed. Dubbed "Elegant Oakey," the flamboyant mayor, known for his trademark pince-nez glasses, enjoyed lavish parties and brilliant company.

This extravagant affair was no different. While butlers circulated among the guests, August secured Selma's elbow and navigated her through the crowd to engage with the high-ranking politicians and entrepreneurs circulating through the mansion's ballroom. William Tweed, sporting his infamous 10.5-carat-diamond stickpin, caught his eye.

"Boss Tweed," August said, extending his hand. "How good to see you."

Tweed looked Selma up and down, his eyes riveted on her slim waist and full bosom, before he returned August's handshake. "I attend all of Oakey's affairs," he said. "I suspect that from all I hear about you recently, you will be a frequent attendee, as well. Keep up the good work, lad. We will talk business soon. Very soon."

With that, Tweed winked and went to speak to Peter O'Flanagan, Gus Cairny, and others of his inner circle. August's skin prickled, but he quickly dismissed the foreboding feeling and continued to work the room. Flashing a bright smile, he regaled guests with inside stories of Willie's races and anecdotes from parties he now attended on a regular basis.

Dinner was an elegant affair consisting of soup, appetizer, salad, and a choice of marbled veal, roasted mutton, or fricasseed chicken. As soon as the main course was cleared away, August stood and went to help Selma out of her chair.

"But August," she protested, her voice cold and her eyes boring into him. "The waiters are about to serve dessert. The night is not yet finished."

"For us, it is," August said. *I have other things to do with my evening*, he thought. *I'm sorry she is disappointed, but I made her no promises, so there's nothing I need to do about that.*

A stony silence passed between them.

"Please fetch Miss Richter's cloak," he said, passing a large gratuity to a butler. "We will meet you at the front portico."

Later that evening, August arrived at Billy Boon's Ale House, just a few blocks from the piers in lower Manhattan, and headed downstairs to a faro table. He had become a master at the fast-paced betting game and was quickly becoming known as a formidable competitor. Even Boss Tweed, accustomed now to drawing promised commissions on August's gambling gains, applauded his overwhelming wins in Tammany tournaments.

During each turn in faro, the dealer turns over two cards, a winner and a loser. Players bet on each series of cards until the deck has been completely drawn. Deceptive in its simplicity, the game required extraordinary counting skills—and August was an expert.

Applause went up as August pulled out a stool at the table.

"There he is," the dealer cheered. "Let's see if you can top last week's winnings, Mr. August Rose."

"Okay, August grinned. "Deal away."

With each round he won, August felt the flush of victory. His heart beat faster, and his face filled with a familiar flush of euphoria as he won hand after hand. His chips built up into higher and higher stacks, quickly becoming taller than any others at the table.

August played well into the night. His wallet was stuffed with bills, and he became giddy with the sense of infallibility that cards, horses, and fights always gave him. Here in the saloon, he was home, king of the roost, someone in control of his fate.

Then, suddenly, a hollow feeling in the pit of his stomach hit him as a large bet went under. *If I had just followed my gut, if I had only counted better, if only. . . .*

"You out?" asked the dealer, triumph crossing his face at the loss of this veteran winner.

August flushed, his face red with rage and humiliation. He forfeited the losing chips on the table, shoving them angrily at the dealer. As a barmaid passed, he took another drink—the fourth of the night-—and gulped it down in one swig.

"Hold your tongue," he said to the speechless dealer. "*This* player doesn't lose. Deal." He reached into his pocket and took out a fresh wad of bills. *The cards will be right this time. I know they will. I never lose, never. But . . . maybe I should go to another table . . . NO, I'm a winner. I'll show them how it's done.*

A crowd gathered as people began to realize that August Rose had lost a hand. The tension grew, and bets were placed among the spectators about August going down with a hand so big he might never rise again. On and on the game went as August piled up chips. The stacks grew higher until August threw his whole wad at a final bet.

The room grew quiet, the only sound the ticking of a clock on the wall. He placed his bet, then rose with victory as he won back all he had lost—and then some. He pumped his arms in the air and ordered drinks all around. Two muscular bettors hoisted him onto their shoulders.

August basked in the moment. *I still have what it takes,* he thought. *I'll always have it.*

The sun was about to rise when August got home. Shocked that the house was lit up when everyone should still be sleeping, his eyes grew wide, and his heart started to pound. Deep howls were coming from the parlor. He raced into the house, perspiration breaking out under his arms and into his eyes. When he reached the front door, he felt as though his legs would fail him.

The howls came from his mother. And she was cradling a dead child in her arms.

Frida

When Frida, Josef, and the children arrived at Temple Emanuel for Gertrude's funeral the next day, the sanctuary was filled to its two-thousand-person capacity, and an overflow crowd waited outside. The congregation had moved into its new building just three years earlier and was the largest synagogue in the country. Located at Forty-Third Street and Fifth Avenue, the Moorish Revival building towered impressively over its sparsely developed surroundings, the style chosen to reflect the pre-Inquisition period when Jews enjoyed relative freedoms in Spain.

As the Roses' carriages pulled up to the synagogue, a cadre of police officers created a path for the mourners. Josef and August supported Frida as they made their way to the back room where the family would wait until the congregants were settled. Josef held Frida tightly, trying in vain to stop her shaking. Her body spasmed in grief as she tried to squelch the sobs that wracked her core. She clung to Josef, turning her head deep into his chest. He rocked her back and forth, his own sobs blending seamlessly into hers.

When the family finally entered the sanctuary for the service, the mourners rose. Josef was pale and drawn, but Frida was bent over, unable to walk erectly. Her cheeks were void of color, and her usually coiffed black hair was dull and disheveled. Dr. Wurman, who had been staying with the family to take care of the twins, followed immediately behind Frida. He held tightly on to his black medical bag. Ernst Reinhard walked beside them.

Next came Willie and Burke. They flanked Elsie and Bessie, all four with solemn and drawn faces. Louise followed, crumpled like an old rag in her wheelchair. Liesel pushed her, while Ida navigated Gertrude's empty chair, its only occupant the dead child's doll. Across the gap between the two, Louise gripped the doll's worn-out hand, tears raining down her cheeks.

What will Louise do without her sister? wondered Frida. *What will I do without her? What if Louise dies, too? Papa. Mama. Jakob. The twins. How will I endure?*

Frida's mind raced back to the evening before when Gertrude had first started to twitch violently and gasp for air. Dr. Wurman, ignoring the Roses' demands to call Ernst Reinhard, rushed to her side when Louise screamed that Gertrude's body had gone rigid. Shouting orders, he told Ida to fetch warm milk and instructed Liesel to give the struggling child a vapor bath. When those remedies didn't work, he tried draining blood from Gertrude's foot ulcers, but the gasping became worse, and her body spasmed into a vicious seizure. Time seemed to stretch out forever. Then, suddenly, her breathing stopped, and she was gone.

As the family were escorted to their seats, Frida and Josef were greeted with solemn expressions from the mourners in attendance. Mayor Oakey, U.S. Senator Ruben Fenton, and other New York dignitaries took up the second row of pews near the bimah. In the first row, Ulysses and Julia Grant stood and greeted Frida and Josef as they settled down next to them.

"Ulysses, Julia. How good of you to come," managed Frida, accepting Julia's embrace.

"We were distressed to hear your sad news," Julia said. "Your friendship is important to us. When we saw you after Ulysses' inauguration, Gertrude seemed to be doing better. Gus Cairny contacted us immediately when he heard about the poor child. And so, here we are to offer you comfort and strength."

The only sounds to fill the hushed sanctuary were the rustles of crinolines as women shifted in their seats. Gertrude's traditional, plain pine coffin rested at the front of the bimah where a small choir was assembled. Bessie stood at the center, music sheets in hand. Her face was streaked with tears, and her eyes were red, but she held her head high.

As Rabbi Adler took his place behind the lectern, he was silent for several moments until, in a departure from tradition, Bessie stepped forward and took her place alongside him. Without introduction, she started to sing "*El Maleh Rachamim*," a Jewish prayer for the soul of the deceased. Her voice trembled at first but then soared with emotion so strong that it shook the hearts of the mourners. In training now as a diva for the Grand Opera, she sang with maturity and grace beyond her years. She filled Frida and Josef's souls.

Throughout the service, Rabbi Adler paused several times to allow Bessie to sing. Often, the choir joined her, their voices rising in mournful tones that enveloped the grieving congregation. When the service was complete, Josef, Frida, and the family made the long walk down the aisle to the carriages that would bring them to the mausoleum for Gertrude's entombment. Several times, Frida's knees buckled; several times, Josef had to be propped up by his sons.

When they returned home at the end of the interment, friends and neighbors had worked with Ida and Henry to prepare food for the mourners. The house was full but silent, except for soulful whispers rippling through the parlor and ballroom where friends and associates had gathered to begin shiva. The crowd parted as Frida and Josef climbed the steps and came through the front door. Martha Reinhard gasped when she saw Frida whose complexion was ashen and her eyes veiled as if she had been swept away by grief.

Dr. Wurman rushed to Frida's side. He was holding a hypodermic needle filled with a clear fluid. "Get her upstairs, right away!" he commanded. "She needs morphine, and she needs it now."

Martha's eyes widened and her mouth fell open. "Ernst!" she screamed, summoning her husband, who appeared at her side immediately.

"What are you thinking, Wurman? Morphine? She's suffering from grief, not pain!" Reinhard shouted emphatically, disbelief in his voice. He thrust himself between Frida and the resident doctor.

"This woman needs to be calmed," Wurman insisted. "Let me do my job."

Reinhard's voice rose. "You've done enough harm already, Wurman. Frida, Josef, do you see what I've been trying to tell you? The girls gradually needed more and more of the healing syrups; they were taking too much. Their skin often became clammy and cold, and they became lethargic. I can see that Louise's pupils have contracted, a bad sign."

The crowd gathered around the two doctors as they locked eyes. Wurman's mouth quivered with rage as rumbles of indignation growled in his throat.

"That's enough," an almost disembodied voice insisted. Quiet and acquiescent until this moment, Frida placed herself directly in front of Wurman. "That's quite enough," she repeated. Emboldened, she drew back her shoulders. "They always craved more. Louise still does. Every few hours, in fact. Josef, Ernst; you tried to warn me. How I wish I had listened!"

In an opposite corner, Louise was propped up in her wheelchair, clinging desperately to Gertrude's doll. She had started to shake violently. Her eyes were darting wildly, and she was shrieking at an invisible monster. "Get away from me," she pleaded, clawing at the air. "Get away from me."

Her breath was coming in uneven gasps, and she suddenly slumped in the chair. Reinhard rushed to her side. Suddenly, he stiffened and ran his hands through his hair. "Someone, anyone," he commanded. "Get me her smelling salts. NOW!"

Moments later, Henry pulled the salts vial from a credenza. Ernst administered them to Louise, who revived enough to sit up. She was deathly white, her lips a ghastly shade of violet.

Edmund Wurman stood on the sidelines, daggers shooting from his eyes. "I told you. Louise needs more of her syrup," he said. "Mrs. Rose needs it as well. I have Mrs. Winslow's in my bag. I'll fetch it immediately."

"You'll do no such thing," said Josef, blocking the doctor's path. "In fact, you will leave this house immediately. You didn't save my child. You probably would have killed Louise, too, with your remedies. Get out. Immediately!"

"You can't possibly agree with Josef, Frida. You need me here."

"You've got another thing wrong, Edmund. I do agree with my husband, and with Ernst Reinhard. It's over. And I will personally see to it that you never practice in this city again."

CHAPTER 30

Josef

Josef got up at 6:50 a.m. after a sleepless night. In the past year, since Gertrude's death, he and Frida had grown the business to unprecedented heights, and it was thriving; but Josef had met with Boss Tweed the previous evening. It had not gone well. Tweed had demanded a place on the Rose Industries executive board.

"It's only fitting," he had insisted, drawing deeply on his Cuban cigar after a favorite meal of oyster pie, roast duck, and thick porterhouse steaks. As he ordered desserts and after-dinner cordials, his eyes narrowed. "Rose," he said, patting his large belly, "Tammany made you. Yes, you've contributed large amounts to our cause, but it's time for me to have a bigger say in the business and in the size of your contributions."

Tweed had paused, readying himself for a burp, then continued. His blue eyes bored into Josef's. "You see, Rose, as you are aware, this November the people will elect multiple state officials. I'll know which office seekers need to be nominated to further Tammany's interests and which ones need the most financial backing. And I'll make sure that Rose Industries' bills go through the proper channels, especially when you round them up just a bit to make bookkeeping easier. I'll make sure that the company receives all the monies it deserves."

Tweed hadn't given Josef a chance to respond. Instead, he laughed. "The truth is, you and I, together, can make Rose Industries into a leading force in determining candidate choices."

Josef's mind had raced as he searched for a way to avoid Tweed's demands. Trembling, he had reached for his wine glass, hoping against hope that it would work the miracles he needed to get out of Tweed's terrifying ultimatum.

If Tweed noticed his victim's angst, he promptly dismissed it. "Rose," he had said, "let me make myself perfectly clear." The huge man's eyes had turned glacial, and the chair beneath him groaned as he shifted his weight and leaned into Josef's face. The alcohol on his breath filled the space between them, and he reduced his voice to a whisper. "I know what's best for this city. I know the inner workings of this town, and as Tammany's leader, it is I who make the big decisions. I will see to it that your board makes the right decisions. You can see the logic here, no?"

Somehow, Josef now recalled, he had managed an affirmative nod.

"Good. It is settled," the boss said. He stood, grabbed Josef's shaking hand, and put an arm around his shoulder. "We'll do great things together, Rose. Tell your board members the next meeting will be the first Tuesday of August, right here at Delmonico's. Seven o'clock sharp. And don't be late. I don't appreciate being kept waiting."

Now, as sunshine filled the bedroom in mockery of his mood, Josef remembered that this would be a special day for Bessie. At eighteen, Bessie had become a beauty. Petite, but slender and shapely, her thick black hair offset her swan-like neck and sparkling black eyes. Still painfully aware of her facial birthmarks, she had turned them to her advantage when she performed. A skilled makeup artist, she used pencils and powders to create a rose out of her deformity. It became her trademark, and she became known as "Bessie, Rose of the Roses." She had just completed a spate of performances as a courtesan in the opera *La Belle Helene,* or *The Beautiful Helen,* which was based on the story of Helen of Troy just before the Trojan War.

Today, Bessie was auditioning for the upcoming musical *Lalla Rookh,* a far-eastern romance, at the same theater, the prestigious

Grand Opera House on the corner of 8th Avenue and 23rd Street. The marble structure was adorned with intricately carved statues of Comedy and Tragedy and could seat up to 3,500 guests. Henry would take her there and retrieve her later to bring her home.

Throughout the rest of the morning into the latter part of the afternoon, Josef was involved with signing a contract with A.T. Stewart's, which had become the city's first major department store. The marble building occupied an entire city block. Featuring five stories and plate-glass display windows, it catered to a wealthy clientele seeking goods ranging from furs to silks, carpets, and toys. Stewart's unique concept of one finely appointed store offering multiple products with standardized pricing had thrived in direct contrast to the chaos of street vendors hawking their specialized wares. With its unique elegance, the store was also known as the Marble Palace and had quickly become a shopping destination.

A. T. Stewart himself had approached Josef and asked to sell Rose Industries' ready-made women's clothing and domestic linens. Today's meetings would tie up the contract details, and Rose products would be in the department store within the next few months. Josef had contracted earlier with smaller stores like Macy's and Lord & Taylor, but Stewart's offered an unprecedented variety of goods, enjoyed a robust mail-order business, and served not only city clientele but customers from all over the country.

The riots started at 2:00 in the afternoon while Josef was in the parlor signing the last of Stewart's paperwork. The Orange Order of Irish Protestants was marching to commemorate its victory over their Catholic counterparts at the Battle of the Boyne back in 1690. A parade marking the Boyne anniversary the year before had resulted in massive rioting that had left eight people dead. There had been few police present, and the public blamed the Catholic-backed Tammany Hall for allowing the violence to go unchecked.

This year was different. Tweed had spoken of the upcoming march in his conversation with Josef the night before. "You know, Mr. Rose, when I make decisions for this town, I listen to the people, and they listen to me."

He chuckled, his belly rippling in great, undulating waves. "Take the parade tomorrow. The Catholics got Police Superintendent James Kelso to deny a permit for this year because of the melee the Orange Parade caused in '70. At first, Kelso denied the permit, but all hell broke loose with the Protestants—so I worked to reverse the decision. Can't have a problem now, can we? The '71 parade for July 20th is on, my friend. They will march tomorrow at two p.m. sharp."

As Josef recalled Tweed's conversation, he winced. He checked the clock. The parade was starting, and his nerves were frazzled. Bessie had insisted on going to the audition, and he started to panic. *I shouldn't have let her go. It will be my fault if anything happens to her,* he thought, as he paced in front of the window watching crowds forming on the sidewalk.

His mouth was dry, and his breath came in deep gasps as parade reports started to filter uptown. When he could stand the tension no longer, he joined the mass of curiosity seekers. Frida was standing among them.

"My God, Frida," he said, "what's going on?"

"It's not good, Josef," she replied. "The Orange marchers met at their Lamartine Hall quarters on Eighth Avenue, right near the Opera House."

An older woman, who sported chin hairs and a particularly wide girth, overheard them. "I hear that the marchers were surrounded by Catholic laborers, and bedlam has broken out. They're throwing bricks and rocks and bottles, and someone said the militia is shooting at people to clear a path for the marchers."

A young boy on a bicycle planted himself on the sidewalk. "I was just down there," he said, tears running down his cheeks. "I'm lucky I got out."

The crowd gathered around him.

"People are falling all over the streets. It's getting bad fast." He began to sob. "I think people are getting killed."

In the distance, Josef could make out the sounds of musket fire as the marchers proceeded up Fifth Avenue. He took Frida's elbow and guided her into the house. "Henry," he called as he entered the foyer. "Get the carriage. We must get Bessie home immediately."

Henry rushed to the stable. A short while later, he returned to Josef. His face was red with effort, and his eyes were cloaked in fear. "It's impossible, sir," he stammered, his voice shaking. "When I took Bessie to the opera house this morning, they were readying the streets for a parade. A simple parade. Everything was orderly. But I just took a horse out to see what's happening. The streets are packed, and there's no way we can get a carriage through. The crowd is surrounded by mounted police and soldiers with muskets and bayonets. They're not afraid to use them, not afraid at all. There's blood everywhere. Hundreds are wounded."

Josef's knees buckled.

Henry paused for a moment, his voice choked and trembling. "There's more, Mr. Rose," he finally said, his voice low. "I heard some marchers chanting that they want to storm Boss Tweed's mansion because he allowed the parade. Tweed's house is almost next door to us at 43rd Street and Fifth Avenue. If they succeed, the marchers will be coming right past us. I'll go out with August and Willie—God knows Willie knows his way around horses—to find Bessie."

Josef sighed audibly. "Please bring Bessie back safely," he said. "Meanwhile, we will ready the house in case the crowds arrive. We can't be too careful."

CHAPTER 31

Otto

Otto Krause was a happy man. Now in his forties, he had been thwarted by the change from clipper ships to steamships, with which he was unfamiliar, and he was no longer able to work on the seas. At first, he was furious at his fate, but he soon found regular work unloading cotton and wool at the docks. Still brawny, his huge arms carried the large bales easily with little strain on the rest of his aging body. Besides, there was also considerable income from Tammany Hall. Boss Tweed was impressed with his ability to wrest bribes and commissions from those in Tammany's debt, and more and more assignments were coming Otto's way.

Still, there was nothing Otto Krause liked better than a good fight. Today, Otto followed the sights, sounds, and odors coming from the parade downtown. By the time the brawling mobs reached Eighth Avenue, the riots were in full swing. Otto was in his glory as he joined the Catholic protestors but would have been perfectly happy to join the Protestant marchers. He didn't care which side he fought for; he just cared about being part of the fight.

As he wound his way through the mounted police, he checked to be sure his Bowie was secure in the holster on his thigh. Smoke stung his eyes and clogged his throat, but he charged through the crowd until he got to the center of the fight at 45th Street. As luck would have it, a young woman was just coming out of the Grand Opera House. Otto's eyes fell upon her slim body and raven hair.

This was a damsel unlike any he had ever seen before. Her painted cheek seemed to rise over her slender jaw in the shape of a rose. Its intricate petals spread from her upper lip to her delicate ear, and its pale green leaves spread to the slope of her sculpted brow. The girl seemed confused—terrified, really—as if she were coming upon the riots unaware of what had unfolded while she was in the safety of the opera house.

She's mine, he thought excitedly, quickly plotting how he would take her. *Offer to assist, to take her safely to wherever home is, win her confidence . . . then do the deed. Sweet . . . oh, so sweet.* Drool dribbled out of his thin lips and covered his chin as he contemplated his moves.

Otto watched patiently to see what his victim would do next. Tears were cascading onto her fine gown, and terror clouded those magnificent black eyes. He knew that look of terror. He thrived on it, his excitement mounting as he elbowed his way to within feet of where she stood on the broad steps of the Opera House.

As he inched his way closer to the girl, she seemed unaware of the huge man who was about to lure her into danger. *She doesn't see me . . . yet,* he thought. *Get ahold of yourself, Otto. Don't let her be afraid of you. Not when you're so close.* He straightened his shoulders and inhaled deeply. He counted slowly to ten, then to twenty, and thirty, never taking his eyes off the damsel. *It will be worth it,* he told himself, swallowing hard, until he was finally ready to make his move. He adjusted his clothing, loosening his shirt collar to relieve the searing heat of the afternoon. Drying perspiration with a dirty rag, he made his way toward the girl whose confusion was growing greater by the minute.

"Can I help you?" yelled Otto. "A young thing like you shouldn't be out in this crowd."

When she appeared not to hear him, Otto changed strategies. Smoothing back his stringy hair, now oily with sweat, he managed to put a smile on his face. "I'll be glad to get you through this mess to safety," he said, approaching her and offering her a hand. He laughed. "I'm a big fella. I can protect you."

The girl's eyes widened, panic contorting her features. Breathing heavily, she hesitated, obviously torn between fear of the crowd and fear of a stranger.

"C'mon now, girlie," coaxed Otto. "This crowd will devour you without me."

Otto watched while his prey wavered. Suddenly, the girl yelped, relief flooding her face as she all but jumped into the air. "Henry, August, Willie!" she shouted, as the three rescuers approached her.

Without warning, a protester threw a handmade bomb directly at the Opera House steps. The girl screamed, hiding her head with her shawl to shield herself from the percussions of the explosion and from the charred debris rising all around her. Immediately, mounted militiamen started to pour into the area. Her rescuers' terrified horses, unaccustomed to battle, neighed in protest and reared up on their hind legs.

"Don't lean backwards!" yelled the lead horseman. "The horses could throw you. Lean forward. Hug their necks and pull the reins downward like I'm doing."

Otto fell to the ground and folded his arms over his head. Furious that he had missed his opportunity with the girl, he screamed obscenities and fought to breathe through the thick smoke. By the time he dared look up, the girl was being pulled up onto the largest of the three steeds by a big blond man with gray eyes. Otto jumped to his feet and started to run after the threesome carrying his would-be victim.

The crowd was starting to disperse, propelled by the authorities to clear the area, but Otto was able to keep track of the girl as the trio made its way up Fifth Avenue. Just as he was about to lose her trail, he stopped and hid behind a nearby tree. The group had halted in front of a huge Fifth Avenue townhouse—with a turret, no less. The big blond fellow dismounted and reached for the girl. She took his hand and climbed down from the horse, falling into her rescuer's arms.

Almost immediately, people poured from the house. They appeared to be the girl's parents, sisters, brothers, servants. *Who knows who they all are?* thought Otto.

Otto was transfixed. The blond man had some kind of mark on his neck. Otto couldn't quite make it out, but it was strangely shaped and dark. And there was something about the parents that seemed familiar. His memory was hazy, but Otto could swear that he knew them from somewhere.

Especially the mother.

CHAPTER 32

Josef

As Josef went downstairs to join Frida in their newly decorated breakfast room, the tensions of the past two and a half weeks since the Orange Riots showed in his pale face. He slipped into the ornate mahogany chair across from Frida, gratefully accepted a cup of steaming coffee from Henry, and sighed deeply. "Aahh, that's delicious. Just what I need on this crisp October morning."

"Good morning, Josef," said Frida. "The news today is mostly about Tammany Hall," she said, somewhat absently, as she handed Josef the morning edition of *The New York Times.*

Josef took a sip of coffee, selected a hot biscuit from the basket Henry had just brought to the table, and took the paper from Frida. As he scanned the headlines, an involuntary shudder traveled down his spine. "My God, Frida," Josef said, putting the paper down on the table between them. "Did you read this?"

"No, not really," Frida responded. "I have other things on my mind today. Louise was up all night. She's doing worse every day, Josef. It is she I must attend to, not the newspapers."

"Well, this time, you need to know what's going on."

Trying to hide his growing fear, Josef read the story aloud. It stated that there were proofs of secret accounts perpetrated by Tammany. As he read, his hands twitched so violently that the paper shook, filling the room with the *slap-slap-slap* of dry pages rubbing against each other.

"This could be a problem for us, Frida. *The Times* is saying that the bulk of the money Tweed paid for his recent courthouse construction was fictitious, that payments came back to the Tammany Ring fraudulently. It states that dates and amounts were altered, including for repairs, cabinets, furniture, and upholstery. It also lists, in detail, what was paid to individuals and companies, and the dates on which work was supposed to be done. The inquiries go back a few years. We did courthouse upholstery, window, and wall treatments. We're not listed, thank God—but we could be."

Though her eyes registered concern, Frida had refused to be perturbed. "Now, Josef Rose, you listen to me," she said, "William Tweed runs this city, and he runs it brilliantly. When he started asking us to pad our bills and adjust dates, it was for a reason. Just look at all he has done for the people of New York. It's not just that he secured food and jobs for the poor, either. Everyone benefits from the Boss's philanthropy. Let's not forget that Tammany helped us to become citizens, to vote, to find a decent place to live when we arrived here penniless." Frida's jaw set into a firm line. She stood and put her hands on her hips, some of the old fire glinting in her eyes. Josef hadn't seen her like this in a while, and it scared him.

"But Frida," he implored, "*The Times* is reporting—right here, in black and white—detailed lists of accounts, including padding yielding significant upcharges. It says the public has the right to see them."

Frida sat down again, arranged her skirts, and took a deep swallow of her now cooling coffee. "Let's be reasonable. Tweed's been a U.S. congressman, a state senator, and the Grand Sachem, the leader of Tammany Hall. This city can't function without Tweed and Tammany. The people would never stand for it." She laughed coldly. "Tweed even paid for Civil War draft substitutes for family men in dire circumstances. Do you really think people will forget his largesse? The clean water he provided? Or the hospitals, firehouses, paved roads, and museums, like the Metropolitan Museum of Art, he helped to build? The taxes he reduced? The list goes on and on."

"That doesn't make us safe. We should never have agreed to providing inflated bills, and it looks like we might have to pay a heavy price for our complicity," Josef whispered. A cold sweat broke out over his body, and he felt as if he were suffocating.

"Pull yourself together. This is a tempest in a teapot. Tweed couldn't have done any of the remarkable things he did without vast income for the city. Besides, it's business," she said, as she rose from the table to start her day. She had walked a few paces when she turned back to address her husband. The steel in her voice sent a shiver down his spine. When she spoke, her voice was firm. "There's a lot in this life that isn't pretty. We do what we must, Josef . . . to survive."

Josef's angst continued to build during the week as more of Tammany's business dealings were at risk of exposure. There had been news reports of a set of three tables and forty chairs purchased for $179,729.60; a contractor who was paid $133,180 for two days working on window frames; a plasterer compensated more than $350,000 in one month; and a sky-high proposal for tile roofing to be constructed with material taken from quarries owned by Boss Tweed.

To make matters worse, Louise was now a patient at the Jewish Hospital, her condition grave. Frida kept vigil over her daughter, rising at dawn and coming home only to change clothes and to sleep restlessly for an hour or two each night. She was unavailable to Josef, and he felt dangerously alone.

Today, as he sat in a forest-green upholstered chair in the dining room, the gentle breeze wafting through the empty house seemed contradictory to the violent tension Josef felt in his gut. The Saturday issue of *The Times* sat perched on an end table, unread. It was with reluctance that Josef accepted the newest issue of *Harper's Weekly* that Henry handed to him.

"I know you are consumed with Louise's condition, sir," the faithful servant said, "but the whole city is buzzing with news of Tammany Hall and its misdeeds. Perhaps it will distract you from the situation."

"Thank you, Henry," said Josef. "Please put it next to *The Times*. I will get to it shortly."

When Henry left the room, Josef reached for the news journal. Hands shaking and chest pounding, he glanced at the front page of *Harper's*. The headlines depicted a furious populace that blamed Boss Tweed for the Orange Riots and the multiple casualties they had caused. Even worse, a drawing by Thomas Nast, an illustrator who was making a name for himself depicting scandalous issues with cartoons that even the illiterate of the city could understand, had a double-page portrayal of the riots. The cartoon was captioned, "Something That Will Not Blow Over." It featured aggregate drawings that included depictions of Irish-Catholic mobs charging an unarmed Protestant parade marshal, images of a lynched Black man, and the burning of the orphanage.

It was the center, bottom panel that riveted Josef. Representing an unconditional surrender of Tammany officials, it was reinforced by images of the Tweed Ring, sitting in chains and guarded by rioters, defiantly commenting, "WELL, WHAT ARE YOU GOING TO DO ABOUT IT?" It was the question Tweed, himself, had posed when faced with corruption charges.

Josef laughed bitterly, recalling another Tweed remark during a recent conversation. "My constituents can't read. But damn it, they can see pictures," a comment he had made in public and that had recently appeared as a caption in a different Nast cartoon.

Shaken and terrified that the investigation into Tweed's business practices could affect Rose Industries, and indeed, his whole family,

Josef reached again for *The Times*. One of the headlines screamed at him. It posted, in full, a reporter's investigational interview of a dealer who had been paid exorbitant fees for carpets provided to Tweed for his New York City courthouse.

Josef's intuition forced him to read as fast as he could. The article quoted a detailed interview with a Mr. Gregg, a dealer who had been paid handsomely for carpets provided to Tweed for his city courthouse. The reporter had hammered away at Gregg, demanding pricing, delivery dates, names of personnel from the controller's office who paid him, and other details that trapped the dealer in a series of shaming denials.

What if I am questioned by a reporter? I have no answers ready. Frida says we did what we had to do . . . what if, what if, what if . . .

Josef's heart raced, but he was compelled to read on. *The Times* featured additional stories that compared the New York County Courthouse costs to the building of the Kings County Courthouse in Brooklyn. It stated that Tweed's new Manhattan building was larger in ground area, but one story lower; amenities and architectural details were similar for both structures. However, in comparison, it reported, the New York Court House under Tweed's commission cost $450,000, while the Brooklyn building cost $70,000. The article went on to state that the history of the New York County Courthouse would be so riddled with scandal that even the children of any of those involved would be forced to live with shame.

Feeling totally alone, Josef started to feel haunted by the emptiness of the house. The children had all left after an early breakfast for business or social events, and Frida was at the hospital. The servants had been given the day off. With only Josef at home, there was no reason for them to be there.

A pounding at the front door wrenched Josef back to the moment. Weakened by his racing thoughts, he was barely able to lift himself from his chair. As he made his way to the foyer, he stayed as close as he could to the walls, grasping onto furniture for support. The pounding became louder and louder, echoing through the empty house like a sledgehammer.

"Open up this instant. It's Tammany Hall calling. I'll give you five seconds or I'll break the door down," shouted a raspy voice.

Terrified, Josef managed to turn the knob. The door started to creak and was then pushed forward to admit a heavy-set man with a huge belly, stringy blond—but graying—hair, and tattoos on his arms. The huge fellow called out and looked around furtively. Satisfied that no one else was home, he grabbed Josef by the shirt collar, lifted him off the ground, and carried him into the parlor.

"Now look here, Mr. Rose. You surprised I know you by name? Well, Gus Cairny instructed me to collect what you owe Tammany. Some one hundred thousand dollars, I suppose. Yes, that sounds about right," he laughed. "It's collateral, you see. Just in case you ever decide to skip town." The man suddenly leered and licked his lips. "Besides, I'm here to pay a visit to your black-haired daughter."

As Otto grabbed Josef and dragged him into the parlor, a picture of Frida with August caught the intruder's eye. He grabbed it, held it up, and studied it. His eyes seemed, to Josef, to fill with glee as he pointed to August's image.

"The girl reminds me of her mother. I saw the whole family, Rose, when I followed your daughter home after the rioting at the Opera House. I even saw this son in the picture, the son you thought was yours."

He shoved the photograph into Josef's face. "Look at his hair, his eyes, his mark. Now look at mine." The thug pulled down the collar of his shirt to reveal his turtle mole, glee lighting up his face as he saw Josef's horror. "That's right, Jew. I had his *Jude Bitch* mother back on the *Holstein*. But never mind that for now. I've had my eye on your black-haired lass for a while. The one with the rose picture on her face. I'll have my way with her, that I will. Can't have her jealous of her mother now, can we?"

Josef managed to kick out his feet, hitting the man's crotch.

Screaming in pain, the intruder lost his grip, and Josef fell to the ground. He picked Josef up again and pinned him against the wall. The tough drew his face up against Josef's, his whiskey and tobacco breath making Josef gag. Then, the man started to laugh.

"I thought I knew you from somewhere!" he howled delightedly. "You're the little Jew from the street. It was a long time ago, but I never forget a face. Especially one that had a Jew beanie. Long time, no see," he rasped.

Josef tried to wriggle out of the intruder's grasp, but the harder he tried, the tighter the man held him. "Guess you're wondering who I am, Mr. Rose. My name's Otto. Say 'Hello' to Otto now, like a good chap. Nice and polite, like a proper gentleman."

Josef gagged as Otto grabbed his neck in one hand and drew his Bowie knife with the other. "I don't like unfinished business. You'll get me my cash, and then we'll see what to do with you," he said, pushing Josef away.

Just then, the veins in Josef's neck convulsed. He broke into a cold sweat and started to pant heavily, his breath coming in shorter and shorter gasps. He clutched his chest and silently begged for air as the color drained from his face. Knees buckling, he fell to the ground, writhing violently in an attempt to get away from his assailant—but also to escape the pressure mounting inside of him.

Emboldened, Otto crouched to the floor and bellowed into Josef's ear. "Think you can fool me with the fainting act?" he sneered. "Not Otto. No one fools Otto." Otto flashed his knife in front of Josef's eyes. He raised his arm and aimed for Josef's neck. "You're mine!" Otto yelled triumphantly. "I always finish what I start!"

The knife sliced across Josef's neck. Blood oozing from the cut, Josef clutched his throat. His pupils dilated so widely that they all but blocked out the irises. His jaw fell open in agony as violent pain traveled down his arm. Suddenly, realization dawned on him. August's blond hair and big build, his narrow eyes, his late birth, the violence, the *Holstein*. The turtle mole. And Frida's scar. It was all clear.

As a powerful convulsion ripped through his body, Josef's life flashed in front of him. *Germany, New York, Peter O'Flanagan, Gus Cairny, and Boss Tweed. Erwin, Roshen, Gertrude, Louise, August, Otto . . . and Frida. Why didn't we tell each other, Frida? Why, why, why?*

CHAPTER 33

Otto

As Josef fell to the ground, Otto Krause panicked. Things had not gone as planned, and Otto wasn't happy when things didn't go as they should. He was supposed to be on his way with $100,000 in his pocket, a sum that Tammany Hall would never have seen. He was supposed to get rich tonight and leave for parts unknown where hard labor and sweat couldn't ever reach him again. And then this Rose fella had to go and die—before he doled out the cash.

There was the picture, too, of some bastard that the *Jude Bitch* from the *Holstein* had. It was inescapable. The Jew son was a well-known gambler, a big-time winner. He was also the spitting image of him. Of Otto.

There was no way Otto could allow that. He'd get his money somehow. But a Jew son walking around? Not if he had anything to do with it. No, he would get away from this house and the dead Jew on the floor as fast as he could. His mind raced. He couldn't escape through the front door. Someone might see him. He'd go through a window in the back. He'd lay low for a while, keep out of trouble. He'd be patient and bide his time. *I'll find a way to get to the money. Then, the Jew bastard son, and his bitch mother, will have to go.*

CHAPTER 34

Frida

Frida did not arrive home until dinnertime. August, who had joined Frida at the hospital, helped her out of the carriage; her knees were too weak to carry her. Louise was gone, her disease taking her as it had her sister.

"We'll tell Papa together," August said gently. "Arrangements can wait until tomorrow."

Frida leaned heavily on her son as they made their way into the house. Except for Henry, who had driven Frida and August home, the family and other servants had not yet returned, and the house was eerily silent. Their footsteps echoed heavily through the foyer as they made their way across the marble floor to the dayroom, an intimate retreat directly off the entryway.

"Papa!" called August several times, his calls unanswered. "Perhaps he went out," August said. "There should be his customary note on the credenza in the parlor. Come, Mama. Let me help you onto the chaise by the fireplace, and I'll go look for him."

Too weak to protest, Frida let August pick her up. The sun had ducked behind a dark summer cloud, and heavy shadows settled throughout the house. Frida sobbed into August's chest as paroxysms of grief overcame her. August pulled a black cashmere blanket from a nearby basket, gently covered his mother, and went to seek a note.

He was gone only a few moments, when the empty house echoed with a gurgling sound as August made his discovery.

"What is it, August? What's wrong?" called Frida.

"You don't want to know, Mama!" August sobbed, as he made his way back to the sofa. He reached for Frida. "Let me protect you!" he pleaded. "I'll take you upstairs immediately, and then we will talk."

Frida wrested herself from August's grasp. Propelled by terror, she bolted upright and ran across the hall into the parlor. Her screams echoed throughout the house.

Josef lay in a puddle of blood, his body stiff and cold. His back had arched involuntarily, and a blue caste had invaded his skin. His open eyes stared at the ceiling, and blood was pooled around his neck.

"NO, NO, NO!" she cried. "Do something, August! Do something!"

August scooped Josef into his arms and ran out of the house. His father's arms and legs dangled and swung as August raced to the street. Instinctively, Frida gathered her skirts and followed, adrenaline making her legs pump wildly as the two made their way across the cobblestones.

"Ernst must be home, Mama. He'll be getting ready for shul," he shouted over his shoulder. "He'll fix Papa. I know he will."

When they arrived at the Reinhard's a few minutes later, Frida pounded at the door. "Ernst! Martha!" she yelled. "Open up!"

Frida could hear Ernst's footsteps running down the stairs. Dressed in his Sabbath best, the doctor threw open the door and hurriedly placed Josef on a loveseat in an adjacent parlor. He grabbed his stethoscope and placed it over Josef's heart. "He's gone," the doctor finally said, tears streaming down his face. "His heart has stopped, and he is gone."

Frida threw herself onto Josef's chest. As she burrowed into him, she tasted the fresh blood on his neck. With horror, realization dawned. The wound was the same as hers and in the same place it was on her neck. Just deeper.

Just before she fainted, *Jude Bitch, Jude Bitch* raced loudly through her head, mixing with the memories of Louise's last breath.

CHAPTER 35

August

Three months later, August drew a sigh of relief when he saw the October 27th *Times* headlines. Orders of arrest had been granted by a judge who pushed Boss Tweed and other Tammany cohorts into a corner. They were to be arrested and taken into custody.

Yes, he thought, as he reviewed the paper over breakfast, *Rose Industries has escaped the jaws of justice unharmed. It's been a long time since I've been out. I'll celebrate today.*

After the twins' and Josef's funerals, Frida had retreated into herself, spending hours alone in her bedroom. Willie, Bessie, Burke, and Elsie, now teenagers, tried to talk to her, to bring her out of herself, to no avail. She barely ate the meals that Henry delivered to her, and she refused to leave the house. During the night, August slept with his door open, offering solace and guidance to the younger children and to Frida when dreams of Josef, Gertrude, and Louise in their coffins awoke her and she called out for them by name. Her screams filled the house with anguish, and she relented willingly when August offered to oversee Rose Industries. The board had readily agreed. Frida was not in any condition to participate in the day-to-day decisions the business required.

As August examined the books over the past few months, the millions in Tammany's enormous bills and payments surprised him. *The Times'* exposures were concerning, but he was able to draw a sigh of relief. The main culprits had been cornered, and Rose Industries appeared to be in the clear.

There was no relief when it came to Frida's state of mind. She cowered at outside street sounds and refused to see friends who came to call. Pale and thin, her clothes hung loosely on her now-skeletal frame, and her body trembled at the slightest provocation. Many were the nights when she shrank into a corner after a terrible dream.

Alarmed at her deteriorating mood, August took matters into his own hands and presented Frida with a five-inch-long pistol. It featured a finely etched barrel with abalone grip plates and could be tucked easily into a purse or a dress pocket. "The gun is for your protection," he insisted, when she balked at the idea. "Just in case."

As the weeks wore on and her nightmares worsened, Frida began to keep the firearm with her at all times. It put August at ease to know she was protected, and he thrust himself into the daily operations of Rose businesses more than ever.

A few days after *The Times*' announcement of impending Tammany Hall arrests, Stefan met with August. With great ceremony, he produced several enormous ledgers. "Are these figures accurate?" August asked, as he sat across from Stefan at Josef's old desk.

"Absolutely," the comptroller replied. "Your father and I worked closely together. He was precise and meticulous in everything he did, and he made sure everyone else was, too."

August grinned. "Still, I'm amazed. These records show a much greater net worth than I anticipated," he declared.

"The business dealings of Rose Industries are complex, August," Stefan said. "I would be glad to meet with you individually on a regular basis, as I did with your dear father. To keep you informed of Rose Industries' finances, of course."

Without warning, August slammed the register covers shut, sending pulsations of heavy thuds throughout the room. "I will be meeting with the board shortly, Stefan, to review how Rose Industries goes forward from here. Colin has agreed to work with Fritz Bayer in taking on some renovations in the factories. Arnold is alert to any legal fallout from the Tammany scandals, and Gottfried informs me that our sales have continued to soar in all divisions. In the meantime, at my mother's request, I will take over my late father's duties in their entirety."

Stefan furrowed his brow. "I must advise you, August, that since Josef's passing, Rose Industries' outlays have increased beyond our income. It concerns me."

August abruptly stood and extended his hand to Stefan. "Thank you for coming in today, Stefan. I am aware of the situation, and I can assure you all will be resolved shortly. Have a good day, and please send my best to Amalia and the children."

Before Josef's death, August had been privy only to the finances of the subdivisions he oversaw. Thrilled with the huge income Rose Industries produced by the total of all its divisions, he decided it was time to get back to life. Selma Richter was still available; it was time to call on her.

Wearing charcoal slacks, a light-gray coat cut to the hips, and a tall beaver hat, August summoned Henry to bring a carriage around. As they approached the Richter mansion, Selma was just stepping out. She was dressed from head to toe in the latest shade of mellow red. Her bustled dress was adorned with ruffles and lace of the same hue, and her gypsy-style bonnet sported egret feathers and long flowing ribbons.

Mama is right, August thought. *She is handsome . . . and, since her father has become a powerful mogul, the connections could be helpful. Quite helpful, indeed.*

"Pull up to the curb please, Henry," August instructed.

He was riding in the Roses' brougham, a box-like coach that conveyed two passengers and was drawn by the family's old mixed-breed horse. *I'll need to get a better carriage,* he thought. *Perhaps a French barouche . . . or a landau that will allow me to be seen as I travel through the city. And I'll get matching Clydesdale horses with the feathery hair around their ankles.*

"Hello, my dear Miss Richter," he said, as Selma saw him and approached the carriage. "Have you a moment to spare? I happen to have two opera tickets for tomorrow evening and would be honored if you would join me. We will, of course, have dinner first at a restaurant of your choice."

Selma glared at him, her azure eyes shooting daggers. "And why should I accept your invitation?" she asked. "The last time we—"

"My dear," he interrupted, smiling his broadest smile, his narrow gray eyes looking directly into hers. "I sincerely apologize for my necessary but abrupt departure on that unfortunate occasion. If you will allow me to make it up to you, I will call for you at five tomorrow evening so that we may become reacquainted."

After several moments, Selma agreed, and the date was set.

That was easy, August thought. *I've got her. Ours will be a marriage of convenience. As Mama always says, we do what we must do. It's business.*

A short time later, August walked into a brownstone just off Fifth Avenue. He was greeted by an elegantly attired gentleman, about fifty years of age, who asked him for a code word.

Always prepared for such questions, August didn't hesitate. "Merrymount," he answered, gazing unflinchingly into the gaming-manager's eyes.

"Yes, sir, step right this way," the fellow replied. "You'll find the Castaway Casino downstairs. The second password will be required. Do you have any problem with that, sir?"

"None at all," August answered, straightening his tie.

"Very well then," said the concierge. "Good luck to you."

When August finally entered the gambling hall, his pulse started to race. He was heady with excitement. No longer would he need to limit his bets. There were millions in Rose Industries' coffers, and August intended to use them. *After all, my winnings will add to our wealth. We'll expand to national or even international markets, build more factories, expand our contacts. Between Selma's family connections and mine, the world will be ours.*

Once inside the protected inner chambers of the gambling establishment, August was recognized by several of the high players and welcomed heartily. He won hand after hand and went home with a considerably fatter wallet than he had won in previous games. That night, as he lay in his bed, visions of a grand city mansion, of a summer home in the stylish new resort town of Larchmont Manor, of travel and power, filled his head.

Perhaps I'll run for office one day. The family's connection to Grant could come in handy. Marriage to Selma, with her connections, could bring even the presidency within my grasp.

He fell asleep dreaming of the robust future that would be his to enjoy.

The next day, when Boss Tweed was arrested, a sheriff, who had obtained his office because of Tweed's support, released Tweed on a $1 million dollar bond. August was pleased. There was nothing at all to worry about. He decided to celebrate by going to Jerome Raceway the following day where Willie had been hired to train Whisper Nights.

That horse will bring good luck for us. Guaranteed.

CHAPTER 36

August

August smiled wryly. Their three-month courtship had been swift, but Selma had eagerly accepted his marriage proposal. He straightened his cravat, put a brilliant red, partially open rosebud in the lapel of his white frock coat, and checked to see that the two-carat diamond wedding band he would place on Selma's finger was tucked securely into his pocket.

She had been pleased with the fashionable wedding dress that, as custom dictated, he had given to her as a wedding gift. Created in the tones of whites that brides often wore these days to reflect chastity, its voluminous skirt featured rows of ruffles and a slightly bustled back. A great admirer of Queen Victoria, Selma had been pleased with the sapphire brooch and a Turkish-diamond necklace and earrings August had made to replicate the queen's wedding jewels.

When August and the family reached Temple Emanuel, the sanctuary was filled to overflowing and included guests from the city, the state, and business's most elite business, social, and political circles. Even the Grants had come in for the wedding. Rabbi Adler would perform the ceremony, and then the guests would attend a reception at August's new mansion on Fifth Avenue.

The residence took up an entire city block. Rising five stories above the street and descending two basement stories down, it featured sixty-one rooms and included a servants' quarters and separate apartments for Frida, Willie, Burke, Bessie, and Elsie. A turret for

Bessie occupied the south corner of the white marble structure, and a covered portico provided protection for visitors during inclement weather. It also included a large study that would allow August to avoid the crowded city streets during business hours when he had work that did not involve other personnel. The empty lot next door had provided space for a sixteen-stall barn for August and Willie's growing posse of Clydesdales, mustangs, and thoroughbreds.

"Willie," August had said one day after a particularly big win at an exclusive saloon, "come with me to the stable. I've a surprise for you." An arm around his brother's shoulder, August opened the stable door and led Willie to a magnificent thoroughbred that had won multiple purses in recent races. Willie's jaw had dropped when he saw the chestnut stallion with its thick black mane and rippling muscles. The animal held its finely chiseled head high on its long, arching neck, and his fine tail whisked gently as if in greeting.

"My God, August," Willie gasped, his jaw dropping open. "It's Whisper Nights. How did you—"

"It's okay, Willie," August grinned. "He's ours."

"But how? When?" Willie stammered.

"The world has been good to me, brother," August laughed, memories of the recent faro wins that had fueled the thoroughbred's purchase dancing in his head. "I've already bought a summer place in Larchmont Manor, up north in Westchester County. I've named it Rose Farms. In addition to a getaway lodge, it's got everything you'll need: a cottage for you, and a stable, paddocks, hurdles, and a track for Whisper Nights. You'll be able to go there for jockey training in time for the Saratoga races next summer."

August had spared no expense in furnishing Larchmont Manor, but he thrilled in decorating the new Fifth Avenue house. He procured antiques from France and Italy and brought in artifacts from all over the world. To entice Frida out of her self-enforced isolation, he hired Frederick Law Olmsted, the architect of Central Park, to design a greenhouse that would lead to a healing garden.

"Mother," August told Frida, "Olmsted is the best there is. He'll work with you to order specimen plants from anywhere you wish. It will be a perfect way, and a perfect place, for you to find solace."

When Frida responded with a shrug of her thin shoulders, August suggested that she create a memorial garden to be named after Josef, Louise, and Gertrude. "I suppose I will agree to consult with Mr. Olmsted about plantings," she said, her eyes flat, "but there will be no solace. There are no memories to be made."

With that, she had continued to stare out of the window, her back hunched and her hands lying limply in her lap.

Even August and Selma's wedding had held no interest for Frida. Reluctantly, she had agreed to attend the ceremony, but when guests arrived back at the house, she retired to her quarters.

"It's too soon for celebration, August," she had told him when the engagement was first announced. "It will always be too soon."

Frida's absence was notable, but the wedding crowd filled the mansion's ballroom to capacity. Servants offered guests an endless array of canapés before a dinner of roast venison, soufflés, and roasted autumn vegetables. Members of the New York Philharmonic Orchestra played waltzes and polkas throughout the evening. Louis Tiffany had been commissioned to provide chandeliers and lamps featuring stained-glass images of August and Selma. Their light cast a glow over the entire room and created an aura that made the cavernous space seem warm and intimate.

At the close of the affair, while Selma was occupied changing into a green cashmere going-away suit, August chatted with guests as they bid farewell and complimented him on a magnificent evening.

"Most weddings we attend are small family gatherings," said Ernst Reinhard. "This certainly was an extravagant affair, indeed."

August drew out his conversations with the guests until the last of them had departed. He was waiting for Selma to appear when he spotted someone familiar lingering just past the door. August wondered who the fellow might be—until he realized that it was Edward Reilly, who had recently been promoted from loan officer to vice president of the Immigrant Savings and Loan Bank.

When janitorial staff came in to begin the cleanup process, Reilly sauntered over to August. "Good evening, Mr. Rose," he said, extending his hand. "Congratulations on your wedding. It seems to have been a fine affair."

August felt the blood drain from his face. "Yes, it was," he said. "And what can I do for you?"

"I apologize for my timing," Reilly said, "but you have not returned my requests for a meeting. Your wedding was announced in *The Times* just a few days ago. You left me no choice but to visit you when, and where, I knew you would be found." Reilly paused, took a deep breath and grabbed a pastry from a tray remaining on the skirted dessert table. "Delicious," he said, as he bit into the Swiss chocolate mousse confection. "But tell me, Mr. Rose, how are you paying for all of this?"

"That's really none of your concern, is it?" August said defensively, his skin prickling.

"Oh, but it is, my dear sir," answered Reilly, as he plucked a miniature raspberry tart from the tray. "You see, defaults on Rose Industries' loans have been increasing since your father's death. I am here to see what you intend to do about it. I will expect answers soon, Rose," he said, starting to make his exit, leaving August trembling and pale.

As Reilly walked out, August caught sight of a figure lurking in the shadows. He was big and broad, with a huge belly and stringy hair. August's skin crawled. The man was holding a knife but scurried away when he caught August's eye.

It's okay, August told himself. *That fellow is a nobody. And Reilly? He is nothing to worry about. I will win plenty of money at the Monte Carlo casinos when we sail on my new yacht for our European honeymoon.*

CHAPTER 37

Otto

When Boss Tweed was arrested a few months after August's wedding, he was charged with fifty-five criminal offenses, each of which cited multiple incidents amounting to several hundred crimes. Otto realized that his days as a Tammany collector were numbered and, with the chances of being charged with Josef's death well behind him, it now appeared safe to come out of hiding. When he was approached by a member of the Whyos, the up-and-coming New York City gang that had emerged from what remained of old street gangs like the Dead Rabbits, he jumped at the opportunity to join their ranks.

Frank "Baboon" Connolly was a wiry fellow with a long narrow face. His dark hair was parted to the side and spilled haphazardly onto his forehead. Small, slightly crossed eyes peered out from under straight dark brows. Baboon hailed Otto as he was leaving Sweeney's House of Refreshment.

"Rumor has it you're a tough guy," the gangster said, his lip curling into a sneer. "Maybe even killed a man. We Whyos like that. Require it, even, to be a Whyo. Come work for us. We need collectors like yourself."

Otto put up his fists. "Who are you?" he demanded. "And why should I trust you?"

"Baboon's the name," laughed Connolly. "And," he said, his eyes veiled and cold, "you should trust me because you have no choice."

The thug pulled out a loaded pistol and thrust it into Otto's ribs.

"Okay, okay," Otto replied, recognition of the famous gangster dawning. "What do you want from me?"

His heart skipping a beat with excitement, Otto followed Baboon back into the saloon where eight other gang members came in through a hidden back door. The ten sat at a back table, ordered beers to celebrate St. Patrick's Day, and talked for a long time over corned beef and cabbage. Outside, the sounds of bagpipes echoed through the street as Irish revelers sang ditties and danced the jig as they paraded through the city for the holiday. It was an opportune moment. Most people were outdoors enjoying the celebrations; the din muffled the conversations taking place inside.

"We know you, Otto Krause. Your reputation with the Dead Rabbits—and Tammany Hall—precedes you," said Baboon. "The Whyos voted for you even before I met you on the street. You're ours. And you know it. We pay our members to perform services." He handed Otto a menu that included payment of:

Punching, $1

Both eyes blacked, $3

Nose, jaw, arms, legs broke, $7

Collections, $8

Collections with weapons, $10

Ear chewed off, $15

Stab, $20

Murder, $100 and up

Otto couldn't read, but he knew numbers and made a pretense of studying the list. A few minutes later, he handed it back to Baboon. "Looks okay to me," he said, nodding his head and drawing heavily on a cigar. *Looks dammed good to me*, he thought. *Those rates will earn me a lot more than I could ever make on the street. Or at sea. Another lucky break has come.*

CHAPTER 38

August

Over a year had passed since Josef's death, and August still spent much of his time attending to family matters. He was particularly worried about Frida, who had reclused herself and spent little time outside her room or her greenhouse. But he also knew the business was in trouble. After a night of drinking whiskey to calm his nerves, he stumbled into his study for a conference on Rose Industries' budget. He had put off a full board meeting for a while now, but he could no longer postpone Stefan's and Arnold's insistence that the three of them meet privately.

"It's a matter of urgency," Stefan had written to him a few days earlier. "There are pressing financial matters that must have your attention."

As he sat in the old leather chair that had been Josef's, August realized that he should have shaved, the stubble on his cheeks a reminder of his mood since he had received Stefan's letter. He knew the books weren't what they should be. Expenses, including the installation of fountains and statuary throughout the house, had been high. There had also been the cost of a mortgage on Rose Farms where sailing, polo, golf, and tennis were a way of life. The nineteen-room lodge needed furnishing, and both the barn and stables had required important additions. Besides, there were threats now from Gus Cairny—and from Edward Reilly, who had started to ask too many questions.

There were also decorating expenses. When he and Selma returned home to Fifth Avenue from their honeymoon, they had brought back several Monets, Van Goghs, Cézannes, and Renoirs, but Selma wanted more.

"We must have murals painted in the drawing room, the parlor, and the dining room," she had insisted. "It's all the rage, you know. I will hire John La Farge, the painter that everyone is using. Perhaps he'll do a sky with cherubs? Or an English landscape? Or a Monte Carlo scene?"

August had relented quickly. Such art was important in their circles.

As the three Rose executives began their conference over scones and coffee, August shifted nervously in his chair. Stefan and Arnold wore grim expressions.

"August," said Stefan, opening several ledgers, "something *must* change. Please look at these entries. For one thing, I don't recognize some of the employees' names."

That's because they don't exist, thought August. *There was no choice. I need their "salaries" for our business coffers.*

Stefan paused, waiting for August's response.

"So sorry, Stefan," August finally said. "I meant to catch you up on the new hires, but I've been extraordinarily busy."

"Rose Industries has never encountered anything like this," Stefan interrupted. "For the first time since the business began, we can't meet payroll. Checks are bouncing, and some of our suppliers are complaining that their bills are not being paid. Reilly says Immigrant hasn't received remittances in a few weeks. We've been tolerating this situation for a while, out of respect for Josef, but this cannot continue."

August reached under his desk for a shot glass, poured some whiskey and gulped down the amber liquid. "There have been a few small setbacks," August stammered, as he forced a smile. "I've had to draw monies from various accounts to cover them. But I promise you that cash will be available within the next few weeks. Rose Industries is doing better than ever. But now, gentlemen," he said, rising from his chair, "that will be all. Please give my regards, Stefan, to Amalia and the children. Arnold, send my best to your lovely wife, Bertha, and kiss the baby for me. We must get together soon. It's been a while."

As August cut them off from further conversation, Stefan and Arnold exchanged furtive glances and exited the room, their faces angry and tense. When they were safely out of sight, August relaxed his aching facial muscles. It was painful to maintain a smile, but he was certain he had convinced them that Rose Industries' finances were solid.

I'll put them off for a while longer. My wins will cover payroll and vendor expenses. And the rest? I'll come up with a plan. I always do.

CHAPTER 39

August

It had been a rough week for August. Gus Cairny had left several calling cards at the office demanding to be seen, Stefan was insisting that payroll not be delayed, and Reilly was threatening—again—to call in Rose Industries' loans. Then, as Friday had drawn to a close, a wiry fellow with a narrow face and slightly crossed eyes showed up at the house, knocking furiously at the elaborately carved entryway. Reluctantly, August answered it, terrified of who might be calling.

"Well, well," the man said as he planted himself between August and the door. "Aren't you going to invite me in?"

August's face drained of color as the intruder shouldered his way to the study, sat down on Josef's old chair, and put his feet up on August's carved mahogany desk. "Nice office!" he exclaimed, his eyes sweeping over the oil paintings, sculptures, and blown glass pieces August had purchased on his European honeymoon.

"Just what do you think you are doing?" August raged, sweat oozing from his pores and his small eyes blazing. "Who are you? And what gives you the right to barge into my home?"

The brute ignored August. "I like this piece especially," he said, as he stood and picked up a Murano glass vase decorated with fusible enamels in golds, royal blues, and forest greens.

"Be careful with that!" August shouted, as the gangster shifted the vase carelessly from hand to hand. Blood coursed loudly through his veins as if it would burst through his skull and spurt over the floor.

"Why? There seem to be more where this came from. Or maybe I should take it as partial payment for what you owe me—and the Whyos—from last night's faro game."

The man paused and surveyed the room. His eye caught the porcelain monkey. Frida and Josef had placed the figurine in the study where they would see it every day. After Josef's death, Frida had not wanted to move it.

"Treasure this always," she had said to August, explaining its origin as her beloved grandfather had explained it to her. "It is truly our story, the story of our family and of the Jewish people. The monkey represents the story of life with all its beauty and all its defects encased in a fragile shell. Remember it in times of love and, especially, in times of trouble."

August watched in horror as the man went over to the secretary desk where the porcelain monkey occupied a prime shelf behind the paned glass. He grabbed it and turned to face August.

"Put that down!" August shouted, his voice urgent and close to trembling.

"Oh, all right," the thug snarled. "I guess you don't want me to have it, right?"

"Give it to me," August said, his hand outstretched.

"Okay," the thug answered, dangling the monkey upside down. He laughed, shrugged, and assumed a pitcher's stance. "Here, catch!" he commanded, as he threw the monkey across the room to August.

Time seemed to freeze as August watched the figurine tear through the air. Propelled by rage, he lunged forward and extended both hands toward the hurtling porcelain. It turned over midair—but August slid to the floor and caught it just before it landed. He clutched it to his chest, Frida's words rushing through his head: "Keep the monkey always . . . and live by its lessons."

As August stood to face the thug, recognition dawned. He recalled the humiliation of the previous night's faro losses at the Castaway. Flush with new cash coming into Rose from a big sale, he had gone to the casino to celebrate. He had easily won hand after hand, and he won big—until he threw down all his chips in a flush of excitement. In seconds, it was all gone as the dice failed to go his way. He had watched in drunken horror as the dealer scooped up his pile and pushed it to the winner, a tall wiry fellow with a long face. August now felt bile rise into his throat as he recognized the thug from the faro game.

"Where's the rest of the money?" the ruffian now said. "You gave the dealer last night only part of what you owe, Mr. Rose, sir. As you well know, there are other outstanding debts, as well. My collector, one Otto Krause, will pay you a visit by month's end. By the way, name's Connolly. But you can call me Baboon."

CHAPTER 40

August

Willie gently guided Whisper Nights into his stall after a jockeying session at Rose Farms. August's generosity in providing the best of everything the farm required had paid off, and the facility was sterling in every aspect. Several trainers and stable hands resided in the cottage, and a handsome room was reserved for Willie when he came to the farm to ride.

Neighboring horses and their handlers were often called in to train with Whisper Nights whose calm temperament and even disposition made him a perfect competitor. Standing at sixteen hands and weighing almost 1,200 pounds, his intelligent face featured a long white star settled between bright, clear eyes. All four feet sported white socks that extended to his knees, and his muscles were hard under his broad chest and short, solid back.

Willie had just taken the stallion out for a gallop on the farm's track. When they got back to Whisper's stall, he checked the horse's hooves, brushed him from head to rear, and washed him down. He was about to take the steed to feed in the pasture when he saw August's new landau carriage pull up. Four Clydesdales pranced elegantly as the driver offered them apples and cubes of sugar.

"August, how good to see you!" exclaimed Willie, as he helped his brother step onto the well-pounded dirt patch by the barn door. "It's been a while," he said. "Whisper and I have missed you."

The brothers embraced briefly. "What brings you here today? You look so serious," Willie said.

"Can we go inside to talk?" August asked, his eyes darting to check for eavesdroppers.

"Certainly," said Willie, "we can use the front room of the cottage. There's no one there at this time of day."

A few minutes later, the Rose brothers were settled in opposite-facing plush couches next to a ceiling-high stone fireplace. A horse-themed rug covered the brick floor, and paintings of recent purse winners were hung in gilt frames on the mahogany-paneled walls. Placed carefully on an overstuffed chair were Willie's new silks. The royal blue jacket was emblazoned with a large rose on its back; smaller roses were superimposed on the blue-and-white-striped sleeves. White jodhpurs were laid out next to the jacket, and a red-white-and-blue cap with a large rose embossed on its peak hung on a nearby hook.

"Is Whisper Nights ready for Saratoga next week, Willie?" asked August, his expression serious but his narrow eyes twinkling with excitement.

"Absolutely," answered Willie. "He's running with a smooth twenty-foot stride, and he can do a three-and-a-half-mile stretch in four minutes. That's more than enough for Saratoga, August. Besides, I can feel the strength and speed on his back when I ride him."

August grinned. "It's his time, Willie. I can feel it. Now, let's get the two of you ready and prepare to rake in the winnings."

The following Tuesday morning, July 16, 1872, August and Selma checked in at the elegant Raceway Hotel as soon as they arrived in Saratoga. They chatted with the concierge for a while, then made their way to their reserved suite next to Willie's rooms on the top floor.

"Does everything please you, my dear?" asked August, as he poured two flutes of champagne.

Selma accepted a glass of the sparkling wine, sipped it daintily from her painted lips, and placed it on an intricately carved table next to a rose-colored loveseat. She strolled through the anteroom, peered into the adjacent bedrooms, and checked her hair in a floor-length wrought-iron mirror. "All seems to be in order," she finally said, examining her perfectly groomed, red-oil-tinted fingernails. "And if you don't mind, August, I will lie down for a while before we get ready for the gala this evening."

"Very well, darling," said August, hiding his immense pleasure at the prospect of being free for the afternoon. "I'll go with Willie to check on Whisper Nights while you rest."

His heart beating wildly, August met Willie in the grand lobby, and the two hired a carriage to take them to the stables where Whisper Nights was settling in after the long journey up the Hudson. *He must be perfect, perfect for tomorrow. Everything depends on perfection. There's no option but a first-place win. None at all.*

When they entered the stable, Willie strode across the raked dirt floor to where Whisper was feeding. "Good boy," he crooned, as he stroked the animal's luxurious mane. "You're going to do just fine tomorrow, aren't you?"

As if he understood Willie's words, Whisper Nights whinnied and reached down to place his great head on Willie's shoulder. He cocked a back leg, nudged the jockey's cheek, and let out a long sigh.

"He likes you," said August.

"Yes, he does," answered Willie. "We've spent many hours together. He is going to be great racing against Longfellow and Harry Bassett. Those two steeds are the only serious threats to us. They're serious competition, you know."

"That's true," said August. "Longfellow has won thirteen races, including beating Harry Bassett by a three-quarter length for the Saratoga Cup last summer. He was named after his long legs for a reason, that's for sure. And Harry Bassett? He's won an outstanding forty thousand so far. Both horses have strong backs and legs, powerful shoulders, and robust loins."

"But so does Whisper Nights," said Willie, reaching out to smooth Whisper's star. "Our boy has already won multiple races in record times."

"Let's hope he adds a win tomorrow," said August. "For now, I'll leave you two to each other. I'll see you at dinner and the opera this evening."

Following a meal of wild salmon with Venetian sauce, Parisian peas, and roasted potatoes, all followed by fresh cherry crepes and rich coffees, August excused himself and left Selma to attend the opera with acquaintances from Manhattan. As soon as she was out of sight, he headed to the crowded bar where he ordered drinks for everyone.

"Cheers!" he shouted, as he lifted glass after glass in jubilant anticipation of the wins Whisper Nights would bring him. He exulted in the adoration of the crowd as he picked up tabs in celebration of the large pot he would reap the next day.

As clouds gathered around the moon, August headed for the clubhouse where its great hall had been converted into a betting parlor, and speculation was taking place at a frenzied pace. August made the rounds of the bookmakers accepting wagers. Finally, he entered the billiards room where he placed bets for the two-year-old pre-race. He also placed an across-the-board Saratoga Cup bet on Whisper Nights with a scrawny bookmaker named Fergus.

"*How* much are you betting, sir?" Fergus asked, his expression incredulous.

"You got it right," August said, a sneer crossing his lips as the bookie examined his six-figure check.

"You are August Rose, aren't you, sir?" Fergus demanded.

"Yes, I am," August replied, puffing out his chest.

"Your reputation precedes you," said Fergus, taking a crumpled list of blackballed players from his pocket. "I can't take your check, sir. Only cash."

August's face turned purple with indignation. "That's ridiculous. I won't stand for it."

"You'll have to stand for it, Mr. Rose. Gus Cairny over at the Union Hotel says checks you've issued recently have come back with insufficient funds. It's cash or nothing."

His mind racing, August took several deep breaths before he responded to the bookie. *Whisper is a sure thing. I must be in this for the Cup. Damn Cairny, damn him. I can't let him stop me, not now when I'm so close.*

Trying to keep his fury in check, August drew an ornate sterling silver flask from his pocket. He took a long swig of whiskey, patted his lips with a Rose Lace handkerchief, and glared at the bookie. "I'll speak with Mr. Cairny myself," he said, "to straighten out this misunderstanding. Where is he?"

"He's not available, sir," said Fergus. "He is on leave from the Union Hotel and will not be back for the foreseeable future."

Don't panic, August admonished himself, pausing to gather his thoughts. *For now, August, just do what you must, and things will take care of themselves.*

"Very well, then," August finally said, his nostrils flaring. "Here's what will happen." He took a deep breath, straightened his shoulders, and took his last bills from his wallet.

Fergus scowled and took the money with a wave of his hand. "I guess you're not going to be such a big winner this time, are you now? What happened to the big bettor and his famous wins, eh? Loser can't beat the odds anymore?"

Anger flooded August's head. Somehow keeping his calm, he stared at Fergus. "What makes you think that I'm stopping with cash? I'm betting the deed to my business, Rose Industries. Do you have a problem with that, Mr. Bookie?"

I have no choice. If I don't win this big, the business will collapse anyway. We Roses do what we must do.

The bookkeeper's eyes bored into August's. "I have no problem. It's you who will have the problem if you lose."

But I won't lose. I know Whisper will do it. I'm about to see to it. Then, after tomorrow, I'll show them all. Cairny, Immigrant, Baboon and his collector, whoever that is . . . even Stefan and Arnold with their payroll and supplier demands. Everyone will be paid off. I'll be free.

That night, August cowered as an angry horde chased past him through burning streets. As he lay in the gutter, dollar bills flew from every direction, eluding him when he tried to catch them. Higher and higher they piled until they covered him in a shroud from which he couldn't escape.

His screams were of no avail until, suddenly, a massive chestnut thoroughbred came thundering down the street, its splendid hoofs pounding the cobblestones until it reached August and came to a sudden halt. It reared up on its hind legs, pawing at the air in a desperate attempt to fly. Its eyes were wild, and its black mane flew in every direction. When it saw August, its screams pierced the air just before August woke, his heart pounding and perspiration soaking his sheets.

"I'm sorry, Whisper," August stammered, as he forced himself back to reality, "but there's no choice." Still shaking, he threw back the covers, tore off the monogrammed silk pajamas hiding his day clothes, and slipped on the shoes hidden just under the bed. He grabbed a waiting satchel and had started for the door when Selma awoke.

"August," she said, her voice heavy with slumber. "It's not even daybreak. What are you doing up?"

"Go back to sleep," he replied, hoping his voice wouldn't betray the fear he still felt from the nightmare. "I'm fine. Just awake early from the excitement of today." He gave Selma a peck on the cheek and waited until her breath was even and her eyes fluttered with dreams. On feather feet, he tiptoed out into the hall.

The hotel was quiet when August reached the lobby. Gratified when he saw the concierge slumped in a chair and snoring lightly, he managed to slip unnoticed into the night. With only a sliver of moon to guide him, he made his way to the stable where Whisper Nights was sleeping in his stall. He woke the stablehand who had been assigned to watch the stallion.

"Okay, fella," August said in a hushed tone, "you can leave now. I'll stay here with Whisper Nights until morning. Get some rest, lad. You'll be working hard later today."

When the great horse saw August, he stood, shook out his mane, and lay his head on August's shoulder. "Good boy," crooned August, stroking the animal's nose. "I've some treats for you."

He pulled a few carrots from his pocket and offered them to Whisper whose soft lips quickly accepted the offering. From the other pocket, August grabbed some carefully measured, crushed coca leaves. He crouched and mixed the stimulant into Whisper's feed. The coca would suppress thirst, pain, and fatigue. It would keep Whisper at top speed on the track.

"Enjoy tomorrow's race," said August, breathing into the animal's ear. "The treats will be good for all of us."

"He's unusually lively today," beamed Willie, as he checked Whisper Night's saddle straps. The animal's muscles rippled under his touch, and he whinnied loudly. "He feels a win."

August grinned and helped Willie climb onto Whisper Night's back. Morning clouds had receded, and a hot sun bathed the parade grounds. Carriages followed each other in constant succession, and spectators dressed in the latest fashions wandered the grounds not caring about the dust clouds swarming about. The enormous crowd waved flags and cheered from the stands, and a brass band added great excitement to the festive atmosphere.

Suddenly, a great roar went up as Whisper Nights, Longfellow, and Harry Bassett strutted onto the parade grounds. Moments later, after all sixteen racehorses had entered the arena, they were off at a gallop past the stands. Their hoofs thundered as they tore up dust and finally came to a ceremonial halt at the two-mile starting post.

Exactly one hour later, the roar of the crowd became deafening as the bugle sounded, the flag fell, and the horses were off. When they passed the stand for the first time, spectators erupted from their seats, clenched their fists, and pounded the air. Some were nervous and trembling; others looked like they would explode with excitement, their faces flushed and the veins on their necks bulging as they shouted for their favorites. The police tried to get everyone to sit, but they were overwhelmed as the crowd jostled to get the best views.

When the horses swept around the lower turn, the jockeys wielded their whips and spurs until they were close together. Bassett was leading by a half-length. Down the quarter stretch came the trio—Harry Basset, Longfellow, and Whisper Nights. Men threw their hats and ladies sliced the air with their parasols.

Suddenly, a groan rose from the crowd as Longfellow stumbled halfway through the race. The plate of his shoe had broken and torn the soft part of his heel. The valiant steed continued to race, managing against all odds to keep only three-quarters of a length behind Bassett and Whisper Nights, but his valiant efforts couldn't overcome his handicap.

In the stands, August rejoiced as Whisper Night's greatest competitor was knocked out of the race. *Now Whisper will definitely make it,* he thought. *He will make it. He must make it.* August pumped his arms and shouted. His voice, already hoarse, cracked as Whisper gained a head on Bassett just as they were approaching the finishing line. He watched Willie stand in his stirrups and ply his whip as the two leading stallions thundered around a bend. The crowd went wild. Ladies forgot propriety and jumped into the air, hair coming undone and shirtwaists separating from skirts. Men hoisted boys onto their shoulders, stamped their feet so hard that the grandstand shook, and screamed encouragement to their chosen steeds.

Suddenly, Bassett got away and gained a nose on Whisper. As they came up the stretch, Whisper put forth a gallant lunge and regained the lead by a length. Then, to August's horror, a stray piece of paper bourn on the breeze landed on Whisper's nose. The stallion spooked and fell back, allowing Harry Bassett to enter the final lap way ahead of the pack. August blanched as hooves flew past the spectators, but Bassett pulled away and thundered toward the gate to finish at three minutes, fifty-nine seconds.

Whisper came in at the back of the pack.

August picked himself up from the grandstand floor and willed himself to leave the track. He stumbled out of the gates, ignoring Selma's and Willie's calls to join them and made his way to The Ale House on a back street near Saratoga Springs' outskirts. A shanty that had seen better days, it offered a dark interior and lots of beer. If he were lucky, they'd have bourbon at the bar but, in that unlikely event, August hoped, they'd have, at least, an abundance of whiskey.

Disheveled and sweaty from the walk to the saloon, his shirt untucked and his shoes battered, August was unrecognizable. Gone were the swagger from his step and the self-satisfied curl of his narrow lip. As afternoon waxed into evening, and then into night, August drank.

"That's it for you, mister," the bartender finally said just before midnight. "It's time to pay up and go home."

"Pay up?" August said, almost choking on his words. "That's a good one."

The bartender flashed an ominous smile. "Yeah, pay up. And leave."

August threw back his head and howled with laughter. "I'm August Rose," he said. "I'll pay you when I get around to it."

From a back room, two men dressed in black appeared. They grabbed August by the elbows, pulled him outside, and threw him to the ground. One grabbed his coat while the other straddled him and rifled through his pockets.

"No money? Let's teach this guy a lesson he'll never forget."

Hours later, August revived. His face was swollen, his eyes were beaten half shut, and blood caked his fine jacket and trousers. His wallet was gone, but in its place was a note: "We'll get you. No free drinks at this establishment."

August moaned and tried to stand but fell back onto the ground immediately. He lay there with his knees pulled to his chin, his tongue and throat parched, until a coral sun started to make its way across the sky to greet a new day. Finally, as the morning crested, he managed to pick himself up and stagger back toward the hotel, his hat pulled closely over his face.

Early risers were up and about, many of them delivery people and workers about to start their labors. No one paid attention to the bum weaving his way unsteadily through the streets. When he arrived at the hotel, he dared not go through the main lobby. Holding himself tight against the building's walls, he made his way to an open cellar door. Nobody saw him as he took back stairs and hallways to his rooms.

Selma had already left for breakfast as August entered his suite. *It all looks so normal,* he thought. *But it's not.* He tried to stifle the huge, hulking sobs that were clamoring to be released, but it was of no use. They came from deep within his chest until he was spent. Then, wiping the telltale tears from his face with the back of his hand, he went to an ornate writing desk at the back of the suite and took out an embossed sheet of stationery.

In a shaky hand, he began to write:

Dearest Mama,

By the time you get this letter, you will know what I have done—to you, to the family, and to Rose Industries. I know that I have lied and most shamefully deceived you, and I find myself reduced to that low state where I am ashamed and unable to talk to you but must take the coward's way out by writing this letter.

When I was gambling over the last few years, I lost a big amount of money and never was able to tell the truth about what I lost. Had I come out with the truth, I would not be in the position I am today. But I have lost Rose Industries and your trust. I must now face the disgust and anger you will no doubt direct toward me.

In the past, I tried to stop playing of all kinds, but when the time came to settle what I owed, my manliness left me. I believed the only way I could pay my debts was to gamble more. I thought I could keep winning, save up to pay my balances and wait for another year when I could come to you with an open heart to tell you what evil I had done, but also to tell you that it was all behind me.

I vow to you now that fate has taught me a lesson. I vow never to play any game or enter any race where there is any chance of losing any amount of money. I will be your devoted servant in rebuilding our businesses. Whatever you decide to do with me, I shall do without saying a word. This I swear to you. You will yet get pleasure from me. Should I ever violate my promise to you, in any way, show no mercy to me, for then I would not be worth recognizing.

Your penitent son,
August

As he put down his pen, he heard an insistent knock. Hastily, August put the letter into a hotel-embossed envelope housed in a slot at the back of the desk's writing platform. He stood, ran a hand through his disheveled hair, and reluctantly walked to the door. Any color that was left in his face drained when he saw the caller.

It was Gus Cairny. "Now, Rose, now," he insisted, holding a gun to August's ribs.

Moments later, August signed another promissory note. For his homes.

CHAPTER 41

August

A few weeks later, August was working in the study at Frida's mansion when Edward Reilly arrived unexpectedly early one morning. The banker carried a briefcase stuffed with legal papers and ceremoniously placed them on August's desk. "That's it, August. I'm leaving these banking termination files with you. I'll expect them signed and back in my office by four o'clock this afternoon."

As August rifled through the documents, his expression darkened, and his lips trembled. "How dare you withdraw our banking privileges? How dare you call in our loans?" he shouted. His veins pulsed wildly, and his eyes threw daggers of hate. "Reilly, you know damn well that Rose Industries has been a backbone of wealth for Immigrant Savings. You'll see. Without us, you'll go under. You won't get our contracts, our interest payments, our investment returns. Mark my words. You'll be sorry, sorry, sorry!"

Reilly coolly turned his back and strode out the door.

August's jumbled mind darted from possibility to lost possibility. *I would have won the race losses back. I would have borrowed from someone. They're not giving me a chance. None of them trust me, know my planning abilities, my resilience . . .*

When Reilly was out of sight, August grabbed the portfolio papers and threw them in the air, watching them scatter throughout the study. He grabbed the heavy inkwell on his desk and threw it into the bookcases lining the window wall. The well hit imported crystal vases and sent them crashing to the floor. His fury building, he threw books across the room, howling incoherently as they knocked lamps to the ground and tore paintings off their hooks.

Finally, August grabbed the inkwell's envelope opener and furiously slashed Josef's old office chair. Again and again, he drew the blade across the aged leather, digging until the chair's down stuffing flew into the air like snowflakes. Next, he turned to his father's secretary desk, the one Josef had so lovingly restored back on Nassau Street when he and Frida were newlyweds. Drawing on the escalating strength of his fury, he pulled the writing platform off its hinges and hurled it across the room.

"Where are you, Father, when I need you most? You would have stopped me! You would have stopped me!" he cried into the empty room.

He fell into a heap, his body shuddering with recollections of the past few weeks. The business was gone, the Rose homes were in court-mandated sales, and his mother—his own mother—had been forced to sell her jewelry. Whisper Nights had been sold, and Willie hadn't talked to him since. And then, there was Burke, who was working with Elsie on a history of racing for *Harper's*. August was terrified that his pre-race visit to Whisper could somehow come to light. The very thought made his mouth go dry and his stomach heave.

After some moments, August managed to upright himself and stagger to the study's bar, where he guzzled whiskey straight from the bottle, chugging it like water until his mind dulled and he passed out on the littered floor.

When he awoke, his body stiff and sore, the sun was starting to set in a blaze of pinks and oranges. He pulled himself to his feet and tried to pick up a few damaged curios when the door was pushed open by a large man with a huge belly and stringy hair. The fear that clawed August quickly turned to rage. "What are you doing in my house?" he shouted.

"Oh, don't you know who I am? Everyone knows Otto, Mr. Rose. Baboon Connolly sent me to collect what's due the Whyos. That's fine with me. There *are* tender young girls in this house, right?" He laughed. "I do like young girls. The younger the better. Besides, you and me have business to attend to."

August lunged at the intruder, his face crimson. "Get out!" he screamed, as Otto swung his fist and hit August in the jaw, drawing blood and ripping a front tooth from its socket. He grabbed August's arm and twisted it behind his back, pushing the limb toward his shoulder blades until it couldn't be wrenched up any further. Throwing his right forearm around August's neck, he squeezed until August felt his eyes start to bulge.

"What do you want?" August managed to stammer. "Let me go!"

Otto threw back his head and laughed obscenely, lightening his pressure and breathing hotly into August's ear. "Bastard son of mine. *Jüdischer* bastard."

"What are you talking about? I have no idea what you're talking about," he replied, as sweat beaded on his brow and his head began to pound.

Otto released his chokehold, rolled down his shirt collar, and pulled August's face to within inches of his turtle mole. "You don't believe you're mine?" he sneered. "What do you see, Rose, what do you see? You look just like me. Your face, your eyes, your mole are the same as mine. *Exactly* the same."

He pushed August back against the wall. August's stomach heaved, and bile rose to the back of his throat. Otto's blond hair, his thin lips, the gray slit-like eyes—the mole, exactly like his own. "But that's impossible," he gasped.

Otto slapped August's face. "You think it's impossible? Ask your *Jude Bitch* mother about her and me on the *Holstein*. Just ask her about our good times on that ship from Germany." He howled with glee. "Too bad your supposed father's not around anymore. Not that a dead Jew isn't a good Jew. Your dear papa," he sneered, "would tell you who put the scar on *his* neck, *and* the one on your bitch mother's. Now let's give you a matching one, shall we?"

Otto grabbed August's waist. He drew his knife and held it to August's neck, teasing it against the skin before the Bowie sliced his flesh. August felt searing pain and clutched his throat. Involuntarily, he sucked in his breath and wheezed as blood poured from his wound onto the floor.

August's belly boiled in fury. He kicked Otto's shins, managed to extricate himself, and tried to throw a fist into Otto's abdomen. Otto ducked and went for August's legs. Still holding the Bowie, he slashed August's right calf, drawing howls of pain from his victim. Mustering strength he didn't know he had, August reared up, grabbed Otto, and the two fell to the floor in a twist of legs and thrashing arms.

"I will *NOT* have a Jew son!" Otto bellowed, as he turned August over and pressed the side of the Bowie to his jugular vein. "You're dead, *Jude* bastard, dead. You hear me? Damn you and your *Jude* bitch mother for having you," he rasped, as he raised the blade to slice it into August's throbbing throat.

August brayed in indignation and pushed Otto off just before the knife could make its mark. He scrambled to his feet and had almost wrested the knife from Otto when Otto stood and counterattacked with a blow to August's abdomen. The air whooshed from August's lungs, but instinct told him he'd be dead if he fell. He righted himself and threw his body against Otto's, knocking him to the ground. With lightning speed, August straddled Otto. He grabbed his wrist, twisted it, and poised himself to grab the Bowie when he heard someone enter the room.

When he heard the voice, he froze. *It can't be,* he thought. *Or could it?*

CHAPTER 42

Frida

Frida was in the greenhouse. She had been refusing to see members of Emanuel, friends, and business associates, permitting only perfunctory visits with the children. Even the porcelain monkey, to which she had turned in times of trouble, could no longer offer solace. The conservatory was the only refuge left, a silent place where she could be surrounded by her plants. Absorbed in their colors, textures, and fragrances, she had come here often to escape her despair.

Josef and the twins were gone. Rose Industries had been forced into bankruptcy. She had been forced to sell her home. Except for faithful Henry, who had insisted on staying with Frida and the children until she could get back on her feet, the servants had been forced to depart. The impending move into a dreary flat in the outskirts of town, the treachery, and the sudden poverty August had inflicted upon her were overwhelming.

There's no use in trying anymore, she thought, as she walked, trancelike, through the greenhouse. But today, even the plants seemed distant. Every leaf blemish, every fading flower mocked her as if to say, "We, too, are leaving you."

Only her oleander, reaching now to thirteen feet, seemed a beacon of peace. As she approached its place of honor at the center greenhouse mound, it called to her, *I can help you, dear Frida. You have cared for me. Let me take care of you. Put one of my red flowers in your hair as a remembrance of me. Then pluck my leaves and crush them against your tongue so my toxins can carry you away forever from your faded life. What use are you to anyone now? You've failed your children. Your friends. God will understand, Frida. Do it, my beloved mistress. Do it, do it, do it.*

Frida felt her knees go weak. The prospect of final peace was in reach, right here in the conservatory. *But the children . . . Bessie, Burke, Elsie. . .They need me. But what kind of mother am I? Will I let disaster fall upon them as I let it fall on August? Despite his lineage, he's still mine, still that adorable baby with fat dimpled legs . . . But he's not that baby anymore. He betrayed me, betrayed all of us. You tempt me, oleander. It would be so easy. . . .*

At that instant, she heard August let out a blood-curdling scream and an all too familiar voice screaming back. The hair on her arms stood up, and bile rose to her throat as she recognized the rasp in the second voice. Her heart pounded, and her veins pumped blood into a boil as her breath came in deep gasps, filling her lungs with searing pain. The screams reached deep into her soul as she forgot the oleander's call and instinctively raced toward the ghastly sounds. Toward her child.

When she reached the study, resolve overcame her as if God were watching and planning her every move. "That's enough!" she shouted, as she saw August pinned to the ground by the brute wielding an all-too-familiar knife.

The conflict came to an abrupt halt as August and Otto looked up to see Frida in the doorway. She was clenching her pearl-crusted pistol, and it was aimed directly at Otto. For the first time in a long time, her posture was erect, and her eyes were on fire.

"Well, well, well," gloated Otto. "If it isn't the *Jude Bitch*. One of my best! Will your daughters be as good?"

"Get up, you bastard," Frida said, her voice unwavering as she approached Otto and pointed the barrel at his heart. "You have done enough damage to this family."

Otto jumped to his feet. He pulled August up and grabbed him around the neck, the Bowie flashing. "You wouldn't dare!" Otto yelled. "You're nothing but a *Jude Bitch*."

August took advantage of the moment. He broke Otto's hold, grabbed the Bowie, and sliced it into Otto's shoulders, drawing streams of blood. Otto rallied and wrested the knife from August. He had poised the knife just above the center of August's chest when Frida's voice again permeated the scene. "Not this time. You don't win this time," she commanded, her voice cold and steady.

A loud report filled the room as Frida pulled the trigger. Gunpowder scorched Frida's nostrils and filled her mouth with the acrid taste of revenge.

Otto fell to the floor, his narrow eyes widening just before the life drained from them. With cold calm, Frida bent over the body. Slowly, she extracted the Bowie from Otto's dead grasp and drew a deep two-inch slice across his neck. Then, she stood and caressed her scar while she watched the blood cake on her dead tormentor's throat. Triumph filled her eyes, and a calm entered her soul. Suddenly, Henry entered the room; questions seemed to fill his eyes. He appeared, to Frida, to be a ghost from another world.

Where were you a few moments ago, Henry? Did you see what happened here?

She walked slowly over to the shelf where the porcelain monkey sat. Gingerly, she pressed it to her chest.

August's eyes asked questions he could not speak. Frida looked from his face to Otto's dead one, the brief moments of peace draining from her. Inextricably, the three had been bound to each other. *Are they still bound to me? My child and also my nemesis . . . ? Will I ever know?* she wondered, shivers running up and down her spine.

Frida stared at her son. She held the monkey in one hand and the

Bowie in the other. The weapon glistened moistly with Otto's fresh blood. She turned to address both August and Henry. In a detached tone, her eyes shaded and unreadable, she managed to retrieve her mantra.

"I did what I had to do. I always do what I have to do."

Author's Note

As a child, I used to sit with my sisters and cousins at the feet of my late uncle (to whom this novel is dedicated) to hear his captivating tales of the family. Uncle Howie was a true raconteur. He would speak and we would listen in awe to the joys, accomplishments, and travails of our ancestors. We were all ears well into our sixties, when he passed away, never tiring of the tales of Grossmama and Grosspapa and their brood of twelve children.

Then, in the 1980s, he gifted all of us with a detailed memoir filled with extraordinary details of where the family lived and summered; where and how they did business; what they wore; the jokes they played on each other; family dinners and celebrations; births and weddings and deaths. He brought not only the people, but the society and the times, alive for us. For example, the candy jar that Josef holds aloft while the children anticipate the yummy treats within; the dinner table seatings from youngest to oldest and the reporting of news at those dinners; the many parties and gatherings; Grossmama standing on the dining room table and issuing orders; the family mausoleum; and many other details from the novel reflect my uncle's accounts.

The Porcelain Monkey was conceived a few years ago when I found a box of scandalous family letters and documents in my cousin's basement. They were yellowed and musty with age, but they were intact and legible. The stories of love, success, vice, and failure they revealed gripped me and motivated my novel.

Frida, the protagonist, is inspired by the real Grossmama. Although her story is highly fictionalized, she was a woman of tiny stature but big ambition who worked with her adored husband to grow a small business into an industrial giant. She also dealt with the tragedy of a daughter who succumbed to a progressive genetic disease and a son whose genius helped to build the business but lost it when he gambled it away. Josef and the children are also fictionalized.

I have strived to adhere as closely as possible to the issues, mores, and societal concerns of the characters' mid-nineteenth century world. For example, the porcelain decrees of Frederick the Great; Rent Day and Moving Day; the Draft Riots; corrupted voting irregularities; Lincoln's death and funeral; the novel's culminating race with Longfellow and Harry Bassett (in which Harry Bassett won) at Saratoga; the Chauncey Vibbard; Grant's General Orders #11; the Orange Parades and riots; the gangs of New York; A.T. Stewart's and other department stores; General and Mrs. Ulysses Grant and their visit to Saratoga; Mrs. Winslow's Soothing Syrup; Fernando Wood, Isaiah Rynders, Bill Poole, Frank ("Baboon") Connolly, Boss Tweed, Tammany Hall, Rabbi Samuel Adler, Temple Emanuel, Thomas Nast, and Abraham Oakey Hall were actualities. Although I have taken liberties in creating the circumstances, actions, participants, and dialogues of some events, agencies, people, and animals, historical factors have been carefully researched and, sometimes, extrapolated to explore what might have been. I have also refrained from using era-appropriate terminology out of respect for current-day sensitivities.

While most characters in the novel are fictitious, the essence of their struggles and triumphs in the New World are inspired by realities revealed in those forgotten boxes in storage for over a hundred years.

This novel is a work of fiction. Any historical errors are totally inadvertent and, with humility, are solely my responsibility.

Discussion Questions

1. Why did Frida feel that the only way she could let her mother know of her departure was through a note? Why didn't she tell her in person?

2. How does Josef deal with temptation? Is he religious, a man of God? How does he justify his departure from the tenets of Judaism?

3. How does Frida deal with ethical dilemmas? With practical problems?

4. Why doesn't Frida share her suspected pregnancy with Josef until it becomes obvious?

5. Why do people respond positively to Frida's demands?

6. Why doesn't Erwin take care of Roshen when she becomes widowed? Is he justified?

7. Why does Frida shun her orthodoxy? Why does she later join Temple Emanuel?

8. Does Frida ever go to the mikveh? How resolute is she? Do you think she goes eventually?

9. What are the characters' flaws? good qualities? Name examples.

10. What do Josef/Frida/August want at different times during their lives? Why? How do those goals evolve during their lifetimes? Are their goals met? If not, why not?

11. To what extent were the various characters' issues products of their era? Which struggles relate to our times? Which do not?

12. How does antisemitism drive the plot's central conflicts and decisions?

13. What do you think happens to Frida? August? Bessie? The children? Boss Tweed, Peter O'Flanagan, and other characters? What is it about their each of their personalities that is central to their fates?

Acknowledgments

The Porcelain Monkey, an historical fiction novel, came to be with the support and input of many people, including my late uncle Howard Baron, who gave our family the gift of a written family history in 1981.

Special thanks to Carol and Gary Rosenberg of *The Book Couple* for their invaluable help, encouragement, and inspiration in the development, editing, and production of the book. Thanks also to developmental editor Carol Hoenig for her insights.

Sandi Skodnik, with her thirty-seven-year background in teaching drama and film, spent hours participating in the planning and development of the story and contributing to the staging of the novel. Karen Mascio read the manuscript multiple times and offered not only technical support but also invaluable insight into the characters' development. Barbara Shapiro, former English literature teacher and librarian, offered structural consultations from early on in the writing. Dr. Bryan Mascio, PhD in Education from Harvard University; microbiologist Carmela Mascio; and Dr. Arlene Kalderon, PhD in Clinical Psychology, offered insight into the characters' reactions to both positive and negative experiences. Dr. Howard Sacher; Dr. Amy Slear; Jane Baron, RN; and Caryn Antriello of the Scleroderma Society were generous with their medical insights and expertise. Udo

Drescher provided German-language translations, and Barbara Feinstein and Terry Kaufman offered the gifts of readings and feedback as the manuscript went through multiple revisions. Amy Robinson always gave me confidence and encouragement when I reached a plateau.

Content advisors Jeffrey Bass, Albert Bleecker, Anthony Colletti, Barbara Weiss, and Sidney Eisenberg provided business expertise. Michael Veitch of the Saratoga Racing Museum generously offered input about horse racing and the Saratoga Cup of 1872. Rabbi Judith Cohen provided religious advice, Professor Richard Walsh read the Civil War segments for accuracy. Jeff Robel of the National Weather Service provided as much weather information as was available for the time scope of the novel. Fred Baron of High Ridge Antiquarian Books provided period maps and commentary for New York City; Jessica Varma of the New York City Tenement Museum provided detail of the Lower East Side in the mid-nineteenth century. Any possible content errors are mine alone.

Many thanks to Beta readers Alan Ring, Mara Robinson, Sheila Zimmerman, Susan Baron, Barbara Elis, Burt Mitchell, Felicia Colletti, Janet Sylvester, Rhoda Zinn, Alice Soskin, Doris Rosenfeld, and David Silverman. Gratitude goes also to the friends and neighbors whose encouragement during the tough times urged me to keep going. You know who you are!

About the Author

Connie Baron Ring is a lifelong resident of Long Island, New York. Formerly, she was assistant to the editor of a national magazine, a writer/producer/editor of K–12 educational materials, a reference librarian, and a school library media specialist.

She is passionate about writing, genealogy, research, gardening, and family. Her historical fiction novel, *The Porcelain Monkey,* was inspired by a box of scandalous family letters found in her cousin's basement that told a tale of love, success, vice, and failure. She lives in Melville, New York, with her husband, Alan.